KP05

B
BW

Deborah Challinor is a freelance writer and historian living in the Waikato. *Blue Smoke* is her third novel, following the highly successful *White Feathers*, and she has written several nonfiction titles.

BLUE SMOKE

The final volume in a three-volume family saga.

On 3 February 1931, Napier is devastated by a powerful earthquake — and Tamar Murdoch, beloved matriarch of Kenmore, is seriously injured. As she recovers, Tamar is preoccupied with the ongoing effects of the Great Depression. When her grandson threatens to leave for Spain to join the International Brigade, she feels a familiar dread — once again her family is threatened by war and heartbreak, as Hitler's armies march.

Books by Deborah Challinor
Published by The House of Ulverscroft:

TAMAR
WHITE FEATHERS

DEBORAH CHALLINOR

◆

BLUE SMOKE

Complete and Unabridged

CHARNWOOD
Leicester

First published in 2003 by
HarperCollins*Publishers* (New Zealand) Limited
Auckland

First Charnwood Edition
published 2005
by arrangement with
HarperCollins*Publishers* Pty Limited
Australia

The moral right of the author has been asserted

British Library CIP Data

Challinor, Deborah
    Blue smoke.—Large print ed.—
    Charnwood library series
    1. New Zealand—Social life and customs—20th century—Fiction 2. Domestic fiction 3. Large type books
    I. Title
    823.9′14 [F]

    ISBN 1–84395–904–6

Published by
F. A. Thorpe (Publishing)
Anstey, Leicestershire

Set by Words & Graphics Ltd.
Anstey, Leicestershire
Printed and bound in Great Britain by
T. J. International Ltd., Padstow, Cornwall

This book is printed on acid-free paper

This one is for my parents, Pat and Brian Challinor, who hardly laughed at all when I said I wanted to write books for a living.

Thanks to the team at HarperCollins for their faith, advice and guidance, to Dexter Fry for designing such a perfect cover, and to Anna Rogers for another excellent editing job. Thanks also to my husband, Aaron, for his financial and emotional support, and for cooking really good dinners.

Prologue

She's too hot and wants to roll over to ease the minor but annoying ache in her back, but can't summon the energy. No matter, the ache will be gone soon. It has always been very hot here, at the tail end of March, and she learned to live with it years ago. So different from the climate she knew as a child, but certainly no worse.

Dying is such a bore. She's ready to go now, and has been for more than a year. There's no pain any more, just this feeling of almost-weightlessness, of still being tethered but knowing that the cord will separate very soon and release her.

Why she can't just go now she isn't sure, and then she remembers. There's one more child she must see before she leaves. It's important, that the ones left behind have these last memories of the one who is going. Soon, in the infinity of the grand scheme of things, she will become just another portrait on a parlour wall, and there will be no one left alive who actually knew her, but that doesn't matter either. Because she has done what she wanted to do. She has loved her men, raised her children, nurtured her grandchildren and stayed alive long enough to meet at least some of her great-grandchildren. Surely a woman can't ask for more than that?

The child is finally here now, and she is weeping. She wishes they wouldn't cry, because

1

it all will be fine. Perhaps when they grow old, they will know that too, but not until then.

Is it growing dark outside, or is it nearly time? They're all here, her family, except for the ones who have been ripped away from her, over the years. But no matter about that, either — she will be seeing them soon enough.

She tells them what they have all meant to her, and they begin to fade away. But only in her vision, never from her heart.

She waits, just a handful of slow heartbeats longer, and then he comes for her, the one she has always loved the most.

She raises her hand to meet him.

Part One

Tamar
1936–1938

1

Keely Morgan adjusted the angle of her hat in
the hall mirror while she waited for her mother
to finish getting ready. The hat was a chic little
affair — peach felt with a narrow, turned-up
brim — and it looked rather good on her, even if
she did say so herself. And it nicely complemented her pale salmon, calf-length dress and
matching heels. Keely's twelve-year-old twin
daughters, Bonnie and Leila, called the ensemble
her 'apricot outfit' — not because of the colour,
they insisted, but because it made her look like
one.

There was muffled giggling behind her. Keely,
without even bothering to turn around, said,
'Run upstairs, girls, will you, and see what's
keeping Gran. Tell her we've really got to be
going.'

Out of the corner of her eye she watched the
girls jostling each other to be first up the stairs
and along the upper hallway to their grandmother's bedroom, then turned back to the
mirror to complete her inspection.

Owen, her husband, had said at breakfast that
she looked 'peaky', and suggested that perhaps
she and her mother should postpone their trip
into Napier if she hadn't slept well. But they
went every week — it was their time together,
with no interruptions from demanding children,

5

or men wanting to know where yesterday's grubby work trousers had disappeared to — and it would take more than a hint of shadow under Keely's eyes to keep them from their treat.

And it was only a hint. She hadn't slept well last night because it had been so muggy, but Owen always fussed over her and she didn't think she looked particularly peaky at all; her eyes sparkled with health, her skin was smooth and supple, and her thick auburn hair shone with its usual lustre. She'd had it cut last year in a short, modern bob with finger waves, but Owen had disliked it intensely; had said, in fact, that if it wasn't for her shapely bust, she'd have looked like a boy from the back with her slim hips and long legs. So she'd let it grow again; longer hair was coming back anyway, and Keely liked to be fashionable.

She adjusted her hat a final fraction of an inch, thinking she actually looked rather good for a woman of thirty-eight with two semi-grown — and extremely challenging — children.

They rarely behaved for her, but then they wouldn't behave for their father either. But he had deep reserves of equanimity on which he was able to draw, and their constant high spirits didn't seem to goad him as much as they did her. She realised, however, that for the most part, the problem was her lack of patience, and she blamed herself for the discord that sometimes abounded in the household. Her discomfort was compounded by the guilt she still harboured for virtually abandoning them during the first few months of their lives. At the time she

6

had been deeply ambivalent about her marriage to Owen, but they'd grown to love each other very dearly, although their road together had never been particularly smooth. They had had to marry, of course, which was ironic in itself, since there had been no sign whatsoever of any further children, despite their very healthy physical relationship.

'Here she comes!' shouted Bonnie and Leila in unison as they thumped back down the stairs.

Keely stepped back from the mirror and looked expectantly up at her mother, who had paused on the landing halfway down the wide, carpeted staircase.

Tamar Murdoch was sixty-nine years old, and looked approximately a decade younger. She walked with freedom and grace, was still slender — well, *mostly* slender, she told herself whenever she consulted her dressing mirror — and the silver in her burnished chestnut hair had confined itself to two wide streaks sweeping back from her temples, accentuating the width of her green eyes. Her hair was long and she wore it up in her habitual, slightly dishevelled style. None of these short fashions for her; one or two of her peers had acquired bobs and they looked, in her opinion, like stringy old ewes after a particularly aggressive clip. No, she wasn't young any more, and was happy to admit it, and as far as she was concerned that entitled her to do whatever she liked with her hair. And her clothes, for that matter. She wore what took her fancy these days, whether it was *à la mode* or not, but was always elegant and still managed to turn heads wherever she went.

Today she was dressed for town, in a flatteringly cut jacket and skirt in copper-coloured linen, with a smart black hat and shoes. There were also gloves, but these were dangling precariously from her handbag, which was currently being swung at great speed around Leila's head.

'Stop that, darling,' Tamar said mildly. 'You'll break something.'

'No I won't! It's an aeroplane coming in to land in the top paddock,' Leila replied breathlessly, and swooped the bag perilously close to her mother's face.

'Leila!' Keely snapped. 'Put that *down!*'

Exasperated, she tugged on her own gloves, then sighed. She loved her daughters very much, but by God they tried a person.

'I'm sorry, girls,' she added after a moment, and in a calmer tone. 'I'm feeling a bit tired and grumpy today. Why don't you go and see if Mrs Heath is baking this morning? She might let you lick the spoons.'

The twins, almost identical except that Leila's hair was honey blonde while Bonnie's was auburn like her mother's, elbowed each other and grinned gleefully, then tore off down the hall to the kitchen at the back of the house, delighted with the idea of invading the elderly housekeeper's domain.

Tamar raised her eyebrows. 'That wasn't a very nice thing to do to Mrs Heath, dear. You know she doesn't like being pestered while she's cooking.'

'No, I know, but if we're still here when Erin arrives we'll never get out the door.'

Tamar had to agree; the combination of the twins and Erin and Joseph's three children — Billy, Ana and Robert — always resulted in a certain level of chaos. 'Did you ask her last night if she needed anything from town?'

'Yes, and she said they're fine.'

Tamar nodded, then added, 'I often think we should talk her into coming with us more often.'

'Well, I've said dozens of times she should, but you know Erin, she's never happier than when she's baking or sewing or doing something *homely* like that.' Keely screwed up her face as if the very idea was anathema to her. 'She says once a month in town is more than enough for her.'

'Well, dear, not everyone needs shopping to make them happy,' Tamar observed, amused. 'And she obviously *is* very happy.'

Keely, who had never quite got the hang of the domestic arts herself, shrugged. 'I know, and I think it's lovely. It's just not for me, that's all.'

'Oh, you have your moments, dear. What about those little iced cakes you make for Owen? The ones he's so fond of? And the outfits we've sewn for the girls over the years?'

'You've sewn, you mean.'

'You chose the fabric and the styles,' Tamar countered, retrieving her gloves. 'Has Lachie brought the car around?'

Keely nodded and preceded her mother out onto the porch and down the sweeping front steps. It wasn't yet eight o'clock so the sun was

9

still climbing in the eastern sky and early morning dew still fleetingly decorated the lawn and extensive flowerbeds surrounding the house. If they didn't get a move on they would be feeling the new day's heat before they even reached town.

In the gravel driveway stood a gleaming and very stylish Chrysler Imperial Roadster. Kenmore Station's second car, currently parked in one of the sheds at the side of the house, was a robust Cadillac sedan that could accommodate seven passengers and was just the thing for family outings. But it really was a big vehicle and Keely had to perch on two cushions to see over the steering wheel, so she preferred to take the smaller but racier Chrysler into town: it required only one cushion. And anyway, it was a much more exciting car to drive, capable of reaching speeds of seventy miles per hour on a good road. Tamar also drove, and had done for years, but preferred not to these days if she could avoid it as she no longer completely trusted her eyesight.

'I see Uncle Lachie's polished it to within an inch of its life again,' Keely said, running her gloved hand along the shining yellow hood.

She glanced at her mother and they both giggled immoderately. Tamar's brother-in-law Lachie McRae loved automobiles, and on the occasions on which he was forced to concede to the increasing stiffness in his joints that kept him off horseback and out of his beloved paddocks, he spent much of his time tinkering with the farm machinery or lovingly grooming the Chrysler, purchased the year before last after

10

much poring over automobile importers' catalogues. As it could comfortably accommodate only two people it had been an extravagance, but Lachie adored it. By the time Keely and Tamar returned home that afternoon its beautiful chrome and paintwork would be covered in a thick layer of dust from the rough unsealed road between Kenmore and Napier, but at least that would give Lachie something to do tomorrow if he couldn't ride.

Keely opened the driver's door, stepped up onto the running board and eased herself onto the cushion. She and Tamar waved gaily to the twins, waiting impatiently on the porch for their Aunty Erin to collect them for school, then roared off down the driveway, trailing a small wake of dust behind them.

* * *

They drove for some miles before they passed the fence marking the south-eastern boundary of Kenmore. It was one of the biggest sheep stations in the Hawke's Bay and had been owned and run by the Murdoch family since its establishment in the 1850s.

The economic depression had so far not laid its mean and fleshless hands on Kenmore. Tamar and Lachie had made some very prudent financial arrangements before the crash of '29, and the steps they had taken since had left the station in reasonably good stead. They were not making the profits that had so characterised the decade after the Great War, but neither had they

11

lost any of their land, or much of the money that had been committed to various investments. As Andrew Murdoch's widow, Tamar had inherited his half of the station after his death during the influenza epidemic of 1918, and the remainder had gone to Lachie after his wife Jeannie, Andrew's sister, passed away in 1926, so the family's considerable wealth was still intact.

When Tamar died, her share would go to her children, including her illegitimate first-born son Joseph, which she considered fitting and fair as he, together with her son-in-law Owen, was more or less running the station now anyway. When Lachie eventually died, which Tamar maintained would be years off yet but Lachie insisted could be any day now judging by his arthritis and the age it took him to get moving in the mornings, his share would go to his daughter Erin, who was married to Joseph.

James and Thomas, Tamar's surviving sons to Andrew Murdoch, were not and probably never would be sheep farmers. Thomas was happy in his flourishing Dunedin law practice and insisted, generously as always, that since he and his wife Catherine had not had children there was no need for them to share in the financial rewards generated by the family business. James, on the other hand, wasn't earning terribly much as a banker, and greatly appreciated the income he received from the station. In fact he depended on it, and this worried Tamar.

She was thinking about James's precarious financial situation, which he believed he'd successfully concealed from her but had not, when, an hour into their journey, she caught sight of something decidedly odd.

'Keely, stop the car,' she ordered sharply.

'What?'

'Stop the car. Look at that.'

Keely slowed and pulled over to the side of the road. A great cloud of dust engulfed them but as it cleared Tamar pointed across golden, drought-parched paddocks at a large flock of sheep.

'Why are they doing that?' she asked.

Keely stared. 'I really don't know.'

The sheep, hundreds of them, were racing wildly up a hill, then stopping so abruptly that many of them were losing their footing, before turning around and racing back down again. And the really disconcerting thing was the quiet; there was none of the monotonous bleating that always ensued whenever more than two sheep were within fifty yards of one another, and the silence and obvious disorientation of the animals was eerie.

Keely eased the car back into gear. 'Is there a storm coming?'

'I don't think so. How bizarre. I've never seen sheep do that before, have you?'

Keely shook her head as she manoeuvred the car off the grass verge and back onto the gravel.

The rest of their trip was uneventful, except for the rapidly increasing temperature, and by the time they reached Napier a little after half past ten they were hot, dusty and desperate for a cup of tea. They parked the car in Emerson Street and set off towards the nearest tearooms, grateful for the cool shade under the shop front verandahs. Somewhere close by several dogs were howling so mournfully that Tamar wondered whether they were hurt; if so, someone should attend to them. But then she caught sight of a bold display in a draper's window, and came to a halt.

'Look at this fabric, Keely. Is it silk, do you think, or rayon? It's getting more and more difficult to tell, unless you actually handle it. It's a lovely colour, though.'

'Not for you or me, it isn't. It would clash horribly with our hair.'

'No, I was thinking more of Erin. The red would be gorgeous on her.'

Keely touched her mother's sleeve. 'Come on, Mam, let's get something to drink. I'm parched. Then we'll look at the shops.'

Tamar nodded, still with half an eye on the material, and turned to follow Keely.

But then something very strange happened. The air around them seemed to suddenly swell and assume such a sense of brittle expectancy that Tamar clutched at Keely's arm in fright. But as she did, the ground beneath their feet heaved wildly and the pair of them staggered drunkenly across the footpath. A second later a deep, subterranean rumbling began, and the telegraph pole Keely had grabbed began to sway alarmingly.

'Earthquake!' she shouted, and pushed Tamar out towards the road. 'Get away from the buildings!'

But before they could take more than two steps, and to the accompaniment of a painfully

14

high-pitched creaking and groaning sound, the surface of the street thrust violently up to meet them. They fell to the ground instantly, the noise both deafening and disorienting them.

Tamar tried to rise, leaning first on one elbow and then the other, but felt as if a huge but invisible weight were relentlessly pinning her down. She lifted her head, astounded to see that every part of the street was rocking — buildings, telegraph poles, staggering people, cars, and the ground itself, rising and rolling like a heavy ocean swell. A crevasse opened in the middle of the street and Tamar grimaced as a woman fell to her knees, then tumbled shrieking into it.

To her left Keely screamed, '*Mam*! Behind you!'

The façade of the shop behind Tamar was bulging ominously outwards, the plate-glass window bowing surreally and almost gracefully before it shattered with a resounding report, propelling millions of shards of sparkling glass out into the street. Tamar managed to duck her face in time, but felt a myriad of burning stings as tiny fragments of glass struck the back of her head and hands.

Dimly she heard Keely shouting again, then something massive slammed down on top of her.

★ ★ ★

'Mam! *Mam*! Can you hear me?'

Tamar drew in a ragged breath to reply but winced in pain, choking on the thick dust that seemed to be filling her mouth. She couldn't see

15

at all and Keely's voice sounded miles away. Something was crushing her, and her ribs and legs ached; she couldn't move, and could barely breathe.

Had she been buried alive? Was she about to die without even the chance to say goodbye to anyone? The thought of expiring right here on a Napier street under a ton of bricks hurled her into a panic, and her hands scrabbled wildly but ineffectually at the rubble entombing her.

'Oh no,' she whispered thickly. 'No, not *yet!*'

Then she took as deep a breath as her searing ribs would allow, told herself sternly not to be so melodramatic and concentrated on trying to get up. It was then that she realised she wasn't lying on her front at all, as she had first thought, but on her side with her right cheek jammed against the rough and hot tarseal. This explained why her face and mouth hurt so much. She couldn't feel the touch of air on her anywhere, and if someone didn't come and move whatever was squashing her soon, she could be in real trouble.

The ground jolted and dropped nauseatingly again, and Tamar's heart lurched as she envisioned even more bricks and rubble crashing down on top of her. But none did, and the movement subsided to a series of trembles. She didn't know it then, but after two and a half minutes of catastrophic upheaval, the worst of the earthquake had passed.

She heard muffled yelling, and felt movement against her left hand as someone dug at the rubble. Then suddenly air trickled across her skin, and fingers were touching her own.

16

'Mam? Can you hear me? Mam?'

Tamar responded by squeezing Keely's hand weakly, and heard her call out to someone, 'She's alive; she's holding my hand! Help me!'

She felt more rubble being dug away, and faint light began to filter into her temporary tomb. After a minute her head was uncovered and she squinted through scratchy, teary eyes at the daylight. And at Keely who crouched several feet away, her hat and shoes gone and covered with thick, white dust from head to toe.

'Oh, Mam,' Keely sobbed, tears cutting shiny tracks down her dirty face. 'Oh my God, Mam, I thought you'd been killed!'

Tamar shook her head mutely. Not this time.

'Are you hurt? Does anything hurt?'

'My leg and my chest,' Tamar wheezed.

Keely panicked momentarily and clutched the arm of the man squatting next to her. 'Oh, God, she's having a heart attack! Get a doctor!'

Tamar coughed painfully and cleared her throat raggedly. 'I'm not, it's my ribs. And I think my leg might be broken.' Then she added crossly, 'For God's sake, Keely, you're a nurse, stop dithering and have a look.'

'I can't see, there's too much rubbish on you!'

'Well, get it off then!'

Keely decided then that her mother certainly didn't sound at death's door, and struggled to pull herself together. A long time had passed since she had nursed, but she didn't think she could have forgotten much. She grasped Tamar's wrist, pressed two fingers against the fat vein at the base of the thumb, and counted; her mother's pulse was fast but strong, a good sign.

She said to the man at her side, 'Could you please help me get her out? I don't think I can do it by myself.'

The man, whose own hat had disappeared and who had several bleeding scratches on his grimy face, nodded and began to dig. He was soon joined by several others, who looked shocked but determined to help.

'Hold on, Mam, we'll have you out in a minute,' Keely soothed as she heaved bricks and pieces of wood off Tamar's prostrate body.

'We should take her down to the beach,' one of the helpers suggested, 'that's where everyone else is heading. In case there's another one.'

Keely stopped digging and watched closely as two men lifted a heavy wooden beam off her mother's legs. Tamar flinched but managed not to cry out.

'No,' Keely said slowly after a moment. 'No, I think we'll be going up to the hospital.'

Tamar's right leg was bent between knee and ankle at a very unnatural angle. The white of bone protruding through torn and bleeding flesh elicited a muffled groan of horror from one of the helpers.

'Right!' Keely declared authoritatively as she stood and brushed dust and dirt off her knees. 'Find a flat board, a door would be ideal, and we'll get her onto it. We have to move her now. If we . . .'

She was cut off in mid-order by another ominous rumbling. They all froze as if playing some sort of children's game, legs straddled against the movement of the earth and eyes wide with fear. Then, mercifully, the tremor subsided.

'Aftershock,' someone said nervously.

Keely squatted down again and spoke quietly. 'Mam, your leg is broken, quite badly. We need to get you to the hospital. It needs setting. Can you hang on until then?'

Tamar nodded, although she wasn't so sure she could hang on. She was starting to feel rather faint, her chest felt constricted and the pain there was worsening, and there was a loud and disconcerting ringing in her ears.

She would be all right with Keely, she knew that, but Tamar wanted Kepa to be here as well. He would know what to do, he always did. And she needed him very much.

★ ★ ★

Keely sat holding her mother's limp hand, waiting patiently for her to regain consciousness after the operation to set her leg.

Most of the buildings at Napier's public hospital had been destroyed in the earthquake; sailors from the navy warship HMS *Veronica*, currently berthed at Port Ahuriri, were still digging through the ruins, including the nurses' home, for survivors. Instead, an emergency hospital had been set up at the Greenmeadows racecourse on the outskirts of town.

It was here that Keely waited. Tamar had been moved from the makeshift operating theatre beneath the main grandstand to one of several large, hastily erected tents on the track itself.

19

Every hour that passed brought more supplies and medical equipment from the ruined public hospital, piling up where it was unloaded. Wounded people lay everywhere, reminding Keely horrifyingly of the nursing work she and Erin had done overseas during the war. But she knew she could help here, and she would, as soon as her mother's condition had stabilised.

The surgeon had confirmed that the fracture was nasty, that several of Tamar's ribs had indeed been broken, and that he'd had to suture quite a number of small but deep lacerations on her head and hands caused by flying glass. But he felt that her prognosis would be satisfactory, providing that none of the post-surgery complications that could often beset the elderly developed. Keely hoped that her mother had been sound asleep when he'd said this — she would be very annoyed to hear herself described as 'elderly'.

She looked up as someone entered the tent.

'Christ, she looks terrible!' exclaimed Owen from the doorway. He was still in his work clothes and had clearly come straight in from Kenmore. 'Are you all right?' he asked. He was shocked both at the sight of Tamar, and at the dishevelled state of his wife.

Keely stood and let herself be enfolded in his tanned arms. 'Her ribs are broken and she has a compound tib and fib. But the surgeon says she'll be all right.' She buried her face in his chest. 'Oh God, Owen, it was absolutely terrifying!'

Owen nodded, his chin resting on the top of

her dusty head. 'I know, darling. It was pretty frightening out at the station too.'

Keely jerked back and looked up at his kind face. 'The children?'

'They're fine. The school wobbled a bit apparently, but nothing collapsed. They're at home with Mrs Heath. We telephoned the post office here in town as soon as it happened but we couldn't get through.'

'No, they say the lines are all down. I tried to ring you too, as soon as we got Mam here. Is there much damage at home?'

'Not really, not to the house itself, except for one of the chimneys. We must have been too far away. A few things were broken, though, the mirror in the hall and some bits and pieces, and that big dresser in the kitchen fell over. And the river seems to have gone right down, so the generator isn't working.'

Keely asked, 'How did you know to come here, to the racecourse?'

'Everyone looking for anyone's being directed here.'

'Did Joseph come in with you?'

Owen nodded. 'He was worried sick until one of the doctors told us you were both still in one piece. He and Erin are talking to the superintendent bloke — we heard quite a few of the nurses were killed at the hospital and Erin's offering to help.'

'I will be too, as soon as Mam comes around.'

Owen glanced down at his mother-in-law lying motionless on the narrow cot, her leg enclosed within a heavy metal brace and bandages

21

covering the cuts on her head and hands. A huge bruise dappled the right side of her face and her top lip was split and swollen. Worst of all she appeared somehow *reduced*, not at all like her usual self. She had never been a big woman, but now she looked like a child, which Owen found very disturbing.

'She's pretty grey around the gills,' he noted hesitantly. 'Are you sure she's going to be all right?'

Keely nodded. 'Half of it's dust.' She waved in the general direction of the grandstand. 'They didn't have time to clean her properly. There are four operating teams going at the moment and they're flat out.'

Joseph and Erin appeared then; Erin rushed straight to Keely and embraced her.

'Oh Keely, are you all right? We've been worried *sick*!'

'I'm fine, and Mam will be too. We got a hell of a fright, though. I thought she'd been killed! It took four of us to dig her out.'

'My God, were you indoors when the earthquake hit?'

'Outside the draper's on Emerson Street. The front of the building collapsed right on top of her.'

Erin stared at her cousin, appalled at how close they had come to tragedy.

Tamar stirred then and started to say something, but the dryness of her throat stifled her voice.

Erin bent down. 'Aunty Tam? It's Erin. How are you feeling?'

'Ill,' Tamar croaked.

'It's the anaesthetic,' Erin said over her shoulder. 'Get a bowl, someone.'

Owen rushed off but was too late; Tamar vomited weakly over the side of her cot and onto the canvas floor while Erin held her hair out of the way.

Joseph, his brown face pale with concern and his dark hair flopping over his temples, asked uneasily, 'Is that normal? Being sick?'

'Yes, it won't last long.'

'Shouldn't we get a nurse?'

'We are nurses, Joseph,' Keely said mildly, excusing her half-brother's unintentional slight because he was so distraught. 'She's doing as well as can be expected. She should be properly awake soon.'

Tamar subsided painfully onto her back and lifted a shaking hand to sweep her hair off her face. 'I'm properly awake now. And my leg hurts.'

Joseph bent over her. 'Don't worry, Mam, Papa will be here soon.'

A light flared in Tamar's puffy red eyes. 'Is he coming? How do you know that?'

'I don't,' Joseph said, 'but I know my father, and so do you. He'll be here as soon as he can be.'

The mention of Kepa had cheered Tamar visibly, and Erin smiled. 'Right, well, I'll organise something to relieve the pain. I've been assigned to the dressing station at Nelson Park, but I'll be back to see you as soon as I can, Aunty Tam, I promise.'

23

Tamar closed her eyes. The idea of sleep was very enticing — she couldn't recall the last time she had felt so utterly exhausted, ill and sore.

The others watched her for a moment, then moved outside as another patient was brought in on a stretcher.

Erin asked Keely, 'Will she be staying here, do you know?'

'I'm not sure. The public hospital certainly won't be taking patients.'

Erin pushed her dark hair, escaping from its customary neat bun, behind her ears and off her sweaty face. On a normal day the high summer heat would be bearable, but today, on top of everything else, it was almost intolerable. 'I was talking to the superintendent just before, and he said the field hospital from Trentham army base has already left Wellington. They should be here on the train tomorrow morning and they'll bring more tents and equipment. Apparently they can do about two hundred and fifty non-ambulatories,' she added, slipping into military medical jargon without even realising it. 'So I expect she'll probably stay on here, for a day or two at least.'

'I'd like to take her home,' Keely said.

'Yes, so would I, but we don't have any electricity at Kenmore at the moment, and don't forget she can't be moved until her leg's been plastered.'

Keely nodded, then frowned as Erin suddenly giggled. It was a high-pitched, slightly hysterical giggle, and very uncharacteristic of her cousin.

'What?'

24

'I'm sorry, it isn't funny really, but you should see yourself, Keely. You look a fright. Not your usual impeccably groomed self at all.'

Keely turned to her husband for confirmation. 'Do I?'

Owen gazed back at her, turning his hat around in his hands. Joseph, at his side, smiled at his sister with rueful sympathy.

'Well, yes, darling, you are a little, um, untidy,' Owen admitted.

Keely's hair was sticking out wildly and caked with brick and plaster dust, her face was grimy and all traces of her carefully applied make-up had long since disappeared. Her smart town dress was torn and filthy, her silk stockings in tatters and her shoes nowhere to be seen. She made an ineffectual attempt to smooth her hair and pinched her cheeks to bring a little colour into them. Then she looked down at her bare feet, and burst into shocked, exhausted tears.

2

Owen handed her a mug of steaming hot tea and went on rubbing her back. 'Are you sure you want to stay?' he asked gently. 'I know you want to help, but you're needed at home too.'

And that was true. With most of the Kenmore adults volunteering their services in town, and Tamar injured, there was only elderly Mrs Heath to look after the five children out at the station. Lachie was there, of course, but Bonnie and Leila were quite capable of running rings around the old man, and God only knew what would happen after a day or two of that. And there were also Erin and Joseph's children — Billy, only a few weeks older than the twins, Ana aged ten, and nine-year-old Robert — all three of whom, although generally better behaved than Bonnie and Leila, weren't above kicking up their heels when they could get away with it, particularly Ana, who often took her cue from her cousins.

The children's little country school — which had in fact sustained some structural damage, although Owen had neglected to tell Keely that — would have to close until repairs were assessed and carried out, so there was no chance of foisting them off on their teacher in the foreseeable future.

And there was also the matter of the appalling and widespread devastation in town. As a war veteran Owen had seen some deeply disturbing things, but had never imagined he'd see such sights again in the place he had come to call his home. He was extremely worried that what had happened here today would revive in Keely all the horrors of war she had finally managed to put to rest.

On their way through the Napier streets, he and Joseph had watched in dismay as people — some still alive but others clearly beyond help — were pulled out of the rubble by furiously digging rescue workers. They'd stopped to help several times, and had already ferried five injured people in the farm truck here to the emergency hospital. The main shopping areas of Emerson, Tennyson and Dickens Streets resembled a bomb site; familiar landmarks had been reduced to piles of shattered bricks, the three-storeyed Government Building at the bottom of Shakespeare Street had split in half, and the Clarendon Hotel next to it had collapsed completely. Napier Technical School was a heap of bricks and splintered wood, and everywhere smaller shops and buildings had disintegrated.

And the fires — they had started almost immediately after the earthquake. Owen and Joseph, approaching the city from the northwest, had been awed by the huge pall of smoke already settling over the central business district, darkening the skies and bringing an unnatural, premature dusk. A brisk wind had risen and cajoled hungry flames through city blocks baked dry after months of hot rainless weather, and almost all the central city was burning. The Napier Fire Department, even with dozens of volunteer helpers, was pushed well beyond its capability. Wooden buildings had been worst hit, but even the solid Masonic Hotel, where Keely had once sat for hours one long rainy night waiting for a man who had never arrived, had been thoroughly burnt out.

She took a final puff on the cigarette Owen had lit for her and replied frustratedly, 'I want to stay and do something. I feel so . . . God, I don't know what I feel!'

Owen empathised. 'Is it the wounded?'

'Yes, it reminds me so much of . . . '

'Ssshh.' Owen placed his fingers gently on his wife's lips. 'Don't say it. I expect all the returned men and women are feeling the same way. But this isn't a war, it's a natural disaster. There will be an end to this.'

'But I want to *help*!' Keely blurted childishly, her normal confidence and sense of equilibrium apparently deserting her.

'Look, love, you don't even have any shoes,' Owen said sensibly. 'At least go home, get cleaned up and see to the children. Then you can come back.' He stared at her thoughtfully. 'In fact, before you do come back in, why don't you call on a few of the neighbours and see if they have anything they can contribute? People will have to be fed and they'll need bedding and probably clothes and all that sort of thing. I heard food depots are being set up, I think the navy's helping with that, and they're bound to want meat and vegetables.'

Keely's face lit up. 'Yes, I could do that, couldn't I?' Then she had a rather dismal thought of her own. 'Oh, but the car, we parked it in Emerson Street. The fires . . . what if it's been destroyed?'

Owen had seen for himself the crushed and burntout wrecks of automobiles on his way through town, but the fact that Lachie's cherished Imperial Roadster might be one of them hadn't occurred to him.

He considered for a moment. 'Take the truck. Joseph and I are going back into town to see if we can lend a hand, but I'm sure someone will give us a lift. We'll look for the car later.'

Keely got to her feet, which were rather sore now. She was filthy and stiff, and covered in bruises and grazes, and the idea of a decent bath at home was very appealing. But something still niggled at her.

'But what if there aren't enough nurses?'

'I think there will be,' Owen replied. 'The girl doling out the tea said she'd heard that civilian medical teams are coming from Gisborne and Taupo, and even Wellington. Apparently the navy's been onto everyone with their wireless link.' He didn't mention, however, that the state of the roads into Napier could seriously hamper many vehicles trying to get in or out of the area. 'The navy's here, the army's on its way and so is the Red Cross, so everything will be all right. Go home, Keely, please. We'll keep an eye on your mam. I'll see if we can track down James and Lucy and they can help as well. The bank's now a great heap of rubble so I doubt even James will be at work today.'

29

Keely drove home to Kenmore, Erin went to work at the Nelson Park emergency dressing station and Owen and Joseph thumbed a lift into the town centre where they joined the volunteers fighting to contain the fires.

At Greenmeadows, Tamar lay on her cot, dozing and trying to ignore the gnawing pain in her leg and all the other bits of her aging body which were protesting mightily over their recent trauma. The surgeon had returned briefly and explained that although the break in her leg had been set, the limb had not yet been encased in plaster to allow the wound to heal, hence the heavy brace to prevent movement. She would not be able to go home to Kenmore until the plaster had been applied, so she could either stay at the temporary hospital at Greenmeadows, which would be fine with him as he wanted her kept under observation anyway, or stay somewhere else suitable in town, if she absolutely must go. Did she have somewhere where she would be appropriately cared for?

Tamar thought; there was the little house on Marine Parade she had bought years ago when she had first come to Napier, and which she still used often when she was in town — providing it was still standing, of course. Or, failing that, she could stay with James and his wife Lucy at their house in town. She preferred the former plan, but then she would have to look out for herself. She hated being fussed over but really didn't think she would be able to cope alone, at least not while she couldn't even get out of bed. She could ask Erin to stay with her, she supposed — and no doubt her niece would offer anyway — but as a trained nurse she was very much needed by others, and Keely had the children to attend to.

No, it would probably have to be James and Lucy's admittedly very comfortable and well-appointed home. They would welcome her, she knew that; it was just that she sometimes found it almost impossible to refrain from saying what she really thought to her second eldest son.

First, there was the matter of how James and his own son Duncan got along, or rather, did not get along — a problem that had dogged the family ever since James had come from the Great War, and worried Tamar constantly.

Duncan, now a big, handsome, confident sixteen-year-old, boarded at Napier Boys' High School. The school was only a couple of miles from his home, but everyone, not least Duncan himself, had agreed he'd be better off boarding, given that he and his father appeared to be so incompatible. And there were the other children too — Andrew, aged eleven and named for his grandfather (although he was known to all as Drew), and Kathleen, aged ten. In Tamar's opinion neither was always at ease with the atmosphere in the Murdoch home — the angry exchanges between Duncan and their father, the shouting, the subsequent frosty silences that sometimes went on for days — and although they loved their older brother, they were relieved when he became a boarder and relative peace

31

descended on the house. Lucy clearly mourned her son's absence, but he came home most weekends and, providing James wasn't in one of his moods, those two days could be relatively calm and pleasant.

Poor James. As a young man he had lived for his career as a professional soldier, but he had been terribly traumatised by his war experiences and had been discharged, although honourably, from the army after an appalling incident involving the death of another officer. The family never referred to it, even after all these years, but they all knew that James still lived under the shadow of what had happened that day on the battlefield. He had never quite recovered — although he was better these days than he had been when he had first come home — and was still prone to mood swings and not infrequent irrational and aggressive behaviour. Unfortunately, he took much of it out on long-suffering Lucy who, although essentially a generous and empathetic soul, had begun to compensate for her husband's behaviour by focusing on less emotionally hurtful things, such as what to wear to social events and the colour of the curtains in their living room. The naïve and gentle young girl, already pregnant when a very different James had proudly introduced her to his family in 1914, had grown into a wary and slightly embittered woman. Their marriage had been characterised by disagreements, silences and sometimes even fear on Lucy's part. Privately, however, Tamar was convinced that they loved each other quite fiercely and that James

32

depended on his wife far more than he would ever admit.

The disharmony between Duncan and James had always been present. Certainly, Duncan had never really overcome his anger at James for coming home halfway through the war and taking his mother off him. It hadn't been like that at all, of course, but James had been extremely unwell and Lucy had been forced to attend to her husband rather than their small son, who had been the centre of attention until then. James had resented the demands Duncan had made on Lucy, seeing in the whining, frightened and unhappy child the same traits he believed himself to have displayed under the stress of combat. It had all been too much for the little boy to comprehend, and now that boy was almost a man himself and all too ready and willing to stand up to a father who was still moody and unreasonable and, if everyone were completely honest, occasionally a bully.

So here they were, James and Duncan, lacking the humility and understanding to set aside their differences. In truth, they were very similar characters, both in looks and personality, and Tamar wondered if they would ever make their peace. She loved them both, her son and grandson, but sometimes it was all she could do to stop herself from banging their stubborn heads together. And she knew that should she stay with James and Lucy for any length of time, she would be unable to refrain from lecturing James yet again on his inability to get along with his son.

But at least Duncan had the company of his cousin Liam, who was also attending Napier Boys'. Liam's father Ian, Tamar and Andrew's youngest son, had died on the Somme in 1916, never knowing he had fathered a child. At the age of three months, Liam had been deposited in Kenmore's kitchen garden following Ian's memorial service, presumably by his mother, a woman who had chosen to remain anonymous. Tamar had raised Liam as her own, grateful to have such an unexpected and precious reincarnation of her youngest son. The boy was fifteen now, uncannily like his father, and had been delighted to go to school with Duncan, whom he had always idolised, even if it did mean having to spend much of his time away from Kenmore Station, which he loved. Tamar would have liked to have kept him at home, but he was a bright boy, and she couldn't bring herself to deprive him of a good education just because she would miss him. And Kenmore was just too far from town for the children to travel in daily for school.

And then there was the other matter over which Tamar and James were entirely unable to see eye to eye — her relationship with Kepa Te Roroa, her lover for the past twelve years. Tamar knew that James hated the idea of his mother having a liaison with anyone other than his father, and especially with Kepa, who was a respected and very powerful man, but also Joseph's father. James and Joseph usually got on very well, but Tamar wondered whether James wasn't sometimes jealous of Joseph's position in the family. She also suspected that he was

34

ashamed that, at her age, she still had physical and emotional needs that could be satisfied only by a man. But after the death of her beloved Andrew, Tamar had thought very hard about what she wanted to do with the rest of her life. She had loved Andrew dearly, and had been absolutely devastated by his unexpected loss but, as her lifelong friend Riria Adams had pointed out at the time, a woman's life did not end just because her husband's had. And, as a widow of many years, Riria was certainly in a position to know.

So when Kepa, a widower himself by then, had asked Tamar if she would consider rekindling the short but intense love affair of their youth — one which had produced Joseph and almost broken Tamar's heart — she had accepted his offer. She had not expected a resumption of the passion they had once shared — although she had been very pleasantly surprised to discover that their physical attraction for each other had not dimmed — but she did want a companion. Someone with whom she could talk about the station and her family, and on whom she could rely for emotional support. Kepa was certainly that someone, and of course Joseph would always be a very strong bond between them. And, over a decade later, their private and extremely discreet arrangement was still working very satisfactorily, despite her continued refusal to marry him.

Now, though, all she wanted was another glass of water. It was almost evening, nearly seven hours after the earthquake, and since she had awoken from the anaesthetic she had been desperately thirsty. Her broken ribs were hurting more, and the pain seemed to be wandering all over her chest. It was unbearably hot in the tent, even though the door had been propped open all afternoon, and she was starting to feel nauseous again too.

She felt a shadow on her face and opened her eyes, hoping it might be a nurse. Kepa stood with his hat in his hands gazing down at her, his dark, lined face a picture of concern and dismay. He was covered in road dust — he must have come in from Maungakakari.

'Hello, my love. How are you feeling?' he asked quietly, his rich, deep voice a balm to her already.

Tamar reached out a hand and sighed. 'Kepa, you're here. I'm so glad.' She swallowed and willed her increasing nausea to go away. 'Did you ride all the way in from the village?'

He stroked her fingers softly and said in his formal, slightly stilted English, 'Yes, I came as soon as I could. I did not drive — the roads are not in a good state.'

Tamar shifted uncomfortably as another wave of pain gripped her. 'How did you know I was here?'

'I did not, but this is your usual shopping day. I presumed that if you were not at any of the medical stations, then you would be somewhere else and I could stop worrying. When I arrived here I talked to the person in charge, and he looked you up on his list.'

It was on the tip of Tamar's tongue to ask, but

what if she'd been one of the fatalities? But Kepa, as he often did, read her mind.

'I did not go to the morgue. I would have known in my heart if you were there.' He bent down and discreetly kissed her cheek. 'And I thank God that you were not. I am so relieved that you are safe, Tamar.'

She blinked hard as tears finally began to break through her rather tattered composure. 'And everyone at the village, are they safe too?'

Kepa nodded. 'A little shaken, but there have been earthquakes before. Although not as big as this one. The horses ran away, including mine, which is why I am late, and so did the pigs and the chickens, but at Maungakakari there is not much to fall down so there is little damage. The artesian well has dried up, so I have evacuated everyone temporarily, but we will be fine. But it is you I came to see.' He noted the sheen of sweat on Tamar's brow and the grey pallor of her skin. 'Are you in pain?'

Tamar nodded. 'Could you get a nurse for me?'

'Now?'

'Please,' Tamar replied through gritted teeth.

Kepa was gone for less than three minutes but by the time he had returned, with a nurse hurrying behind him, Tamar's heart had spasmed violently, just once, and ceased to beat.

★   ★   ★

James put his brandy glass down on the polished mahogany sideboard and rubbed both hands

37

wearily over his stubbled face. His eyes were sunken and rimmed with red and he felt utterly wrung out and exhausted. When he looked up again, Lucy was watching him intently.

'Are you feeling all right, James?' she asked from her seat on the sofa.

'No, I'm not bloody well feeling all right!' he snapped back. 'What do you think!'

Lucy flinched. She hated it when James became upset — it made him almost impossible to deal with. Grief and fear, especially, caused him to lose his temper. But she'd spent the days since the earthquake trying her best to hold everyone and everything together and she was exhausted too. She didn't have the energy to pander to her temperamental husband.

'I think you should at least try and make an effort to manage your emotions, James, that's what I *think*! You're not the only one who's grieving and in shock; we're all feeling it, you know. It's been terrible, all of it. It's been hard for everyone!'

James glared at her, then had the grace to lower his eyes, knowing in his heart that he was being unreasonable but finding it very difficult to stop. He picked up his glass again — one of the very few not broken in the earthquake — drained it, then forced himself to take a good look around his living room. Some of the more solid pieces of furniture had survived unscathed, although anything taller than hip height had fallen over and broken, and ornaments and pictures had been smashed, as had most of the windows. The damage was similar throughout

38

the house — the coal range had come away from the wall and its flue in the kitchen, and in the bathroom the toilet pan had cracked and the bath had travelled from one side of the room to the other. Worst of all, neither the water nor the electricity was back on yet. Fortunately the house was built almost solely of wood and had flexed rather than collapsed when the earth had buckled, but still, a lot of repair work would be needed.

He contemplated his wife, still very pretty with her ash-blonde hair and bright blue eyes even though she was getting on for forty, and sighed. She was right, as usual; he was finding it difficult to manage his emotions. And damn the repair work on the house — the past few days had reminded him very unpleasantly that there were far more important things to be mourned than the damage to four walls and a roof.

'I'm sorry, Lucy. I'm just . . . ' He trailed off, thinking I should say I'm just a bad-tempered old bastard, but then Lucy already knows that. Instead he said, 'God, I'm so damn *tired*. It's just all been so bloody awful.'

Lucy went over to him. More and more these days she was having to be the strong one; they both knew it, although neither would ever acknowledge it openly.

She said gently, 'I know, but we'll manage somehow. We always have, and we will this time too.'

'I wish I could turn back the clock. Things will never be the same, you know.'

'Perhaps not, but sometimes good can come out of something as terrible as this.'

'I can't imagine what,' James replied shortly. 'We don't even have the children with us. I miss them, Lucy. Even Duncan.'

Napier Boys' High School had been temporarily closed until the earthquake damage to several of the main buildings had been repaired, so the boys had been sent out to Kenmore, together with Drew and Kathleen. So all nine grandchildren were at the station now, with only Lachie and Mrs Heath to look after them. Erin was still acting in her capacity as a temporary nurse, and at the moment Keely was also in town more often than she was at home, keeping herself as busy as possible.

For the first few days after the earthquake, she had helped co-ordinate the relief effort for the townspeople — and there were hundreds and hundreds of them — whose homes had been destroyed. Refugee camps had sprung up almost immediately. Shocked and dazed survivors spent their first night under army-issue canvas, eating food salvaged by seamen from HMS *Veronica* and the merchant navy ships *Northumberland* and *Taranaki*, and prepared and served by volunteer helpers.

The beachfront along Marine Parade had been the most popular place to go, despite the rumour that earthquakes were often succeeded by tidal waves. There was no tsunami, fortunately, but the regular and frequent aftershocks that continued for some time had kept everyone in a high state of tension — apart from one group of children Keely had seen sitting on a fence at Nelson Park chanting gaily, 'Here comes a . . . *nother* one!' at the beginning of every fresh tremor. Other people set up camp outside their ruined homes, sleeping under the stars on mattresses dragged outside, eating whatever they could salvage from their own pantries, cooked over fireplaces made from bricks and rubble. But almost everyone, regardless of whether their homes had been destroyed or not, chose to sleep outdoors.

By the following day the aftershocks were tapering off but the fires in the central streets still burned. Navy reinforcements — in the form of the warships HMS *Dunedin* and *Diomede*, both of which had quickly been dispatched from Auckland — had arrived at 8.30 in the morning. On board was a large medical contingent from Auckland Hospital, as well as first-aid supplies, stretchers and tents, and seamen who would be working on shore. Their efforts were added to those of teams of ex-servicemen, as well as the Red Cross, the Salvation Army, extra police and other emergency services converging on Napier to begin burying the dead and start repairing the roads, railway lines and telegraph network.

Then at the end of the week came the announcement that evacuation from Napier would begin for those who wished to leave; the water supply and drainage systems were still not functioning, and there was concern about an outbreak of disease. Nelson Park had been designated as the official evacuation centre, and medical cases would be moved to Green-meadows before being transported out of the area. Initially all evacuees would go to Waipukurau, and then on to Palmerston North or to other parts of the country. Keely, therefore, was elbow deep in paperwork, and hadn't been home to Kenmore for two days. She was desperately tired, but grateful to be so usefully occupied. She lived on tea and cigarettes, slept when she could and dropped around to James and Lucy's house whenever she was able to grab an hour to herself. Joseph, Owen and Erin were doing the same, as if converging there could somehow make things better.

Only Erin was there at the moment.

There was a discreet cough and James and Lucy turned to see her standing quietly in the hall.

'Sorry to interrupt, but she's awake and she'd like to talk to you, James.' Erin paused. 'Oh, and Kepa's here too. He's waiting outside.'

'God, *again*,' James said. 'He might as well be living here.'

Both Lucy and Erin ignored him. They understood — Kepa was reassuring himself that Tamar was not going to slip away from him after all.

The doctor had worked on Tamar desperately for some minutes after her heart had stopped, and just as he had been about to tell the tall Maori gentleman — who had gripped her hand during the resuscitation as if he were having a heart attack himself — that Mrs Murdoch had gone, he'd detected a faint hitching of her chest.

When he had applied his stethoscope to her breast he'd been delighted to be able to confirm that she was breathing again, and the Maori man had wept. Not loudly, but in a manner the doctor had found profoundly moving.

Kepa had stayed with Tamar all that night and the following day, and had never been far from her side since. He was sleeping at Tamar's house on Marine Parade, which hadn't fallen down in the earthquake, but was certainly worse for wear, and doing what he could to tidy it up in case Tamar wanted to recuperate there before she went home to Kenmore. But that seemed unlikely, with no water or electricity and the drains in the town beginning to stink revoltingly.

Lucy, Erin and Keely were all touched by his obvious dedication and his efforts to make Tamar comfortable, but James wasn't. He deeply resented Kepa's involvement in Tamar's recovery, and was even more annoyed that his mother was so clearly benefiting from the old man's ministrations. He turned up at James's house at least twice a day, sometimes with flowers — God knew where he got them — and sometimes with fresh fish or some other food or drink he insisted Tamar have because it would be 'good for her heart'. Tamar ate everything he brought along, and James found it particularly galling that neither Erin nor Keely, the two nurses in the family, had told the bloody annoying, arrogant old man to stop interfering in Tamar's recuperation.

Tamar had been transferred to James and Lucy's home a few days after her heart attack.

The doctor overseeing her medical treatment had been most concerned when she refused to be evacuated to Waipukarau with the other injured earthquake victims, and had said very crossly that if anything happened to her because she wasn't able to receive the appropriate medical help, he wouldn't be held responsible. But he'd visited Tamar twice since she'd been moved to James and Lucy's, and had examined her at length both times. In his opinion the leg wound was healing well, and a plaster cast could probably be applied soon, which meant Tamar could go home to Kenmore.

But James knew that wouldn't happen for another day or two, so he would have to put up with Kepa fawning all over her. But he dared not refuse the man access to his mother; she would be extremely annoyed, and even James had to concede that Kepa's visits were having a positive effect on her.

'Oh, let him in then,' he muttered, reaching for the brandy decanter again. 'But not for long, I don't want her getting overtired.'

The two women gave each other a quick, exasperated look before Erin went to see Kepa in.

* * *

Tamar lay propped up against a bank of soft pillows. Her face was still unusually pale, although a little colour had finally crept back into her cheeks, and her eyes were regaining a little of their sparkle.

44

'Hello, my dear,' Kepa said. He sat down beside the bed and reached for Tamar's hand. 'How was your afternoon sleep?'

'Fine,' Tamar replied truthfully. 'I believe I'm finally on the mend.'

Over the last two days she had been feeling better and better, physically anyway, and was very much looking forward to going home.

She shifted slightly, smoothed the fine satin coverlet over her lap and added, 'Although I have been thinking, Kepa.'

He raised his eyebrows; such a statement from Tamar usually signalled an announcement of some consequence. 'About?'

'Well, about the earthquake, and my health and the children and what have you.'

He waited, knowing there would be more.

'I have to admit,' she continued, 'that being crushed by a collapsing building then having a heart attack has rather made me reconsider my . . . well, my own mortality, I suppose you would call it.'

As it would, Kepa agreed silently.

Tamar was silent herself for a moment, then looked up at his handsome face and silver-streaked hair. 'The time that you and I have had together since Andrew died has been wonderful, you know that, and I wouldn't have missed it for anything, but, really, apart from that, all I seem to have done over the past ten years is fiddle about arranging flowers, making clothes for the children and playing at doing the station accounts.'

'Lachie says that you do a superb job of it,

45

too,' Kepa said. 'And do not forget, Tamar, that you are getting on in years. It is time you relaxed.'

Tamar snorted. 'That's good coming from you. You're older than I am.'

Kepa smiled benignly. 'But only by one year.' Then he became serious again. 'We are growing old, my dear. Time does not stop even for a man and a woman lucky enough to come together as late in life as we have.' He almost added *finally*, but stopped out of respect for Andrew's memory.

'Oh, I know all that,' Tamar replied, waving a hand dismissively. 'But I've been thinking about who will run things — Kenmore, and the family itself — when I finally do go. Which,' she added firmly, 'I fully intend won't be for some time yet.'

Kepa settled back in his seat. 'You are not pleased with the way Joseph is managing the station?'

'Oh, I am, I'm delighted. He and Owen are doing a fine job. And of course Lachie's input is still invaluable.' Her face clouded momentarily. 'Although Lachie won't last forever either. No, it's really James I'm worried about. It disturbs me greatly to think about what he might do with his share of Kenmore when I'm gone, and perhaps even the others' shares. I know he's starting to make a name for himself as a banker, but I suspect that his personal finances are a shambles. Well, no, I don't suspect it, I *know*. I'm concerned that he might sell his share — or be coerced into selling it — and I would hate that. And so would Andrew, if he were still alive.

I would be extremely opposed to any Kenmore land passing out of the family.'

Kepa opened his mouth to speak, but Tamar held up a hand. 'So I've decided to play a more prominent role in the management of Kenmore, after consulting with Joseph and Owen and Lachie, naturally, and I'll be setting up a series of trusts so that none of the land can be sold off, or passed on to anyone outside the family, without the approval of a majority of the trustees.'

'And who will the trustees be?' Kepa asked, although he thought he already knew.

'Well, after I'm gone, my children, of course. All of them. And Erin, when Lachie goes.'

'James will not like that.'

'I don't care, Kepa. I love James dearly, but I will not allow him, or any of the others if it comes to that, to jeopardise Kenmore. Andrew and Lachie put their lives into the station, and it must stay in the family.' She reached for a glass of water on the night stand and took a sip. Her face now took on a very determined expression. 'So while I am still here, I am going to do my utmost to make sure that all of the children, and that includes Joseph and Erin, and James, regardless of what he might think about it, retain access to what is rightfully theirs. They are my family, Kepa, and I will fight for their interests until my last breath.'

3

Kenmore, 1933

Napier rebuilt itself in the years after the earthquake. Ruined shops, offices and houses were gradually cleared and replaced with brand-new, starkly modern buildings. An elegant and poignant memorial to those who had died was built on Marine Parade. Bridges and roads were repaired, and the local economy began to recover — as much as the Depression allowed. Many unemployed men found work in the city's reconstruction, which prompted more than one optimistic local to note that every cloud had a silver lining.

Tamar was left with a limp — which, to her extreme annoyance, necessitated the use of a cane (at least while she wasn't in public) — and a warning from her doctor to heed the weakened state of her heart. She ignored him, and threw herself into her family's affairs with enthusiasm and a vigour that amused Lachie, startled James, delighted the grandchildren and heartened everyone else.

She became more involved with the children's schools, although this year, much against her protestations, Bonnie and Leila had gone off to board at Iona College in Havelock North. It had been decided, though, as much for the sake of peace and quiet as anything else, that it would be for the best. And the twins loved it, although it

48

was less clear whether the school loved having them. Their academic progress had been, for the most part, quite acceptable to date, but both had already been reprimanded for 'conduct unbecoming to young ladies'. Drew had joined Liam and Duncan, now in his last year, at Napier Boys', and Billy had started there as well, Joseph having refused to even contemplate sending him to Te Aute College, which he had loathed. Now only Ana and Robert remained at Kenmore, and James and Lucy's daughter Kathleen would soon be joining Bonnie and Leila at Iona College.

Tamar had also become more involved in the business of the station. Since Andrew died she had thoroughly enjoyed managing Kenmore's books, finding real satisfaction in seeing the numbers entered squarely into the black columns of her ledgers. Over the past two years, however, as a result of the Depression and the associated drop in wool prices, Kenmore's profit margins had been reduced significantly. But the station was much better off than smaller landowners, many of whom had been forced to walk off their land, leaving behind paddocks and homes and lives they had worked years to establish. Heartbroken on their behalf, Tamar gave such men work at Kenmore whenever she could, even when the station could barely afford it. Lachie sat her down one day and pointed out, kindly but bluntly, that if she did not stop hiring unemployed farmers and farm labourers because she felt sorry for their families, they could well be walking off their own land in the not too distant future. Tamar had told him not to be ridiculous, but had not taken on anyone new since.

Keely and Erin were also doing what they could to help those hit hard by the Depression. Once a fortnight they went into town and worked in the soup kitchens set up at relief depots, although often it was a thankless task. Many in the queues were children and women whose men were away on relief work, although some were unemployed men themselves, periodically stood down from the miserably paid government-subsidised schemes. Keely and Erin both felt extremely uncomfortable standing behind the bare trestle tables doling out soup to disheartened and haggard women dressed almost in rags, their children shoeless or with sacks wrapped around their small feet for warmth. Or to men who had been skilled or even white-collar workers before the Depression but had humiliatingly lost almost everything since, and were often unable to meet anyone's eyes because of their shame and despair.

The cousins took care to wear their plainest clothes, and after April of the previous year, when the mayoress of Dunedin was attacked by protesters after handing out parcels of food while wearing her best outfit complete with elegant dress gloves, were very pleased they had. The work was depressing but neither would contemplate not doing it. Not even Keely, who found herself having to bite her tongue on several occasions when the mood in the queues became unpleasant. And it frequently did. There was bitterness, sometimes pronounced, among the unemployed towards those they perceived to be better off.

One day a barefoot little girl, dressed in a frock that looked suspiciously like a man's work shirt, muttered something to Keely as she was ladling soup.

'I'm sorry, dear?' Keely had responded pleasantly.

'I *said*,' replied the girl, her face screwing up in a scowl, 'my mum said yous are all stuck-up bitches and you're only doing this to make yourselves feel righteous!'

Keely froze, then slowly put down her ladle. 'Did she now?'

'Yes, I did,' said a grim-faced woman behind the child, the straight line of her lips echoed by the brim of the unadorned cloche hat jammed low on her forehead. 'And I'm not the only one as thinks that either, Mrs Fancy Landowner.'

Keely, astounded at such rudeness, opened her mouth to retaliate, but closed it again as she felt Erin tread heavily on her foot.

The woman continued, warming to her theme. 'You all think you're doing us such a favour, doling us out soup and bread when we can't afford to buy our own, but whose fault's that? Not ours! We didn't ask to be unemployed!' Mutters of approval around her spurred her on. 'It's the fault of the likes of you. Yes, it is! You on your big sheep farms with your cars and money and fancy schools for your kids. And your ruddy government that couldn't see this coming and won't even stump up with a few miserable shillings for those that can't find work. How am I

51

supposed to feed me kids, eh? This soup isn't even enough to nourish a kitten!' She whipped open her baggy brown coat to reveal her advanced pregnancy. 'And what about this one, eh? Due in two weeks and I'll be lucky if I can feed it meself, I'm that hungry. And me man's away working up north on the roads for next to nothing, too far away to come home during the stand-down, so God knows when he'll see this new one.'

Keely had relaxed now. Behind the woman's anger she could sense fear and frustration, and realised that the attack wasn't really personal.

The woman bit her lip, only just winning her battle against encroaching tears. 'If you really want to do something useful, you tell your husbands to get on to the government and that bloody Coates and get them to change the economics. Telling the unemployed to eat grass! It's the economics that's got us where we are today!'

'Yeah!' declared the little girl enthusiastically, soup dribbling down her grubby chin.

Keely stopped herself from pointing out that the woman had only moments ago blamed sheep farmers.

'You been listening to that man of yours too long, Lottie Baker,' another woman said. 'That's his words.'

'Too bloody right I have, and it'd do you good to listen to them and all.'

There was a lull then, which Keely filled by asking as politely as she could manage, 'Would you still like this soup then, Mrs Baker?'

The woman's head came up, and she straightened her back. 'Yes, I would,' she replied with dignity, her hand resting protectively on her distended belly. 'I got me new one to think of.'

Afterwards, when Keely and Erin talked the incident over, they both agreed that what had struck them most was not the invective the woman had hurled at Keely, but the desperate, trapped look on her face when she'd said she still wanted the soup. As mothers themselves, it was something they both thought they understood.

Not long after that, when the government had reduced the pay for relief work even further, had come the riots and the looting. They started in Dunedin where members of the Unemployed Workers Movement rampaged through the centre of town, breaking windows and taking what they could, and spread to Auckland a few days later. The riots there were worse and continued over several days, ending only when the military was called in to restore order. Then it was the turn of Wellington, where the destruction and looting were the most widespread and violent yet.

* * *

Tamar had known for some time that something was up with James. Since July of the previous year, he had begun to show excessive interest in the economy, even for a banker, and had become very enthusiastic about a new political organisation called the New Zealand National

Movement, which was busy convening meetings with sheep farmers and businessmen throughout the Hawke's Bay. Then one day he arrived out at Kenmore unexpectedly, asking Tamar if he could speak with her in private.

When they'd settled themselves in the parlour, Tamar looked at her son for a long moment, taking in his high colour and the uncharacteristic sparkle in his eyes.

'What's this about then? You certainly look excited about something.'

James sat forward eagerly. 'Yes, I am, actually. I've just been elected as an officer of the New Zealand Legion,' he declared triumphantly.

'I'm sorry, dear?'

James raised his voice. 'The New Zealand Legion, Mam. The political movement destined to put an end to the Depression and change the way New Zealand is governed for ever.'

'Thank you, James, I'm not deaf yet.' Tamar reached for her cup of tea and balanced it carefully on the wide arm of her chair. 'The New Zealand Legion? I thought you were following the New Zealand National Movement?'

'I am. The name's been changed.'

Tamar said something she knew she would probably regret. 'Oh yes, I read about it in one of the papers recently. Isn't it a Fascist group?'

James looked thoroughly appalled, and Tamar had to stop herself from smiling. 'No, it most certainly is not!' he said.

'Oh, well, I'm very sorry, James, but the editor of this particular newspaper implied strongly that the New Zealand Legion has definite Fascist leanings.'

'Rubbish. The papers can never write anything without distorting it one way or another. No, we're a group of conservatives bound together by a common interest in saving this country from social and economic ruin resulting from state paternalism, overly liberal social policies and reckless borrowing. The legion aims to maintain law and order, and encourage and stimulate what is best for our public life. We fully support nationalism and self-reliance.'

'Really, James, you sound as though you're reading straight from some sort of political pamphlet.'

James reddened. 'Certain words and phrases are particularly apt to describe what we hope to achieve. And I support their sentiments whole-heartedly.'

Tamar took a sip of her tea. 'But isn't the government we already have quite conservative? Didn't you even vote for it yourself?'

'It's not doing what it was elected to do, and it has to be changed before matters in this country deteriorate any further, don't you see?'

Tamar noted he had sidestepped her question. 'All right then, dear, but what does this have to do with me?'

'You don't see, do you?' James sighed in exasperation and sat back, ignoring the cup of tea going cold at his elbow. 'Look, what sort of prices have you been getting for Kenmore wool lately? Not very good ones, I'll bet.'

'No, they're not very good, as a matter of fact.

They've dropped almost fifty per cent since the crash. And you know that, James, so why do you ask?'

'Because I want to make sure *you* know it.'

'Well, of course I know it. How could I not? I've managed Kenmore's accounts for years.'

'And do you know *why* the prices are so low?'

'I'm sure you're going to tell me.'

'Because the Coalition government has mismanaged the market, that's why. There must be rigid demarcation between state and private enterprise. An unbridled socialist government will be the death of New Zealand.'

Tamar was beginning to lose her patience. 'Oh, get off your soapbox, James. Go back into town and have a look at the queues outside the soup kitchens and tell me again about our unbridled socialist government. That soup is the only meal some of those people get each day. Little children, James, and pregnant women surviving on one bowl of soup! It's an absolute disgrace.'

'Yes, but if the government wasn't doling out that soup, those people would be encouraged to find work and support themselves!'

Tamar stared out through the french doors and breathed deeply through her nose until she had regained control of her temper. 'What exactly was it you wanted to talk to me about, James?'

'There's not much point now,' he replied truculently. 'I can see you've a bee in your bonnet about what I've said already.'

Tamar fixed her son with a cool, controlled gaze. 'There are no bees whatsoever in my bonnet. Please do go on.'

James, too enamoured with what he was about to say, missed the warning signs. 'Well, you may or may not know that a lot of the members of the legion, those from this area anyway, and from the south, are sheep farmers. There are plenty of businessmen too, bankers and lawyers and what have you, but sheep farmers really are very well represented.'

'Small landowners, or big station owners?' Tamar asked. 'Because a lot of the small farmers don't have their land any more, a fact of which I'm sure, as a banker, you'll be thoroughly aware.'

'I mean station owners, farmers with substantial holdings. In fact, several out this way have joined just recently. And what I was considering . . . well, we, really, what we were considering . . . '

' "We"?'

'I and my colleagues, at the bank and in the legion. We'd like to extend an invitation to you, as part owner and manager of one of the largest and more profitable sheep stations in the Hawke's Bay, to join us, to become a member and support and contribute to our policies and help change New Zealand for the better. And Uncle Lachie too, of course.'

'But James, I'm a woman.'

James missed his mother's sarcasm completely. 'In fact, Roland Peacocke suggested it himself. He had a word with me this week so I

57

said I'd talk to you about it as soon as I had the opportunity.'

Tamar replaced her teacup on a side table. 'The manager of the bank would like Lachie and me to become members of the New Zealand Legion?'

'That's right. It would be a great opportunity. Think of what could be achieved. If we could change the government, we could end the Depression here in New Zealand, improve profits for landowners, which of course includes us, and help get the country back on an even keel. It's a tremendous thing to be involved in, Mam, it really is. And it would almost certainly mean an end to the Labour Party, which can only be good for New Zealand.'

Tamar judged correctly that this would be the wrong time to reveal to James that she had been voting for Labour ever since it was formed. She looked at her son and her heart almost broke — because of his naïveté, and because of his obvious ignorance of her beliefs and the way she saw the world.

She'd been pleased to see in him the sort of enthusiasm he'd shown as a younger man, before he went away to war, but was disturbed to discover that it was for something as crack-pot and ominous-sounding as the New Zealand Legion. It was reasonably common knowledge that the movement consisted of wealthy men made nervous by increased taxation, and enraged by the Coalition's introduction of vaguely socialist measures. Tamar was not a socialist — not a politically active one anyway

— but her working-class roots gave her a sympathy with the so-called lower classes, despite her now privileged station in life. But James obviously didn't feel the same way, not any more.

It was true he'd been raised at Kenmore in a very comfortable and happy home, had received a good private education and then gone straight into the army where his social status had helped his military career. But he'd had a real knack for soldiering too, and an affinity with his men that had guaranteed their commitment and loyalty. That had been proved both here in New Zealand and while James had been overseas. In fact, Tamar suspected that the loyalty of James's men — ordinary blokes from farms and blacksmiths' forges and factories and coal mines — had been all that had kept him from the firing squad in France.

But that had been a long time ago, and James had changed enormously since then. His war experiences had isolated him, made him judgemental and narrow-minded, and turned his fear into sanctimony. And now it seemed to Tamar that his feelings of inadequacy, his desperation for respect and maybe even redemption, had propelled him into a situation where he was floundering, and he didn't even know it. She wasn't mistrustful by nature, but more than seventy years of life had made her wise and very shrewd, and if she wasn't mistaken — and she hardly ever was these days — her son was being taken advantage of.

'And what manner of support does Mr

Peacocke have in mind?'

James looked at her, and for a moment a shadow of discomfort flickered across his face. 'Well, public backing of the legion's policies, of course, attendance at meetings, that sort of thing. And perhaps some financial assistance.'

Ah, thought Tamar. 'How much financial assistance?'

James shrugged. 'The local members have all made donations.'

'How much have you given?'

James looked affronted. 'Really, Mam, that's a bit personal. Oh, all right, five hundred pounds.'

Tamar closed her eyes briefly. 'And how much has everyone else given?'

'It's not the sort of thing one bandies about, the amount one has donated.'

'So you don't know?'

'No.'

'What if you're the only one?'

'Oh, *really*, Mam, why must you be so suspicious! Everyone has given something, or at least made a pledge to!'

'So would I be correct in assuming that this legion of yours is not very well funded.'

'It's early days yet.'

'But aren't most of the members wealthy landowners and businessmen?'

At this point James didn't know what to say to his mother — she was right, and he wasn't entirely clear regarding why there was so little money to finance the legion's activities.

He changed the subject. 'It's not just money you could contribute. It would be wonderful to

60

have the Murdoch family name on the members' list. Or even on the national council of delegates.' He was starting to sound desperate.

'Your name's already on the members' list. What's wrong with that?'

'Well, nothing, of course. But . . . '

'But what?'

James looked his mother directly in the eye, and she had the distinct impression that he was blaming her for something. '*I* don't run this station, Mam, you do. You and Lachie. I may be a Murdoch but I don't have any influence at all when it comes to the family business. You've made sure of that.'

Tamar couldn't deny this. 'You will when the time comes, James, you know that.'

'When the time comes!' he exploded. 'And when it does, there'll be Joseph and Keely and Thomas and Erin as well!'

'I don't really expect that Thomas will be all that interested.'

'You know what I mean! *I'm* the eldest, Mam, I'm the eldest Murdoch. When will that ever be acknowledged?'

Tamar stared at her son for a long moment; this tantrum had gone on long enough. 'But you're not my eldest child,' she replied, though not unkindly.

James jerked back in his seat as if he had been slapped. Then he raised his hands and put them over his face, and Tamar wondered if he was weeping. But when they came down again to rest limply in his lap, she saw that his eyes were dry. Unfathomably weary, but dry.

'Mam, you have to understand. I must be someone, I have to *mean* something. This is my chance to do that.' He reddened again, embarrassed to have revealed so much of his private torment. 'So will you consider lending your support to the legion? Please don't let me down.'

And then he added something that he didn't really mean, and it made everything so much worse, but as he sensed his mother gathering the words to turn him down he was suddenly overwhelmed with panic and despair.

'You've always favoured Joseph, and you treat Owen more like a son than you do me. I think I'm entitled to your support at least just this once.'

Tamar thought of the opportunities that James had been given during his life and, after he'd come home from the war, all the support and second chances and tolerance and forgiveness and patience.

'No, James. I'm sorry, but I'm afraid I can't help you. Not this time.'

He picked up his hat and rose to his feet in one swift, angry movement. When the parlour door slammed behind him, Tamar remained seated, gazing unseeingly across the room.

★   ★   ★

'Aren't they a pack of malcontents with too much money and nothing better to do than whine about taxes?' asked Lachie, helping himself to another large dollop of Creamoata

62

and slopping it into his grandson's Sergeant Dan bowl, made redundant now that Robert had decided he was too grown up to use it. There were flecks of porridge in Lachie's white beard and down the front of his work jersey.

'Something like that,' Tamar replied. 'They seem to stand for just about everything I don't. And do you know what really upset me, Lachie? The fact that he thought it would be something I'd actually want to support. He knows we give meat and what have you to the soup kitchens every week, and he knows how much I support what the girls are doing.' Angrily, she buttered another piece of toast. 'What on earth made him think I would want to join an organisation that wants to do away with social services, especially these days?'

'Aye, it does demonstrate a wee lack of thought. Anyway, I thought their main aim was to end the Depression?'

'Apparently, but you and I would like to do that too, wouldn't we? And we're not advocating taking food out of the mouths of babes.'

'Tamar, love, you always see things in black and white, don't you?'

Tamar cut her toast in half. 'Perhaps. Andrew used to say that too. But sometimes things *are* either black or white.'

Lachie blotted his lips, beard and jersey with a table napkin and burped discreetly. 'Well, I'll not be joining any New Zealand Legion. I've enough to do as it is without gallivanting about the countryside attending dreary meetings and throwing good money after bad.' He looked

63

across the table at Tamar and pulled a wry face. 'And the lad wasn't too happy about your turning down his invitation?'

'No, he wasn't. He stormed out without a word. I'm surprised you didn't hear the door slam from up in the top paddock.'

'His pride, do you think?'

'I expect so.' Although she knew that desperation had also been driving her son. 'I think he feels I've let him down in front of his friends.'

'Well, he should have discussed the matter with you first, rather than the other way around.'

'Actually, I suspect his 'friends' approached him about it. I've never particularly liked Mr Roland Peacocke — far too arrogant and oily for his own good. I much preferred old MacGregor Sinclair before he retired.'

'Perhaps the lad felt he had no choice in the matter.' Lachie folded his napkin, took a last noisy slurp of his tea and pushed his chair back from the table. 'God knows I'm fond of James, Tamar, but I think it's high time he stood on his own two feet and stopped trying to curry favour from that crowd he's mixing with. He didn't used to be like that.'

'He didn't used to be a lot of things, Lachie,' Tamar said harshly.

'Aye, well, I can understand you being angry.'

'I *am* angry. He said some very unkind things about the others. And about me. This bickering and bullying and mistrust of anyone who ever tries to do anything good for him has gone on for years, Lachie, *years*! Lucy's oppressed by him,

64

Duncan despises him and he scares Kathleen and Drew silly whenever he's in one of his moods. I've had enough, I really have. This time he can get himself out of trouble.'

Lachie raised his eyebrows.

'Yes, trouble. You know it's always his 'trouble' when he gets this desperate.'

4

'I've bailed James out before, you know,' Tamar said to Kepa.

They were in the living room of the little house on Marine Parade, with the french doors fastened open so that the smell of the sea wafted in on the spring breeze, together with the sound of seagulls screeching raucously over something dead on the beach.

'And will you do it again?' Kepa asked, his feet propped comfortably on a low table in front of him and a small glass of whisky on the arm of his chair. He loved these rare times when he had Tamar all to himself. Today they had all afternoon, and all night too, if they chose.

Tamar took a small sip of her brandy and shifted in her seat; if she sat too long in one position her bad leg would invariably become stiff, then she would have to use the despised cane the following day.

'No, I won't.'

'Really?'

'Really.'

'He does not want money for himself, though, this time, does he?'

'Well, no, he didn't ask for it directly, but he might as well have. I very much suspect that his fine and upstanding colleagues in the New Zealand Legion have him over a barrel, Kepa.' She rubbed a finger around the top of her glass,

66

hoping to hear the crystal sing. It didn't. 'Well, I say 'colleagues', but I suspect that only a handful are behind this particular nasty little manoeuvre. Perhaps even only one. I don't believe that the legion is inherently bad, just somewhat mis-guided. But James must really have outdone himself this time to be in this sort of pickle.'

'It may be your standing as a very successful station owner that they are wanting. You have influence in this area, after all.'

'Not in those circles, I don't.'

'You do, Tamar. Obviously James has gambled himself into serious debt again, has borrowed from the bank and now cannot pay it back. Someone, perhaps this Roland Peacocke, has offered to cancel the debt if you agree to support this political organisation of his.'

'How do you know that?'

Kepa shrugged. 'I am simply guessing. But is that not what you are thinking?'

'More or less, yes. I hope he's only borrowed money. I hope he hasn't taken out a mortgage on their house — Lucy would be devastated if they lost that. She would die of the shame.'

'I doubt it. She would feel humiliated, yes, but I do not think she would die.'

'But it would be disastrous for them, especially the children. I'm more than happy to do whatever is needed for my grandchildren and my daughter-in-law, but I've come to the point where I really have no compunction about letting James finally reap what he's been sowing these last years.'

'That is certainly a relief to hear,' Kepa said,

who would happily have abandoned James to his own inept devices ages ago if he'd had any say at all in the matter. He had never interfered in Tamar's family, except where Joseph was concerned, and had no intention of starting now. Tamar had very rarely denied her children anything, and in his view this recent change of conduct was not an altogether bad thing. 'So that is that, then?' he added, a note of admiration in his voice.

'Yes,' she replied adamantly. 'It is.'

But he saw in her eyes how much it was hurting her.

★ ★ ★

In an elegantly decorated office not even a mile away in town, James sat on a rather uncomfortable chair with his legs awkwardly crossed and a large glass of brandy in his hand. The seat was low — deliberately, James thought, to place whoever was sitting in it at a disadvantage.

Opposite him, behind an enormous, highly polished mahogany desk, sat Roland Peacocke, leaning back in his high-backed leather chair and pondering James as if he were some sort of unique insect mounted on a card.

'And she said no? Well!' he said with some amusement. 'And you were so sure she would be absolutely delighted with the idea!'

'No, sir, I believe that when you made the suggestion I said she could well be interested,' James replied.

He hated Roland Peacocke with a passion, and

hated even more having to call him 'sir'. He would give anything to cross the room and deliver a good hard punch to the man's smirking, imperious, red-veined face. If he had the guts, of course, which he didn't.

'Now, James, I think you implied more than that,' Peacocke said, swirling brandy around in his cut crystal tumbler and sniffing it pretentiously. 'I think, given what's at stake, you implied a *lot* more than that.'

James said nothing, simply sat and waited for the next snide, derogatory comment.

'If I remember correctly,' Peacocke went on, 'you took out the mortgage on your house six months ago. To date you have been unable to meet a single repayment.'

I know that, you bastard, James answered silently. And you know it too, because you approved the transaction and you've dangled the bloody thing over my head like a guillotine ever since. He cringed at the thought of Lucy ever finding out — it would break her heart.

'Yes, sir,' he said out loud, 'I'm aware of that, but I'll be able to pay you soon.'

Peacocke suddenly leaned forward. 'You know you can't pay it, *I* know you can't pay it, soon *everyone* will know you can't pay it. And nobody admires a bankrupt, do they, James? Especially one from a family as illustrious as yours. And of course you'd lose your position here. So I strongly suggest that you go back and speak to your charming mother again. I'm sure she'll be very keen to give us her full support if you just try a little harder.' He reached for the brandy decanter and poured himself another tipple. 'She's an imposing and well-respected woman, and her commitment to the cause would be a real incentive for new members. She's also known to be a very generous benefactor, which would certainly not go amiss as far as the legion's coffers are concerned.'

James nodded in meek agreement. He was being blackmailed and he knew it, but had no idea about how to extricate himself. He'd managed not to gamble for over a month so had avoided losing anything more — not that there was much left to lose these days: his savings had gone long ago and the bank now owned his home. In a way he'd felt immense relief as he had pushed his chair away from the card table that last time, knowing that if he didn't go near the cards, or the horses, or the dogs, he could not continue to come to grief.

Some men were ruined by alcohol, and others by women or the poppy, but his nemesis had turned out to be gambling. Only for those brief moments when he was winning — and even, perversely, when he was on the verge of losing — did he feel vital and alive again. It was completely irrational, he knew that, but the terrible elation gambling gave him was almost exactly the same as the dreadful but utterly seductive sensation he'd lived with night and day throughout the war — not knowing whether this time would be the last, whether he would live or die, win or lose. It had driven him insane then, and it was doing the same thing to him now, but he needed it. God only knew how long he would be able to keep himself away from it this time.

And now there was Peacocke. It had taken James some time to work out what lay behind his boss's goading and insidious persecution, but he thought he'd finally narrowed the possibilities down to one or two likely motives. There was Peacocke's commitment to the New Zealand Legion, of course, but James suspected that had only a minor role. More than anything, Peacocke was jealous — jealous of the Murdoch family fortune, of Tamar's standing in the community and of her reputation as a shrewd business-woman, and of James's privileged life. It was rumoured that Peacocke himself had not come from a monied background, that he had clawed his way up through the banking hierarchy to reach his exalted position of manager, and as a result bitterly resented those who, like James, had not had to start at the bottom, and who would ultimately inherit more money than Peacocke could ever hope for.

How delighted the bastard must have been to discover that James was in such financial strife. And — even more rewardingly — why. James should have known from the cloying sympathy in the older man's voice, the hand of condolence on his shoulder and the assurance that, yes, of course the bank could see its way to some sort of arrangement. But the minute the mortgage documents had been signed, everything had changed. Peacocke had started making thinly veiled remarks about James's situation in front of other bank staff, men whom James hoped had come to respect him, and sending unnecessary memoranda — inside sealed envelopes, thank God — reminding James when his repayments would fall due. But, James, having paid off a sizeable portion of his gambling debts, had not been able to make even one payment. His incomes from both the bank and the station were going straight to various card-playing opponents and bookies around town, leaving just enough to deter Lucy from becoming suspicious. Or so James hoped.

He had lost everything and now, just as Peacocke had hoped, his own mother had turned away from him and refused to help. Tamar's rejection had wounded James to the very depths of his soul. No matter what had happened in the past, she had never shut him out like that before. She did not know the full story, the true magnitude of his problems, but she should have been able to sense that something was severely awry.

'So, what's it to be, James?' Peacocke said cheerfully. 'Another trip out to magnificent Kenmore Station, or do I need to start proceedings to foreclose on your mortgage?'

'My mother made it quite clear that she didn't want to be involved, sir. It really isn't her sort of thing.'

'That's not what you said the other day.'

'I was wrong.'

'Go on, James. One more try, eh? Otherwise I might just be forced to have a very close look at the accounts Kenmore holds at this bank as well. These are hard times, James, hard times.'

James drained the last of his whisky and closed

his eyes for a moment. 'I'll see what I can do,' he mumbled.

He felt sick, but he couldn't tell whether it was the alcohol or his conscience.

★ ★ ★

His mother would not even speak to him this time, and as he drove away down Kenmore's long driveway, humiliation, anger and hurt burning in his belly, he knew for certain that he could not rely on her for help.

But in the end he did not need to. A little over a week later he found himself sitting alone in his study, in the house that was no longer his, weeping hot, muffled tears of relief and shame. In his hand was a note from his brother Thomas, pinned to a personal cheque generous enough to repay what he owed the bank, and most of his remaining debts.

The note read:

Dear James,
I won't beat about the bush. Keely hinted in her last letter that you might be in some sort of financial strife again. I telephoned Mam, who refused to talk to me about it, so I knew then you must have really excelled yourself this time.

You have to stop this, James, now. If not for your own sake, then for the sake of Lucy and the children. I know what this is about — I was there too, remember — but it was a long time ago. Let go of it, for God's sake, before it's too late.

The money is to get you back in the black. If you don't think you can trust yourself to use it for that, please give it to Lucy and have her sort things out. Or does she not know? Tell her, James, trust her, she's a good woman, and very capable.

Trust yourself — I still do.

Your brother,
Thomas

James reflected for a moment on the inherent goodness and generosity of his younger brother, and burst into tears again, his face in his hands. He didn't know whether Thomas could afford this gesture or not — he seemed to know so little about his own family these days — and vowed to pay it back as soon as he could. Thomas had always supported him, and Keely and Ian too, even when they'd been children and had all teased him mercilessly for being so sensitive and gentle. Dear Thomas, the one who was always quiet, rational and unfailingly fair. Over the last few years, James had barely given him a second thought.

Through his tears he felt his shame burn even more intensely, remembering those terrible, surreal, fragmented days he had spent locked in a French farmhouse not far behind the front lines, awaiting court martial for killing his colleague and one-time friend, Ron Tarrant. Suffering from advanced shell shock, he'd barely been able to speak or to make any sense of what was happening to him. But he had recognised Thomas, who'd arrived from his unit as soon as he heard what had happened, and had used his lawyer's skills before the trial, talking on the quiet to everyone who might help his brother's case.

James had been acquitted for lack of evidence, sent to a convalescent hospital in England to recuperate, then returned to New Zealand. Thomas had known he'd killed Ron Tarrant, but he had also known why. And James had never really thanked him for his support, choosing instead to sink further and further into his own anguish, guilt and self-doubt. Yes, there had been a short period after he came home when he'd thought he could manage life after all, but then, without even realising it, he'd slipped gradually and inexorably back into his own private morass of misery. Now, nearly seventeen years later, he was still floundering around, up to his neck in fear, bitterness and bad decisions. For a fleeting, terrifying moment, his thoughts strayed to the shotgun locked in the cupboard behind him.

He rubbed his wet face with shaking hands and swallowed painfully around the lump in his throat that threatened more tears, and realised he had probably reached his lowest point. He had finally, truly, become what he had always feared being — weak, inadequate, and a coward.

And, once again, his brother had come to his aid. But could Thomas be right? Could he stop this awful, destructive behaviour and turn himself around? Because perhaps — just perhaps — it wasn't too late. James felt something deep within himself shift — only a fraction, but it was enough to give him the first prickle of hope he'd felt in years.

'James? Is there something wrong?'

He lowered his hands to see Lucy poised in the doorway of the darkened room. She was balancing a tray bearing cups and a plate of biscuits, and peering at him worriedly.

'Yes. No. Well, yes.'

'Why is the light off?'

'I wanted it off.'

'Well, I want it on, I can't see anything.' She carefully put the tray down on a low table and fumbled across the wall for the light switch, a sharp intake of breath coming when she saw her husband's swollen red eyes.

'Have you been crying? Why, what's happened?'

James blinked hard in the bright electric light. 'It's all right, it's not bad news.' He hesitated briefly. 'It's good, really.'

Lucy sat down opposite him and began to pour the tea. She knew better than to force him to divulge information — past attempts had usually resulted in him losing his temper and accusing her of nagging or interfering. Passing him a cup with two biscuits balanced on the edge of the saucer, she sat back and waited.

He put the biscuits aside, took a sip of his tea, then reached for the whisky bottle on his desk.

Lucy made a pinched face, hoping it wasn't going to be one of *those* nights.

He caught her look and shook his head. 'No, it

really is good news.' He poured an uncharacteristically small measure of whisky into his tea and replaced the cap. Then he cleared his throat, took another sip and cleared his throat again.

To Lucy it seemed he was struggling to say something momentous, something that was going to cost him very dearly indeed. Then she glimpsed the immense sadness in his eyes, and her own heart lurched in response.

'Lucy, I need to talk to you about something quite ... well, *very* important.' He held up Thomas's letter. 'This is from Thomas. It's only a note but he's sent a cheque too. A rather big cheque.'

She gazed impassively back at him, her pale, waved hair gleaming in the light and her hands clasped loosely in her lap.

'Look, this is extremely difficult for me to say. But I am saying it, and it's probably the first really honest thing I've said in years. I'm terribly sorry, Lucy, I really am. I'm sorry for my behaviour and I'm sorry for the decisions I've made and the way I've treated you and the children. But most of all I'm sorry ... ' and here he drew a deep ragged breath, 'I'm sorry for gambling away all of our money. I've had to mortgage the house to meet my debts. If this money hadn't come from Thomas we would have been out in the street.' Then, almost as an afterthought, he added, 'And I'm being blackmailed by Roland Peacocke at the bank.'

A silence ensued, into which the ticking of the clock over the fireplace expanded until James thought his head might explode.

77

'Then all I can say is it's lucky your mother is paying the children's school fees, isn't it?'

He stared at his wife, his face a picture of confusion. 'Lucy, did you hear what I just said?'

'Yes, James, I heard. We've no money left whatsoever and our house is currently owned by the bank.'

'But, aren't you . . . I thought when I told you, you'd . . . ' He trailed off.

'Yes, I might have, if I hadn't known. But I did know, James. I've known for the last three months. About the mortgage anyway. You shouldn't leave important documents lying around in your desk drawers.'

'But that drawer was locked!'

'It came open one day when I was dusting in here.'

'You went through my private papers?' James, momentarily forgetting the magnitude of his own sins, was outraged.

'You mortgaged our home,' Lucy responded quietly.

He flushed deeply, unable to meet her eyes. Instead, he handed her the cheque. 'Take it. Go into the bank tomorrow and have the mortgage discharged.'

She took the cheque, put it to one side and read the note.

Moments later she looked up and regarded him steadily. 'No, you take it, James. Do you trust yourself?'

'Do you?'

'That's irrelevant at the moment. *You* go and discharge the mortgage, then *you* go to each and

78

every person to whom you owe money, and pay them back.'

James began to grin then, the real, genuine sort of smile he could barely remember. Whether she trusted him or not — and he certainly didn't blame her if she didn't — she was giving him the opportunity to salvage at least a shred of his dignity. 'Yes, I could, couldn't I? In fact,' he added excitedly, 'I could . . . '

'You could what, James?'

★   ★   ★

James didn't go into the bank the following morning. Instead, he drove out to Kenmore — at a rather reckless speed — to talk to his mother. At first she wouldn't see him, but in the end, James went thumping up the stairs and barged into her bedroom, where she was reclining on her chaise longue pretending to read a book. She sat up quickly as he appeared breathlessly at the door, but after a single glance at the wide smile and buoyant expression on her son's handsome face she knew immediately that something had changed.

'I have to talk to you, Mam, please,' he blurted, before she had a chance to say anything herself. Then he went very red.

She nodded her agreement and listened as he stood shamefacedly in front of her, like the small boy he had once been, and delivered a litany of his more recent misdemeanours — unvarnished and with not even the smallest unsavoury detail left out. She was so relieved at his apparent

79

willingness to at last speak openly and honestly that she didn't even reprimand him for his appalling behaviour and staggering lack of sense.

When he'd finished, he sat down on the edge of the big bed his parents had shared all their married life. 'So that's it, Mam, all of it. I'm so sorry, and I'm especially sorry for trying to coerce you into that business with the New Zealand Legion. I really believed I had no choice, but that's no excuse. It was an awful thing to do to you. I know it upset you.'

Tamar nodded her acceptance of his apology. 'And what does Lucy say about all of this?'

James looked uncomfortable again. 'Well, that's sort of what I've come out to talk to you about.'

Tamar's heart sank. 'She's not left you, has she?'

'Left me? No, thank God, because I imagine plenty of women would. No, I think she's relieved.'

'Relieved?'

'Because now she knows exactly what's been going on, although she already knew about the mortgage on the house. And we want to make some changes, Mam. *I* want to make some changes.'

Tamar had heard this before. Warily, she asked, 'But you will use Thomas's money to pay off your debts?'

'Today, as soon as I get back into town. And while I'm at the bank I'm going to hand in my notice.'

Tamar's eyebrows went up.

James took a deep breath. 'Mam, I need to ask something of you. We'd like to move back out to Kenmore, Lucy and I and the children. I'm not cut out to be a banker. I thought it would be the ideal career for me. I thought . . . well, I thought a lot of things, and I was wrong. I think I'd like, I *need*, to do something completely different.'

Tamar was intrigued. 'Such as?'

'I want to grow fruit.'

Several moments ticked by as Tamar absorbed this.

'Fruit? You'd like to grow fruit?'

'Yes, peaches and apricots and cherries and that sort of thing, here at Kenmore. Jim Wattie from Hawke's Bay Fruitgrowers is apparently looking into setting up a cannery and he's going to need contract growers. I think I could be one of them.'

'But James, dear, you've never grown anything in your life.'

'I can learn,' he replied stubbornly. Then, anticipating her next question, 'And we won't need to live here in the big house because I'll build us a new one. How hard can it be? Joseph managed a really good job of his and Erin's.'

Yes, Tamar thought, but Joseph is considerably more practical than you.

'But what I'm really going to need is land, enough to set up an orchard, just a small one at first. I was hoping you and Lachie could perhaps see your way to selling me ten acres or so. I'm not sure exactly how much I'll need yet.'

'If we were to sell you land, James, how would

81

you pay for it? You're not exactly financially secure at the moment, are you?'

'No, but I could get a loan.'

'Not from the bank you're about to resign from this afternoon?'

'Hardly.'

Tamar shook her head. 'No, James, you're not borrowing money from an institution, not even one that isn't associated with Roland Peacocke. What a pig of a man. I think I'll go into town myself in a few days and transfer Kenmore's accounts to another bank.' She thought for a moment. 'How much do you really want to do this, James?'

He didn't hesitate, and the passion in his voice told her as much as his words. 'As much as I wanted to lead men in battle.'

'Then let me talk to Lachie. I imagine he would agree to lease you the land you need at some sort of peppercorn rental to start with. Ten acres isn't much, and I'm sure the sheep won't mind having to go and stand somewhere else. When would you want to start this new venture?'

'As I'll no longer be employed by the bank by five this afternoon, as soon as possible.'

'And you're sure Lucy is happy about all of this?'

'It's her decision too, Mam. And yes, she is happy.'

Tamar was suddenly overwhelmed with the heart-swelling realisation that her son might just have finally come home from the war.

'All right then, dear, let me talk to Lachie. But

82

it will have to be on a proper business footing, mind.' Something occurred to her. 'And I'm sorry, but I still can't allow Kenmore's name to be associated with the New Zealand Legion, so you'll have to have your meetings somewhere else.'

James said, 'Bugger the legion.' Then he laughed out loud, darted over to Tamar and crushed her in a hug that almost knocked the pins out of her hair. 'You won't regret this, Mam, you really won't. It could be the start of a whole new empire for the Murdochs.'

'Is that what you really want?'

He stepped back from her, and frowned. 'No, it isn't actually. I just want to grow things. I want to get up in the morning and do real, physical work and get my hands dirty and watch the trees grow and the blossom come and then the fruit. I want to do something quiet, Mam, something *peaceful.*'

Tamar felt her eyes prickle with tears as she reached out and took his hand. 'James?'

'Yes?'

'Your father would be very proud of you.'

★   ★   ★

It was a very determined-looking James who walked into the bank that afternoon. Ignoring the startled looks of the tellers in the foyer, he pushed through the heavy wooden door that led to Roland Peacocke's office. Without knocking he went straight in, bypassed the pair of disconcertingly low visitors' chairs and parked

83

his backside on the edge of Peacocke's desk.

The man himself rocked forward in his plush manager's chair with a crash and exclaimed in shocked and angry tones, 'Get off my desk, James.'

'Not until you get off my back, *Roland*.'

'I beg your pardon?'

'I'd like the mortgage documents to my house, if you don't mind.'

'What?'

'The mortgage documents. I'm about to pay it off. In full.'

Peacocke's stunned look of disbelief mixed with disappointment was so comical James almost laughed.

'This is highly irregular,' he sputtered.

James leaned menacingly forward over the desk, bumping Peacocke's half-finished cup of tea so that it spilt messily onto some papers.

'No, it isn't. I took out a mortgage, now I'm paying it back. Get the papers, please. Now.'

Peacocke swivelled around in his seat and unlocked a cabinet, then extracted a small sheaf of papers inside a folder. The look on his face had changed rapidly from arrogant incredulity to one of ill-concealed fear.

James withdrew his chequebook from his coat pocket and opened it. 'What was the amount again? With interest to date?' He knew full well what the amount was, but wasn't going to let Peacocke know it had been burned forever into his memory.

Peacocke stated the figure and James wrote the cheque, tearing it briskly out of the book and handing it over.

Peacocke said, 'How do I know you have the funds to cover it? I don't believe you do.'

'It's valid, and I couldn't give a toss what you believe.'

After checking the amount, Peacocke reluctantly took a large rubber stamp from his desk tray and banged it violently onto every page of the mortgage document, leaving the word 'Discharged' in red as he went.

'Now sign it as well, if you don't mind,' James ordered. He was thoroughly enjoying this.

'What?'

'Sign your name on every page. I'd hate there to be any confusion at a later date.'

Peacocke scribbled his signature beneath each stamp mark, then passed it to James to do the same.

'I'd like a receipt as well, thanks.'

Peacocke glowered as he wrote one out and handed it over. 'You can get off my desk now,' he said through clenched teeth.

James stood up. 'Thank you, Roland, I appreciate that,' he said cheerfully. 'Oh, and there's just one more thing,' he added, delving into his coat again. 'Here. It's my letter of resignation, in effect as from now. I've suddenly discovered that I've got much better things to do than work for someone like you.'

He walked out then, leaving Peacocke sitting behind his desk with his mouth agape and the door open so that everyone walking past was treated to the spectacle of their boss looking like a fish stranded in a bucket.

85

Whistling, James raided the storeroom for an empty box, collected his things from his office, then marched back out through the foyer, waving jauntily to the tellers as he went.

5

Lachie died on the first day of the New Year. He had gone out early, as was his habit on the first day of January, to ride up to the topmost crags of the station when no one else was about and survey in solitude the land rolling away beneath him. It was his way of marking the transition between the old year and the new, and collecting himself for whatever the coming twelve months might bring. He left the big house at dawn, but when he hadn't returned by three that afternoon, Tamar became worried and walked slowly over the hill to Erin and Joseph's to check that he had not stopped off there on his way home.

He hadn't, and when she shared her concerns with her son and daughter-in-law, they decided unanimously that someone should go out and look for him. He was an old man of eighty-two now, still very sound of mind but not always entirely hale. Over the past year Erin had been suggesting — at first tactfully, then quite bluntly — that it might be time for him to put his horse-riding, hill-roaming days behind him, but each time he had smiled, patted her on the cheek, thanked her for her concern, and then ignored her completely.

'I'll go,' declared Joseph, who had spent the morning teaching Billy and Robert how to repair eeling nets, and then had to start all over again at lunchtime because Ana insisted it was unfair that her brothers learn such fascinating skills while she had to stay inside making boring scones and darning whiffy, worn-out old work socks. 'I'll get Owen as well.'

They set off on horseback twenty minutes later, not knowing what they might find but both feeling distinctly uneasy.

'He could be sitting on a rock having a leisurely smoke and thoroughly enjoying the lovely day for all we know,' Owen pointed out, his hat pushed low on his forehead so he wouldn't have to squint into the sun. A long rope was looped about the pommel of his saddle, and he'd tucked a bottle of brandy in his rucksack as well, just in case.

'Or having a bit of a sleep in a sunny spot somewhere,' agreed Joseph.

They were silent for several minutes, then Owen said, 'I wonder if we shouldn't have brought the truck.'

'No good if he's somewhere difficult to get to,' Joseph replied, thinking of some of the deceptively deep ravines in the top paddocks.

But Lachie wasn't enjoying a smoke on a rock, or having a sleep, or stuck in a ravine. When Joseph and Owen found him he was lying motionless on his back on the side of a moderately steep hill, his horse some yards away, cropping the short, brown summer grass and favouring a front leg.

It was immediately clear to the two younger men that Lachie was dead. His head was bent at an unnatural angle and his eyes were open and lifeless, but his face looked peaceful and relaxed. Some yards above him the surface of the hillside, pitted in all directions with rabbit holes, had been gouged and there were grass and dirt stains on his clothes.

'Shit.' Joseph felt his heart begin to ache and his throat swell with loss. 'What are we going to tell Erin?'

Owen had taken his hat off. 'The truth, I suppose. His horse fell and he broke his neck. God, what a tragedy.'

But in the end everyone at Kenmore accepted that the accident had been the best way for Lachie to go. He'd had a morbid fear of becoming infirm, or even worse, mentally decrepit, and having to depend on others to take care of him. Instead, he had died happy, riding the paddocks and hills he'd loved for more than sixty years. And, buried in the small family cemetery in the daffodil paddock next to his wife, he would never be far from the life he had cherished.

The children missed him enormously, their cheerful white-haired old grandfather who'd always been willing to spend time with them and who'd good-naturedly tolerated their pranks, no matter how irritating. Erin, of course, missed him desperately too, and mourned the fact that both her parents had now gone. But Tamar, stuffing down her own grief over the departure of a real friend, her business partner, and her closest link with the life she had shared with Andrew, rallied the family and both the Deane

89

and Murdoch households gradually adjusted to their loss.

★ ★ ★

The next event of note also had an impact on the station, but in an entirely different way, when Mrs Heath, old herself now and in deteriorating health, reluctantly announced that the time had come for her to retire. So, in March, amidst copious tears and promises to visit soon, she moved into Napier to a small cottage which a very generous farewell bonus from Tamar had helped her to purchase. Her departure was the end of an era; she had been with the Murdochs for sixteen years and knew them all almost as well as they knew each other. Once again Tamar was reminded of how much life at Kenmore had changed over the years, and of the uncomfortable fact she herself was aging.

After Mrs Heath had gone there was some debate over whether she should be replaced, but now that the Depression had come to an end, the number of women still willing to work as domestic servants had tapered off dramatically. Erin, who had always done the cooking and housework for her family anyway, declared at dinner one evening that in her opinion housekeepers were a thing of the past, even very good ones like Mrs Heath, and should stay there.

'That's very modern of you,' James commented dryly, hoping that if Kenmore was not to have another housekeeper, he wasn't going to be expected to do any sort of 'inside' work.

He couldn't anyway, even if he'd had the slightest desire to do so: he was too busy with his trees these days to do much else. After two and a half years of very hard but satisfying work, his orchard was now bearing fruit, and making money. He and Lucy were living in the house Owen and Joseph had built for them — James had indeed turned out to be somewhat less than a dab hand with a plumb line and a saw — and although it was nowhere near as grand as the one they'd had in Napier, neither of them really cared. They were happier than they had been in years.

Drew and Kathleen were at boarding school, and Duncan had gone down to Otago University to study medicine, where he was notably underachieving. According to Thomas, who seemed to view such behaviour as fairly normal if not particularly admirable, he preferred to spend his time in various public bars and generally getting into trouble — news which James, despite his genuine attempts at tolerance, was finding difficult to countenance. He had, however, so far kept his opinions to himself, mainly on the advice of Tamar, who believed that Duncan was simply sowing his wild oats before settling into what would surely be several years of earnest and dedicated study. James and Lucy had both laughed hard at this — out of Tamar's earshot, of course — but had decided not to broach the subject with Duncan as he was still refusing to have anything to do with his father. The New Zealand Legion business, even though it had happened three years ago, had been the

91

last straw for him, and since then he had remained convinced that James was a dyed-in-the-wool Fascist, on top of everything else. He rarely came home and, when he did, he spent as much time away from his father as he could.

Although this concerned James, and hurt him quite badly, he understood Duncan's attitude. Or at least he thought he did. James knew that, for most of his son's life, he had been difficult to live with and a bad father. It would take time for the young man to accept that James was doing his best to rectify past mistakes and avoid new ones. It was hard, knowing that his eldest son wanted nothing to do with him, but James hoped that one day Duncan would accept that his father really was a changed man. He'd talked to Joseph and Owen, and to the veterans they sometimes drank with at the RSA in town — a new habit he'd developed last year and was rather enjoying — and the advice he'd received from everyone was just to wait, preferably with his mouth shut. The first move towards reconciliation would have to come from Duncan.

Lucy also found the ongoing rift in her family upsetting, but was determined not to dwell on it. She was far too busy enjoying her husband again. It seemed to her that after those long, grim years of black depressions, emotional withdrawal and relentless nightmares, of which James himself was only half aware, he had at last come to terms with his war experiences. Each passing month brought back a little bit of the old James — or, rather, the young James she had fallen so hopelessly in love with — and she thanked God for it. He was even looking younger: his eyes sparkled, he had lost the pot belly he'd developed during his time at the bank, and he was tanned and very pleasingly muscled again. If, in exchange for that, her new house was smaller and she'd swapped clothes shopping for housework and pruning prickly little trees, then she was more than prepared to make such a sacrifice. She and James were still relatively young and, as far as she could see, they had the delightful prospect of a whole new life stretching out in front of them.

'Actually, I've come to a decision about a housekeeper,' Tamar said conversationally as she sliced into her beef. 'I really think we should do without. Hardly anyone has one these days, and I see no real need for one. Do you?' she asked, glancing around the long, gleaming dining table. They no longer dressed formally for dinner, unless it was a special occasion, but at her insistence the table was still elegantly laid with silver and fine china for the evening meal.

'No,' said Erin immediately, 'but then I've just said as much. And anyway, it's none of my business, we don't live here,' she added cheerfully, helping herself to another new potato. She and Joseph had been invited to dinner at the big house so they could all sample some of James's vegetables, a sideline that kept him occupied when his trees didn't need attention. 'These potatoes are absolutely delicious, James.'

'Thank you, Erin,' he replied, swelling almost visibly with pride. 'But you should be complimenting Joseph, really. And Kepa. They showed

93

me the best way to cultivate them. Traditional method, apparently. I'm just doing them in bulk.'

Erin already knew that — Joseph had rows and rows of them behind their own house — but she said nothing because it was such a delight to see James smile these days.

Keely used her fork to prod unenthusiastically at a dish of small, lumpy, orange vegetables. 'What are these things?'

'Yams,' James replied. 'I'm trying them out. They're quite nice, rather subtle in flavour. Try one.'

They looked to Keely like brightly coloured huhu grubs, and even the thought of eating one was making her feel sick.

'No thanks.' Then, tentatively, she asked, 'Mam, if we're not having a new housekeeper, then who's going to prepare all the meals?'

'Well, you and I can, can't we, dear? There are only three of us, after all.'

Keely stared at her mother.

'Except during the school holidays, of course,' Tamar added. 'Bonnie and Leila will be home then.'

Joseph and Owen exchanged swift, surreptitious glances before concentrating very hard on their meals.

'But I can't cook.'

'It's about time you learned then, isn't it?' Tamar replied, a no-nonsense edge creeping into her voice. 'I'm sure Erin won't mind giving you a few lessons. And Lucy, you're very good at pastries and desserts, I'm sure you'd be happy to give Keely some tips, wouldn't you?'

'I'd love to,' Lucy said, kicking James under the table as she spied him working hard to suppress a wide grin. 'When would you like to start?'

Keely said grudgingly, 'Oh, well, thanks, whenever it suits you, I suppose. But Mam, what about the laundry and the cleaning and that sort of thing? Who's going to do all of that?' she added in increasingly appalled tones.

Tamar made a regretful face. 'Well, I'd like to be responsible for that side of things, of course, but my leg does give me more than a little trouble at times, as you know. And winter will be here in a few months, which will only make it worse. No, I feel that those duties would be best left to you, dear. I'm sure you'll manage, though, you're a very capable little homemaker.'

There was a choking sound as Owen struggled with a green bean that had gone down the wrong way.

Keely blotted her lips with her napkin, then touched the linen to her forehead where a thin sheen of perspiration was forming. 'The sheets and everything?'

Tamar nodded enthusiastically, then took a closer look at Keely, who really had gone very pale. Perhaps she had taken the joke a little too far. 'No, dear, not the sheets. Actually I'm thinking very seriously of asking if Mrs Pike would consider taking on the cleaning and the laundry. If she's interested, of course.'

Mrs Pike was the wife of one of Kenmore's live-in farm labourers, and Tamar knew that the young woman would be pleased to get out of the quarters she shared with her husband and small baby, because she had already been to see her several days ago. Mrs Pike had agreed immediately, providing Mrs Murdoch didn't mind the baby coming with her in a basket. It had all been arranged.

Keely muttered, 'Really, Mam, sometimes you can be very mean.'

'I'm sorry, dear, I was only teasing. I didn't realise it would upset you.'

'Well, it did. Oh . . . God!'

Keely lurched to her feet and rushed out of the room with her hand clamped to her mouth. They all heard her heels clacking across the wooden floor in the hall then through the kitchen, followed by the bang of the toilet door on the back porch. Tamar glanced across the table at Owen questioningly; shrugging in reply, he pushed his seat back and rose to follow his wife.

James stared bemusedly at the bowl of orange vegetables. 'They're only yams. They're not *that* exotic.'

But after a further fortnight — during which yams were not served once — of Keely rushing from the dinner table in some distress, Tamar felt compelled to contrive a brief chat with her daughter in private.

'Is it the food making you ill, do you think?' she asked as they took a late morning wander around the garden looking for flowers for the vases.

Keely withdrew a pair of secateurs from the pocket of her gardening overall, and stooped to cut a champagne-hued rose.

'No, I don't think so,' she said over her shoulder. 'I'm fine at breakfast and lunch. It's just dinner, and during the preparation of dinner. That's when I start feeling seedy.' She carefully stripped a few superfluous leaves from the stem and laid it gently in the bottom of her trug. 'And it's not because I don't like cooking either,' she added, turning to her mother. 'I'm actually beginning to quite enjoy that.'

Tamar looked at Keely thoughtfully. 'Is anything else amiss?'

Keely spied a late bearded iris and deftly clipped its slim, green stem. 'What do you mean?'

'Well, is there anything happening that shouldn't be? Or, should I say, anything not happening that should be?'

'Such as?'

'Such as your monthlies.'

'Oh, Mam, don't be . . . '

Keely froze. Tamar waited, watching as her daughter's face went from its customary fairness to a deep flush, then to a shade that could only be described as bloodless.

'Oh my God! Surely not!' Keely whispered in horror. 'But I'm forty-three years old!'

'When was your last period?' Tamar's tone was gentle, and ever so slightly amused.

'Oh, about three months ago, I suppose. I haven't been taking much notice lately. I thought it was the beginning of the change.'

'Well, you know, dear, change of life babies aren't unheard of.'

97

'But surely, in all the years we've been married . . . ' Keely faltered, then looked at Tamar beseechingly. 'God, Mam, do you really think so?

Tamar shrugged. 'I really don't know, darling, but I think you'd better get Doctor Fleming to call, don't you? Just in case.'

At her somewhat reluctant request, the doctor came the following day. In the bedroom she and Owen shared, and with Tamar in attendance, he asked her some pertinent questions, gave her a physical examination, said yes to a cup of tea, then washed his hands in a bowl of warm soapy water.

Towelling them dry, he gazed thoughtfully at Keely, perched nervously on the edge of the bed. She in turn stared back at his round whiskered face, and wondered how on earth he managed to fit his considerable belly behind the steering wheel of his car.

'And you're forty-three now?' he asked.

Keely nodded.

'Mmm. It certainly isn't unheard of. Quite common, actually,' Fleming said cheerfully, unknowingly echoing Tamar's words of the day before. 'And you're fit and healthy. Did you have any problems delivering your twins?'

'It was hard work and I certainly didn't enjoy the experience, but no, no real problems, given that there were two of them. Look, Doctor Fleming, am I expecting or not?'

'Dear me, didn't I say? I'm so sorry. Yes, Mrs Morgan, you are.'

'Oh, how lovely,' Tamar exclaimed, clapping

her hands together in delight.

'In six months, according to my calculations, give or take a week,' Fleming continued. 'Please accept my warmest congratulations. Although I should point out now that we will need to keep a fairly close eye on your progress, given your advanced years.' Noting Keely's scowl, he added quickly, 'Advanced in terms of child-bearing, I mean.'

'Owen will be delighted,' Keely said. 'He's always wanted more children.'

'And you're not?' said Fleming, rolling down his white shirt sleeves and looking around for his suit jacket, which Tamar had hung neatly over the back of a chair.

'Well, it's not exactly what I was planning for my middle age.' Keely thought for a moment, then a slow smile began to spread across her face. 'But on the other hand, and despite the horrendous shock of discovering that I'm in such a condition during my *advanced* years, I think I *am* delighted, actually. My first pregnancy was . . . well, let's just say I wasn't in a position at the time to really appreciate the experience. This time I am.'

Owen, of course, was absolutely thrilled. Having resigned himself several years ago to the likelihood that there would be no more children, he was overjoyed to discover that he was to be a father once again at the age of forty-five. He immediately told Keely to sit down and take things gently, and she immediately told him not to be so silly. But still, she wrote straight away to Bonnie and Leila, now in their last year at Iona, to tell them the good, if thoroughly unexpected, news that they could expect a new brother or sister some time in September.

August, 1936

The anticipation of the forthcoming addition to the Morgan family was eclipsed, at least temporarily, by a telephone call from Thomas in Dunedin early one evening in August.

Keely answered the telephone in the hall, and spent a few moments chatting to her brother about her excellent health, her huge waistline and Owen's constant requests that she put her feet up. 'Honestly, Thomas, you'd think I'm made of porcelain. I've never felt better. I was like this with the twins, too, I think he's forgotten that.'

'Perhaps he's worried because you're a bit older this time,' said Thomas, his voice crackling over the telephone line.

'Well, I'm fine and I've no intention of getting fatter than I have to through lolling about on the sofa all day doing nothing.'

'No, but perhaps you could humour him and rest up occasionally.'

'I suppose,' Keely replied grumpily. 'Did you want to talk to Mam?'

'Yes, I did, thanks. About Duncan. Is she handy?'

When Tamar came to the telephone, Thomas said without preliminary, 'Mam? I've just telephoned James and Lucy ... '

'Yes, we heard James's ring,' Tamar interrupted, referring to the system the family had

100

adopted to accommodate the party line catering for all three households on Kenmore Station.

' . . . but I think you should know as well.'

'Is something wrong?' Tamar felt a small spider of anxiety beginning to inch its way down her spine.

'Sort of. I went around to Duncan's earlier this evening to see if he wanted to come out for a meal, and he wasn't there. In fact, no one was. So I went to the pub he favours, and one of his classmates said the last he'd heard he was off somewhere with a group of his cronies planning an expedition to Spain to fight in the Civil War. On the side of the Loyalists.'

'What?' Tamar was astounded.

'Exactly. I laughed at first, but the boy insisted it was true. Or so he'd heard, anyway. He gave me an address in Stuart Street so I shot around and banged on the door and barged my way in and there they were, this group of university students hunched over a kitchen table, poring over maps and lists and what have you. They got a hell of a fright when I barrelled in.'

'What were they doing? Was Duncan there?'

'No, he wasn't, but I got it out of them. They were in the middle of getting ready to go to Spain to join one of the International Brigades. Some of their 'comrades' have apparently already left. I'm sorry, Mam, but it seems that Duncan was one of them.'

'He's left? For *Spain*?'

'Almost. The ship leaves from Wellington tomorrow afternoon. He's on his way there now.'

'But what's the war in Spain got to do with Duncan?'

'I don't know, but they were all extremely passionate about it, going on about hating the idea of the Spanish being forced by the Fascists and the Nazis to live under a totalitarian regime, and not being able to stand by and watch it happen. I can't say I disagree, either.'

'But why would he want to fight another country's war, Thomas? *Why*?'

Thomas heard the note of despair in his mother's voice, but elected not to respond to her question. Why? Quite possibly because Duncan's father and all his uncles had done it, that's why.

Instead he said, 'If I leave now, I might be able to catch up with him before he gets to Wellington. He'll have to wait for the ferry across Cook Strait. I could catch him there.'

Tamar thought quickly. 'When did he leave Dunedin?'

'This morning, according to his mates.'

'Then you'll be too late. No, we'll stop him from this end.'

'But can you?' Thomas was doubtful. 'God knows I hate the very idea of any of my nieces and nephews going off to war, Mam, you know that, but he's twenty-one and can do what he likes now. I'm not sure you can stop him. I'm not sure I could, either, much as I'd like to.'

'I can and I will,' Tamar shot back.

At that moment the front door banged open and Tamar whirled as James crashed into the hall, his face thunderous. Tamar said into the telephone, 'Thomas? James is here. I'll phone

102

you back later, all right?'

She replaced the black mouthpiece of the telephone in its cradle, and turned to her son.

'Was that Thomas?' James demanded before Tamar could get a word in. 'Did he tell you what that fool boy has done? Only gone and volunteered to fight in the bloody Spanish Civil War! I have to stop him, Mam, the stupid bloody little bugger! He could be *killed*!'

Tamar knew that Duncan was neither stupid nor little, but she thoroughly agreed with James that he had to be stopped. By now Keely and Owen had come into the hall and were staring in consternation.

'We'll leave immediately,' Tamar snapped. 'Bring the car around, Owen. Keely, will you help me pack a bag, please? We've no time to lose.'

Keely demanded, 'What are you talking about, Mam? What's happened?'

'Duncan's decided to run off and be a freedom fighter in Spain. He's leaving tomorrow afternoon.' James grimaced in frustration and rubbed his eyebrows wearily, fear and worry quickly overcoming his initial anger. 'We have to stop him.'

'But *you* can't go, Mam,' Keely protested. 'What about your heart?'

'Never mind my heart! My health won't be worth anything if I lose my eldest grandchild. Please, run upstairs and start on my bag, there's a good girl.'

Keely noted the fierce determination in her mother's eyes — a clear indication that she was

103

in no mood to be argued with — and without another word hurried off.

Tamar suddenly reached out and touched Owen's hand. 'Will you come with us? Duncan respects you a great deal so he might listen to you.'

The unspoken implication in her words was that Duncan did not respect his father, and the look of resignation on James's face demonstrated that he knew it only too well.

Tamar said, 'Is that all right with you, James, if Owen comes?'

James nodded. 'I don't care who comes, as long as we keep him off that ship. I'd appreciate it, Owen, if you don't mind.'

'Not at all. Joseph can hold the fort for a couple of days.'

So within half an hour, the car had been packed and Tamar, James and Owen had set off down the long tree-lined driveway out to the road that would take them in towards Napier then on to the main road to Wellington.

They drove throughout the night, stopping only briefly at Woodville for a toilet break, and whenever the car needed refuelling from the petrol tins stowed in the trunk, and once to change a tyre. Tamar slept for much of the trip, slouched uncomfortably in the passenger seat with a heavy woollen rug tucked over her for warmth, while James and Owen took turns driving. They said little, both staring out into the darkness and trying not to think about what might befall Duncan if they did not reach Wellington in time to stop him.

Tamar woke to a barely rising sun as they went through Masterton, but nodded off again almost immediately. Then, some hours later as James drove along the Wellington streets towards the docks, the car bumping heavily over tram lines, she woke again. She was stiff and sore, her leg ached abominably and she was desperate for a cup of tea.

'What time is it?' she asked, pushing herself upright and untangling the rug from her feet.

'Just after one o'clock,' James replied from the back seat. His eyes were red from lack of sleep and his chin and cheeks frosted with stubble. 'We're going straight to the docks to find out what time the ship leaves.'

'What's the name of it?'

'The ship? I don't know, but there can't be too many ships heading for Spain, surely, although he'd probably go to England first.'

After a frustrating amount of time mucking about locating an office with a person in it who could tell them which ships were leaving that day and whose names appeared on the manifests, they were finally informed that only one was bound for the UK — the *Northern Sun*, departing for Southampton at five o'clock that afternoon. And yes, Mr Duncan Murdoch was listed as a passenger.

James breathed a sigh of relief. 'Well, at least we know what time he's expected at the dock. That gives us an hour or so to freshen up.'

'And then what?' Owen asked.

'Then we come back here and wait for him to board. We can at least talk to him about whatever the hell it is he thinks he's doing. And if the worst comes to the worst, I'll . . . ' He faltered, not sure at all of what he might do.

Owen thought for a moment. 'James, I don't mean to be presumptuous, but is that the right attitude to take with him, do you think? Throwing your weight around?'

'No, it isn't,' Tamar said. 'James, I know you're worried sick, but bullying the boy isn't going to get you anywhere, is it? It never has in the past. Just talk to him, don't argue. Tell him how worried you are. Tell him you don't want him to go.'

James rolled his eyes. 'That's no going to make any difference, is it? He's never listened to me before.'

'But things have changed. *You've* changed.'

'Yes, but he doesn't know that, does he? Or if he does he won't acknowledge it. I've barely seen him since we moved back out to Kenmore. He's made damned sure I haven't, by hardly ever coming home.'

Owen sighed. 'Look, there's no point in going on about what's past. I don't know about you two but I could do with a decent bath. Why don't we find somewhere to tidy ourselves up?'

They booked rooms at a hotel in nearby Willis Street, and Tamar went straight to her room, ignoring the uniformed bellboy's inquisitive glances at her dishevelled appearance as he carried her bag up the stairs.

She ordered a pot of tea, then ran the bath and

gingerly eased herself into it, taking care not to put too much weight on her bad leg, luxuriating in the swirl of hot, scented water around her aching limbs. What would Kepa say if he knew she had gone racing off to Wellington on an errand of mercy without a moment's notice? He knew she could look after herself, and she had James and Owen with her after all, but still, he would not be pleased. He had fussed over her incessantly ever since her heart attack five years ago, but knew her well enough to retreat whenever he sensed she was about to lose her temper. No doubt he would, however, have something to say when she got back to Kenmore.

She stayed in the bath until the water had grown cool, then dressed in a simple grey suit fastened snugly at the waist with a black belt. Her hair needed a good comb so she let it down, brushed it thoroughly then twisted and refastened it in her customary chignon. As usual she wore little make-up, firmly believing that too much on an older woman served only to accentuate the negative rather than the positive. She applied only a hint of rouge to her cheeks and a light sweep of russet-coloured lipstick that complemented her hair. She added a small black hat, a pair of black heels and matching gloves, picked up her dark tweed coat and decided she was ready.

In the hall she rapped on James's door and waited impatiently until he opened it. She noted with approval that he'd had a shave and changed into some decent clothes, as opposed to the work shirt and trousers he'd worn all yesterday and last night.

'Ready?' she asked.

He stepped out, tugged down the sleeves of his jacket, took a deep breath and nodded. 'But ready for what, I'm not sure.'

On the docks a cold, aggressive wind had risen and Tamar had to keep a firm grip on the brim of her hat. The sound and smell of the sea, the screeching of seagulls and the bustle and shouting of stevedores reminded her with a sharp pang of a dock she had once waited on almost sixty years ago, thousands of miles away in a different world.

Owen trotted up the gangway of the *Northern Sun* to wheedle out of someone which passengers had already boarded. Squinting up at him, looking small and wind-buffeted on the ship's deck, she saw him talking with a crewman, then handing something over. She smiled to herself; compensation for the man's trouble, no doubt. The crewman disappeared, then returned several minutes later. She and James hurried over to the base of the gangway as Owen came back down.

'They're leaving in an hour. The ship carries mostly cargo so there won't be many passengers. That bloke I just talked to reckons that, according to the purser, no one called Duncan Murdoch has boarded yet.'

James exhaled in relief. 'Good, we haven't missed him then.'

'Missed who?' came a voice.

The three of them whipped around; behind

them stood Duncan, his feet planted wide and a look of grim determination on his handsome young face. He wore a sailor's black knitted cap over his bright bronze hair, a black jersey and old work pants, and a pair of sturdy boots. Slung over his shoulder was a well-scuffed duffle bag and a heavy coat. He looked a complete ruffian.

Although Tamar almost had another heart attack at his sudden appearance, she still noted that he had grown even taller, surpassing his father's height by several inches, and had filled out considerably. He'd lost the chubbiness that had dogged him even after his school years, and replaced it with what appeared to be solid muscle.

She stepped up to him, stood on her toes and kissed him on one chilly cheek. 'Duncan, you've grown!'

'Hello, Gran,' Duncan said fondly, and nodded amiably at Owen. Then he turned to James and his voice became harsh. 'What are you doing here?'

In a strained voice that indicated that he was struggling to control his temper, James replied, 'I was about to ask you the same question.'

'Well, you obviously have a rough idea. I just saw Uncle Owen coming off the ship. And no, I haven't boarded yet, but I will, very shortly.' He turned to Tamar. 'How did you know I'd be here?'

Before Tamar could speak, James said, 'Thomas telephoned last night with some story he'd been told by friends of yours about going to Spain to fight in the war. Unfortunately, you'd already left Dunedin by the time he found out, so the only way we could stop you was to come down to Wellington ourselves.'

Duncan looked almost amused, but his eyes narrowed all the same. 'Stop me?'

'That's right.'

'Why? Why would you want to stop me, and what makes you think you could? I'm twenty-one and I can do what I like now. You've no control over me any more, *Dad*.'

James visibly bit back an angry retort. 'We, *I*, want to stop you because you've no idea of what you're getting yourself into.'

'I bloody well have. I know *exactly* what's going in Spain and it has to be stopped. Bloody Nazis and Fascists!' He spat out the last word and gave his father a dangerously contemptuous look.

In response James clenched his fists, but when he spoke his voice was still controlled. 'The fighting, Duncan, I'm talking about the fighting. The fear, the blood, the screaming. Death.'

'What would you know about that?'

Tamar breathed in sharply — Duncan had just made a very serious error. This was awful. She stepped between her son and grandson and held her hands up, palms out. 'Stop it, the pair of you! *Stop* it!'

Owen moved forward as well, nearer to James, just in case. 'That's enough, Duncan. Leave it.'

Oblivious to the curious stares of people going past, Tamar continued, angry herself now. 'Duncan, you don't know what you're saying, so shut up.'

'I do,' Duncan said with a sneer, all traces of amusement gone. 'He was sent home because he couldn't cope. The great and glorious Captain James Murdoch cracked up on the battlefield.'

Tamar's arm snaked up and she grabbed Duncan by the lobe of his right ear, pulling his face down to the same level as hers. 'I want a word with you.'

Ignoring his cries of 'Ow, Gran!', she marched him away so swiftly that his bag and coat slipped off his shoulder and landed in a heap on the ground. When they were far enough away from James and Owen, she turned to face him and finally let go of his ear.

'Your father might have come home because of shell shock, young man, but it wasn't the result of cowardice. He shot and killed someone, Duncan, a captain in his own company, because the man was endangering the lives of those around him. Your father went against all military convention, and what was seen to be morally right, and protected his men from certain danger and death the only way he knew how.'

As Duncan's mouth fell open and he stared at her dumbfounded, Tamar knew that James had never once mentioned any aspect of his horrendous war experiences to his children.

She went on, still angry, 'And then, when he realised what he'd done, even though it was the only choice he believed he had at the time, he retreated into himself for a long, long time. There was a court martial, during which your father insisted he was guilty, but he was acquitted, mainly because his men thought so

111

highly of him that they chose not to provide the evidence that could have condemned him. Which is very fortunate for us, because if he'd been found guilty, he would have been shot. You won't remember because you were too small, but he was in a convalescent home in England for almost a year after that, before he came home to us with an honourable discharge.' Her tone softened. 'I know he's been difficult to live with, and not a particularly good father, and so does he, but get off your high horse, Duncan, and at least recognise your father for what he is. He's a decent man, despite his problems, and he was a damn good soldier, highly respected, well liked and very, very good at what he did. He knows exactly what he's talking about when it comes to war, because he was one of the best.'

Duncan gazed at his grandmother for a moment, looked at his boots for a few moments more, then adjusted his cap so that his sore ear was under it once again.

'Well, how was I supposed to know any of that?' he said truculently.

'You weren't, but you do now. So what are you going to do about it?'

Duncan looked back at his father. 'I could at least talk to him, I suppose.'

And that's what he did. Tamar and Owen left father and son on the docks and went in search of a cup of tea. They sat in a steamy-windowed tea shop on Custom-house Quay savouring the warmth and comforting aroma of their drinks until they judged that James and Duncan had had sufficient time to either come to some sort

112

of terms, or batter each other senseless, then retraced their steps to the wharves.

They found Duncan and his father sitting on a wooden seat, deep in conversation. On the *Northern Sun*, the gangway had been hauled up and the heavy mooring ropes tethering the ship to the dock were being disconnected one by one.

The two men rose.

'Well?' Tamar demanded, coming to a standstill in front of them, at least eight inches shorter than either and with her hands jammed aggressively on her hips. Her leg was giving her absolute hell now and she hoped this distressing business had been sorted out once and for all so she could back home and put her feet up for a couple of days.

'I've decided not to go,' Duncan said evenly.

'Good, I'm pleased about that.' Tamar could hear Owen behind her blowing out his cheeks in a release of pent-up tension.

'Not to Spain, anyway,' Duncan added. 'I'm going to England.'

'England?'

'Yes,' James said. 'To learn to fly with the Royal Air Force.'

The look on Tamar's face made both James and Duncan burst out laughing, but she didn't really mind — it was probably the first time they had laughed together in over a decade.

'Explain, please,' she asked resignedly.

Duncan did. 'I was going to fly planes when I got to Spain, with the Brits or the French, or maybe even the Poles. We heard they're desperately short of pilots.'

Tamar raised her eyebrows enquiringly.

'It's all I want to do, Gran. I don't want to be a doctor, and I've been failing miserably at medical school for the last two years. I've spent most of my money — well, your money, actually — on flying lessons, and I'm at the stage where I can go up by myself now. Well, almost. So I thought if I could get to Spain I could get in some real flying time.'

Owen said, 'So this business about wanting to fight the Nazis and the Fascists was all rubbish?'

'Not at all, I detest them, all of them, especially that absolute bastard Adolf Hitler. But flying is the way of the future, don't you see? If there is another war, it will all be about air supremacy and I want to be in on it.'

Tamar waited for either James or Owen to say that there wouldn't be another war, but neither of them obliged.

Seeing the look on his grandmother's face, and knowing how much she disliked any talk of war, past or future, Duncan added quickly, 'But mostly I just want to fly. It's the most incredible feeling. The sense of freedom is indescribable.'

Tamar said to James, 'So why does he have to go to England? Why can't he fly here?'

'He doesn't have to, but he wants to. It's a compromise. In exchange for my supporting his efforts to join the RAF in England, he's not going to Spain.'

'That sounds like blackmail to me,' Tamar said.

Duncan had the good grace to look vaguely embarrassed.

The expression on James's face suggested he thought it sounded like blackmail too. 'Yes, well, that's what we've agreed. And I think we all have to admit that the two years at medical school have been a complete waste of time. Although if Duncan ever sprains his ankle leaping out of a cockpit, he'll be able to apply his own bandage. And he can't really train here, not comprehensively, not in the sorts of planes he wants to fly. He'd have to join the army to do that and, well, I'm not prepared to support that. There's a chance he might end up having to serve as an infantryman.' He paused briefly, then added flatly, 'Like I did.'

Owen said, 'Didn't I read recently that the army's giving up control of the air arm in favour of a permanent air force? Couldn't you wait until then?'

'No,' Duncan said quickly, 'I couldn't.'

There didn't seem much else to say. The following day Duncan left for Dunedin to remove himself from medical school and collect the rest of his belongings, and Tamar, James and Andrew began the drive back to Napier.

Tamar wasn't entirely pleased with the compromise, but at least it seemed that James and Duncan had had some sort of a reconciliation. The relationship between father and son hadn't been this good since Duncan was small boy.

Part Two

The War Years
1939–1945

6

Kepa switched the radio off at the end of Prime Minister Michael Savage's measured and sober declaration, then sat down heavily on the sofa and sighed.

'That is that, then.' He plumped a cushion angrily. 'I suppose they will all be going off again. Christ.'

Across from him Tamar sat with her arms folded defensively over her stomach, her face pale and eyes bright with tears. She looked at him and shook her head wordlessly.

He moved to sit next to her, uncrossed her arms and took her hands in his own. 'I'm so sorry, my darling. This will be very hard for you, I know.'

Tamar sniffed and dabbed beneath her brimming eyes. She hated crying, especially in front of people, even Kepa. 'And for you. They're your grandchildren as well as mine. They're ours.'

This was true, and Kepa could think of nothing to say that wasn't trite. War again, a mere two decades after the last, great, worldwide conflict that, according to the politicians, would end all wars. Joseph would not be involved this time, thank God, but his children almost certainly would be.

Unaware that she was echoing the sentiments

119

of thousands, Tamar exclaimed vehemently, 'I thought that after the last time they would have learned. I thought it would never happen again.'

Kepa knew she was seeing her son Ian in her mind's eye, for ever twenty years old and lying for eternity in the cold, dense clay of a French field. He released her hands to stroke her fading hair, and kissed her temple softly. She was old now, and so was he. Even together, would they have the heart, or the strength, to see their families through another war?

* * *

On 3 September 1939, New Zealand, together with Britain, Australia, France and India, declared war on Germany. It was not really news, because everyone who owned a radio or had access to a newspaper was well aware of the events unfolding in Europe, and had at least a vague notion that New Zealand's defence forces were preparing for war. The new machine guns for the army had been arriving from Britain since April, and the previous month it had been widely reported that a company of New Zealand soldiers had been sent into the Pacific to guard a cable station on Fanning Island. The long period of waiting, in which international crisis had followed international crisis, was finally over.

Seven thousand men volunteered in the first four days, twelve thousand by the end of the first week, and recruitment posters went up everywhere. Almost every organisation in the land pledged support for war in one form or another, and the Public Works Department set about building huge military camps at Burnham, Trentham and Ngaruawahia.

Ordinary people were caught up in the excitement, and some panicked and began to hoard. Staples such as sugar, flour, tea and some tinned goods were bought up so quickly that shop shelves were left empty and grocers found themselves compelled to ration their stocks. Petrol was also rationed for several weeks, and prices were frozen. But the initial panic passed after a few days, and for many New Zealanders day-to-day life did not change much. The country was at war, but they weren't in it yet.

Things did change at Kenmore, though. Farmers were affected immediately, and some complained almost as quickly; overnight they were asked to produce more, mainly by extending their hours of work, but at the same time access to farm labour was being whittled away by recruitment campaigns and by the temptation of better money to be earned in war-related work. And, on top of that, the government would be paying set but low prices for farm produce, with no compensation against rising costs. This was a potential blow for the account books at Kenmore, Tamar thought, but probably wasn't going to lead the family to penury.

Duncan was already in England, of course, flying with the RAF — and Tamar's heart plummeted in dismay every time she thought of how offhandedly they had allowed him to swan off to become a pilot. Liam had come home from Canterbury Agricultural College, where he'd been studying for the past two years, to enlist in the newly formed Royal New Zealand Air Force — in the hope, Tamar suspected, of meeting up with Duncan overseas; Billy, Joseph's eldest boy, had signed up with the Maori Battalion; and Drew was thinking about joining the New Zealand Division of the Royal Navy.

Tamar herself had tried desperately to dissuade her grandsons from becoming involved, but her protests fell on deaf ears, as she knew they would. Her sons had not listened to her during the first war — and neither had her daughter — and Joseph had ignored her advice (although she had to admit he'd done it with due consideration for her feelings) when the war had broken out in South Africa decades ago and he'd run off to join up under age.

But Henry would be safe. Henry Murdoch Morgan — almost three years old now, a delightfully bright, bouncy little boy adored by his parents and sisters and spoiled dreadfully by everyone at Kenmore. Contrary to Doctor Fleming's concerns about her age, Keely had had an easy time with the birth, and this time was delighting in being a mother. From the moment she'd held her red and wrinkled little son in her arms and gazed into his dark blue eyes, she had been utterly and irretrievably captivated. Tamar had been delighted too, for Keely especially. Although she now loved them dearly, when the twins had been born she'd not been in a fit state to mother them. Now, with this extra, unexpected, arrival, she'd been given another chance.

At least the army would not claim her granddaughters, as none of them were nurses, although there were rumours already — unfounded, Tamar hoped — of women being recruited for various types of war work if necessary. At twenty, Bonnie and Leila were certainly old enough, and at eighteen Ana and Kathleen both soon would be. Joseph and Erin's youngest son Robert was seventeen and therefore probably safe from conscription, if it was introduced, for a couple of years at least. But surely this new war wouldn't go on for that long? Surely there simply couldn't be a repeat of the protracted, dragged-out horrors of the last one?

To Tamar's annoyance — or perhaps it was disappointment, she wasn't sure — neither Joseph, Owen nor James seemed to have made an effort to talk the boys out of their plans to enlist. It was already too late for Duncan, but as veterans themselves she felt they could at least have *tried* to talk some sense into them. One evening, after dinner, she walked over the hill to Joseph's house — leaning heavily on her stick, as she so often had to these days — to berate him for not doing so.

For company, she took Henry with her. He adored his grandmother and relished every opportunity he could get to have her all to himself, and this fine spring evening was no exception.

They found Joseph sitting in his favourite ratty old wicker chair on the verandah, smoking a cigarette and watching the lengthening shadows as they stretched across the lawn in the wake of the sun setting behind the hills. His artificial leg was propped against a verandah post, and he pushed himself up on his good leg and grabbed his own stick as she approached.

'No, sit down. God, what a pair of old cripples,' Tamar grumbled as she carefully negotiated the three steps up to the porch.

Henry scrambled up behind her, wielding his own little 'Granny' stick that Owen had made for him. Unfortunately he spent far too much time using it to irritate the farm cats and poking it into places it wasn't meant to be, but Tamar didn't have the heart to take it off him.

'You should have asked Owen to bring you over in the truck,' Joseph admonished as she hitched up the knees of the trousers she customarily wore at home and sat down opposite him.

'He's busy, and anyway I wanted to talk to you privately. You can tell him off after I've told you off, though. And James.'

'Oh yes?' Joseph laughed. 'What for?'

Tamar frowned at her firstborn son, whom she proudly considered was still an extremely attractive man, despite the silver that was creeping from his temples back through the thick black hair he seldom cut. Very like his father, he was, although considerably less arrogant.

'For not talking to those boys about what they think they're getting themselves into. And they are only boys, Joseph, they've no idea of what really happens on the battlefield.'

'No, probably not. But they'll find out, like all

lads who heed the call of empire and go charging off to war.'

Tamar gave an inelegant snort. 'I don't think they actually are heeding the call of empire, are they? Liam wants to go because Duncan's already there, Drew's bored and I strongly suspect Billy's only keen on going because you did. And his mother. Henry, leave Uncle Joseph's leg alone. It's not a toy.'

'You're quite possibly right about Billy. But look at us, Mam, look at all of us. We're a family raised on war. From as far back as John Adams, who might as well have been family, and me in two wars, and James and Owen and Ian and Keely, and even Thomas, who hates conflict of any sort. How could the young ones not be influenced by all that? And it's not just us. I expect just about every lad in this country has a father or an uncle who served in the last one. It's what makes us New Zealanders, isn't it? And Billy's got a double dose, really. My people have a great warrior tradition, and it's a matter of mana, you know that. Ask Papa.'

'I have asked him, and I got almost as little sense out of him as I'm getting from you. But that's not all of it, is it? There's more to it than that. Or is it less?'

Joseph knew exactly what his mother meant. Reaching for his tobacco pouch before Henry found it and emptied the contents all over the verandah, he set about rolling another smoke.

'Mmm, sometimes it is less. Young men everywhere like . . . no, not like, they crave adventure. Sometimes that's all there is to it.

125

And of course blokes put their hands up to get away from bad marriages, or trouble at home. I met plenty dreading being nailed by nagging wives or the coppers when they finally did get back. But I've no doubt that others really feel they have a duty to go, plenty of them, in fact. And on top of all that there's this need blokes have to prove their manhood, or whatever you want to call it, that they can take everything that's thrown at them.'

'What a lot of rubbish!'

'Rubbish!' echoed Henry.

Joseph licked the edge of his paper, tamped the cigarette into shape then lit it. Blue smoke drifted up around his head, confusing the moths beginning to congregate around the outside light.

'Perhaps, but that's the way it is.'

They were silent for a minute as they watched Henry crawling around, head down, humming tunelessly to himself and looking for insects to investigate.

'So, you won't try to talk them out of it?'

Joseph looked at his mother sadly. 'Believe me, Mam, I have tried. We all have.'

'Oh. Didn't you tell them how awful it was?'

'We did, but it doesn't mean much to anyone who wasn't there. And war stories from old soldiers — and military nurses, I might add, because Keely and Erin have said their piece too — don't mean anything to young blokes champing at the bit to get away and prove themselves. I'm sorry, Mam, we did try.'

Tamar slumped back in her chair dejectedly.

126

Joseph knew she was thinking about Ian, and about the state James had come home in twenty-two years ago, and about his own lost leg. He reached out and put his brown hand over her smaller, time-weathered one.

'Please try not to worry.'

'That's an easy thing to say.'

'I know it is. I'm worried too.' Joseph bent down, scooped Henry up and sat him on his knee. 'Erin and I both are.'

There was a noise behind them and Erin stepped out onto the verandah. In the dim light she looked overly pale and tired. Wiping her hands on a tea towel, she said, 'Hello, Aunty Tam. Is someone taking my name in vain?'

Henry immediately reached his arms up towards her. 'Aunty En! Need a bicky!'

Erin took him, balanced him on her hip with practised ease and planted a quick kiss in his ivory white curls.

'You're up late, little one. Are you keeping Granny company?'

'Mmm, an' I need a bicky.'

'Oh, all right then, let's go and see what's in the tins, shall we?'

Tamar waited until Erin had gone inside before she said, 'She looks very tired, Joseph. In fact she looks exhausted.'

'She is. She's cried herself to sleep for the last four nights. She won't let on to Billy because she's said her bit and won't say any more, but I think she'd give almost anything if he didn't sign up. But he will, you know. They all will.'

1940

One by one, the boys went away.

Billy went into camp with the Maori Battalion at the Palmerston North showgrounds late in January for three months' training, the technicalities of which he took very seriously, especially the weapons training. He didn't take much else seriously. In his first letter home he described in colourful detail the sight of hundreds of volunteers, accompanied by friends and relatives, arriving at the showgrounds dressed in their Sunday best and carrying banjos, unkuleles and accordions. According to Billy, it gave Major Dittmer, the commander of the battalion, a 'bloody good fright', which, also in Billy's opinion, served the army right for appointing only Pakeha as senior officers. Joseph shook his head in disbelief as he read the letter — it sounded exactly the sort of shambles he'd experienced himself when he'd trained at Avondale in 1914.

Liam also went to Palmerston North, but to Ohakea Air Force Base some distance from the town. There, he was to train as an observer, then probably go on to Britain where he would serve with the RAF, most likely with Bomber Command. The RNZAF had agreed to implement an intensive training programme for Dominion pilots and air crew for the RAF in the event of war, and many New Zealanders were now destined for the UK. Canada was doing the same thing. Liam intended to apply to one of the New Zealand squadrons in Britain — already making a name for themselves — and in which

Duncan was currently flying.

Drew, however, much to his disgust and frustration, was compelled to sit around out at Kenmore for several months kicking his heels while the admiralty sorted out its recruitment procedures. He'd initially gone into town to sign up for the navy, but was told by the local naval authorities that only reservists and yachtsmen/mariners were being accepted. He was neither, and had come home in a foul mood grumbling about ineptitude and ingratitude. In the end, and after several semi-clandestine meetings with like-minded acquaintances over beers in town, he decided to join a group who were planning to make their own way to Britain to join the Royal Navy and left in May.

England, August 1940
Flight Lieutenant Duncan Murdoch awoke to the feel of someone shaking the hell out of his shoulder.

'Sir? *Sir!* Time to wake up, sir!'

Duncan groaned and opened one eye, then snapped it shut again — the light of the hurricane lamp was too bright, his mouth was dry from sleeping with it open and his head pounded painfully, which was bloody irritating, as he hadn't had a drop to drink last night.

The airman orderly had another go. 'Wakey, wakey, sir. Time to get up and polish the Spitfire.'

Cheeky bugger, Duncan thought. 'Yes, all right, I'm awake,' he muttered and heaved himself upright with a monumental effort. It seemed that these days the only thing that had the power to wake him immediately from a deep sleep was the word 'Scramble!'

He pulled his jacket on over his shirt — he'd not bothered getting undressed at night for nearly three weeks now — shoved his feet into his flying boots and lit a cigarette.

'How's the weather looking?'

'Probably fine, bit of high cloud,' the orderly replied morosely.

'Bugger.'

Today would therefore no doubt be a repeat of yesterday, and the day before, and the day before that. Duncan was averaging three sorties a day, and he was utterly exhausted. The Luftwaffe had been bombing the hell out of shipping convoys and coastal towns, airfields and radar stations relentlessly for almost six weeks now, and Fighter Command was starting to seriously feel the strain.

He went outside, stopped off at the latrine for a quick pee, then trudged across the wet grass to where his squadron's aircraft were lined up along the edge of the concrete runway. He flicked his fag end away before he got too close — petrol fumes were everywhere. His Spitfire was second from the end, the rising orange sun reflected in the glass of the cockpit's small windscreen. The fitter was just climbing out.

'Morning, Tosh,' Duncan said. 'All ready?'

'Aye. Chute's sitting on the tail and the tank's full.'

'Good-oh.'

Duncan climbed into the tiny cockpit, easing his long legs into the cramped space under the instrument panel, and began to check that everything was functioning correctly and set for a quick getaway. A last look to ensure that the oxygen and R/T leads were fully connected to the mask hanging with his helmet, goggles and flying gloves, then he hauled himself out and headed back towards the hut for some breakfast.

Biggin Hill Airfield, just outside London, served fairly unspectacular food, but there was plenty of it. Duncan ate as quickly as possible, had two cups of tea and another cigarette, then returned to the latrine, hoping that the call to scramble wouldn't come while he was there. More than once he'd seen pilots dashing out of the little wooden building, hurriedly doing up their flies and swearing all the way to their aircraft.

The sun was almost completely up now, which meant the call could come at any time. He returned to his cot and carried out his ablutions. After a quick shave in tepid water and a thorough brush of his teeth, he slicked his hair down with water, buttoned his jacket, buckled on his Mae West and checked that his service revolver was in his jacket pocket. It always was these days — he never went anywhere without it.

Outside the hut chaps were congregating in the deckchairs arranged around several low tables set on the grass. On wet or windy days they sat inside, but when it was fine they made the most of the sun. Besides, being outside gave them a head start when the call came. This morning, the cards were already being dealt for a round of poker. Some days lately, they hadn't managed to finish even a single game.

Duncan flopped down in a chair next to Terry Finch, a pilot and good mate from Canterbury who had also trained with the RAF in England before the war. There weren't many of them left now — every day 'old' hands disappeared to be replaced by new, fresh-faced and virtually untried pilots from the RAF training schools or the Empire Air Training Schemes in New Zealand and Canada. Duncan had lost so many acquaintances and friends that he'd given up bothering to make any new ones. It was a form of self-protection.

Terry, a short, solid man of twenty-six with a shock of blue-black hair that refused to be tamed, even after a day flattened in a sweaty flying helmet, said, 'Did you hear about Gus Reidy? Bought it late yesterday afternoon.'

Duncan nodded and picked up his poker hand. Gus, a member of Seventy-nine Squadron, also stationed at Biggin Hill, had a been a decent bloke, a New Zealander with plenty of guts and a very skilled pilot. He'd gone down with his aircraft over Coulsdon and his death had been confirmed early this morning. Nothing more would be said about him now.

Duncan was losing badly — and struggling to stay awake — when the call came over the Tannoy to scramble. He could hear the orderly shouting, 'Estimated fifty bandits coming in from south-east!', and before the words really registered he was automatically on his feet.

132

At his Spitfire he tugged his parachute on over his Mae West and accepted a leg up into the cockpit from one of the ground crew. The engine was already running. Once seated he swiftly strapped himself in, pulled on his gloves, helmet and goggles, and fixed the oxygen mask over his face. His stomach was churning and he felt the familiar surge of adrenalin flood through him as he taxied out onto the runway, then manoeuvred the Spitfire into the correct position in preparation for take-off. By the time he'd switched on the R/T he was already in the air, watching the ground drop away and at the same time glancing around to make sure everyone was in formation.

Below him, the ground crew turned into ants scurrying in all directions and the barracks, huts and hangers became toy buildings. The end of the runway was cratered from an attack on the airfield four days ago, and littered with the husks of three Spitfires that had been destroyed and already scavenged for any retrievable parts.

Terry was positioned on his left and to his right was Jacko Ebbett, a pilot who'd only been with the squadron for a few weeks. Duncan waved to them both, a habit they'd developed only recently. None of them had been shot down since they'd started doing it and, being as superstitious as most service personnel, they didn't dare stop the ritual in case it was the only thing keeping them safe. They banked sharply, climbed and the squadron headed south-east for the coast.

Over the R/T, Duncan stated calmly, 'Red Panda airborne.'

Through the crackle the female ground controller replied, 'Okay, Panda leader, fifty plus bandits southeast of Ashford heading north-west. Vector 130, go get 'em, glamour boys!'

They flew for several minutes more, then suddenly they had a visual fix on a phalanx of bombers, escorted by fighters, moving towards them on their left.

Duncan said, 'Here we go. Go for the Dorniers but watch the 109s, they'll be coming out of the sun. Jacko, pull in a bit, you're too far out.'

He was referring to the Messerschmitt Bf 109s, the scourge of the RAF. Checking that the setting on the gunsight mounted above his instrument panel was calibrated for the wingspan of the 109s, he then gave the order to climb higher to compensate for possible fire from above. In the tight confines of the cockpit he smelled his own sweat, and the involuntary tightening of his sphincter was an all too familiar sensation.

'Panda Squadron, I repeat, aim for the bombers.' His voice had risen a notch in the excitement of the impending battle. 'Here they come! *Break, break!*'

He banked sharply and broke formation. Suddenly the sky around him shattered in a confusion of banking and swooping aircraft, some so close he could see the faces of the German pilots inside. He sensed someone on his tail and jinked, then dived and banked again, climbing at the same time so he came out above the mêlée. The R/T buzzed with snatches of commands, swearing, bellowed warnings, victory yells and cries of sheer terror.

He caught sight of Jacko Ebbett's Spitfire beneath him, a 109 directly on his tail, and winced as a trail of bullets tore through a wing. Jacko jinked, rolled and recovered. Duncan squeezed his trigger and sent a prolonged squirt at the 109, spraying the German aircraft with bullets the length of its fuselage. A thick stream of smoke began to pour from the Messerschmitt, and Duncan let out a loud, triumphant whoop.

'Got ya, ya bastard!' he bellowed and banked again, turning for a split second into the sun.

A voice shrieked from his R/T, '*Duncan*! Snapper at eleven!'

He barely had time to register the 109 coming at him directly out of the sun before the German fired. The Spitfire's cockpit glass crazed, but did not shatter, and Duncan was flying semi-blind. He rolled quickly, but not quickly enough to dodge the bullets; a line of them tore into his fuel tank, positioned directly in front of the cockpit. The tank was armoured, but not invincible. The needle on his fuel gauge began to drop immediately, meaning one of two things — he could lose all of his fuel and plummet out of the sky, or another bullet could cause a spark that would blow him to kingdom come. He decided to turn back.

'This is Panda leader; tank's hit, I'm heading home.'

He acknowledged the squadron's responses as

he banked and headed back for the airfield, feeling frustrated and cheated. This had happened to him once before and it had pissed him off then, too. He would miss the rest of the fight, and not be there to guide his men.

The needle on the gauge was still falling, but he calculated he would make it back. Barely. He could see the airfield and was almost home anyway.

Then, from nowhere, a 109 swooped in from his right and fired another barrage that raked his right wing heavily. There was a count of several seconds when Duncan thought he might have got away with it, then a great sheet of flame erupted in front of the cockpit and blew the glass in. Heat surrounded him instantly, the flames blasting directly over his face, hands and chest. He was on fire and screaming. The ground controller heard it over the R/T and dispatched an ambulance immediately.

But Duncan didn't know this — he was still inside the Spitfire spinning faster and faster as it sped towards the ground, a great trail of acrid, dirty smoke pouring from the fuselage. Following a drill that had been drummed into him time after time during training, he pulled the split-pin out of his sub-harness and ripped the oxygen and R/T leads out of his helmet. Then, shoving upwards with both blazing hands, he opened the hood of the cockpit and felt an almighty bang as an explosion hurled him up and out. He had just enough wits about him to tug frantically on his ripcord before he passed out.

7

At that very moment Liam was sitting nervously in the parlour at Kenmore waiting for Tamar to come downstairs. Next to him perched the girl he planned to marry. He was going to marry her no matter what, but he did want Tamar to meet her first. She had, after all, been more or less a mother to him while he was gowing up, even though she was really his gran.

'You'll like her,' he said reassuringly. 'She's been marvellous to me. She's probably been the most important person in my life. She raised me, you know.'

The girl did know. He'd told her the story more than once about how he'd been discovered under the beans in the kitchen garden after his father's memorial service, and how there had been a note from his mother — whoever she was, because to this day still nobody knew — asking that he be looked after because she couldn't do it.

'Yes, sweetheart,' she replied, laying a hand on his uniform sleeve. The nails were lacquered a very deep red. 'You've told me several times now.'

Liam looked at her and laughed. 'Yes, I suppose I have, really, haven't I? I can't wait for you to meet everyone. Duncan and Drew are away of course, but the girls are floating about. You'll like them, too, I know. They're great fun.

Especially the twins.'

The girl uncrossed her legs, rose to her feet and walked smoothly on three-inch heels across to the china cabinet where Tamar kept her best pieces.

'This is all gorgeous stuff. Mind you, it goes with the house, doesn't it? Your grandmother must be loaded,' she said, bending down to look more closely.

Liam couldn't keep his eyes off the taut, rounded globes of her bottom as it strained the fabric of her snugly fitting dress. He got an erection immediately, and moved his uniform hat onto his lap; she always had that effect on him, and it could be very embarrassing.

In fact, he'd been sporting bloody great stiffies at the very thought of her, and at the most inopportune times, ever since they'd met two months ago when he'd first arrived at Ohakea.

It had been at the end of the second week; he'd been absolutely knackered from the gruelling training regime, even though he'd been fit before he'd arrived and was intellectually very capable, and had at first declined his barrack mates' offer of a ride into Palmerston North to sample the night life. But they'd given him such a hard time about it that in the end he'd decided to go, despite his fatigue.

They'd gone to a pub and had quite a few beers until closing time at six, had a feed of fish and chips then headed for a dance at the community hall where, it had been rumoured in the bar, there'd be plenty of girls just dying to be swept off their feet by dashing young airmen.

138

There were, and Liam's mates lost little time 'bagging' the ones they fancied and whizzing them out onto the dance floor, ignoring the dirty looks from the sour-faced civilian blokes. Liam, who couldn't dance to save himself, was left sitting on a wooden bench against the wall, wishing he'd taken more notice of the dance lessons he'd been forced to attend at Napier Boys' High.

He was resigning himself to a night of bum-numbing boredom interspersed with surreptitious dashes out to the car for a quick bottle of beer, when suddenly his view of the dance floor was blocked by a pair of very shapely calves and the outline of equally curvaceous thighs beneath a floaty floral skirt. He'd looked up and into the face of the most enchanting, vivacious girl he'd ever seen.

She bent over so her face was on the same level as his, at the same time giving him both a lovely view down the front of her blouse and a great waft of perfume. 'Hello, love,' she said loudly over the noise of the band. 'Has she left you sitting here all by yourself?'

'Who?'

'Whichever girl has been silly enough to leave you alone and unguarded for five minutes. If I was her, I wouldn't let you out of my sight.'

Liam didn't know what to say. Never in his life had a girl spoken to him like this.

'Er, no, I'm here by myself. Well, those are my mates over there on the dance floor, but I don't have a girl.'

The girl's artfully pencilled eyebrows shot up.

'Is that so? I don't think I believe it, a big, good-looking young bloke like you.'

Liam blushed and hoped the lights were dim enough for her not to notice.

'No, I'm by myself,' he said, then surprised himself by seizing the initiative. 'I don't suppose you'd like a glass of punch?'

The girl sat down next to him. 'I'd love one, thanks. What's your name, love?'

'Liam. Liam Murdoch.'

She stuck her hand out with a clatter of bangles. 'And I'm Evelyn, Evie to my friends. Lovely to meet you.'

Liam smiled, dashed over to the canteen and came back with two glasses of punch. Evie took hers and put it beside her on the bench. Then she opened her purse and withdrew a small flask and unscrewed the lid.

'Gin. Want some?'

'I don't think we're allowed alcohol in here.'

'Oh, don't be such a stick in the mud. Here, give us your glass.' She poured a decent measure into Liam's punch, then topped up her own and swallowed a third of it in one go. 'That's better. Shall we dance?'

Liam felt embarrassed again — he was bound to make a fool of himself. 'Well, I don't dance, really.'

Evie stood up, took his glass out of his hand, and pulled him to his feet. 'Of course you do, it's easy. I'll show you.'

And it was. He stood on her toes twice — it must have hurt because she was wearing open-toed shoes, though she didn't say anything

140

— but after that he found the rhythm and started to feel more comfortable. She was a good dancer, if rather a close one, and the pressure of her thighs against his and her hand on his back helped him to work out which way he should be going. He relaxed and was starting to think he was actually doing quite well when someone jabbed him hard from behind. He looked around ready to apologise, and encountered not an irate dancer but the smirking face of Dick Curtis, one of his mates.

'Doing well,' he said in a stage whisper. 'She's a real looker. I'd hang on to that one if I were you!'

Liam couldn't help it — he smirked back and whirled Evie around in a burst of confidence and enthusiasm.

'That's the ticket!' she said, laughing up at him. 'You're really getting the hang of it!'

The song ended then and the band segued into a slower number, the woman vocalist dropping her voice from the rather strident pitch she'd been using to a semi-seductive croon that seemed to encourage the dancers on the crowded floor to move even closer together.

Evie's hand slid down to the small of Liam's back and her hips pressed against his groin. He felt the stirrings of a very healthy erection and hastily sucked in his middle in an attempt to avoid poking her in the stomach. But it was too late — she'd already noticed.

She laughed again and said teasingly, 'I see you're enjoying yourself.'

He was mortified. 'I do beg your pardon.'

Her hand came up and she laid a finger gently on his lips. 'Ssshh. It's all right, love. You can beg anything you like from me.'

This did absolutely nothing to minimise the lump in Liam's trousers, and he gave up trying to hold himself away from her. He didn't dare let his hand slide any further down her back than her waist, though he was itching to run his palm over her round bottom under the silky material of her dress. Her breasts pressed against his chest and he imagined he could feel their heat even through his uniform jacket. Dipping his head to her bright blonde hair, he smelt Palmolive soap and her perfume — strong, but heady and provocative.

As they danced slowly among the other swaying couples, her body against his and the smell of her in his nostrils, he marvelled at the fact that he very nearly hadn't ventured out at all tonight. If he hadn't let himself be persuaded, he would at this very minute be lying on his bunk in his service pyjamas reading something exceptionally turgid about how to master topographical maps and recognise heavily camouflaged German ammunition factories. This was infinitely more alluring.

And then she did something that tipped him right over the edge.

Their hands had been intertwined and resting against the front of his shoulder. Now she leaned back slightly and slid her hand out of his. Then, very slowly — lightly scratching his skin with her long nails as she went — she encircled his wrist with her fingers and thumb and held him in a grip so strong he could barely move his hand. He didn't even want to; he felt caught, overpowered, and deliciously *trapped*. Then she lowered her head and licked the inside of his wrist, bit him gently there, then slid his thumb into her warm, soft mouth. It was so incredibly erotic that he had to bite his lip to stop himself from groaning.

He wondered desperately if he could convince her to come outside with him to the car. Or even for a wander in the paddock behind the hall. If he missed his ride back to Ohakea, too bad — she would be worth having to stick his thumb out for.

In the end he didn't need to convince her at all. When she suggested they go outside for a breath of fresh air, he agreed willingly.

'We could sit in the car,' he said hopefully. 'There should be a few bottles of DB left.'

Evie said, 'Well, only for a minute. We don't want to miss the supper.' Then she burst into laughter at the sight of his crestfallen face. 'Don't worry,' she giggled, linking her arm through his, 'I'm only joking. I can think of much more interesting things to do than scoffing scones. Come on, Mr Airman, let's go!'

They threaded their way through the crowd of unattached men congregating around the door, then down the wide concrete steps and out onto the road. Dick's battered Austin Seven was parked a short distance away under a tree; they walked towards it hand in hand, their shoes scrunching loudly on the gravel of the road.

Liam opened the passenger door, took two bottles out of the almost empty crate on the floor, then stood there dithering about whether Evie would be offended if he opened the door to the back seat for her. But she opened it herself and climbed in, moving across so there was plenty of room for him. He clambered in beside her.

Swivelling on the leather seat she turned to face him. 'Well,' she said.

'Yes,' he said back, wondering what to do next.

He considered opening his bottle with his teeth, but decided that such a show-off gesture could pose a needless risk and result in an enforced visit to the base's somewhat cavalier dentist. Instead he took his penknife out of his pocket and prised the lid off with that, then did the same for her.

But she put her bottle on the floor, where it promptly fell over and emptied its foaming contents everywhere. She reached for him and began to kiss him, and not chaste kisses either. Deep, tongue-probing, passionate kisses that smeared lipstick all over his mouth and set his trousers bulging again, while shivers of excitement raced up his spine and across his buttocks.

And she just didn't stop. Within minutes she had his flies open and her cool hand burrowed into his trousers, skilfully caressing his penis in a manner that made him suspect he wouldn't be able to hold on for much longer. She unbuttoned her blouse and opened it wide, positioning one of his hands encouragingly. He fumbled for a few moments, not altogether inexpertly, until she lost patience, removed her blouse completely and unhooked her best Berlei bra so he had full access to her heavy, satin-skinned breasts.

His breath caught in his throat at the sight of them — their whiteness seemed to reflect the moonlight — and he moaned involuntarily as his damp hands felt their smooth, inviting warmth and weight.

She moaned, too, and nuzzled his neck and nipped his ear. She had his penis out now in the cool, silky air and he knew it would only be a matter of seconds.

So did she.

'Ready?' she asked huskily.

He didn't trust his voice and could only nod.

She leaned back then, along the seat, and slithered her skirt up to her waist. Tucking her thumbs into the waistband, she wriggled her knickers down and kicked them off, revealing a suspender belt attached to gleaming silk stockings and a dark, lush triangle between pale thighs.

In the semi-darkness of the moonlight, Liam thought her lips and eyes looked like black shadows.

She reached for him, and he came to her, pushing his trousers down to his knees and settling himself between her welcoming legs. Two tentative pushes then a deeper thrust and he was inside her. Her feet, still in their high-heeled shoes, settled across his back and the car began to rock gently on its springs. He could smell the leather of the car seat, her perfume and the scent of their sexes mixing together, and lost himself completely.

And that had only been the beginning. He saw her as often as he could after that, borrowing Dick's car or thumbing a lift into town whenever he could get away from the base. Sometimes they had sex in the car, or under trees in paddocks, getting grass in their hair. Once they did it in a haystack, and on two memorable occasions they went to the house of Evie's married sister, while she and her husband were out.

They had sex in every position they could think of: she straddled him and smothered his face with her breasts; he sat her on his lap or held her up against a wall. She sucked him and bit him and held him down; he licked her and stroked her and left small bruises on her thighs. They groaned and giggled and cried out in their lust, and Liam, realising he would be going overseas in a matter of weeks, came to a decision.

Which was why they were now sitting in the parlour at Kenmore waiting for Tamar.

When she did appear, Liam leapt to his feet, smiling broadly. Tamar crossed the floor and kissed his cheek.

'Liam, darling, what a lovely surprise. We weren't expecting you for at least another fortnight. Your embarkation date hasn't been brought forward, has it?'

'No, but I managed to wangle a weekend pass, and there's something I need to tell you,' he said, holding his hand out to Evie who was standing in silence by the china cabinet. 'Gran, this is Evie Jones. She's from Palmerston North, and we're getting married.'

Tamar took one look at the girl, who was now holding Liam's hand and smiling broadly herself, and her heart sank. The girl's smile conveyed a hint of something that Tamar didn't like at all. Ownership, certainly. Triumph? Quite possibly.

And that wasn't all. The girl was wearing heels that were too high to be anything but tarty, her cheap green and red dress was a little too tight across her considerable bust, there was at least quarter of an inch of brunette visible in the part of her otherwise blonde hair and her lipstick was an altogether inappropriate shade of red for day wear.

Tamar's face remained set in a welcoming smile. 'Hello, Evie, how nice to meet you. Please, sit down.'

As they arranged themselves Tamar glanced surreptitiously at Liam. She took in his glossy fair hair, still tending towards curls in spite of the best efforts of the base barber, his big frame and long legs, and the handsome, open and perennially cheerful face that so resembled his father's. She noted his soppy smile as he gazed at Evie, and allowed herself a moment's reflection regarding his sweet, trusting nature.

Then she turned all of her attention to the girl.

'Now, Evie, tell me all about these wedding plans.'

★ ★ ★

147

'God, Kepa, she was awful.'

Kepa, who had not arrived at Kenmore until after Liam and Evie had gone, sat at the kitchen table eyeing a steaming loaf of bread just out of the oven.

'Awful in what way,' he asked, succumbing to temptation and cutting himself a thick slice. 'I should not be eating this. My trousers seem to have become smaller.'

Tamar struggled to find words that would not sound too judgemental, and gave up. 'She was a bit of a tart.'

'Oh yes, and how do you define a tart?'

'I can't say exactly, but believe me, I know one when I see one. And so I should,' Tamar added, thinking back to her long ago brothel-keepings days. 'Myrna's girls were good sorts, most of them, and a few even went on to respectable marriages, I'll grant you that, but there's something about a woman who's prepared to sell herself. For whatever gain. Much as I liked them, Myrna's girls had whatever it is, and so does this Evie.'

'And what is it that makes you think she is selling herself?'

'Well, I could say the way she was dressed. Really, Kepa, you should have seen her frock — it was so snug I could see the outline of her suspender belt underneath. And her shoes, I'm surprised she made it up the front steps without toppling over.'

Kepa raised his eyebrows, but said nothing.

'But it wasn't just her outfit,' Tamar went on, picking at a corner of the loaf herself. 'It was more than that. It was the expression on her face. She looked at me, right into my eyes, and I swear she knows that *I* know damn well what she's up to, but couldn't give a hoot!'

'And what is she up to?'

'She's taking advantage of poor sweet Liam, that's what!'

'Really?' Kepa was interested now. 'How?'

Tamar gave a derisory snort. 'She's *trapped* him, of course. She's bewitched him into marrying her. And I know how, too. He couldn't keep his hands off her.'

Kepa smiled broadly. 'There is a name for his condition, but I will not tell you what it is.'

'It's not funny, you know,' Tamar snapped. 'And I am familiar with the term. I've seen more than enough men with the same problem silly enough to do just about anything for a woman's favours. Including spending a week's pay.'

'Do you think Liam is paying this woman?'

'No, of course not. But he's agreed to marry her, hasn't he? And he is an heir to the station; she must know that. She was taking a damn good inventory when I walked into the parlour.'

'Ah, a . . . what is it? A gold-digger?'

'Yes, I suspect so. She can't be anything else.'

'Why not?

'Because . . . because she *can't* be, that's why.' Tamar was horrified at the idea that this girl might genuinely love Liam and that he might love her back. She was just so *unsuitable*.

Kepa brushed crumbs off his shirt, then thoughtfully eyed the woman he loved across the big kitchen table.

'You, my dear, are becoming a snob.'

Tamar, a piece of warm crust halfway to her mouth, stopped, aghast.

'A snob! What do you mean, a snob?'

'You are judging this woman when you do not even know her, and you are judging her based on your own expectations and standards.'

'Rubbish! I'm looking out for my grandson!'

Kepa smiled in the knowing way that irritated Tamar intensely. 'Are you?' he replied. 'Who are you to say what is right for him?'

'I've known him since he was three months old. I raised him, Kepa, you know that. And I *know* that a girl in high heels and a too-tight dress is not the right person for him. Liam needs a sensitive girl, someone who's loyal, and decent and honest. This Evie is eminently unsuitable, doesn't even appear to have had an education, and . . . and I just don't trust her!'

Kepa raised his eyebrows again. 'I was unsuitable, I did not have a Pakeha education and you certainly did not trust me in the beginning, did you? But that has not stopped us enjoying what we have now.'

'That's different. And we are not married.'

'Only because you will not accept my *frequent* proposals.'

Tamar stared at the loaf moodily — Kepa was not reacting as she had expected.

He said, 'Did you talk to him about your concerns?'

'No, I couldn't really. They weren't here long enough, and then they went back into town, at *her* insistence, I expect.'

'If she really is a gold-digger as you say, surely she would have relished the opportunity to have a good look around the house?'

'I think she's too cunning for that. I think she knows she has Liam well and truly on the end of her hook, and that when she's his wife she'll have all the time in the world to wander around out here.'

Kepa shook his head sadly. This was not amusing any more — Tamar was getting herself into a state, which would not be good for her health. He rose, moved around to her side of the table and stood behind her, gently and wordlessly massaging her tense shoulders. He noted that her hair, which smelled like lavender, was now almost entirely silver, with only a few faded streaks to remind him of the glorious colour it had been when they'd first met. He thought now that she was more beautiful than she had ever been.

At the touch of his big hands, Tamar made a noise that was halfway between a sigh and a sob. 'I just don't want him to make a mistake, Kepa!'

He bent and wrapped his arms around her, and she covered his hands with her own.

'I know, darling, I know,' he murmured, 'but the fact is he is old enough to make a mistake, if that is what he chooses.'

'But he doesn't know what he's doing!'

'I think he does.' Kepa's words were blunt but his voice was gentle. 'And is it not better that, if there should be a child, it should have two parents to raise and care for it?'

'Well, we did quite well with Joseph, in the

151

end, and we weren't married.'

'No, but do you think this girl would be able to do that?'

'I'd have the child.'

Kepa sat down then, and touched Tamar's cheek softly. 'You are too old now to be raising children, and you know it. Let him be. He is going away soon. Life changed very much during the last war, do you remember? And it will again during this one, I am sure of it. It may be for the best that he have this, if only for a few weeks before he goes. It may, as you say, turn out to be a grave mistake. But you cannot make his decisions for him, Tamar, you cannot stop him.'

★ ★ ★

And in the end she didn't.

Liam and Evie were married a week later, just days before he left for Britain. The ceremony was modest, as weddings often were these days, and apart from Liam's family was attended only by Evie's sister and brother-in-law, and her parents, a mousy, pleasant, middle-aged couple from Palmerston North who looked rather grateful to be passing the responsibility of their daughter on to someone else.

Tamar, for their sake and for Liam's, made up her mind to be at least pleasant and polite to Evie, although she would certainly not be inviting the girl to stay at Kenmore while Liam was away, as she had when James had bought Lucy home on the eve of the last war. This one was not pregnant — she hoped — and had a job

152

and therefore her own means, so there was really no need.

She sat quietly against the wall of the small reception room the Jones's had hired for their daughter's wedding breakfast, watching her family and wondering how Evie would ever fit in with them.

Joseph and Erin had come, with Robert and Ana, who had left school now and had grown into a very pretty, dark-eyed girl. James and Lucy were here, too, with Kathleen, and so of course were Keely, Owen and Henry, marching about in his little suit with a mutinous expression on his face. Thomas and Catherine had sent a telegram from Dunedin expressing their regret at not being able to attend, but public transport was increasingly being redirected to the war effort, and everyone understood that it would have been impossible for them to get train and ferry passages at such short notice.

The twins, Bonnie and Leila, had turned up too, dressed in the most modern of outfits with very smart little hats perched on their identically coiffed hair. They were not identical themselves, however — for which the Murdochs had always been eternally grateful: God only knew what extra mischief they might have caused had they looked exactly the same. Leila was still almost as blonde as she had been as a child, while Bonnie's thick auburn hair had deepened only a shade. They were both very attractive girls, perhaps not classical beauties, but very pretty with slim, curvaceous figures, ready smiles and wicked senses of humour. Of the pair, Bonnie was possibly the more level-headed, but both were well known for their energy, gregariousness and sheer *joie de vivre*. They had been holy terrors as children, were only marginally better now and Tamar loved them dearly.

After they had graduated, with not very flying colours, from Iona, they had come home to Kenmore and lounged around the house for almost a year deciding what they wanted to do with themselves. As female children of a wealthy farming family, they were not really expected to do anything except marry suitably and have babies, but neither of them was particularly keen on that idea. They were, they insisted, having too much fun being single. And it was true, they had both had suitors telephoning them constantly — which had greatly entertained their cousins listening on the Kenmore party line — or roaring up the long driveway in their jalopies, tooting horns and generally making nuisances of themselves. That had all been marvellous fun, until the novelty of not having to go to school any more had worn off and they had become bored.

They decided they should get jobs. They didn't want to be nurses or teachers — really the only two professions open to women of their social standing — and they couldn't go on to university, like some of the Murdoch men, because they had not done anywhere near well enough at secondary school. So what was left? Shop assistants in town? Hardly. Hairdressing? Too common. The public service? Possibly. After several days of seriously debating their options,

154

they drove into town to investigate the possibility of employment in a government office. They could both type and do basic shorthand — they'd taken these subjects as a lark at school — and there were certainly vacancies for young women with those skills, so clerical work it was. And it didn't sound too difficult or demanding.

Tamar thought they were being awfully cavalier and rather irresponsible in their attitudes towards working for a living, especially so soon after the Depression when many people were still trying to recover from the economic havoc, but she held her tongue, knowing that the girls would soon tire of having to get up at a reasonable hour every morning, turn up somewhere on a regular basis and put in an acceptable day's work. Owen kept his mouth shut too, for more or less the same reason, but Keely had been too busy with Henry to notice what her girls had been up to, beyond asking Owen if he thought they would be safe.

Then of course they'd had to move into town, as the return trip from Kenmore five days a week by car was just too gruelling and time-consuming, and anyway petrol rationing put an end to that. Their mother and father had refused to buy them a house of their own, so they'd been forced to board with an elderly woman who, fortunately for Bonnie and Leila, was hard of hearing and retired to bed early, and was therefore unaware that her charming and beautifully behaved boarders were climbing out of their windows for night-time jaunts with the local 'in' crowd.

But although their social lives flourished, performing typing and shorthand duties soon palled almost as quickly as had sitting around at Kenmore. And the twins suspected that their efforts were not being taken seriously by the senior members of their department — although they were often called in to take shorthand in the office of Mr Dimbly who, they decided, had an eye for a nice pair of legs — and certainly not by their younger female colleagues. In fact, their initial reception had been distinctly frosty, and had barely thawed since. Although they genuinely tried to make friends they were just too casual about everything, and perhaps, they were forced to admit, considered by some to be just a little too privileged to be doing that sort of work. They didn't mind it themselves, apart from the fact that it was dull, but they were not stupid and were aware that others resented their presence. But, rather than throwing in the towel and going home to listen to their grandmother telling them I told you so, they'd decided to stick it out for a little longer just in case anything interesting developed.

Nothing had, in the department, but then the war had been declared and almost immediately there were rumours about women being called up to do various types of work for the war effort — even men's work! — so they had stayed on for a few months more until the rumours had become a little less ephemeral, then resigned and a week ago had returned to Kenmore to 'wait for the call-up'.

Tamar disapproved of their attitude towards

this as well. In her opinion women were already 'doing their bit' by waving goodbye to sons, husbands and brothers, perhaps forever, but there was no telling Bonnie and Leila that. They were young and simply did not, or could not, understand.

Tamar caught Bonnie's eye, and crooked a gloved finger at her.

Both girls came over, and sat down on either side of their grandmother.

'What a very nice wedding,' she said to them as diplomatically as she could. 'Simple, but very pleasant.'

Bonnie and Leila looked at each other and grimaced. They had not met Evie until today, and had been a little surprised, to say the least, by the woman their beloved cousin had chosen.

'Her wedding outfit is, well, it's quite unusual,' Bonnie said.

They all glanced over at Evie, who was holding Liam's hand, chatting to her sister and laughing uproariously. Her pale pink suit was fitted at the waist with sleeves that puffed slightly at the shoulder, and her hat matched her white lace gloves. The ensemble itself was fairly harmless, apart from the fact that it was rather tight across her bottom, but Evie had brightened it up by adding an enormous red silk flower to the band of her hat, and was wearing high heels in the same startling shade. The whole effect was rather tropical, and not, in Tamar's view, entirely suitable for a late winter wedding in Palmerston North. But that was certainly not something she was going to say out loud.

Instead, she said, 'A lot of brides haven't been wearing the full white costume lately.'

'But still,' Leila said, 'red silk flowers?'

'That is unnecessary and unkind, Leila,' Tamar responded somewhat hypocritically. 'Do remember that not everyone is as privileged as you two.'

Bonnie asked, 'Does, er, does Liam love her?'

'He certainly thinks he does,' Tamar replied in a tone that suggested to both girls that they should not pursue the subject. Not with their grandmother, anyway.

Later, after they had all enjoyed a hearty wedding breakfast of cold chicken and ham, peas and potatoes, fruit salad and trifle and a small, iced, single-tier wedding cake, Bonnie and Leila asked Liam himself.

He went pink, because it was a very personal question and these were his *girl* cousins, after all, but replied gamely, 'Of course I do. She's the best thing that's ever happened to me.'

The girls had their doubts, which they shared with a kind of fascinated dismay in their hotel room later that night. Evie seemed to be a very confident, *worldly* girl, and not at all the sort of wife they would have expected for their quiet, slightly naïve cousin. He was twenty-four, granted, and not completely inexperienced when it came to the opposite sex — they knew because they'd heard Duncan teasing him about it some time ago — but still . . .

'I hope he knows what he's doing, that's all I can say,' said Bonnie as she hopped into one of the two single beds in their room.

'Well, if he doesn't, it's too late now, isn't it?'

8

Duncan was in so much pain he could easily have chewed off his lower lip. That was, he thought, if he still had one — he wasn't sure. His skin itched appallingly under the bandages swathing his head and hands, and he very much needed a pee.

He turned his head slowly and said to his neighbour, 'Pete? Get us a nurse, will you? I'm dying for a slash.'

The man lounging on the bed next to him, dressed in an odd assortment of casual clothing, obliged by ringing his bell repeatedly, holding the handle between his teeth and shaking his head vigorously. A minute later the sound of a nurse's shoes came squeaking down the linoleum floor of the ward.

Peter Nash was a flight sergeant with Bomber Command who'd passed out at altitude through lack of oxygen without his gloves on, and had been severely frostbitten. Last week, as a final resort, his fingers had been amputated, although he still had his thumbs — which meant he would still, eventually, be able to grip things.

'Pete, what can I do for you?' said the nurse cheerfully, as if she were a shop girl behind a counter.

Her name was Claire Pearsall and she loved working at Queen Victoria Hospital in East

159

Grinstead, although she had to admit that caring for her charges in Ward Three was sometimes emotionally very demanding. The 'Boss', though, Doctor Archibald McIndoe, was a truly gifted plastic surgeon and an outstanding and refreshingly informal man. His ability to give back to his patients their faces, their hands and limbs, and therefore their self-esteem, was extraordinary, and they and his staff alike revered him.

'Duncan wants a wee,' Pete said.

'Then what's wrong with ringing your own bell, Duncan?' she chided gently.

She had a voice that was low and pleasant, but her laugh was boisterously loud, and she laughed often. Like her colleagues, she had been personally chosen by Doctor McIndoe for her looks and her cheerful nature, as well as her nursing skills. He had a policy of employing only nurses he considered capable of communicating with his patients, regardless of their deformities and scars, and of relating to them as the young, virile men they still were, in spite of their injuries. As for the girls being attractive, McIndoe believed it was good for his men to have pretty faces to look at, and that it helped them with their confidence.

Claire Pearsall was aware that most of her patients were at least half in love with her, and she and her colleagues, also objects of affection if not lust, used that knowledge shamelessly to get the men to do the things they disliked, such as exercising their shattered bodies, and to jolly them out of succumbing to bouts of black depression, an all too common occurrence.

But Duncan knew only Nurse Pearsall's voice, and what a delightfully rich, seductive voice it was. His eyes had been bandaged since he'd arrived at East Grinstead, and the Boss had not yet decreed that it was time to remove the gauze, preferring to give the ruined skin and muscle the best chance of recovery. And although no one had said anything, Duncan also suspected that Doctor McIndoe was giving him an opportunity to come to terms with the possibility that he might be permanently blind.

So over the month he had been in hospital, he'd become very familiar with his ward mates and the ward itself, although he had never seen either. He could put a name to every voice now, and knew in which part of the big room each man's bed was located. He was not very clear, however, about the injuries of his fellow patients, because most of them did not speak in detail about what had happened to them. There were frequent references to being 'fried', and comments such as, 'Stop your moaning, you've only been singed' and 'Buck up, you were bloody ugly before anyway', but no one ever seemed to refer to their injuries directly. Perhaps such a cavalier attitude helped them come to terms with the awful damage their bodies had suffered. But they all seemed to be very decent chaps, mostly from the RAF and injured during the Battle of Britain which, thank God, seemed to be easing off now.

He also knew intimately the daily routine that had become central to his existence. The ward was a very noisy place — except when someone was very badly off, and then everyone would

161

tiptoe around until the man came right — and at times seemed nothing less than chaotic. Patients and nurses referred to each other by their Christian names — except for the Boss, who was always addressed to his face as 'sir'. The radio played all day and there was a piano the chaps thumped away on regularly, people talked loudly and laughed uproariously and seemed to come and go whenever they felt like it, and ever since Duncan had arrived someone had been teaching themselves to type, clacking away for hours at a time. There was a keg of beer permanently on tap for the patients, and he knew that groups of the chaps — the mobile and the semi-mobile — would frequently go out to the Whitehall, a pub in town, sometimes just to let their hair down, and sometimes to meet up with nurses or the local girls. Already, two patients had become engaged to their nurses, even though one of McIndoe's rules — not always adhered to — was that the men were not to touch them.

There were all sorts of stories, related repeatedly and at length, about the time that a certain patient toured East Grinstead after a night at the Whitehall and diligently uprooted every single road sign, about wheelchair races down the main street, and about very under the weather patients being delivered back to the hospital by civic-minded civilians, then put to bed with tea and toast by tolerant nurses. Duncan heard a fair bit of the latter himself. The chaps steered clear of the booze only the night before they were due to go under the knife; that was an unwritten rule that was never ignored.

162

They were extremely proud of the fact that a local clergyman had been heard to refer to them as the most ungodly people he had ever come across.

It was unorthodox, but it worked. The Boss condoned the rather undisciplined behaviour, and at times even joined the chaps in the pub or at the piano. It was rumoured he had asked the people of East Grinstead to support his patients, and it was clear that the town was more than happy to comply. In fact, members of the community often turned up at the hospital to visit the patients or take them out for the day, or home for a meal.

The place seemed to run very smoothly and efficiently and the medical side of things was very professional. In fact, Duncan doubted he could have tolerated lying on his back for all these weeks in a silent room filled with other patients weighed down by their own doom and misery.

After the ambulance crew had picked him up only yards away from the wreckage of his Spitfire, a couple of miles from Biggin Hill, and while the skin and tissue on his hands and face was already blowing up as if he were a human balloon, he'd been taken to the nearest hospital equipped for burns injuries. Then, when he'd stabilised enough to be moved, Doctor McIndoe had come to collect him and bring him back to East Grinstead, fortunately before he'd been given the tannic acid treatment, which often caused more permanent scarring than the original burns.

The first few weeks in Ward Three had been a blur of agony and uncertainty, of morphine injections and not knowing whether he was awake or asleep, and of the Boss continually assessing the damage to his face, head and hands. It had been too early then to start any grafting procedures, but Duncan knew that within the next few days he was due to go 'on the slab' to prepare him for what would be the first in a series of skin grafts.

After the shock of his prang had ebbed, Duncan had been on the verge of sliding into a very frightening depression, but he simply had not been allowed to do it. The other chaps had joked and chatted with him about nothing in particular, just to stop him from withdrawing into himself, and the nurses had been tremendous too. Especially Claire Pearsall, in Duncan's opinion. She had never been far from his side during those bleak weeks, and even now was only ever seconds away if he needed anything. Such as the urine bottle, which he required desperately.

'I can't find my bell,' he said through the bandages covering his lips. 'I must have knocked it off the table.'

'I'll look for it later,' Claire replied. 'I'll get you a bottle, that's more urgent.'

She squeaked away, and was back again almost immediately. Duncan felt his sheet being pulled back and hands undoing the cord on his pyjama pants. He spread his thighs a little as he felt the bottle being placed at the base of his groin, then heaved a great sigh of relief as Claire held his penis inside the neck of the bottle and he let go. He couldn't direct himself because of the boxing glove-sized bandages on his hands. He had almost died of embarrassment the first few times this toileting had happened, but he was quite used to it now, and anyway it was far better than wetting the bed, which he'd also done. It was rather pleasant, really, having your penis handled by lovely, smooth hands attached to a gorgeous-sounding nurse.

'Better?' Claire asked. 'Good. Don't leave it so long next time, it's bad for you. And by the way, the Boss says you're going under the knife the day after tomorrow, but before that we'll be taking the bandages off. Actually, we'll be doing that this afternoon.'

There was a brief silence as the last few drops of urine emptied out of Duncan's bladder, and he digested what she had just said.

'Off my eyes?'

'Yes.'

This was momentous. In only a matter of hours he would find out whether or not he could still see. He suddenly realised that he was absolutely terrified. Being scarred he could cope with — even not having the full use of his hands would be manageable — but to never again see the sky, or the sea, or the green and brown hills of Hawke's Bay was unthinkable.

'If it's gone, my sight,' he asked so quietly it was almost a whisper, 'will the Boss be able to bring it back?'

Claire's eyes filled at the hopeless naïveté of the question. They both knew it was an absurd

165

thing to ask, but Claire understood very well how desperate Duncan Murdoch must be feeling.

'No, not if it's the eyes themselves,' she replied gently. 'If it turns out that they haven't been damaged too badly, and it's only the tissue around your eye sockets and brows, he should be able to do something. He usually can, you know.'

'The chaps keep saying how good he is.'

'He's a miracle worker, in my opinion. I keep forgetting — you haven't seen any of his before and afters, have you?'

Duncan shook his head.

'Well, you will soon, I'm sure.'

Claire thanked God he couldn't see that she had her fingers crossed; she had become very fond of Flight Lieutenant Duncan Murdoch from New Zealand.

★　★　★

Just before dinner late that afternoon, the Boss himself helped Duncan into a wheelchair and, to a hearty chorus of 'Good luck, old boy' from the other patients, wheeled him out of the ward and along the cream and green hall to a smaller room, known as the clinic, one of the few private places in the hospital. This was for Duncan's convenience, not McIndoe's. Once inside he closed the door, pulled the drapes against the deepening dusk outside, and set about laying out a tray of the instruments he would need to remove Duncan's bandages.

Archibald McIndoe, a dapper man of medium

166

height with horn-rimmed spectacles and a touch of grey at his temples, was a New Zealander, originally from Dunedin but now resident in Britain with a private plastic surgery practice in Harley Street, a very impressive medical reputation and more young men to practise on now than he'd ever imagined in his worst nightmares.

'So, Duncan,' he said conversationally as he inspected a pair of small scissors for sharpness. 'How was the weather in Napier before you left?'

Duncan was slightly startled at the question. 'Before I left to fly in England?'

'Yes.'

'Well, it was four years ago now, sir.'

'Yes, that's right. How was the weather?'

'Ah, it was quite nice I think, sir, if I remember rightly.'

It was a very strange question but it had served its purpose — Duncan was no longer focusing on what might or might not be under his bandages.

'Been there myself a few times,' McIndoe went on. 'Lovely beach. Well before the earthquake, of course. Lose anything in it, did you?'

'In the earthquake?'

'Mmm.'

'Well, not personally. I was at school at the time of course, and the assembly hall came off pretty badly. And our beautiful new Chrysler Imperial Roadster was flattened in Emerson Street.'

'My God.'

'Yes, it was a tragedy.'

167

Duncan heard the door open.

'Claire's going to be giving us a hand,' McIndoe said. 'Don't mind, do you?'

A light hand rested on Duncan's shoulder, and he knew she was there to lend moral support, just in case.

'No, that's fine,' he replied. He was nervous again, and feeling rather sick, but trying not to show it.

'Right then,' McIndoe said, and Duncan felt the outer layer of bandages begin to come away.

The surgeon's hands were gentle, but there seemed to be yards and yards of the stuff wrapped around his head.

Eventually, McIndoe stood back again.

'We're down to the last few layers and then the gauze. Are you ready?'

Duncan nodded. He wasn't, but there was no point in delaying what was inevitable.

He felt the last two turns of bandage lifted off, followed by a single clicking noise. Then the gauze, peeled carefully away with what he assumed was the aid of a pair of tweezers. The air felt strange on his skin, which felt wet but tight at the same time, and there was an odd, not altogether pleasant smell coming from somewhere under his nose. He didn't know whether he had his eyes shut or not.

No one said anything, but he felt Claire's hand tighten on his shoulder.

He struggled to move the muscles of his face, feeling an appalling stiffness and a dull, ragged pain, then he blinked once, and then again.

He suddenly felt embarrassingly helpless, and

swore in frustration, anger and despair.

'Jesus *bloody* Christ.'

'What?'

'I'm sorry, sir, but . . . oh *shit*, there's nothing.'

'Settle down, Duncan,' McIndoe said blandly. 'We've turned the lights off. It's pitch black in here.'

'Oh.' Duncan felt even more pathetic now.

McIndoe said, 'I'm going to turn a torch on, but I'll keep my hand over it, all right? I want you to tell me if you can see anything. Anything at all.'

There was another tiny click, a pause of the deepest silence, then Duncan started to laugh.

'Ow!' he yelped. His bandaged hands flew up to his mouth, freed now of the heavy dressings and unaccustomed to stretching far enough to accommodate a decent laugh, and he swore again as they came in contact with the raw skin of his face.

'Careful,' Claire warned. 'Now, what can you see?'

'Mostly nothing, but I can just see four pink sausages, or something like that, with lines of red between them. In a sort of a ball.'

In the barely lit room, both Claire and McIndoe smiled.

McIndoe took his hand off the torch and positioned it on the table facing away from Duncan. 'What about this?'

'I can . . . yes! I can see an outline of a chair, and the bottom of some curtains, and a cabinet or something, with shelves on it.'

McIndoe turned the torch around then, so that the room was at least half illuminated.

And Duncan turned himself around, so he could see what he had been longing to look at for weeks now.

Claire Pearsall's hair was a thick, unruly dark brown and framed a bold face set with sparkling brown eyes, an aquiline nose and a wide, full mouth. Her skin was creamy and smooth like that of so many English girls, and her generous figure looked firm and toned, probably from belting about the wards all day and lifting patients like himself. And she was smiling at him.

Duncan smiled back, but carefully so as not to hurt his mouth.

'Well, then,' McIndoe said, 'I don't think we have to worry too much about your vision now, do we?'

Duncan couldn't say anything; he was still gazing at Claire.

McIndoe switched a reading lamp on and the torch off. 'We have to bandage your face again, although we'll leave your eyes uncovered. Do you want to have a look at the damage now, or leave it for a bit?'

Duncan took a deep breath. 'No, now, thanks.'

McIndoe nodded. He took a hand mirror off the implements tray and passed it over.

Duncan slowly raised the mirror to his face and looked into it.

After a minute he lowered it to his lap, where it rested, mirror side down.

Billy Deane also had his eye on a girl.

He nudged his mate, Harry Tomoana, sitting next to him in the bar of a small English country pub, and said, 'I'm going to ask her out, I've decided.'

Harry took a huge drink of his beer, then wiped the froth off his top lip. 'You'll be lucky. You're too black and ugly.'

This wasn't true. Billy had grown into a handsome young man, with his father's pale brown skin and striking bone structure, and his mother's enormous dark eyes. But Harry could be right — the local people hadn't seen many dark-skinned men before the Maori Battalion had arrived at Camp 49B, and although they had been friendly, especially after the boys had received their new uniforms with the 'New Zealand' shoulder flashes, the village fathers might not take to the idea of their daughters going out with the big, brown 'Moo-ree' men.

The battalion had been in England now for several months, and being on dry land after six weeks at sea had been an almost universal relief. The ocean voyage to Gourock near Glasgow in the luxury liner *Aquitania*, requisitioned for the duration of the war for use as a troopship, had at first been exhilarating, especially the send-off in Wellington when the whole ship had sung 'Now Is the Hour' when the governor-general came out in a launch to farewell them. They had then joined up with the rest of the convoy carrying the Second Echelon, and had felt immense pride in the fact that they were all going off to war.

But then had come the seasickness, followed by increasing boredom with the shipboard menu, lavish though it was. Used to fairly basic fare, most of the men had been startled to be presented with such dishes as Salisbury steak served with creamed spinach and French-fried potatoes, or roast beef with horseradish sauce, or pressed beef or Oxford brawn, followed by sago or custard pudding and then coffee. The problem was soon solved, however, by one enterprising entrepreneur who broke into the large supply of mutton-birds stored in the ship's hold, and sold them at a healthy profit to those who preferred more traditional food.

The convoy had stopped at Fremantle for a couple of days to give the troops a chance to go ashore, but after that the monotony of life at sea began to set in. Then they were told they weren't going to Egypt after all and that the convoy was changing course, which had disappointed all those raring to go into battle.

There were meal times, and there was frequent training, but the growing heat began to fray tempers even further, which led to fights and worse — two stokers working in the engine room committed suicide by jumping overboard. Concerts and community sing-alongs went some way towards alleviating the lethargy and boredom, and new songs did the rounds like wildfire. The tune adopted by the battalion as their marching song, with its rousing, home-grown lyrics about victory and glory, was very popular. But perhaps even more favoured was a

172

song introduced by a mate of Billy's, one Ruru Karaitiana, a Ngati Kahungungu man who in peacetime was a piano player in a band.

He called his song 'Blue Smoke', and its melancholic opening words — 'Blue smoke goes drifting by into the deep blue sky/And when I think of home I sadly sigh . . . ' — could be heard all over the ship at various times. Billy was very fond of it himself, and even went as far as writing down the words and the chords and sending them back to his family in one of his infrequent letters.

There were the official housie games with a heady, threepenny limit, or the unofficial games of poker and two-up, at which Billy excelled, having picked up the skills from the farmhands and drovers who had passed through Kenmore over the years. By the time the battalion disembarked in the UK he had a very tidy sum stashed away in his kitbag.

At Cape Town, the *Aquitania* was too big to go into port, and they were forced to gaze in frustration at the awesome sight of Table Mountain towering above the town. They had already been warned that the white South Africans might be more than a little frosty, and the fact they couldn't go ashore did little to improve the prevailing mood. When they were able to disembark for less than a day after the *Aquitania* moved to the port of Simonstown, they were taken on a tour of local vineyards in buses, then driven to Cape Town for a cup of tea and a bun. Then those who hadn't already absconded were let loose for an hour and a half to explore and spend all their money, though it was actually only twenty-five minutes after they'd sat in a drill hall listening to a lecture on how to behave.

The battalion, though, had its revenge. By the time the scores and scores of huge, green lobsters filched from the clear waters of the bay at Cape Town were discovered on board the *Aquitania*, it was far too late to do anything about it.

Eventually, the convoy was told its destination. Zigzagging through the English Channel, now accompanied by a flotilla of destroyers, the convoy passed the wreckage of torpedoed Allied ships. The New Zealanders watched in awe as an oil tanker ahead of them blazed until it sank in a boiling cloud of steam hundreds of feet high.

On 16 June, the convoy docked at the Scottish port of Gourock, and soon afterwards the Maori Battalion headed for the south of England to begin training for its defence. The four days' leave in London on the way down had been interesting, especially the underground railway system, which had been a real novelty, but the general consensus had been that the city was big, old, dirty and very expensive, and no one was particularly sorry to be moving on. Ewshott, on the other hand, had been a small, very pleasant village surrounded by gentle fields and meadows criss-crossed by tree-lined lanes. Viscount Bledisloe had visited the battalion there, and so had King George VI himself.

On 9 July the battalion had packed up and

marched about five miles to the little hamlet of Dogmersfield, where they were now stationed. Since arriving they'd taken part in endless exercises and manoeuvres designed to thwart and repel the Germans should they land. It was during one of these that Billy's company fell under a cloud of suspicion when a disgruntled farmer complained that a mature pig had disappeared from its paddock at about the same time that D Company had passed through. The inference was that the pig had been disposed of in the traditional Maori manner, and the battalion subsequently received a bill from New Zealand Force Headquarters for twelve pounds, to go towards compensating the irate farmer. A newly promoted Colonel Dittmer was compelled to make several visits to HQ to argue that his men would never do such a thing, which increased his mana considerably. Together with the recent memory of an excellent feed of fresh pork, it raised the troops' spirits markedly.

But between the route marches and intensive exercises there had been time for leave, and it had been on one of these breaks in their training, late in September, that Billy had met Violet Metcalfe. He, Harry and another mate named Rangi were in the village one morning when the alluring smell of fresh bread had compelled them to follow their noses to a small bakery at the end of the row of shops that made up the short main street.

The shop window displayed a selection of loaves and buns, and inside they could see more arranged temptingly on the counter and on the wooden racks behind it.

'I'm starving,' Billy said. 'Let's go in.'

Ferreting through their pockets they came up with enough change to buy themselves a decent feed, and jostled each other through the doorway to get in first.

The day was already warm, but inside the air was hot and humid, the vicious heat from the big brick ovens permeating the entire shop. A sweating, red-faced man in a cook's whites was removing steaming loaves with the aid of a long tool like a flat shovel, and at the counter stood a young girl.

'Good morning,' she said shyly in a lilting Surrey accent. 'Can I help you?'

Oh yes, Billy thought immediately, I'm sure you could help me. The girl had shoulder-length hair that was almost white and as fine as silk, parted to one side and clipped back above her small ears to keep it off her face. Her eyes were the most vibrant blue, and her lips a natural, strong pink, almost matching the flaming patches on her cheeks and neck caused by the heat. Elsewhere her complexion was alabaster, and her eyebrows and long lashes were fair, but not as pale as her hair. To Billy she looked like a patupaiarehe, a fairy, for some reason condemned to stand behind this shop counter flogging loaves of bread to mere mortals.

The three soldiers filled the small shop, but she did not seem intimidated.

'Morning,' Billy said. 'We'd like, um, what do we want, boys?'

'Two loaves, the ones with the seeds on, and

six of those buns with the currants,' Harry said immediately.

'That won't be enough to go around.'

'No, that's just for me. You can order your own!'

The girl dipped her head, and Billy was sure she was trying to hide a smile.

'All right then, we'll have four of the loaves, and a dozen buns, thanks, love. No, make that fifteen. And two of those custard things, eh? They look nice.'

The girl set about putting the baked goods into bags and lining them up along the top of the counter. When she'd finished, she added up the amount and Billy handed the money over.

'Thanks, love,' he said. 'And have you got a name?'

'Yes,' she answered. 'Have you?'

Billy whipped off his cap. 'Billy Deane, Private, D Company, Twenty-eight Maori Battalion, Second New Zealand Expeditionary Force, at your service.'

'A Moo-ree?'

'No, a *Maori*.'

She blushed then, at having pronounced the word incorrectly. 'Oh, beg your pardon. Violet Metcalfe.'

Billy thought Violet was the perfect name for her — it matched her eyes. He stuck his hand out over the counter.

'Pleased to meet you, Violet Metcalfe.'

Her hand was small and damp, but her grip was firm, not at all what Billy had expected.

The man came out then, wiping his hands on

177

his apron. He nodded and said, 'Lads,' then, to the girl, 'You've work to do, Vi.'

Billy took the hint and they left.

Outside, when he opened the bag containing the custard buns, he found that Violet had given him three instead of two. Turning around, he thought he caught a glimpse of her watching him through the window, but couldn't be sure.

Now, sitting in the pub, after having thought about her almost constantly for four days, he'd made up his mind to go back to the bakery and ask her out, even if Harry did think he was wasting his time.

'That might have been her old man,' Harry added unhelpfully. 'Don't think he liked the idea of her chatting up the customers, especially us. He was a big fella, too.'

'Not as big as me,' Billy shot back.

'No, not as tall, but he was built like one of your koro's prize bulls.'

'So? I'll just have to make sure I charm him.'

Harry finished his beer, and burped satisfyingly. 'Away you go then.'

The next time Billy was in Dogmersfield village he made a point of dropping in to the bakery, having first checked his reflection in a shop window a few doors down, slicking down his hair under his cap and making sure his teeth and face were clean.

She was there behind the counter, as he'd prayed she would be.

'Hello again, Violet Metcalfe,' he said as he sauntered casually into the shop, although his heart was skittering in his chest.

'Hello yourself, Billy Deane,' she replied, a smile lighting up her face.

Billy chanced a quick look towards the ovens, wondering if the old man was there.

'He's out, if it's my da you're looking for.'

Billy nodded, slightly relieved. He cast about for something clever or impressive to say, but failed. 'Thanks for the extra custard bun. They were really nice.'

'I'm glad. They're one of our specialties, although we might not be doing them for much longer, because of the rationing.'

'Is that right?' Billy said with just the right note of interested concern, although he couldn't really give a stuff about custard buns.

He stared at Violet, wondering how to ask her to come to the pictures with him on Saturday night in Farnham, without just blurting it straight out. Today she was wearing a V-necked pale green dress with short puffed sleeves, under an apron patterned with brightly coloured pansies, and her face was flushed again from the heat of the ovens. He had no idea how she managed to work in here all day without dying of dehydration. She was even prettier than he remembered.

He thrust his hands in his pockets. 'I was thinking, well, I was wondering whether you might like to come out with me some time.'

Violet raised her eyebrows, but said nothing.

'Perhaps to the pictures over in Farnham? Would your father let you do that?'

'He might.'

Billy sighed exasperatedly to himself — she

wasn't helping him out much here.

'Would I have to ask him first?'

'No, but it would be a good idea if you at least met him and my ma. They're not against me going out, but Da especially is quite strict about who with.'

'Right. Fair enough.'

Billy was about to ask for her address when he realised she hadn't accepted his invitation.

'Well, I mean, would you like to come out? I've got leave this Saturday night, and we could get the bus into Farnham.'

She studied him thoughtfully for a few moments.

'Yes, thank you, Billy Deane. I think I'd like that very much.'

9

October 1940

Billy had been ribbed mercilessly by the boys while getting ready to go out, and when he'd taken the lid off his jar of hair pomade he'd found that someone had thoughtfully put a condom in it. Harry, probably.

But by the time he was ready to leave, he was spit-shined and polished, had money in his pocket and two tins of fruit in his rucksack for Mrs Metcalfe, and the loan of a bicycle for the evening.

It took him less than twenty minutes to cycle from the camp to the village, and he arrived with time to spare so he wobbled up and down Violet's street for another ten minutes, looking at the quaint little red-brick cottages lining both sides. Violet lived in the one second to the end, so he kept clear in case she was looking out of the window and saw him dithering about.

Finally, at half past six exactly, he parked the bike against the fence outside Violet's house, straightened his cap, tugged his jacket down and walked purposefully up the path to the front door.

His knock was answered almost immediately by Violet, who smiled shyly as she ushered him into the short front hall.

'Ma and Da are in the parlour. Ma's made scones and a pot of tea, so we'll have to stay for

181

at least a little while.'

Billy looked at his watch. 'That's fine, we don't need to go yet.'

Violet took his hand and led him into a compact, low-ceilinged parlour room. There was a small fire going in the grate, even though it was still more or less summer, the blackout curtains were drawn against the encroaching dusk and the atmosphere was somewhat stuffy. Mr Metcalfe, who really was almost the size of one of Kepa's bulls, was ensconced in an armchair next to the fire wearing slippers and smoking a roll-your-own. His wife, a small woman with greying hair and laughing eyes that Violet had clearly inherited, was perched on one end of a sofa, its threadbare cushions covered with a crocheted rug. A large radio sat on a bureau against the opposite wall, its volume turned down but still audible, several small highly polished tables held an assortment of china ornaments placed carefully on lace doilies, and two or three faded prints of innocuous rural scenes decorated the whitewashed walls.

Violet made the introductions, and Sid Metcalfe stood and shook Billy's hand while Nancy Metcalfe smiled at him nervously. Billy thought his height in the small room might be putting her off, and was relieved when Violet's father invited him to sit down.

When he handed her the tins of fruit, however, she seemed to relax a little. They'd been told that if they were ever invited to one of the locals' homes for tea they had to take something. It was koha, really, which was fine with the battalion, for most of whom the gesture was customary anyway. They'd also been warned not eat the local community out of house and home, so when Mrs Metcalfe encouraged him to eat a third scone with butter, cream and jam, he refused, although he could have eaten at least two more quite easily. There was probably plenty of flour, the Metcalfes being bakers and everything, but at camp there was talk of jam and butter being scarce, and Billy didn't want to risk depriving Sid Metcalfe of his breakfast.

'So you're a Moo-ree from New Zealand then?' Violet's father said after they'd finished their tea and scones.

'Yes, sir, *Maori*, from Napier. That's on the east coast of the North Island.'

'Very good. And what does your father do, lad?'

'He's a sheep farmer. My family has a station in the hills outside Napier.'

'Oh, aye? A few acres then?'

'A few.'

'And you work for him?'

'Yes, sir. Well, I did before I joined the battalion.'

'Well, you can't go wrong with farming, and I say that even if I am a baker myself. Brothers and sisters?'

'One of each. My brother Robert is only eighteen and won't be eligible for conscription until he turns nineteen next year, so he's still working on the station. Ana's twenty, but she's not married yet so I expect she'll be getting herself involved in something soon.'

183

'And is soldiering in your family?'

Billy nodded. 'My father went to the war in South Africa, and the last one. And Mum was a military nurse in Egypt and here in England. At Brockenhurst, I think it was.'

'You don't say?' Mr Metcalfe was impressed.

'My two uncles went as well. Well, three of them did, actually, but only two came home.'

Sid Metcalfe nodded. 'Terrible business, that. Let's hope this one will be a lot easier to stomach, if such a thing is at all possible. The Americans could help, of course, if they got off their bloody backsides and got involved. It could all be over by Christmas if we had them on our side.'

Mrs Metcalfe gave her husband a reprimanding look, whether as a result of his language or his opinion of the Americans, Billy couldn't tell. She was fiddling with her serviette, folding it and refolding it until it was a tiny, compressed square.

Finally, she said, 'On the radio the other night we happened to hear a German propaganda broadcast, because you can get them here, you know, if you're on the wrong station, and they had someone on saying that the, the . . . ' she struggled with the correct pronunciation and gave up, 'that your people, and I beg your pardon for repeating this, that your people are the descendants of cannibals and head-hunters. I said to Sid, 'What a lot of rubbish that is,' but some folk, even from around here I'm sorry to say, are likely to believe that sort of thing.'

'Let it go, Nancy, love. Sorry, son,' Sid said, embarrassed.

His wife lowered her eyes and began the long, complicated process of unfolding her serviette.

Billy was amused, but kept it to himself. 'It's true, there was some cannibalism among my ancestors and now and again they took heads. But it was more of a ceremonial sort of thing, and it was all a long time ago.'

He didn't want to add that such practices had been most common in times of war, just in case the Metcalfes got the wrong end of the stick.

'See, Ma?' Violet said, laughing as her mother let out an audible sigh of relief. 'I told you it was just a lot of codswallop put out by the Germans. Cannibals don't bring people tins of peaches.'

'Oh, I knew that, dear, of course I did.'

Billy glanced surreptitiously at his watch again; it was almost quarter past seven.

'Should we be on our way?' Violet asked.

'We should if we want to catch the bus into Farnham in time for the pictures.' Billy stood up. 'Thank you very much for the tea and scones. My mum makes a good scone, but not as good as yours, Mrs Metcalfe.'

Nancy Metcalfe went pink with pleasure.

Outside, as they stood at the bus stop, Violet said, 'You've got the gift of the gab, haven't you, Billy Deane? Da will think you're just marvellous because your family are farmers *and* soldiers, and Ma will tell everyone what you said about her scones.'

Billy laughed. The bus was already half full, but as they climbed the step he saw Harry, Rangi

185

and two other lads from the company, Maru and Boy, sitting towards the back, and he groaned.

'What? Oh, look, it's your friends, Billy.'

'Yes, I can see that,' he replied miserably, envisioning an evening at the pictures with the lot of them sitting right behind him and Violet, throwing things and generally making a nuisance of themselves.

But when the bus finally arrived in Farnham, after a very slow trip with the headlights almost obliterated, Harry and the lads got off and headed straight for the nearest pub, pausing only to give Billy a series of exaggerated, salacious winks.

The film was *The Philadelphia Story*, starring Katharine Hepburn. Billy was interested in, and rather chastened by, the British Pathé war newsreel that preceded it, but in all honesty wasn't that fussed about the main feature. He was too busy trying to casually drape his arm around Violet's shoulder in a manner that would encourage her to lean into him so they could enjoy a cosy and intimate cuddle. Her hair smelled of something lovely and flowery, and her hand, when he took it in his own, was warm and smooth.

He managed one or two quick kisses before the end of the film, but it seemed that Violet really was interested in whether Katharine Hepburn ended up with Cary Grant, John Howard or James Stewart.

After the film they wandered down the High Street to wait for the last bus back to Dogmersfield. The moon was big, bathing the

186

old town in a still light. It was the sort of night that Fighter Command hated and the Luftwaffe relished, but there were no planes in the skies, and the countryside was quiet except for the muffled lowing of cattle in nearby paddocks and the odd boisterous shout from the pub still open at the other end of the street. The shops and pubs here were allegedly built with timber beams that had come ashore from the wreckage of the Spanish Armada, the vanguard of an earlier nation of invaders. Above the town loomed a hill, black in the moonlight, topped by an old ruined castle that Billy had a good mind to visit one day soon.

At the bus stop they sat down to wait on the wooden bench thoughtfully provided by the town council. Billy noticed that Violet was shivering, and considerately put his arm around her shoulders again.

'Cold?'

'No, not really. I think a goose just walked over my grave.'

Billy chuckled at the image, but Violet was serious. 'Don't laugh,' she said. 'It's not something to laugh at. Sometimes it can be an omen.'

'An omen of what?'

'Of something bad that hasn't happened yet. That's what my gran says, anyway.'

'My gran doesn't hold with that sort of thing.'

'Doesn't she?' She turned to look at him. 'You're not a proper Maori, are you?'

'Your pronunciation is getting better. Of course I'm a proper Maori.'

'Then why aren't you as dark-skinned as your friend Harry?'

'Harry's parents are both Maori. My father is half-Maori and my mother is Pakeha.'

'What's that?'

'European.'

'Oh. So which side is your gran from?'

'She's European, from Cornwall, actually. She came out to New Zealand in the 1870s. She's my dad's mother.'

Violet thought for a moment, her face a picture of concentration. 'Oh, never mind. So your gran isn't superstitious? The Cornish usually are.'

'I didn't say she isn't superstitious, but she doesn't believe in omens. At least I don't think she does. She's a very practical person. My father believes in them, but then he has Maori blood. In fact the story goes that when I was an unborn child my life was saved by an old witch woman who my dad says was ancient when he was a boy.'

Violet looked at him sceptically, and he laughed again.

'It's a family story. I don't know if it's a hundred per cent true.'

He bent his head then, and kissed her. Her bare lips tasted faintly of peppermint from the boiled sweets they'd shared at the pictures, and they were warm and incredibly soft. She was confident enough on the outside, and in the short time he had known her she had revealed a rather determined streak, but he sensed that she wasn't very experienced when it came to the opposite sex. At least he hoped not; he didn't like to think that she had been with anyone else.

He moved his other arm slowly until his hand rested lightly on her stomach, from where, he hoped, it would be able to wander to other, more intimate parts of her body. His hand began to creep up the front of her fluffy jumper, and he let his thumb stroke the underside of the delicious curve of her breast.

'Unhand that woman, you cad!'

Billy almost leapt out of his uniform, and nearly gave himself whiplash swivelling around on the bench.

Weaving up the street came Harry with the rest of the lads trailing behind him like ducklings after their mother. They had clearly enjoyed a very hospitable evening in the pub.

'Harry, you bastard.'

'Billy, you jack-the-lad.'

Billy was rather annoyed at having been so rudely interrupted. 'What are you doing here?'

'Waiting for the bus, same as you.'

'Can't you wait a bit further away? There's another bench down the other end of the street.'

Harry squinted and pointed an unsteady finger in Billy's general direction. 'Oh, no, I don't think so, eh? Me and the lads aren't in any condition to run after a bus, so just to be sure we're waiting right here.'

Billy sighed, and moved over so Harry could sit down. Rangi, Maru and Boy sat down as well, shoving along so that Violet almost fell off the end of the bench. She clutched at Billy's arm, but when he looked he saw she was smiling.

189

There was a companionable silence for several minutes, broken only by the sound of someone stifling a burp.

'Good night for it,' Harry said.

'It was,' Billy replied sourly.

Silence again. Then Boy muttered something about going for a mimi. He trudged up the street a short distance until he came to a convenient alleyway, then turned his back. In the quietness of the night the sound of his urine splashing onto the cobbles reached them like a miniature waterfall. Harry started to giggle, then the others joined in, and finally even Billy had to allow himself a smile.

'Sorry,' he said to Violet, who was ostentatiously looking in the opposite direction.

She shrugged as if to say, what else can you expect after an evening of holding up a bar?

Mercifully, the bus arrived then, crammed with soldiers returning to camp as well as locals on their way home after a Saturday night out, and Billy and Violet squeezed together in a seat near the back. The Maori soldiers sang at the tops of their voices, almost raising the roof of the rickety little bus, and the locals looked on with amusement. They even applauded after particularly fine renditions of 'Now Is the Hour', 'Pokarekare Ana', and 'Blue Smoke'.

Billy said, or rather yelled, over the noise, 'Will you come out with me next weekend, on Sunday?'

Violet nodded, her eyes shining.

'Shall we go up to that old castle? The one at the top of the hill? I'll see if I can scrounge something nice from the mess to go in a picnic basket.'

'And shall I get some of those custard buns you like from the shop?'

Billy nodded enthusiastically. He gazed down at her sparkling eyes, her soft lips and her pale, pale hair, and decided he just about couldn't wait.

★ ★ ★

Sunday started out fine, but by the time he and Violet had carted the picnic basket up the hill above Farnham, heavy clouds were scudding across the sky. But the view was stunning. Climbing up the crumbling ramparts, hanging on to each other and giggling madly, they found they could see in all directions across miles and miles of green fields cross-hatched by stone walls, hawthorn and holly hedges, and narrow lanes. Billy, more used to seeing great open expanses of farmland uninterrupted by any form of fencing, found this amusing, and said so. Violet, for her part, thought the idea of having your stock wandering everywhere totally unfettered equally strange.

'Don't they run away, your sheep?'

'Yes, but it doesn't matter, because they come to a fence eventually. And it isn't as if we need to milk them every day or anything like that.'

Violet giggled again.

Billy talked about his family then, and about Kenmore. But he played down the actual size of the station — an English country girl could have no concept of the magnitude of a large New Zealand property anyway — and did not labour the point that his family was really rather well off. And he mentioned his ancestral home at Maungakakari only briefly. He was discovering how important it was that she like him for himself, and not for the wealth or status of his family or for any novelty value he might have as a 'Moo-ree'. This came as quite a surprise to him, but then he'd never quite felt for any girl what he was starting to feel for Violet Metcalfe.

Their picnic was very pleasant, in spite of the rain that was threatening in the form of dark clouds gathering on the horizon, and Billy was sorry when it was time to go. But before they got off the bus in Dogmersfield, he'd extracted from her a promise that they would go to the pictures again the following Saturday.

Then for two weeks, as July became August, he did not see her at all as the battalion was out on long-range exercises that prevented him from going into the village. It was one of the longest fortnights of his life. Thoughts of her beautiful face, her lovely, lush body and her shy, giggling laugh hovered constantly in his mind, almost but not quite interfering with his daily activities. He was enchanted with her, he had to admit, even if only to himself and Harry, but was not prepared to allow that to get in the way of his training, especially when the battalion had finally been declared fit for front-line duty.

They had been able to go to the pictures together twice more after that, and had afternoon tea and got their picture taken by the enterprising village photographer earning himself extra shillings by capturing the slightly blurred images of soldiers and their sweethearts. And once they went on a long bike ride that left Billy, who wasn't used to pedalling for miles and miles, with a sore backside as a result of the mean little saddle on his borrowed bicycle. When his fingers weren't doing their best to burrow under her top or up her skirt, he kept them crossed that she would finally let him make love to her, but so far she had fended him off with what he considered to be unnecessary vigour. It was driving him to distraction, being so close to her and not being able to have her, but he knew that to push too hard would ruin everything, and he desperately wanted to keep seeing her, even if his balls did ache after they'd been out together. And time could soon run out: the threat of the Germans coming across the Channel looked very real; they had been told to be ready to move at any time.

He knew that if he wasn't able to express his love for Violet — and that's what it was now, he was sure — physically, he would miss his chance for God only knew how long, perhaps for ever. He'd already decided he would come back for her after the war, but he desperately wanted a little more of her to take into battle with him. Harry said he was getting confused, and mixing up his hopeless need for a leg-over with love, but Billy was convinced his friend was wrong. He did love Violet, and he would come back for her, no matter what.

But Violet, too, had heard the rumours about

the battalion moving, and was well aware that Billy could be on his way any day now. And if she were completely honest with herself she had become tired of fighting him off, because in her heart, and in other newly aware parts of her body, she didn't want to. She thought she might have fallen in love with him, and she wanted to share something, a special part of herself, with him before he went. And why shouldn't she have that? Her parents would certainly not approve if they ever found out, but so what? She was a good girl, and always had been, but she was nineteen now and had never in her life met anyone as handsome, exciting and *wonderful* as Billy Deane. So one day at the very end of August, after an afternoon session at the pictures in Farnham, she made up her mind.

Instead of waiting for the bus to take them back to Dogmersfield as usual, she took him by the hand and began to lead him up the hill.

'Where are we going?'

'Up to the castle,' Violet replied over her shoulder as she preceded him up the old beaten path. 'There's something I want to show you.'

Billy was mystified. It couldn't be the view, he'd seen that twice already now. But he kept hold of her hand as she climbed, pulling the lapels of his battledress jacket together to keep out the rising wind.

In a few minutes, when they were almost at the top, Violet led him around the base of the stone ruin, beyond the wind that was threatening late summer rain and out of sight of the town. In a sheltered alcove between two crumbling walls, she stopped and turned to face him.

When Billy saw the expression of longing in her eyes, he realised what she was up to and grinned in delight.

'I want to show you that I love you,' she whispered. 'Because I do, Billy Deane, I do.'

He kissed her, and this time it wasn't a kiss driven by fumbling frustration, it was the sharp, passionate coming together of two people who wanted each other more than anything else in the world.

There was no question of taking all their clothes off — it was too nippy for that — so Billy removed his jacket and draped it over Violet's shoulders, where it hung on her small frame. He took off his cap, opened the buttons on his shirt so she could put her cold hands inside, then took her face in his own hands and kissed her again and again.

It didn't take them very long at all. He picked her up and she wrapped her legs around his waist as he held her against the wall and thrust into her. She cried out just once, when he first entered her, but after that pressed her face into the side of his neck and went with him in silence. As he came he cried out himself, a great, gasping groan that told of weeks and weeks of frustrated desire and lust.

Then came the cramp as his bare legs and buttocks began to shiver in post-orgasm release and in the growing chill of the late afternoon air. He gently released Violet and set her back on her feet, yanked his trousers up then helped her to rearrange her underthings. There was a large hole torn in one of her stockings, and her thighs were slippery with his seed. He dug in his tunic pocket for a handkerchief and used it to carefully wipe her clean. She smiled at him for his tenderness, then bent to retrieve her knickers, which had been trampled underfoot.

'I'd better wash these myself or Ma will be wondering how I got grass stains on them.'

Billy laughed. 'Oh, throw them away, go on! I'll buy you a dozen new pairs, beautiful silk and lace ones.'

'No! I'm not going home on the bus without my knickers! What if the wind blew my skirt up or I fell down the steps or something?'

Billy laughed even harder. 'Then you'd really give all the old fellas on the bus something to talk about, wouldn't you?'

He couldn't keep the grin off his face. He felt elated and utterly delighted with himself, and with Violet. She was a gorgeous loving girl, a beautiful, precious living doll, and she was his and his alone.

He rearranged his tunic across her shoulders, and set his cap on her white-blonde hair at a rakish angle.

'Aren't you cold?' she asked him.

'Not likely, not after that. Come on, I think it's going to rain in a minute.'

It did start to rain, just as they were nearing the bottom of the hill, and they ran hand in hand over the last few yards, laughing and cursing as their feet slipped on the wet grass.

At the bus stop, which they shared with a dour-faced old woman who was as wide as she was tall and who kept looking at them and sniffing suspiciously, they cuddled into each other for warmth. It was really bucketing down now, and they would no doubt get soaked walking from the bus stop to Violet's front gate where Billy had left his bike.

They did, and under the meagre shelter of the front door porch, Billy kissed her wet face.

'Marry me, Violet Metcalfe, and come back to New Zealand with me after the war.'

She jerked back and stared up at him with wide eyes.

'Marry you? I can't marry you.'

'Why not?'

'Because there isn't time. You'll be away soon, everyone's saying so.'

'But if I wasn't, would you? Marry me, I mean?'

She didn't have to think about it for long. 'Of course I would, Billy. I'd like nothing better.'

'Well, I'm off to talk to the major then, and if that doesn't work, I'll talk to the colonel himself!'

But there was no time for Billy to talk to anyone because the next day the Luftwaffe's massive raids on London began in earnest and the Maori Battalion, as part of the Seventh Brigade, deployed almost immediately to the Folkestone-Dover area to help repel what was assumed to be the beginning of the German cross-Channel invasion. He barely even managed to say goodbye to Violet, and if Harry hadn't covered for him in the temporary chaos of moving out of Dogmersfield, he would have missed her completely.

In the thirty minutes they managed to snatch together he promised he would be back as soon as could, and urged her to tell her parents about their plans to be married so that if the opportunity arose before the battalion shipped out to the Middle East, if that was still on the cards, they could take advantage of it.

She cried when he left her standing in the lane, watching him pedalling madly off in an effort to get back to camp before he was missed, but she wasn't the type of girl who gave in to tears very often and she wiped her face on her apron after only a few moments of indulging herself. He would be back, she knew it.

★ ★ ★

The brigade spent several weeks camped in tents under trees in the Kentish countryside waiting for the invasion. They dug in, went on route marches and bolstered themselves by cheering for the RAF engaged in vicious dogfights in the skies above them. Billy hoped Duncan wasn't up there.

By the time the green leaves on the trees had turned the colour of flames and the weather had really begun to chill, it had become clear that the Germans had missed their chance of invasion; to attempt to cross the Channel during the October gales would be profoundly stupid, even for Adolf Hitler. So Seventh Brigade moved out of their muddy tents into billets, and on 8 October were finally disbanded.

Billy had not managed to get away on leave at all, and was delighted when the announcement came that the battalion would be returning to the Aldershot Command area for the winter. And everyone was very pleased to discover that they were to be billeted in decent accommodation near Farnham — in stately English manor houses, no less! Billy's company was allotted Bradshaigh on Gong Hill. Well housed they might have been, but the winter was so cold that when not out on exercises they sat around in their greatcoats wrapped in scarves and gloves warming their freezing extremities in front of fires made miserable by fuel rationing.

There was time again to go on short leaves, and Billy made the most of these to visit Violet. She must have told her parents about the seriousness of their relationship because when he arrived on her doorstep they immediately made their excuses and went out. Not, Violet was convinced, to allow Billy and her to do what they did on the floor of the fire-warmed parlour, but to give them time alone in case Billy was sent off somewhere else at a moment's notice.

He had asked his company commander for permission to get married and, like many others recently, had been declined. The major did not approve of rushed marriages in times of war, although it had been pointed out to him by more than one senior officer that rushed marriages were surely better than fatherless children. But he stuck to his guns. In his experience young soldiers tended to agree to anything for a bit of comfort if they thought they might be off to the

199

front any time soon. By turning down their requests to marry local girls, pretty though they may be, he felt he was actually doing them a favour, for which they would one day thank him.

Billy was mildly put out, but he believed from the bottom of his heart that Violet would wait for him no matter how long it took. He was content with the situation as it was, convinced they would marry sooner or later.

Halfway through November, Billy received a letter from his father telling him the terrible news about Duncan. When he realised that East Grinstead was actually not that far from Farnham, he immediately asked the company commander for forty-eight hours' leave. When it was denied, because 'things were afoot', he stole a motorbike and a tin of petrol from the camp and headed off wearing a leather jacket under his greatcoat, two scarves, a woollen hat under a leather cap, goggles and thick sheepskin gloves.

He rode all day and arrived at Queen Victoria Hospital about eight that evening, frozen almost stiff and barely able to walk. He was such a sight when he wandered into the main reception area that the woman on duty at the front desk gasped in fright when she looked up from her papers and saw him.

'Hello, sorry, I'm looking for Flight Lieutenant Duncan Murdoch. Is he here?'

'What are his injuries, do you know?'

'Burns.'

'One of McIndoe's army then?'

'Pardon?'

'If he's a pilot and he's been burned, he's

probably in Ward Three. Just a moment please and I'll look him up for you.' She flicked through a list then nodded to herself. 'Yes, Duncan Murdoch, Ward Three. Outside again and to your right — it's a group of temporary buildings. Are you a relative?'

But Billy had already gone.

As he walked towards a wooden ramp leading up to what was presumably the door of Ward Three, he could hear a hell of a racket coming from inside. Someone was singing tunelessly and banging away on a piano, and there seemed to be some sort of yelling match going on, punctuated with bursts of raucous laughter. Perhaps he'd turned the wrong way when he'd come out of the main hospital building and this was the wing for mental patients?

He went up the ramp anyway, and found himself in a wide corridor smelling strongly of antiseptic and something else a little less pleasant. There were no signs advertising which part of the hospital he was in, so he stopped the first nurse he saw.

'Excuse me, is this Ward Three?'

'It is. Are you here to visit someone?' the woman replied. She was very pretty.

'Yes, I'm looking for my cousin, Duncan Murdoch. He's a pilot with Fighter Command and I've only recently heard he's here.'

'Yes, Duncan's a patient here. And you're . . . ?'

'Private Billy Deane, Second New Zealand Expeditionary Force.'

'Well, it's lovely to meet you, Private Deane.

201

I'm Nurse Pearsall. Duncan will be thrilled. He doesn't get many visitors, mainly just the chaps from his old squadron, when they can get away. Perhaps you'd care to leave your coat out here? And perhaps your jacket and your scarves, and maybe your hats, and probably your gloves and goggles as well? It's very warm in the ward. Then would you like to follow me?'

She waited patiently while he struggled out of his multiple layers and piled them onto a wooden bench against the wall.

'I should warn you though, Private Deane,' she said in a low voice over her shoulder as she started walking, 'this is a burns ward and most of the men here are very injured. Not sick, you understand, injured. You may find some of what you see disturbing.'

Billy felt embarrassed by the possibility that he might look like the sort of person who would be upset by disfigurement. 'I'll be fine, thank you, Nurse,' he replied just a tiny bit frostily.

Claire smiled to herself — they always said that.

She opened the door to the ward — a large, open room, and still rather noisy — and ushered him in. 'Duncan's in here somewhere, well, he was five minutes ago. Just wander along and you'll see him.'

Billy took a few steps forward, then stopped in front of a man in a wheelchair with an open book propped against his heavily bandaged hands. This clearly wasn't Duncan, but he nodded hello anyway. The man smiled back. It wasn't until he started moving again that Billy

202

realised that there had not been any feet poking out from the bottoms of the man's trousers.

The piano had stopped, but someone else was singing now, although Billy couldn't see the singer.

He looked at the next group of men, gathered around a card table, smoking. Some of these blokes had the use of their hands, but two or three of them had extremely strange-looking faces.

The man facing him now, smiling — at least Billy *thought* he was smiling — appeared to be missing his nose. Where it should have been there was just a flat piece of taped white gauze, which moved in and out slightly as the man breathed. And instead of eyelids there appeared to be two miniature sausages stitched to the front of his brows. His top lip was also unnaturally flat and a shiny pink colour, and he was missing several of his top front teeth.

The ears on the man next to him had been burned down to small twists of skin, and the flesh on the back and sides of his skull was a mass of lumpy, shiny scar tissue. His face was untouched from the nostrils up, but below that his lips were a shapeless border around a mouth that revealed far too much of his gums.

The next man had most of his face bandaged, while the fourth, his face unscathed, held his cards in heavily scarred hands that had only thumbs.

They were grotesque, but what really horrified Billy was the realisation that these weren't old men, they were young blokes probably only a year or so older than himself. He hoped his shock wasn't registering on his own face.

Everyone in the room seemed to be looking at him now, as if *he* were the odd man out. He supposed he was, really.

'Looking for someone?' said the man with the missing nose.

'Er, yes, actually, Duncan Murdoch.'

'*Anyone seen Duncan?*' the man bellowed to the ward at large.

Another man wandered over and said in a parched, wheezing voice, 'In the bog, I think. Who's this?'

Billy was fascinated by the sausage of rolled skin that protruded from the man's collar; it was stitched down to the base of his neck and looked bizarrely like a fat caterpillar about to take a leisurely walk up the man's throat towards the large dressing on his right jaw and cheek. His mouth also appeared to have been badly burned.

The invisible singer turned up the volume a notch. Billy stuck out his hand and introduced himself.

'Good-oh, welcome to Ward Three,' the man replied, returning Billy's handshake. He touched the protrusion on his neck. 'It's called a pedicle, for skin grafting, in case you're wondering. Duncan shouldn't be long. Mind you, he might be — we had beans and cabbage last night. Have a seat while you wait,' he added, indicating a spare chair at the card table.

But just as Billy sat down someone sauntered into the ward, a tall man with large squares of gauze over his chin, cheeks and nose, and a heavier dressing on the underside of his jaw. From the confines of a bandage wound around his head, set low over his brows and covering one eye, tufts of bright bronze hair stuck up untidily. His hands were a vivid pink and had the telltale shine, but they seemed to function adequately as he was carrying a rolled-up newspaper in one and a packet of cigarettes in the other.

He stopped when he saw his cousin. 'Billy!' he cried in delight. 'What the hell are you doing here?'

Billy didn't know whether to laugh or cry as he suddenly realised who he was looking at. 'Duncan! Bloody hell. How are you?'

Duncan pulled up a chair, his one visible eye twinkling with pleasure. Above it the eyelid was raw and puffy. 'Well, I've been better, I must admit, though I'm starting to come right. What about you, just passing through?'

'No, I only just heard you were here, and the battalion's only over near Aldershot so I thought I'd come and see how you are.'

'Give you leave, did they? That was unusually thoughtful of the army.'

'I'm AWOL.'

'Oh, right.'

The invisible singer hit a particularly high note then, and immediately followed it with a very clearly enunciated curse.

Duncan said, 'Ray's dropped his pipe again,' and one of the card-players got to his feet and headed towards a screen near the end of the ward.

'We've got a saline bath. The chaps spend

hours in it, especially Ray. He copped it just about everywhere.'

Billy nodded. 'Where did you cop it, apart from what I can see?'

Duncan pulled a face that was half grimace, half dismissal. 'I was lucky, really. I had my gloves on so the burns on my hands weren't too bad. I'm getting the use back quite quickly, see?' He held his hands up and waggled his fingers to demonstrate. 'I've had six grafts on my face so far, three on my eyelids, although one of those didn't take, one on my cheeks and nose, and two on my lips, which finally look like lips again. Fortunate, really, because they looked pretty bloody queer before.'

They didn't look a hundred per cent now, Billy thought, but compared with some of the other men here, Duncan didn't appear too badly off at all.

'And there's a bit of a mess under my chin, but the Boss says he can tidy that up with a few more grafts. I broke my arm as well, when I came down, but I didn't even know about that for the first ten days.'

Billy didn't know what to say. He couldn't come out with something as trite as 'Well, you look really good,' because it just wasn't true. And 'She'll be right' was hardly appropriate either.

'Will you go back to flying?'

Duncan's face darkened. 'No, I won't, my eyes were damaged. I'm not blind, thank God, but my vision's no longer good enough to fly. I've had it checked,' he added morosely.

'What about a desk job?'

'Who the fuck wants to spend the rest of the war behind a desk?'

Billy nodded in agreement; surely there could be nothing worse. 'So will you be off home soon?'

'Not for at least another twelve months, according to the Boss, so I'm stuck here for a while yet. But, you know, it's not too bad. There's beer on tap, cards and chess, plenty of stuff to read, the food's all right and we get out quite a bit. The villagers are really good.'

Claire walked past them then, and to Billy's surprise she gave them both an enormous wink.

'And of course,' Duncan added in a stage whisper, 'there's Nurse Claire Pearsall. She doesn't know about this yet but I'm going to marry her in the not too distant future.'

★   ★   ★

When Billy got back to Farnham he discovered he'd barely been missed. He was subjected to a quick five minutes on the mat in front of the company commander and a lecture about not nicking off with battalion equipment, then was told to go and pack his kit because they were on the move again.

The gen was that they were finally off to much warmer climates, and he realised his own wedding plans really would have to wait. Speculation was rife, but most agreed that the battalion's likely destination would be Egypt, and this was unofficially confirmed when they were issued with tropical kit and ordered to paint the battalion vehicles in yellow desert camouflage. They were all very grateful that the Luftwaffe had almost ceased daylight raids: the finished vehicles stuck out like dogs' balls against the white Surrey snow.

Christmas came and went while they were waiting, although celebrating Christmas in freezing temperatures with no sunshine and no pohutukawa trees, and not even any decent stones for the hangi, wasn't very festive, and some of the boys began to feel really homesick for the first time. But on 3 January, they were finally ready to go.

10

Leila swore inelegantly as she attempted, once again, to sit on the lid of her suitcase heavily enough to force the latches shut.

Her mother looked on, bemused. 'Bonnie's managed to close hers quite successfully.'

'Bonnie's managed to close *hers* quite successfully!' Leila mimicked rudely.

Keely ignored her; it was always for the best when Leila was in one of her moods. It was frightening really — sometimes Leila's behaviour was uncannily like her own when she'd been that age.

'What on earth have you got in it?'

'Oh, just stuff. Clothes, my new winter coat, shoes, my make-up kit, some hats — which will no doubt be squashed beyond recognition now — my swimming costume, spare towels, linen . . . '

'Leila, you're only off to Auckland, darling, not a six-month tour of Europe. And won't you be given a uniform when you get there?'

Leila finally managed to shut her case, and got off it. Her blonde hair was escaping from its fashionable roll, and her face was red from exertion.

'Yes, but I'm not living in it for the duration! There are *bound* to be opportunities to go out dancing. I'll need dresses and shoes for that at least.'

Keely shook her head. She supposed that of all the war activities her girls could have signed up for, the Women's Auxiliary Air Force was a reasonably safe option — providing of course that they didn't end up having to go overseas — but already she pitied whoever would have the misfortune of overseeing them. To think that they'd actually had to go through a selection process and they'd passed! But, to give them their due, their typing and shorthand skills had improved markedly during their stint in town, and when they'd left they'd both been given excellent references. By someone called Mr Dimbly, if Keely recalled correctly.

Bonnie came in then, Henry shrieking ear-piercingly as she held him upside-down by his ankles.

'Mum!' he squealed. '*Mum*! She's going to drop me, *help*!' But he was giggling helplessly all the same.

Keely noted his beet-red face. 'Put him down, Bonnie, he'll be sick.'

'No, I won't,' he squawked, 'breakfast was ages ago!'

But Bonnie put him down anyway; he was nearly five now and getting quite heavy.

'All done?' she asked Leila.

'I think so. I've managed to get everything in, just.'

'Good, we'll take our bags down then, shall we?'

They looked at each other and grinned.

Owen used precious petrol filched from the station supply to drive them into town to catch the train to Auckland. Henry was wildly excited as the engine came whooshing into the station platform, hissing and blowing steam exactly like the dragon in the book Gran was helping him to read at the moment.

But he had to be held by the hand, crying and stamping his feet, when he suddenly realised that Bonnie and Leila were going away somewhere without him. He didn't even perk up when they hung out the window and promised they would send him something nice from Auckland, which could have been on the moon as far as Henry was concerned. They had to get their handkerchiefs out then at the sight of his tear-stained little face.

Then Keely cried because Henry was upset and because she didn't know when her girls would be home again, and Owen had to blow his nose because his entire family was weeping and all because of this bloody war.

But by the time the crowded train had gone through Hastings, Bonnie and Leila had cheered up considerably, stashed their hand luggage and coats in the racks and settled in for the long journey. They were actually travelling in the wrong direction at that point, but would change trains at Palmerston North, then head back up the main trunk line through Taumarunui, then Hamilton, and on to Auckland. There was of course a road between Napier, Taupo and the railhead at Rotorua, but petrol rationing meant that the trip was just not feasible by car.

They were tired, grubby and grumpy by the time they arrived in Auckland the following morning. They changed trains at Newmarket, then got off at Henderson where they waited to be collected. They would have been amazed, had they known that the bench on which they were sitting impatiently for what seemed like ages was exactly where Tamar had also waited years ago for a train that would take her on to her own new life.

An air force driver eventually turned up, in a smelly great truck that looked big enough to take a whole platoon of new recruits.

'Are you two Miss B. and Miss L. Morgan?' he called. 'Hey, are you two twins?'

Bonnie and Leila nodded in unison, wishing for the thousandth time that they had a pound for every time someone had asked them that.

He jumped out, took their cases, tossed them none too gently over the tailgate, then he helped them up into the cab.

'You'll have to hop in the back before we get to the base, though,' he informed them as he manipulated the gear stick with a bone-shuddering crash and pulled away from the station.

'Why?' Bonnie was mystified.

'Because it's *fraternising*, that's why. Airmen are not allowed to fraternise with airwomen, it's the rules.'

'Oh, right. Well, we don't want to break the rules, do we?' Leila gave Bonnie an exaggerated nudge in the ribs.

'No, actually, I'm only teasing about the truck. But not about the fraternising,' admitted the driver.

He pointed out various sights on the way, the bush and farmland, the road to the other air base at Hobsonville off to their right, and Waiarohia Inlet directly in front of them, until they eventually drove through the gates of the rather bleak and windswept Whenuapai Air Force Base.

'Here we are,' he announced cheerfully as he climbed out to retrieve their cases. 'Home sweet home, for the duration anyway. Unless you get transferred, of course. That happens. The administration block is dead ahead. Enjoy yourselves!'

They soon discovered that they were the last of a group of thirty new recruits to arrive at Whenuapai that day. They were given a cup of tea and a biscuit, and a talk from a stern-looking woman in uniform who introduced herself as Mrs Buckley-Jones, the WAAF supervisor. Like the others, Bonnie and Leila had had their medical and eye examinations, and their measurements taken for their new uniforms, before they'd left home, and Mrs Buckley-Jones explained that their uniforms would be available for collection from stores later that afternoon. Then the commanding officer, the station adjutant and the administration officer arrived, and the new recruits were required to stand and take an oath of allegiance to the king. It was a very serious, if brief, procedure, and even Bonnie and Leila felt rather humbled by the gravity of the moment.

The next stop was the mess, where they were given a filling but not very inspired meal and a cup of stewed tea, then it was back to the administration block to be issued with registration numbers and 'meat tickets', identification discs — one red and one white — to which each newly sworn-in airwoman had to add her name, number and blood group. There was general agreement that this particular bit of the induction process was somewhat sobering.

After that they were taken to the women's barracks — known collectively as the 'waafery' — where Bonnie and Leila received their first major shock. Instead of the cosy, private, single rooms they'd envisaged, there were several long huts, partitioned into small cubicles just big enough for one person. Each contained a single wooden bed, a chest of drawers and a narrow wooden wardrobe with a shelf at the top for hats. The walls were bare, as was the floor, and there wasn't a blanket, sheet or pillow to be seen. A quick inspection revealed that the furnishings in each cubicle were identical.

Mrs Buckley-Jones gathered them together again and told them that they would have to draw their bed linen and so on from stores, that the ablutions (where on no account could clothes of any description be laundered) were in the hut behind this one, that barracks cleaning day was always on a Thursday and that next door was the recreation room, where they would find some rather more comfortable chairs and sofas, a radio and a sewing machine for their off-duty use.

Leila raised her hand. 'Excuse me, Mrs Buckley-Jones, but I brought my own linen. May I use that?'

There were several titters, but unfortunately none of them came from Mrs Buckley-Jones. 'No, I'm afraid you cannot. This is the air force, there is a war on and you are required to use, and *only* use, regulation air force stores and equipment. I suggest you send your personal linen back home, Miss Morgan.'

Leila stared defiantly at Mrs Buckley-Jones, and Mrs Buckley-Jones stared defiantly back, but Leila was the first to drop her gaze.

The supervisor went on. 'You are all expected at stores at 1500 hours to collect your uniforms. You can pick up your bed linen then as well. Oh, and there is usually a photograph of new recruits in their civvies before you put on your blues for the first time, so I suggest, girls, that you take the opportunity to freshen up and reapply your lipstick. I will see you at stores, which is to the rear of the admin block, in twenty minutes.'

'Well!' exclaimed Leila when she'd gone, flopping onto one of the beds and grimacing because the mattress was even harder than it looked. 'It's not quite what we were expecting, is it?'

'And what were you expecting? A five-star hotel?'

This was from a tall, solid girl with dark hair and a cheerful face.

'No,' Leila replied, 'but it's all very . . . communal, isn't it?'

'I think it's great,' the girl said. 'Sheila Sullivan, from Kaitaia. Where are you girls from?'

Bonnie said, 'Napier. I'm Bonnie Morgan and

215

this is Leila. We're twins, before you ask.'

'You don't say?'

'We applied to get in before Christmas but we weren't called up until just a couple of weeks ago,' Leila added.

'It was the same for me,' said another girl with freckles and huge hazel eyes. 'I didn't hear for ages. Oh, sorry, I'm Eileen Parr.'

'Well, Sheila Sullivan and Eileen Parr,' said Leila as she got up off the bed, 'you heard what Mrs Buckley-Snooty-Jones said, get your lippy on and let's go and have our photograph taken.'

'Actually, she isn't really snooty, you know.'

Leila turned to face an attractive, fair-haired girl leaning against the edge of one of the partitions. She was wearing a smart grey-checked suit over a fine, baby blue jumper, and a pair of very good pearl earrings.

'Is that right?'

The girl nodded. 'My mother knows BJ really quite well, and apparently she's quite a good stick once you get to know her.'

'BJ?' Bonnie echoed. 'That's good, I like that. Much less of a mouthful than Mrs Buckley-Jones.'

'Quite, but don't rub her up the wrong way.'

'Mmm, perhaps not. Anyway, what's your name?'

'I'm Peggy Buchanan. I live out at Kohimarama, so I haven't come far.'

Bonnie laughed out loud. 'Peggy? We had a dog named Peggy once.'

'Really?' Peggy replied coolly. 'When we were kids we used to have a nasty old donkey called

Bonnie. Dad said she went to heaven but I think he sent her to the knacker's.'

There was the briefest of tension-filled silences, then Bonnie and Leila burst into shrieks of hysterical laughter that soon set the other girls off as well.

'What's happening?' someone called from the other end of the hut.

'Nothing,' Leila called back. 'It's all right, my sister's just making an ass of herself!'

This set them off again and all five were still giggling as they set off to find stores and their uniforms.

They weren't feeling quite so amused, however, as they staggered back to the barracks an hour later laden with great piles of clothing and their bed-packs. They had been issued with almost everything the air force had decreed they would need. This included: kitbag; brushes (one hard and one wire); cap badge; two belted jackets and two skirts (of barathea, air force blue); tie; gloves; low-heeled shoes (leather, black); two felt slouch hats; shirts and stockings (lisle, dark grey). There was also a cardigan, which Leila tried on immediately and declared 'positively dire'. The girls destined to work in the mess or as medical or dental orderlies also received white overalls and shoes, and the drivers blue overalls. The air force did not provide underwear, much to everyone's relief — they were to wear their own — although sanitary supplies could be discreetly obtained via one's WAAF supervisor.

It was exciting, though, having a uniform,

especially one so smartly tailored and decorated with shiny buttons and buckles, and the girls couldn't wait to get changed. It made them feel, after more than a year of watching the men in their lives going off, that they were finally doing something for their country.

★ ★ ★

Tamar was going over the books. At nearly twelve and a half shillings per pound of clipped wool, Kenmore was not doing at all badly out of the war so far, contrary to what she had expected. Occasionally she felt vaguely guilty about this, but New Zealand's wool clip had been commandeered by the British government for the duration and the price negotiated fairly, and she knew the wool produced by Kenmore was destined for military purposes. And, privately, she believed that was only fair; if Britain insisted on dragging her family into yet another war, then it should pay a decent price for the raw materials required to dress them. And especially after what had happened to poor darling Duncan. He always played down the extent of his injuries in his letters home, but Tamar knew he must be in a dreadful way if he expected to remain in hospital for another six months at least.

She was just adding up a final column of figures, squinting at the numbers in spite of her relatively new reading spectacles, and reflecting that it really was time she handed this job over to Owen and Joseph, when she heard

Keely calling out to her.

'I can't hear you, dear, I'm in the office!' she called back as she underlined the figures at the bottom of the page.

Keely appeared in the doorway, with a basketful of freshly picked leeks, carrots and an enormous savoy cabbage from the kitchen garden. She put the basket on the floor and sat down on the sofa near the fireplace.

'Mam?'

Tamar looked up at the plaintive note in her daughter's voice. 'Something troubling you, dear?'

'No. Yes. I'm not sure.'

Tamar put the lid on her pen and swivelled around in her seat.

'It's the girls,' Keely began. 'You know how we've only had two letters from them so far?'

'Yes, darling, but then they've only been gone a month.'

'I know, it isn't that, it's what's in the letters that worries me.'

'I thought they were having a lovely time?'

'They are, that's the trouble. They seem to be spending more time going to dances and into town and gadding about than they are working at the air base.'

Tamar was amused to hear this, especially from Keely, who had spent as many of her early years 'gadding about' as she could get away with.

'Well, I'm sure they're doing a wonderful job. Girls have to work very hard in the services, you know. They're taken very seriously.'

Keely frowned, then nodded resignedly. 'I

219

expect they are working hard, but I'm still worried, Mam. There are a lot of men in Auckland — *unattached* men, I might add, looking for a last chance for a good time before they go away — and the girls have never been backward about being forward.'

Tamar could see that Keely really was worried, and she had already been thinking about what could be done to help keep her granddaughters safe.

'Look, why don't I telephone Aunty Ri and let her know that the girls are in Auckland? She seems to know everyone who's anyone up there, and I'm sure she could keep some sort of eye on them.'

Keely eyed her mother sceptically; Riria Adams must be seventy-eight by now, almost the same age as Tamar.

'Would she be up to it, do you think, chasing a pair of energetic, twenty-one-year-old girls around Auckland?'

Tamar removed her spectacles and let them fall on their chain against her chest.

'I very much doubt that Riria will chase them around, darling. She may visit them once or twice, or invite them to her house in Parnell for tea, but no, she won't chase them.'

'Well, then, what good will that do?'

'She will give them good advice, and they will listen.'

'I'm not sure that they will.'

'I am. You know what Riria's like. She can be very persuasive when she feels like it.'

Keely certainly did. When Andrew had died,

Riria had come down from Auckland to be with Tamar during her period of mourning. Keely had been in a state herself, with the loss of her father coming so soon after her unplanned pregnancy and hasty marriage to Owen. As Riria had been quick to inform Keely in a private and very pointed little chat, she had been 'neither use nor ornament', and the shock of realising the truth of that, particularly when her mother needed her support, had chastened her considerably. She had respected Riria Adams ever since, and had admired and almost envied the lifelong friendship between her mother and the imposing, regal and wise Maori woman.

'I suppose,' Keely said after a moment, 'that if nothing else she might frighten them into behaving well. And if not, then at least she can keep us informed.'

They both laughed, although admittedly Keely's laugh was not particularly hearty.

'Good, I shall telephone her tomorrow,' Tamar said, then glanced at Keely quizzically and cocked her head. 'Is that someone crying? Is it Henry?'

Keely could hear it now too, the sound of someone wailing in the distance. She rushed down the hall and outside, and stood on the front steps straining to see across the paddocks. And there he was, small and forlorn, trotting all by himself along the track that led from Erin and Joseph's house on the other side of the hill. As she watched he fell down, then got up again and staggered forward once more.

She leaped down the steps and ran across the

221

lawn. 'Henry! *Henry*! What is it?'

At the sight of her, Henry wailed even harder. By the time Keely reached him and knelt down in front of him he was almost beside himself, his eyes red and streaming and a liberal coat of snot smearing his upper lip.

'What is it? *What is it*?' Keely almost shrieked.

'Uncle Joseph's gone all funny!' the little boy cried. 'And Aunty Erin won't stop screaming! It's awful, Mummy, it's *awful*!'

Keely had no idea what he was talking about, but she knew something must be terribly wrong. She gave him a quick cuddle.

'Can you be a really brave little man and run and get Daddy for me? Tell him to get Gran and come over to Uncle Joseph's. And then, I want you to go down to Aunty Lucy's house and stay there, all right?'

Henry hiccupped, sobbed just once more, then nodded.

'Good man, off you go then. Quickly!'

Keely watched him for a moment to make sure he was all right, then whipped off her shoes and ran as fast as she could up the track.

Erin and Joseph's cosy and comfortable house looked perfectly normal from the top of the hill, surrounded by Erin's carefully selected trees and bright flower gardens and Joseph's neat rows of vegetables, but as Keely hurried down the track she heard something that froze her blood — the sound of a grown woman howling and keening with almost insane intensity. With her heart in her mouth she raced the last few hundred yards and up the front steps onto the verandah.

'Joseph!' she yelled, unable to keep the panic out of her voice. '*Joseph!*'

There was no answer, and the keening went on and on. Then Ana appeared in the hallway, her tear-streaked face the colour of uncooked dough.

'What is it, Ana? What's happened?'

Ana's face crumpled, and huge, fresh tears squeezed from her dark eyes. 'It's Billy, we got a telegram.' She ran to Keely and clung to her tightly. 'He was in Crete, Aunty Keely, he's been killed!'

Keely thought she might faint, but her arms went around Ana and she began to stroke the girl's hair, slowly and rhythmically.

'Is that Mum crying out?'

Ana nodded.

'Let's go and see if we can help her, shall we? Where's your dad?'

'He's in the kitchen; they both are.'

Her arm still around Ana, Keely walked down the hall and into the kitchen.

Joseph was sitting at the table, his face whiter than Ana's, the telegram with its hateful news unfolded in front of him. His green eyes were dry and he was staring steadfastly at nothing at all, although his throat was working violently as if he were trying to swallow something unpalatable.

Erin was standing at the sink. She seemed unable to stop wailing; her eyes were bulging alarmingly and the cords in her neck stood out like taut ropes. Keely let go of Ana, went over to her cousin and slapped her briskly across the face.

223

The noise stopped immediately; the only sound in the kitchen now was the low buzzing of a fly stranded upside-down on the windowsill.

'Erin, Erin! Can you hear me?'

Nothing.

'*Erin*! It's Keely.'

Erin turned slowly, and deep in her eyes there was a flicker of recognition. Even more slowly, she slumped into Keely's arms.

'Oh, Keely, we've lost him. We've lost our baby.'

★ ★ ★

Because there was no body, there could be no real tangihanga. But at Maungakakari there was a kawe mate, a traditional service to bring Billy's spirit home. As he had been the mokopuna of Kepa Te Roroa, an influential and respected rangatira, and the son of Joseph Deane, the veteran of two wars, the ceremony was well attended by mourners from far and wide, including everyone from Kenmore.

There were haka in honour of Billy's prowess as a warrior, veterans of the Maori contingents that had served in the Great War came proudly dressed in their old uniforms, and there were speeches and prayers and songs, including a beautiful and haunting rendition of 'Blue Smoke', the tune that had so touched Billy when he was away.

There was only one day of public grieving, instead of the traditional three, but it helped those who had known, loved and respected Billy

224

to begin to come to terms with their loss. Even his close family would eventually accept his death, however bitterly or begrudgingly.

What none of them knew, however, was that in a small village in southern England, a young girl still waited for Billy. Harry Tomoana, who knew how deeply Billy had loved his pretty English girlfriend, would eventually write to Violet and tell her about Billy's death, and how he had saved the lives of two men even while he lost his own in a bayonet charge that would go down in history. But Violet would not receive the letter until after the battalion had been evacuated to Egypt some weeks later and Harry had recovered from his own wounds.

Billy's death left everyone at Kenmore with a feeling of emptiness and something approaching hopelessness. Duncan was still in England, Liam and Drew were away, Bonnie and Leila were in Auckland, and now Billy would never be coming home. Erin was plummeted into a deep, black depression that lasted for some months until she was able to claw her way out of it, while Joseph also retreated into himself until he realised that his two remaining children still needed him, perhaps even more than before, as did his parents, both of whom had taken Billy's death very badly.

Robert, nineteen now and old enough to be sent to war, had registered with the National Service Department and was awaiting his call-up for service overseas. He could have appealed against his impending conscription on the grounds that he was engaged in essential employment on a sheep farm, or chosen not to register at all because of his Maori blood, but he wanted to go. And almost everyone who knew him suspected, correctly, that he wanted the opportunity to avenge his brother's death. In the event he did not have to wait long: his papers arrived one wet and windy afternoon late in August. Three weeks later he was away to camp.

Ana was even more determined to do something for the war effort. At twenty, she was eligible for a range of wartime occupations, but what she really wanted to do, and what she felt she knew best, was working on the land. So when the idea of a women's land army based on the British model had been mentioned the year before she had been delighted. Opposition from various quarters had ensured the idea came to nothing so Ana had contented herself with working at Kenmore, taking the place of one of the drovers who had gone off with the Second Echelon, and learning more and more as the days passed about the practical business of running a sheep farm. However, the land army idea had resurfaced in January, and now she was merely waiting for the scheme to become official so she could sign up.

Her cousin Kathleen was a different matter altogether. Ana had valiantly tried to interest her in farming and gardening, because normally they got on very well together, but Kathleen had other ideas. James would have loved his daughter to have taken an interest in horticulture, about which he was so passionate himself, but she just wasn't an outdoors sort of girl. She was certainly industrious, a great help to Lucy in the kitchen and around the house, and a built-in babysitter for her young cousin Henry, but she found the thought of getting dirt under her fingernails totally repulsive. The closest she ever wanted to come to fruit and vegetables was the finished product, on a plate, at the dining table.

James and Lucy had warned her several times already that if she did not find some way of contributing to the war effort, then she could very likely be manpowered into some occupation she would loathe, and then she'd be sorry; it was clear to just about everyone now that conscription of women into essential industries would be inevitable, whether it came this year or the next.

Auckland, August 1941

Tamar's plan to manage, or at least monitor, Bonnie and Leila's behaviour in Auckland had been forgotten in the shadow of Billy's death, until a telephone call had come from Riria herself expressing her sincere condolences after seeing Billy's name in the casualty lists in the paper. She would have come down herself, she'd said, but she was finding it more and more difficult to travel these days, and then there was the petrol rationing.

Tamar had been very pleased to hear her dear friend's voice, as always, and had not been surprised when Riria had agreed to the favour she asked of her.

It was a favour that led to Bonnie and Leila sitting at a table near the entrance of the King

227

George Grill and Tearooms in Queen Street one Friday afternoon, waiting for Gran's best friend to arrive and have tea with them. Riria was late, and the girls were deciding whether they should leave or wait a little longer when there was a small commotion outside.

'What is it?' Bonnie asked curiously as Leila got to her feet for a better view.

'It's a car, a really ancient one with one of those foldup tops, parked in the middle of the street.'

Bonnie snorted derisively.

'Hang on,' Leila exclaimed, 'someone's getting out and they're wearing the most extraordinary hat. Oh my God, it's Aunty Ri!'

Bonnie leapt to her feet. 'Where? Oh, it is too. Has she seen us?'

'Well, unless she's waving to someone behind us, yes she has.'

The girls sat down again, and waited in pleasurable anticipation for the inevitable.

When Riria Adams stepped through the door, standing tall and with her head held high, everyone stopped what they were doing and stared. Despite her age, Riria had lost none of her spectacular looks and regal bearing. Her hair, the thick wavy tresses now a uniform steel grey, still tumbled unfettered almost to her buttocks, which admittedly were a little more ample now than they had been in her youth. Her lined face was still pleasingly contoured and the cheekbones as pronounced as ever, but the lines of the moko on her chin had faded to a pale green and seeped across her skin to such an extent that the pattern was now only just discernible. Above the moko her lips remained full and proud, and her eyes glittered with their usual intelligence.

Her costume was old-fashioned, to say the least. She wore a long, full black skirt that reached almost to the ground and revealed, when she walked, a pair of side-buttoned, Louis-heeled black leather boots. The top half of her outfit consisted of a short, fitted velvet jacket in deepest black done up over a black chiffon blouse. A greenstone brooch gleamed softly at her throat, and long greenstone pendants dangled from her ears. Her hat, as Leila had observed, was indeed extraordinary, a confection of black net around a wide brim trimmed with a velvet band and two very long pheasant feathers.

But perhaps, as far as the twins were concerned, the most interesting part of their Aunty Ri's ensemble was the young, dark-skinned man at her side. He was tall, smartly dressed, rather good-looking, and seemed very protective of her.

Riria raised a black-gloved hand in greeting as she came towards them. 'Kia ora, tamariki, kei te pehea koutou?'

Bonnie and Leila stood to receive the kisses Riria always planted on their cheeks.

'Hello, Aunty, we're fine,' they chorused in unison.

'You are both looking lovely as usual, I see,' Riria added as her young companion pulled a chair out for her. 'Sit down, sit down. This is my mokopuna, Hemi, Rose's youngest son. He has errands to run for me so cannot stay.'

She smiled slightly as she noted the crestfallen expressions on the girls' faces. Hemi nodded to them, then gave his grandmother a peck on the cheek. The three women watched him go.

'He is such a good boy, Hemi,' Riria noted, 'especially to his old Nanny. Always does what he is told and never gets up to mischief.'

She regarded Bonnie and Leila thoughtfully while they gazed back at her, eyes wide with innocence.

'And how are you finding working at the air force base?' she went on. 'Your uniforms are very smart.'

'Oh, it's no end of fun, Aunty,' Leila replied. 'We march everywhere and salute until our arms nearly drop off and spend ages trying to get our hats to sit just right.'

'Really? And this is going to help us win the war?'

'Of course not, but our work will. We're both in the SWO's office — that's Station Warrant Officer to civilians — and we type and file and duplicate and rush around with messages and memos and organise leave passes and records. According to the SWO, we're 'essential cogs in the wheels of the machine that is our nation's magnificent air force' '.

'And do you enjoy it?'

Bonnie said, 'Yes, we really do, don't we?' as Leila nodded enthusiastically. 'When we first joined and saw the barracks and had a few mess dinners and found out about all the rules we'd have to learn, we thought, oh dear, what have we let ourselves in for? But now it's almost like second nature. And we really feel we're doing something useful for the war effort, and it's the most wonderful feeling. Well, barrack cleaning and laundry and parades aren't *that* much fun, but the rest is.'

Leila added, 'We're not too keen on the handicraft classes our supervisor keeps trying to push us into when we've time off, but some of the other girls enjoy them. And there's basketball and hockey and PT for the more active types. But it's all great fun and we've met loads of nice girls. It's all a bit like school really.'

Riria was pleased and relieved to see that the twins really did seem to be happy in what they were doing; in her experience contented and satisfied people were less likely to go looking for trouble.

'And what of the social life?' she asked casually.

'Oh, that's marvellous, too,' Leila replied. 'There are occasional dances on the base, and leave to go off base, although we haven't had an overnight leave yet because we haven't been there long enough. We've been to a couple of dances here in town too, at the Peter Pan.'

'Oh, yes, Hemi tells me that the Peter Pan is the place to go.' Riria fished. 'And I imagine there are plenty of gallant young airmen to escort you to all of these dances?'

The girls glanced at each other and burst out laughing as if their aunt had just said something unbearably funny.

'There are plenty of airmen, Aunty Ri,' Bonnie

said, 'but I don't know if you could call them gallant! They seem to think that every girl joined up for the sole purpose of sewing buttons back onto airmen's jackets and making them cups of tea because they're too busy doing vitally important, top secret work. Especially the pilots! Really, just because they can coax an old crate into the air they think they're God's gift to women!'

'And are they not?'

'No, of course they're not. They're just ordinary New Zealand lads with wings sewn on their uniforms. What we do is just as valuable, even if it isn't as exciting. They're good lads, but that's all they are.'

'So there is no one special, for either of you?'

The girls shook their heads in unison, and Riria gave a small internal sigh of relief. Their mother, it seemed, had nothing to worry about, at the moment anyway.

'Well, children, I am here for you if you need help with anything.'

Almost ruefully, Leila said, 'Thank you, Aunty, but it's going to take someone a lot more glamorous than our boys in blue to sweep us off our feet.'

11

Kenmore, March 1942

'How is Duncan getting on, have you heard?'

Kepa placed a cup of tea on the small wicker table next to Tamar's verandah chair, then sat down himself. It was a sultry, stifling afternoon and the concern wasn't that it would rain, but that it would not. The paddocks were dry and almost bare in places, and a good downpour to break up the hard, parched earth would be more than a blessing.

'Quite well, apparently,' Tamar replied as she inspected the almond biscuits on her saucer. Keely really was becoming quite an accomplished cook these days. 'James and Lucy had a letter about a week ago, and he's out of the hospital now, although apparently he has to go back fairly regularly to make sure his skin grafts are holding up.'

'So he is quite fit again?'

'Well, reasonably, or so he says. He can't go back to actual flying of course, because of his eyesight, but the RAF have given him a position on the ground helping train new fighter pilots.'

'Mmm,' said Kepa, who had always been fond of Duncan and admired the boy's mettle. 'How has he taken to that, I wonder?'

'Not well, initially. I had a letter from him myself at the time, you know, and he seemed very disappointed that he would not be flying again. I think he'd hoped that his eyesight might improve, but it hasn't. But the only other possibilities were a desk job somewhere, or an honourable discharge, neither of which he would even contemplate.'

'No, I could not see Duncan behind a desk, not while there is a war on.'

'Quite. But he says in his latest letter to James and Lucy that he's finding this new work really quite satisfying. He feels he's making a difference, and I suppose for Duncan that really is the main thing, isn't it?'

Kepa nodded and helped himself to a biscuit. 'And this young lady of his?'

'Claire? Apparently they're still planning to marry. She's still working at the hospital so they're apart a lot of the time, but she sounds a real treasure. She must be made of extremely stern stuff to do that sort of work, and then happily take on a man who will possibly have problems of one sort or another for the rest of his days. But she loves him, and that makes anything possible, doesn't it? Duncan seems to be absolutely head over heels about her.'

'Good. He will need a good woman. And what of Liam?'

'Well, the last time we heard from him he was still going on sorties with Bomber Command 'somewhere over Germany', but he sounded cheerful enough. Although he did mention that he hadn't heard from Evie for several months, and wondered if I could telephone her in Palmerston North to find out whether she's all right.'

'And have you?'

'Twice now, in the evening, but it seems she's out rather a lot.'

Kepa didn't dare look Tamar in the eye because he knew very well the disapproval he would see there.

She rushed on, as if to override any uninvited thoughts she might be having about Liam's wife.

'And Drew is floating about on a Royal Navy battleship somewhere, so it's very difficult to ever know where he is. James and Lucy haven't heard anything from him for a while, so we're hoping he wasn't involved in the fall of Singapore. But I'm sure we would have heard officially if anything had happened to him,' she added, more to reassure herself than anyone else. 'Robert, on the other hand, has written numerous letters.'

'I know, I have received four already myself. Fiji seems to suit him, although he was not very pleased when he was sent there originally, was he?'

'No, he wanted to go to North Africa. But James seems to think the Pacific will become the latest battleground now that Japan has come into the war, and if that's the case then I'm sure Robert won't be left to languish in Fiji much longer.'

'I doubt that they are 'languishing', my dear.'

'Oh, you know what I mean. He wants to be in the thick of it.' Tamar fanned her face with her hand. 'My God, I wish it would *rain*. Do you really think the Japanese will come this far?'

Kepa shrugged. There had been two sightings

of Japanese submarine-launched planes over Wellington and Auckland recently, which had done nothing at all to allay public fears that New Zealand was about to be attacked.

'I cannot say, Tamar, and neither can you, so do not worry about it.'

Tamar hated it when Kepa was so relentlessly calm and philosophical, but he was probably right. He usually was.

'Did you stop in at Erin and Joseph's on your way here?' she asked, bringing her tea cup to her lips.

'Yes, I stayed for half an hour and had a beer with Joseph.'

'How did they seem to you?'

Kepa reached for another biscuit and examined it closely while he considered his reply. 'Erin is more like her old self these days. It has been almost a year now; I think that they are over the worst of it.'

'Is there a time limit to accepting the loss of a son? I still think of Ian almost every day.'

'But do you remember Ian's death, or do you remember Ian as he was when he was alive?'

'When he was alive, of course.'

'Then you have not lost him at all, have you? And we have not lost Billy, as long as we remember him.'

Tamar sighed in acquiescence, and they sat in companionable silence for several minutes. The brooding clouds were swelling above them, but still there was not a single drop of the longed-for rain.

'Did you talk to Ana?' she asked eventually.

'Briefly. She seems very excited by the prospect of this land army business.'

'Oh, we've heard about nothing else, ever since she found out she'd been accepted. It's a shame, though, that the land army girls aren't permitted to work for relatives. We could have paid her for all the months and months she's been working here.'

'Still, it is only about thirty miles away; she will not be too far from us.'

'No, and I'm sure she'll be a great help to this farmer she's going to.'

'Of course she will. She is our grandchild, after all,' Kepa said proudly. 'What was the man's name?'

'Leonard. Jack Leonard.'

'Do you know of him?'

Tamar shook her head. 'The farm must be fairly small. It is a sheep farm, though.'

'Well, Ana has always been a very mature child, and extremely capable. I am sure this Jack Leonard will be very grateful to have her working for him.'

★ ★ ★

Ana wasn't so sure about that. At her interview with the Women's War Service Auxiliary recruiting committee she had been warned about 'rural conservatism' and, in a veiled sort of way, of the potential for unwanted attentions from employers, and even more obliquely of the reception she might receive as a part-Maori girl. She had not, of course, told her mother and

237

father about this, in case they worried or, even worse, stopped her, and besides she was sure she could manage both problems should they arise.

She checked her watch; she was due at the Leonard farm by three o'clock this afternoon. The National Service Department was liable for paying her transport costs, but when she'd discovered that they would not pay for her horse, she'd decided to ride the distance cross-country. Mako, a very fine seventeen-hand bay gelding she had owned and ridden almost every day for the last two years, was her pride and joy and she could not even contemplate a job on a new farm without him.

It had been a pleasant journey so far, and last night she'd stayed at the home of an old school friend, which had been a nice interlude. But she was looking forward to getting settled and sorting out the gear she'd been issued as a member of the new Women's Land Service. Crammed into a saddlebag behind her she had gumboots (her own, because the WWSA had run out owing to the rubber shortage) and an extra pair of leather work boots to match the ones she was wearing, trousers, overalls, socks, work shirts, a woollen jersey, two pairs of leather gloves, her underthings and her personal toiletries. In front of her saddle she'd rolled and tied her leather jerkin and her oilskin coat and leggings.

Mr Leonard was a widower, which was both good and bad as far as Ana was concerned. Good, because it meant that there would be no Mrs Leonard watching her suspiciously through binoculars all day in case she 'fraternised' with Mr Leonard, an unfortunate situation already experienced and recounted by a land girl Ana had recently met, and bad because Mr Leonard might have ideas about Ana as a replacement for the late Mrs Leonard. He also had a son, who had been overseas since 1940, but his farm labourers had deserted him one by one until there was only Mr Leonard left to run the place by himself. With the continuing, and ever louder, call for primary producers to increase production he'd evidently finally been compelled to contact the district manpower office to ask for help.

That help was Ana. The WWSA had promised that at least one other girl would be sent to join her as soon as it could be arranged, but that as the numbers joining the Land Service were still low she could be on her own for several months. Ana didn't mind that, she was quite happy with her own company, but she did wonder if the work might be too much for just one farmer and a land girl, especially when shearing time came around.

She pulled Mako up and dismounted; it was midday and she was starving. Leaving him in the shade of a tree to munch on a patch of nice green grass she sat down to eat her own lunch — sandwiches made with her friend's mother's homemade cheese and pickle, two apples and a thermos of tea. The heat up here in the foothills of the northern reaches of the Ruahine Range was intense, but tempered today with a welcome breeze. The Leonard farm was just south of the small settlement of Kereru. The holding was relatively small, compared with Kenmore anyway, and divided by a tributary of the Ngaruroro River, and Ana had been told that although much of the block had been cleared, there was plenty of bush still standing. She hoped she wasn't going to be expected to clear bush as well as attend to the day-to-day farm work.

It took her another three hours to reach her destination, and by the time she had she was parched, tired and a little saddle-sore. She found the letterbox, with L and M Leonard written on it in black, hand-painted letters, and followed the long driveway through several small paddocks towards a cluster of tall trees some distance from the gravel road. She noticed as she went that several gates were off their hinges and that the wire in the fences could do with some tightening.

Beyond the trees she came to the homestead, a reasonable-sized house that had seen better days. The yard was part gravel, part grass and part bare earth, and what had obviously once been cultivated flower gardens were now sad little boxed areas of weed-infested soil. The house itself was in dire need of a good paint, the curtains at the windows faded and crooked, and the verandah at the front seemed to be on an angle to the rest of the building.

Ana dismounted and called out, 'Hello the house! Anybody home? Mr Leonard!'

When no one answered she looped Mako's reins around the verandah rail and walked around the side of the house to find the back door. To the right was a cluster of ramshackle buildings — a couple of sheds, a pumphouse and an open-sided shelter — and beyond the house was an overgrown backyard. There was an expansive pig pen housing a sow and five or six porkers at the far end, not far from a lonely little building that could only be the outhouse, and a dozen chickens wandering around foraging in the dirt. Three or four cats eyed her dolefully from the shade of an overgrown hydrangea. Mr Leonard clearly also kept his dogs here, as she noted gnawed bones abandoned in the grass in front of several kennels that looked in better condition than the homestead itself. She called out again, and when again there was no answer she stepped over a pile of boots at the back door and knocked loudly. She stood there for several minutes feeling silly and mildly annoyed — hadn't he received the notification that she would be arriving today? — then decided that since the door was open she might as well go inside.

The back door led straight into the kitchen, which meant she had no time to prepare herself. The room was in a shambles and something in it stank horrendously. There were dirty dishes piled up in the sink, pots on the coal range still with food in them, and used cups and plates scattered across an oilcloth-covered kitchen table among half a loaf of bread, a saucer of melting butter, a bottle of fly killer and a dish of sliced meat curling up at the edges that Ana thought might be corned beef. The smell wasn't coming from that, though, it was emanating in evil clouds

241

from a bucket of slops on the floor next to the sink. The bucket was jammed with food scraps and crawling with buzzing flies and maggots. Ana, her shirt pulled up over her mouth and nose, stood staring at the mess and wondering when the bucket had last been emptied.

She didn't hear the footsteps on the back porch until the owner of the feet was standing in the doorway.

'What the hell are you doing in my house!'

Ana jumped and turned at the same time, her foot slipping in something greasy on the floor. Confronting her was a man in his early fifties dressed in work boots and pants, his muscled, heavily tanned arms and shoulders bared in a grubby singlet, and a wide-brimmed hat pushed to the back of his head. His face, which might have been rather handsome once but certainly wasn't now, was covered with three-day-old stubble that was grey, like his brutally short hair. From where she stood, Ana caught a definite whiff of old sweat.

'Mr Leonard?'

'Yes. Who the hell are you?'

Ana waited until her thudding heart was back where it should be. 'I'm sorry, Mr Leonard, I called out before but I thought no one was home. I'm Ana Deane, from the Women's Land Service. I believe you were expecting me today?'

Jack Leonard looked Ana up and down, from the dark curls around her pretty face to the toes of her size six work boots, and snorted in disgust.

'Jesus Christ, I told them if I had to have a

bloody female I at least wanted a decent-sized one! You're nothing but a slip!'

This was the wrong thing to say to Ana; slip or not, she knew she could do the work required of her.

'I think you'll find, Mr Leonard, that I'm perfectly capable of managing myself on a sheep farm.'

'I don't give a toss about you, it's me sheep I want managed!'

Ana jammed her hands on her hips. 'Well, you're stuck with me for now, I'm afraid. The regulations state that I can't leave for at least seven days, and you can't fire me for at least seven days.'

'Oh, for God's sake.' Jack Leonard scratched the back of his hairy brown neck angrily. 'Well, while you're here you can bloody well make yourself useful. See what you can do with this kitchen, it's got out of hand. I have to feed the dogs.'

He turned and went out again, but Ana was close behind him.

'Hey, Mister! Don't you speak to me like that! I'm not a house maid. Clean up your own pigsty of a kitchen!'

Leonard stopped, and turned back slowly. His eyes had narrowed and his face had gone an alarming purple colour.

'Right, Miss *Land* Girl, have it your way. I need a pig killed. The knives are in the shed.'

'Not until I've sorted out my horse,' Ana shot back. 'We've come a long way these last two days.'

She marched around to the front of the house, untied Mako, brought him back round and led him into the nearest paddock. It took her less than ten minutes to unsaddle him and give him a thorough rub down, then lead him to a water trough where he drank greedily.

When she'd finished, she saw that Leonard had already got the knives out and was standing at the gate to the pig pen, his face wreathed in a smirk. She took the biggest knife and tested in along the ball of her thumb.

'It's a little blunt. Do you have an axe?'

Leonard snorted again, but handed her an axe that was propped against a nearby chopping block. She tucked the knife into her belt.

'Now, do you singe or scald?'

'Singe.'

'We'll need a fire then, won't we?' Ana said as she climbed into the pen and selected a good-sized male porker with plenty of condition.

Shooing the others away, she stood astride the pig, raised the axe and brought the blunt side down onto the animal's skull with a calculated but very solid blow. The pig dropped without a sound. She rolled it onto its side, withdrew the knife from her belt and thrust the blade into its neck close to the shoulder, then down into the heart. A glut of thick, dark blood welled up immediately and the pig, still unconscious, quickly began to bleed to death. When the blood had subsided Ana reached between its back legs and deftly sliced the testicles off to prevent boar taint getting into the flesh.

She turned back to Leonard, and saw he'd

begun piling up wood for the fire that would singe the hair off the pig before it was gutted and hung.

He added a few more dry branches, lit them and straightened up. 'I suppose you'll be wanting a wash now,' he said, nodding at the blood that had spurted onto her hands and over the front of her trousers.

'That would be nice, yes.'

'The pump's over there,' he replied, and walked away.

In his paddock, Mako was trotting up and down the fence, mirroring the actions of a big, good-looking brown mare in the next field.

Ana washed her hands, then rummaged in her saddlebag for a pair of clean trousers. She changed behind one of the sheds, and left the bloody pants to soak in a bucket filled with cold water.

She couldn't leave, and she was damned if she was going to admit defeat already, so she did the only thing she could — she picked up her gear and went inside again.

Jack Leonard was sitting at the kitchen table eating dried-up corned beef.

'I forgot you were coming,' he said through a mouthful. 'Nothing's ready.'

Ana shrugged.

'Put the kettle on and I'll show you where you can sleep.'

When Ana didn't move he sighed, got up and put the kettle on himself. She thought he might have muttered, under his breath, 'Could be a bloody long week,' but she couldn't be sure.

She followed him into the living room beyond the kitchen. It was surprisingly tidy, although it looked as if it hadn't been used for ages, possibly even years. Thick dust coated everything — the mantelpiece, the occasional tables between the sofa and chairs and even the wooden floor where the floral-patterned rugs didn't reach. Three framed photographs stood on the largest table, the middle one of a sweet-looking woman in her late forties, flanked by images of two young men in uniform who looked very much as Jack Leonard must have in his younger years. It looked like a room that had been decorated with thought and care by a woman, then abandoned.

Four bedrooms and a bathroom branched off from a central hallway that ran the length of the house from the front door. Leonard led Ana to a room at the far end of the hall, and opened the door.

'Like I said, nothing's ready.'

The room contained a wardrobe, a chest of drawers, a straight-backed wooden chair and a single bed without sheets or blankets. Here, too, everything was covered in dust.

He caught the lingering look of doubt on her face. 'The shearers' quarters are in a state so you'll have to stay here in the house. Do you mind?'

'Do you, Mr Leonard?'

He was walking back down the hall now. Over his shoulder he said, 'Yes, I do.'

★　★　★

246

He left some bedclothes and a pillow outside the bedroom door. The sheets were clean, if very slightly musty smelling, and so were the blanket and pillow. She made the bed and lay down on it just for a minute; she woke up three hours later as the sun was going down. Jack Leonard was nowhere to be seen, and Ana had a quick wash in the bathroom and made herself something to eat in the disgusting kitchen.

Off the back porch opposite the washhouse was a small, airy pantry with a cool safe and shelves and bins holding a stock of dry goods and cans, including an ancient tin of custard powder and an even older one of Andrews Liver Salts. There was also, on the floor, a tub filled with cold water; in it were several bricks on which stood a crock of milk, a slab of butter in a dish, a bowl of eggs and a baking pan full of raw and bloody chops, all draped with a large damp square of muslin.

She fancied a chop but, unable to find a clean frying pan and refusing to clean either of the two filthy ones on the bench, she settled for a cheese sandwich and a cup of tea. Afterwards she went outside to talk to Mako, who seemed to be settling in well. The dead pig had been rolled in the fire and debristled, hung up on the block and tackle at the end of one of the sheds and gutted. Ana felt slightly irritated — she had wanted to do that.

She slept surprisingly well that night, considering how worried she was about the fact that there was no lock on her bedroom door, and she didn't hear Leonard when he finally came back to the house. The next morning she was up at five o'clock in the hope of beating him to it, but she was disappointed again; he was already in the kitchen, frying chops and eggs.

'Breakfast,' he said without looking up.

Ana eyed the greasy frying pan. 'Thank you, but I'll make myself a sandwich,' she replied politely, wondering how much longer she could go on eating cheese sandwiches before she caved in and did the dishes.

She made her sandwich and watched while he ate his chops and eggs, leaving strips of fat on his plate that the flies would no doubt home in on as soon as the sun came up properly. The sight made her sick, so she looked somewhere else.

'Milk's fresh,' he said, getting to his feet and jamming his hat on his head. 'I'm crutching and dagging today. I've done some lunch, if you care to come and watch.'

She bridled at his sarcastic tone, but followed him outside anyway.

'You're early,' she commented.

'What?'

'With the crutching.'

'No, I'm very bloody late, is what I am.'

The dogs, she saw, had been fed, there was grain sprinkled on the dirt for the chooks, and the cats had their heads down in a large saucer of milk. He might not look after himself particularly well, but he certainly seemed to care for his animals. His dogs especially were fit and healthy, lean but not underweight and their coats gleamed.

'Why don't you feed that bucket of slops in

248

your kitchen to the pigs?' she asked as she patted one of the dogs.

'Usually do, too busy yesterday.'

By tonight, Ana thought, the kitchen could well be infested with bubonic plague. She sighed and went back inside for the bucket. Leonard ignored her as she staggered back out of the house, holding the reeking thing as far away from her body as she could manage. Not even pigs could eat this.

'Where's your offal pit?'

He inclined his head towards trees behind the outhouse, still shrouded in the long blurred shadows of dawn, and watched silently as she headed off to dump the offending rubbish.

She caught up with him as he was saddling the brown mare. She saddled Mako, and fell in beside Leonard as he headed through the open gate and out across the paddocks, the four dogs trotting happily beside them.

'What's her name?'

'Who?'

'The mare.'

'Pandora. The wife liked it, said it was exotic.'

'Nice-looking horse.'

Leonard grunted and fell silent. Ana thought he was lucky the army hadn't commandeered his horse — they'd been out to Kenmore and taken two of theirs. As they rode across pasture and through stands of cabbage trees and native bush, she noticed that the farm was in a state of disrepair, but she didn't think it was because Leonard wasn't a good farmer. He'd obviously been out here by himself for some time, and it showed. She knew there was one son away, but what had happened to the other one, the second boy in the photograph on the living room table? She wondered, but had the distinct feeling that if she asked Leonard outright, she could well be the first land girl in New Zealand to be fired in under seven days.

They came to the shearing shed, looming on tall piles so that sheep could be penned under it. There were gaping holes in the sides where slats of wood had come off and not been replaced, and it was fronted by a maze of post-and-rail yards complete with a long race closed off at the end by a swing gate. On the hillside above the shed sheep wandered slowly, concentrating at pulling at the meagre, dry grass.

'I've done half,' Leonard said. 'Sit over there in the shade if you like; it'll be cooler.'

Ana couldn't tell whether he was serious or having her on, so she stayed where she was, on Mako.

Leonard whistled and his dogs sprinted away, not towards the sheep but beyond them, then dropped flat on the ground while they awaited their next command. Leonard whistled again and they began to move slowly, slinking on low bellies towards the sheep, who were equally slowly waking up to the fact that they were being rounded up.

They were good dogs, and in no time they had the first mob of about a hundred through the gate and milling around in the yard. Leonard whistled a third time and the dogs jumped the rails, bounding across the backs of the sheep

250

until they found open ground, then dashed about, herding the complaining animals towards the first race.

Leonard withdrew a set of hand shears from his voluminous back pocket, swung the gate open and let the first animal in. Bending over it, he clipped the dag-matted wool from around the sheep's backside, then started on the longer wool on the backs of its legs and around its head. The sheep bleated piteously and shot off still bleating when Leonard had finished with it. He let the next sheep in, clipped it, and then the next, and the next.

Ana looked on impassively, although she knew it must have taken him days and days to crutch and dag as many sheep as he already had, and it would take him days more to finish the job. This was ridiculous. She stuck two fingers in her mouth and whistled piercingly.

Two things happened: Jack Leonard's hairy shoulders, the big muscles standing out already, ceased to move, while the dogs looked from Ana to Leonard, and back to Ana again, their ears pricked with interest.

She whistled again, and they raced out of the yard and up the hill where they stopped, waiting. At her next command they rounded up another group of sheep and brought them down off the hill.

Ana got off Mako. 'Where do you keep your shears?' she called.

'Shed,' Leonard replied, but he didn't look up. Slowly, he started clipping again.

Ana went into the shearing shed, feeling at

home with the sharp, sour smell left behind from decades of past clips, and looked around for the hand shears. They were lined up along a stained wooden bench, oiled and wrapped separately to keep the dust off the blades. Behind them, hanging neatly on the wall, were the modified shears that, come shearing time, would be attached to the cables hanging above a long platform down the centre of the shed. When the Anderson engine was going, the mechanical shears would clip ten times faster than any set of hand shears.

She selected a set small enough for the size of her hands and went outside. The sun was well up now; it would be a scorcher.

By midday her back and arms were aching horribly, because that's what this sort of work did to a person no matter how fit they were. She knew Leonard had been watching her out of the corner of his eye, but he hadn't said anything until about eleven o'clock, and that had only been to tell her that there were bottles of water in his rucksack.

They ate their lunch in silence, had a cup of tea each from the thermos and went back to work. By two, the dogs had retired panting to the shade of the shed and the horses had wandered off to the nearest tree and were standing nose to tail, flicking flies off each other.

Ana's face, hair and shirt were soaked with sweat; at home she worked in a singlet and shorts like the men, but here she preferred to keep herself a little more modestly covered. She wondered if she smelled; Leonard in the race next to her certainly did. But then they were both tainted with raw greasy wool and sheep shit, so she didn't suppose a bit of body odour would matter much.

At six o'clock, Leonard put his shears down, groaned as he straightened up and said, 'That will do for today.' Then, as if it had only just occurred to him, he added, 'You did all right. For a slip.'

That was the way it went for the rest of the week — eight hours every day up at the woolshed crutching and dagging, followed by another three hours or so of miscellaneous work. There was rabbiting — dropping carrots baited with strychnine around the farm, and shooting any of the pests silly enough to poke their heads up when Ana and Leonard were about, then going back a few days later to collect the dead ones and lay new bait. The pig Ana killed had to be salted, wrapped and stored in the cool safe to prevent it from going off too quickly. Every morning the two house cows needed milking, and in the evening the animals required feeding. Leonard killed a sheep once a week for the dogs, and the cats stole the scraps to augment their daily diet of rats and mice. There was the kitchen garden to attend to — and the anti-rabbit slab fence surrounding it to be checked vigilantly every night — thistles to grub, fences to mend and farm equipment to maintain and repair.

Every night after a quick dinner and a wash Ana collapsed into bed and slept the sleep of the truly exhausted. She barely had the energy to wash her hair, never mind setting it to make the most of her curls as she had occasionally done at Kenmore, and she certainly couldn't be bothered putting on the dress or lipstick the ads in the women's magazines insisted were essential to morale and the war effort. She doubted that Jack Leonard would notice anyway — she had gone rather quickly from worrying about not having a lock on her door to wanting to belt him one for completely ignoring her most of the time. The only question of any substance he'd asked was who had taught her to ride, manage sheep and kill pigs. She'd answered that her father had, and when he'd asked if her father had Maori blood in him, she said yes. He'd said, 'I thought so,' and left it at that.

The dishes had eventually been washed, and she noted that the slops bucket was being emptied regularly now, but the rest of the kitchen was still a mess.

On the sixth night she was forced awake by the oppressive heat and a vicious, dive-bombing mosquito. When she'd tracked down the offending insect and smeared it bloodily against the faded wallpaper on her bedroom wall, she noticed something else, a stifled, snorting sort of noise coming from another part of the house. At first she wondered if it was one of the dogs snuffling around with something outside, a rabbit perhaps, but the longer she listened the more human the noise became.

Opening her bedroom door carefully so it wouldn't creak, she walked softly down the hallway until she came to the door of the living room.

In the pale darkness, Jack Leonard was sitting on the sofa in his vest and underpants. He had the photographs of his wife and sons held tightly against his chest, and was rocking slowly backwards and forwards and crying. It was an intensely private and personal moment, and Ana knew it. She backed away quietly and went back to her room, aware that she had just seen a side to Jack Leonard that told her more about him than she'd been able to fathom all week, a side he could probably never reveal to her even had he wanted to.

Early in the morning of the eighth day, as they were saddling up in the growing dawn light, Leonard turned to her and said gruffly, 'If you clean up the kitchen, you can stay on.'

Ana tightened the girth on Mako's saddle, giving him a gentle knee in the guts because he was belligerently holding his breath.

'No, if *you* clean up the kitchen I won't leave.'

It was the first time Ana had seen him smile.

★ ★ ★

By the end of the third week, he had mentioned, far too casually, that his wife had died four years ago from cancer, that his youngest boy, Anthony, had been killed in Greece last year, and that David, his eldest, was away fighting in North Africa.

Ana in turn told Jack about her family, in this war and the last. Jack said he'd served in the Great War too, and what a bloody disaster that had been all round, and didn't her family have

255

an impressive military pedigree?

After that they found they had a lot to say to each other, about horses and working dogs and sheep farming, and what were the best fruits and vegetables and crops to grow in the Hawke's Bay climate, and the benefits of singeing your slaughtered pig compared with bunging it in a hot bath to get the bristles off, and about the war in general. But never, after that first time, about what losing someone so close to them meant.

Over the weeks Ana came to like and respect Jack Leonard very much, and she was almost sad when a letter arrived to say that he would be allotted at least one more land girl within the next fortnight. On the other hand, she was relieved. There was still far too much work on the farm for only two people. They were barely keeping up at the moment; when it came to shearing time, they wouldn't have a prayer. She sincerely hoped, though, that she and Jack wouldn't be lumbered with a silly city girl who couldn't lift anything heavier than a bottle of nail varnish, who didn't like the way farms smelled and who fainted at the sight of blood.

12

Keely concentrated on patching a pair of Henry's shorts. She was heartily sick and tired of the rationing, and Kenmore was almost self-sufficient, so she didn't know how on earth people in town were getting on.

In April of last year, books of ration coupons had arrived for everyone who lived at Kenmore, even Henry. First it had been for sugar — twelve ounces per week per person, so there went baking and sugar in her tea (except for during jam-making season, when the allowance went up) — then the damned tea had been rationed, followed by butter in October. But the butter hadn't been a problem because she, Erin and Lucy were making their own from the house cows these days, even if it was considered slightly unpatriotic. And thank God they were; they'd dutifully tried the recipes in magazines for butter substitutes, such as dripping combined with lemon juice and bicarbonate of soda, and almost gagged at what it had done to their baking. They were making cheese, too, and there were always eggs and plenty of fruit, courtesy of James's orchards.

Meat was all right, because they killed their own, but it had been rumoured lately that pork might be rationed soon, and Kenmore didn't keep pigs. However, there were pigs at

Maungakakari, and as Kenmore supplied the village with the odd sheep, the arrangement was bound to be reciprocated when the time came. The government did not encourage swapping, bartering and giving away surplus produce or ration coupons, but it happened all the time, and most people turned a blind eye. And some grocers and butchers were also not averse to keeping scarce or sought-after items under the counter, in exchange for the right amount of money or perhaps a carton of smokes.

Cigarettes and tobacco were not rationed, but they were usually hard to get hold of. James, however, had some sort of arrangement with a bloke he knew in town; in exchange for a case of fruit and a quarter of lamb or hogget every few weeks, he came home with several cartons of Lucky Strikes, Pall Malls or Chesterfields, and six packets of tobacco. Where the bloke got the cigarettes and tobacco from nobody knew, but James strongly suspected it had something to do with the Americans.

Rice was also extremely hard to come by, unless you were Chinese, and so were potatoes if you didn't grow them yourself. But Joseph did, in quantity, so that was all right. There were three large vegetable gardens at Kenmore, including James's in which he was frequently trying something new and exotic, so fresh vegetables were never in short supply.

But regardless of rationing, the women of New Zealand were still being urged to 'bake for the boys' and send parcels overseas. Keely, Lucy and Erin had all become rather skilled at producing baked goods that would reach their destinations in an edible state, but there was an art to this. You had to be careful not to use milk or nuts in anything, and you had to put the baking in tins inside a piece of linen or a washed flour sack, sewn tight to make a neat package to keep the air out. In the beginning there had been baking disasters, and much subsequent hilarity at the dinner table when the failures were served disguised with cream or custard, but Henry was usually happy to dispose of them, and if they were really awful, the farm dogs were never picky.

But petrol had been rationed for ages and was very difficult to get; there were no regular trips into town any more. Sometimes a bit of petrol could be 'borrowed' from the station supply, such as it was, but fuel was now in such short supply that they were back to using horses to plough the paddocks they used to grow winter feed for the sheep. But, despite their best efforts, the army had not taken all of the horses the men relied on every day for droving and mustering, and Kepa, who bred horses at Maungakakari, had sent out three or four really good ones in the last six months, including two Clydesdales, so the station wasn't too badly off. And really, Keely had to admit, there was not much to go into town *for*, these days.

Buying decent clothes, or even the material to make them, was difficult to say the least. Some women managed to save the coupons for clothes or material, but not the money, and others, like Keely, had the money but not the coupons. And more often than not, if you had both, there was nothing in the shops anyway. The daughter of a friend of Lucy's had been married a month ago, and organising a dress for her had been a terrible job. In the end the mother had paid through the nose and under the counter for a length of écru moiré taffeta and some cream satin, and had made something rather nice from that, but Lucy's friend had almost had a nervous breakdown during the process.

Stockings had been rationed first, especially silk ones. They were extremely hard to get now, although the rationing was supposed to ensure that every woman over the age of sixteen could buy a pair once every three months. There were alternatives that weren't quite so hard to find — wool and lisle, which most women under the age of fifty-five loathed, and cotton or rayon — but it wasn't the same. Decent, flattering stockings had always been made of silk, even if it did come from Japan. Wearing no stockings at all was becoming more acceptable, in the summer, but you needed good legs for that. You could reproduce the effect of stockings with a cream and a brown pencil down the back of the leg to create a 'seam', but the process was fiddly, the finish patchy and the cream came off on clothes and furniture. And then there was the problem of stopping your corset or your 'easy' from rolling up and causing unsightly bulges when it wasn't anchored by stockings. Keely didn't wear a corset but Lucy, who did, was always bemoaning the fact that hers invariably ended up under her bust before the day was out. Tamar said did it really matter — why not go without a corset in summer or wear trousers when it was cold? — but Lucy, who had been brought up very strictly, found it a little more difficult to say goodbye to her foundation garments in quite such a perfunctory manner.

Then in May last year the rationing of clothes had come in in general, and at first it had seemed that, unlike silk stockings, there would not be a mad rush to purchase everything in the shops before stock ran out. Some garments required rather a lot of coupons, though, and it soon added up, especially when wardrobes were limited and clothes worn frequently. At Kenmore making their own clothes was the norm, but now even material and knitting wool had been rationed. But Keely could not in all honesty say that they were hard up. The women had all had well-stocked wardrobes when the war had started — unlike many families who had still not quite found their feet after the Depression — and the men were happy to wear their work gear until it fell off them.

Henry, however, who was extremely hard on his clothes, created more of a problem. Fence-climbing always seemed to result in a tear, eeling in the streams was mucky work and bound to require a full dip in the water, and playing with the horses meant at the very least sweat and hair-covered garments. Last week one of the Clydesdales had bitten Henry on the backside — something to do with attempting to count its teeth, apparently. His bottom had remained intact, but his shorts now had a very large hole in them. Keely had recently made him some farm clothes from an old suit of Owen's, but while they served their purpose she had no intention of letting him be seen in them anywhere outside the station gates.

Household linen was also rationed, and china and crockery, and so were chocolate and sweets. Many other items were in short supply. Cosmetics were not rationed, but they were becoming scarce. It was all very dreary, but Keely knew it might have been a lot worse. She'd read in the newspaper recently that in England you couldn't get any sort of fruit at all, and that there were children who did not even know what a banana was!

And at least she had Owen, even if her daughters and her niece and nephews were away. Not that Kenmore's menfolk had a lot of time these days to spend with their women. In fact, Keely was starting to worry about how hard Joseph, James and Owen were working. They not only had the station to look after, and the government's demands for wool and meat, but they'd also joined the Home Guard. They weren't young men any more, especially Joseph, and they were constantly tired, worried and overworked. But they kept on going, just as everyone in New Zealand seemed to be doing. Keely knew that the work the men did on the station, and the work she, her mother, Erin and Lucy did — feeding the men and tending the vegetable gardens and helping with the sheep, then finding the time and energy to prepare parcels for overseas and knitting and fund-raising — was all making a difference but, God, she wished it would all be over soon.

Auckland, March 1943
Bonnie and Leila didn't — they were having a marvellous time. They weren't sick of the rationing and shortages, either. As servicewomen they were fed very well, if unimaginatively, and since the Americans had arrived they'd barely gone short of anything, not even real silk stockings — or, even better, the new nylons.

Everything had changed so much since June last year when the first of the American servicemen and women had arrived in New Zealand. There had been a mad flurry of construction as the Public Works Department had rushed to build camps from Whangarei to Wellington in time for their arrival. That had been a thrilling day in itself, with the convoy of seven huge grey ships steaming unannounced into a dull, wintry Waitemata Harbour and berthing at Princes Wharf. Crowds had flocked to the harbour the next day to see the marvellous Americans, who had no doubt come straight from Hollywood. Bands on the wharves played 'The Stars and Stripes Forever' and the Americans tossed oranges and cigarettes and money to the New Zealanders below. There was a welcoming parade a week later: the Thirty-seventh Division of the US Army marched up Queen Street to the cheers and flag-waving of thousands of Aucklanders, and a general sigh of relief because now that the Yanks were here New Zealand would surely be safe. Throughout June thousands more arrived — the Marines, the army and the navy — and soon New Zealand had been thoroughly if benignly invaded.

Bonnie and Leila had missed the parade because they had been on duty, but stories soon filtered back to Whenuapai of the Americans' charm, charisma and largesse. This delighted many of the WAAFs, but left more than one New Zealand airman with a sour look on his face.

At the first opportunity, Bonnie and Leila, together with Sheila, Peggy and Eileen, had gone into town to taste for themselves the excitement being generated by the new arrivals. From then on, they'd had an absolute ball. With their days filled with busy work at Whenuapai and their nights, when they could get leave, a whirlwind of going out and dancing, they sometimes felt completely rushed off their feet.

The Americans were so utterly charming and exotic. They had lovely manners and gorgeous accents like liquid honey, and they called a girl 'ma'am' until they got to know her, and then it became 'sweetheart' or 'sugar', which was just so exciting after years of being called 'dear', or at best 'darling', by keen New Zealand lads. Or, at worst, 'mate'. And their olive drab uniforms were smartness personified, especially when they were out on the town. They were meticulously groomed and wore beautifully tailored and well-fitting jackets with gleaming leather belts at the waist, and trousers with creases you could cut yourself on, and smart caps and brilliantly shined boots. They even wore ties!

On top of that they seemed so sophisticated, although Bonnie and Leila noted that many of them were actually very young. They were friendly and enthusiastic and seemed to be quite enamoured of New Zealand, even though the country was so different from their own. There were constant good-natured complaints about the scarcity of hard liquor, and the parsimony with which the two per cent beer was doled out by New Zealand bartenders — and then only between five and six in the afternoon. Then there was the terrible coffee, the lack of hotdogs and hamburgers, and the blue laws, which decreed that there were to be almost no forms of public entertainment available on Sundays.

But the Americans were amazed at the cheap prices of everyday commodities — a large plate of steak and chips for less than half a crown, tuppenny tram rides, penny phone calls, a bottle of beer for one and six, and a shoe shine for whatever they felt like paying. And they loved the abundance of thick, creamy milk, the lamb, mutton and beef, the scenery, the opportunities to go fishing, hunting and shooting, and, most of all, the generosity of the New Zealand people themselves, many of whom were liberal with invitations to meals in their homes. Bonnie and Leila suspected that the GIs were also very keen on the fact that New Zealand seemed over-populated by lonely, bored, unescorted girls.

They were big spenders and bought jewellery, watches, curios and souvenirs at such a rate that shops often sold out, spent thousands of dollars on restaurants, taxis and goods from the PX to thank host families for their hospitality, and were especially generous towards the girls they went out with. Bonnie and Leila frequently received red roses or corsages delivered (somewhat thoughtlessly) to Whenuapai on the afternoon before a 'date', much to the sneering disgust of the men on the base who told anyone who would listen that the Americans were nothing more than overcocky, big-mouthed 'flash Harrys'. And they were brash and loud, but their charm and generosity were irresistible to many women sick to death of sitting at home night after night.

Their presence had certainly enlivened Auckland. The milk bars in Queen Street now looked as if they had been transported straight from the States, with their cosy booths and long counters, Coca-cola and over a dozen ice cream and milkshake flavours. The Grand Hotel and the Waverly had been taken over by American officers, and the Hotel Auckland had become the American Red Cross Centre for enlisted men. The Downtown Club in Customs Street, run by the YMCA, was nearly always full of GIs, even though it was supposed to be a club for all Allied soldiers and was dry because it was next door to the YWCA, and the Peter Pan Cabaret, the Orange Hall in Newton Road, the Masonic Hall and the Crystal Palace on Mount Eden Road were all popular dance venues. And there were numerous pubs — although the Americans insisted on calling them bars — such as the Empire, the Queen's Head and the Imperial, but women, unless they were unusually thick-skinned or 'working' girls, only ventured into the lounges, if they went at all.

If you fancied somewhere a little 'racier' and less public, there was always the El Ray out in Hillsborough for T-bone steaks, illegal liquor and a great band that played swing tunes and Glen Miller covers. For somewhere really sophisticated you could go to the Wintergarden Cabaret beneath the Civic Theatre to dance to an orchestra that played on a golden barge, or watch the amazing Wurlitzer organ that rose up through the floor, or ogle (or avert your eyes from, depending on your sense of modesty) the Lucky Lovelies chorus line which performed the Can-Can, and Freda Stark who appeared on stage naked and covered in gold paint. For posh dining there was the silver service restaurant at Milne and Choyce, or you could go to Burlington's, or Forsyth's in Queen Street which had a very 'American style' menu, but if you were desperate and it was late there was always the nearest pie cart.

To date, and despite having been to almost every venue in town at least once, there had been no one special for the twins — in fact they prided themselves on the fact that they went out with as many different Americans as they could manage while still keeping their reputations intact — but all that had changed one night early in March.

They were off to a dance at the Peter Pan in Queen Street, and despite having to hitch a lift into town in the back of an air force truck, they wore their party dresses and best shoes and were made up for a big night out, much to the disapproval of BJ when she had spotted them heading over to the transport depot.

Bonnie's emerald green frock was sophisticated and figure-enhancing with a square, low neck and a fitting waist; Leila's was similar in style but in mauve. Peggy looked exquisite as usual in pale lemon and pearls, and Sheila and Eileen both wore dresses with short puffed sleeves, sweetheart necklines and wide satin sashes.

They coerced the driver into letting them out at the top of Queen Street, then walked the short distance to the cabaret. Inside it was already crowded — girls in bright dresses and men in uniform as far as the eye could see — and the noise was considerable. There was an enormous American flag on the wall at the back of the stage and the band seemed to be in the throes of warming up.

'Don't they look handsome!' Leila exclaimed to Bonnie for at least the hundredth time, speaking loudly to be heard over the din.

'Divine! Look at that one over there, he looks *exactly* like Tyrone Power!'

'I would have said Ronald Colman, myself. Come on, let's go and get a drink. I'm parched already.'

They headed to the bar, ordered an orange juice each, then went out through the foyer to the ladies' and waited for the others. When Peggy, Sheila and Elaine arrived, each clutching their own drinks, Bonnie hoisted her skirt and retrieved a hip flask tucked snugly into her suspender belt. They all took deep sips of their orange juice to make room, then Bonnie splashed a liberal measure of gin into each glass. They toasted each other and drank thirstily.

'God, that's good,' Peggy sighed. 'I've been waiting all day for that.'

'I'll say,' Sheila agreed. 'Certainly hits the spot.'

'Have you got the back-ups?' Leila asked.

Peggy and Elaine nodded. Everyone knew that although the men were often searched at the door for alcohol, women never were, beyond a cursory glance. Now that they were inside, Bonnie slipped the illicit flask into her evening bag.

They trooped out, and found themselves an unoccupied table to one side of the dance floor while the band, having warmed up sufficiently, launched into a very lively rendition of 'In the Mood'. Almost immediately, a tide of soldiers descended on the unescorted women, the Whenuapai girls included.

'Excuse me, ma'am, can I please have this dance?' drawled a Marine in Leila's ear.

She looked him up and down, liked very much what she saw, and smiled warmly.

'Why, thank you, honey,' she drawled back, making the other girls giggle madly.

The Marine smiled too, the grin lighting up his handsome face, and he extended his hand, palm up. Leila rose to her feet, and they stepped out onto the dance floor, disappearing quickly into the crowd.

'That was quick,' Peggy said admiringly.

Soon they were all up, spinning and twirling and completely ignoring the large sign on the wall declaring 'No full skirts when jitterbugging'.

Leila stayed on the floor for the next five dances, and when Bonnie whirled past she winked at her broadly. She really rather liked her Marine. He was well built and towered over her by at least a foot even though she was in heels, and was dark-haired and very good-looking in a slightly dangerous sort of way. He hadn't said much to her so far, but then you couldn't really carry on any decent sort of a conversation when you were hopping and bopping and being flung about.

As the band changed tempo and slid into the slightly more gentle 'You Are My Sunshine', he asked, 'Would you care for a drink?'

Leila nodded and led the way back to the girls' table; the Marine pulled her chair out for her and she sat down.

Still standing, he asked, 'Would you like a juice, ma'am?'

Leila glanced at her almost empty orange and gin, and nodded. He was back within minutes, having elbowed his way through the crowd to the bar, and carefully set two drinks on the table.

Leila looked casually to left and right, then bent over and reached into her bag. The Marine looked on in amusement, his dark eyebrows only slightly raised, as she discreetly withdrew her flask and poured gin into both their drinks. He laughed out loud in obviously genuine delight, and Leila's stomach did a slow, sensuous flip.

Then he said, 'You sure look just like Lana Turner,' with such feeling that she had to laugh too.

'I bet you say that to all the girls.'

'Only the ones who look like Lana Turner. Can I ask what they call you?'

His accent was gorgeous, and it sent shivers up and down Leila's spine.

'Leila Morgan.'

'Leila? That is *such* a pretty name!'

'Thank you. And yours is . . . ?'

'Jake Kelly, ma'am.'

'Well, it's very nice to meet you, Jake. Where are you from?'

'Harper County, Oklahoma, and it's great to meet you too.'

They gazed at each other for a long moment, and Leila thought she'd never seen such beautiful dark eyes and long lashes on a man in her life.

'I see you're a Marine,' she said eventually.

'Yes, ma'am, with the Nine/Three.'

'Sorry?'

'The Ninth Regiment, Third Marine Division, US Marine Corps.'

'Oh, yes, you lot have just arrived, haven't you?'

He nodded. 'A couple of weeks ago. We're camped at Waikaraka Park,' he said, thoroughly mangling the Maori word.

'It's Wai-*kara*-ka,' she enunciated carefully.

'That's right. You sure have some funny place names here.'

271

'Oh, sorry. Shall we have them changed for you?'

Jake looked at her sharply. 'Pardon me?'

'It's a joke. You're right, some of our Maori words are very hard to pronounce.'

'Oh. Yeah.' He lit a Chesterfield and squinted at her through the smoke. 'You're not like the New Zealand girls I've met so far.'

He pronounced New Zealand as 'Noo Zeellind'.

Leila said, 'Really? That looks nice.'

When Jake realised what she was referring to he flipped his packet open and offered it to her, then he leaned forward and lit her cigarette.

'Thank you. What exactly do you mean, I'm not like the girls you've met so far?'

'Please don't be offended, but put it like this — most of the New Zealand girls I've met wouldn't say boo to a goose. I think you would.'

Leila, who was beginning to feel the effects of the gin, said, 'Boo.'

He frowned again. This girl was gorgeous but cheeky with it. He thought he liked it.

Leila laughed. 'Don't worry, I'm only poking the borax.'

'Pardon me?'

'I'm having you on. It was another joke.'

She could see he was dying to get out his *Pocket Guide to New Zealand 1943* and see what it said under 'New Zealanders, sense of humour'.

She wondered if she might have gone too far, and changed the subject. 'Do you know how long you'll be here, in New Zealand?'

Jake looked relieved to be on safer conversational ground. 'Hard to say. We're training for an assault on . . . '

Leila reached out and pressed her fingers to his lips.

'Shush. Loose lips sink ships.'

Her fingers tasted of orange juice. Through them he mumbled, 'Well, yes, ma'am, but how many Japanese do you know?'

Leila took her hand back. 'Sorry. None, actually. I'm a WAAF, and it's second nature. And please don't call me ma'am. It's lovely to talk to a man with such beautiful manners, but 'ma'am' makes me feel like I'm somebody's grandmother.'

He nodded in acquiescence, then said questioningly, 'A waf?'

'Women's Auxiliary Air Force. I'm stationed at Whenuapai Air Base and so is my sister Bonnie.'

Jake exclaimed, 'Ah, the redhead who looks like Rita Hayworth? I thought you might be sisters. I said to my pal Danny, those two have to be sisters. You look very similar, except for the hair colour. Danny likes a redhead.'

'We're twins, actually.'

'I knew it! Me, I like a blonde. So you're both in the services? You must be on a liberty, dressed like that.'

'Sorry?'

'A liberty. I think you call it leave.'

'Oh, yes, just an evening pass, though. There's a truck picking us up at midnight. We have to be back at the base at quarter to one.'

Just then the band struck up the opening bars

273

to 'Boogie Woogie Bugle Boy', and Jake jumped to his feet.

He towed Leila back out onto the floor and they hurled themselves into a jive, belting out the song at the tops of their voices. He was an excellent dancer, throwing her out in a spin then reeling her back in, lifting and turning her effortlessly, his feet never missing a beat and his hips snaking from side to side. He was sweating now and small damp patches were appearing under his arms, but Leila for some reason found this sexy rather than off-putting. Then the song changed to 'Blueberry Hill', and he pulled her close. She could smell him now, a delicious, musky and very masculine scent.

They danced until Leila thought her feet might drop off and she had to plead thirst as a reason to sit down.

Bonnie was already at their table with another Marine who had a pleasant, open face with regular features, light brown hair cropped in the traditional short military style and a very sweet smile. He stood up as Leila approached.

Bonnie said, 'Leila, this is Danny Hartman. Danny, my twin sister Leila.'

They shook hands as Bonnie added, 'Danny and Jake are best pals. Isn't that a coincidence?'

'Absolutely,' replied Leila as she sat down. 'Did you realise that you and I are on a liberty?'

'A liberty?'

'It's what these boys call leave.'

Jake said, 'You can have a forty-eight, or a seventy-two, or even longer if you're lucky.'

Bonnie shook her head. 'Some of the terms

you use are very strange.'

'Oh, not really,' Danny replied with a glint in his eye. 'It starts as soon as you're a ductee in boot camp, see. Mind you, half of it's horse shit on a platter, if you'll pardon the expression, a real snow job. Some of those mustangs sure think the sun shines out of their arse, not to mention the skipper. I don't know if it's the same for the doggies, but it is in the corps.'

Bonnie and Leila glanced at each other in incomprehension.

Then Leila sat back and said, 'Still, the Kiwi lingo must be pretty hard yakka for yous blokes, not to mention your day's graft. Getting up at sparrow's fart out in the wops at that Waikaraka possie, traipsing to the dunny before yous even get the chance to sling the billy for a cuppa, then slogging your guts out 'til smoko. Strewth, you'd have to be hard as nails, wouldn't ya? It's enough to make you crook. Pardon my expressions,' she added, 'but I am the daughter of a cocky.'

'Bloody oath,' Bonnie said, and giggled until her eyes watered.

It was Jake and Danny's turn to exchange bemused looks.

'Excuse me?' Danny said.

'Isn't it strange?' Bonnie observed. 'We all speak English, but we don't understand each other very well at all.'

'But does that matter?' Danny asked. 'We seem to get our messages across, eventually. And isn't that what being in a foreign country is supposed to be about? Learning about how other people live? I love it here; it's a great place. If we

275

weren't in the middle of a war, this would be the most fun I've ever had.'

He sounded wistful, and the girls wondered where these boys were heading after New Zealand.

'I'm thirsty. Do we still have any . . . ?' Bonnie raised her eyebrows.

'Only just,' Leila said. 'We've nearly finished it.'

'What about Peggy and Eileen?'

Leila shrugged. 'Probably not, knowing Peggy.'

'Are you girls looking for a drink?' Jake interrupted. 'There's a great little bar down the street where a nice girl can feel safe. Isn't that right, Danny?'

'It is,' Danny agreed. 'The New Criterion. We had a drink there earlier.'

'Or how about the El Ray?' Jake suggested hopefully.

Bonnie looked at her watch. 'Sadly, it's too far out of town. We'd miss our ride.'

'The New Criterion it is then.' Jake stood and offered Leila his elbow. 'Shall we go?'

Outside it was still warm, but the slight breeze was welcome after the heat inside the Peter Pan. Leila and Jake walked arm in arm down Queen Street, Jake with his uniform jacket slung casually over his shoulder, while Bonnie and Danny walked some way behind them. The footpath was crowded with couples and servicemen — mostly American — out for a good time, swaggering or staggering according to the extent of their inebriation, and they had to step out onto the road several times to avoid being actually pushed there.

'That's the Auckland Town Hall on our left,' Leila pointed out, 'and further down is the Civic Theatre. It's really spectacular inside, really grand. And after that there's Smith and Caugheys, that's an enormous department store. Right down the bottom of Queen Street are the wharves, but you would have seen them when you arrived. And all of these tracks and wires across the road are for the trams.'

Jake gave his surroundings a cursory glance. 'It's okay, for a dinky little town.'

'Auckland is not a dinky little town, it's one of New Zealand's biggest cities!'

'You want to see New York then. It's a hundred times bigger than this.'

Leila pouted. 'Well, perhaps I will see New York one day!'

'You might just at that,' Jake replied, and kissed her chastely on the nose.

While they waited at the door of the New Criterion for the others to catch up, he asked if she had a steady boyfriend. When she said no, he asked if she had any sort of boyfriend. She said no again and he smiled and slid his arm around her waist. It was nice, and Leila snuggled into his broad chest.

'You guys go inside, we'll meet you in there,' he said when the others caught up, and when Leila gave him a questioning look he bent down and whispered in her ear, 'Honey, you and I are going for a little walk.'

Taking her hand he led her further down the street until they came to a narrow, dimly lit lane running at right angles from the main street. He ducked up it, had a look around and then beckoned to her. She walked up to meet him and he pulled her into a doorway that looked like a back entrance to one of the Queen Street shops.

'What are we doing here?' she asked, although she had a very good idea.

'This,' he replied. He dropped his jacket and slid his arms around her, kissing her gently but firmly on the lips.

She responded immediately, feeling the thrill of his touch jolt all the way through her. His lips were full and warm, and he tasted faintly of cigarette smoke.

'Mmm, you're delicious,' he murmured.

'So are you,' Leila responded, and rested her head on his chest.

But Jake had other ideas. Tilting her head up, he kissed her again, nibbling her lips and sliding his tongue into her mouth.

They kissed for several minutes, teasing each other, his tongue darting and probing, then slipping out of her mouth to lick her throat and ears.

He was sporting a very firm erection, and Leila could feel it pushing urgently against her stomach.

'Oh, honey, you're gorgeous,' he said again. 'I don't think I'm going to be able to stop.'

His hand crept from the small of her back down and over her buttocks, where it rested briefly then began to massage the taut muscles insistently.

'You sure have a beautiful fanny. Firm and round and high.'

Leila was slightly startled. 'I beg your pardon?'

'Your fanny, your bottom. It's gorgeous.'

Leila giggled. 'Oh, I thought you meant something else for a minute.'

But Jake didn't seem to have heard; his hand had slid around to her front and cupped one of her breasts, his thumb flicking over the jutting nipple.

'Mmm, these are nice too.'

Leila sighed in pure pleasure, the electric shocks from his caresses shooting straight down her body to ignite between her legs. She was starting to feel weak at the knees now, and leaned back against the wall behind her.

She reached up with both hands and touched his face, feeling the hard planes of his cheekbones and the stubble on his chin and upper lip. He was so handsome, and his body under the starched material of his shirt and trousers felt hard and muscled.

His hands reached for the tiny buttons running down the front of her dress and opened them to her waist, then he lowered his head and began to lick around the edges of her bra, groaning as he reached the place where her breasts met and sliding his tongue down between them as far as it would go.

'Can I take this off?'

Leila had an unwelcome vision of someone wandering up the lane and discovering them, him with a huge erection and her with half of her clothes off and her breasts exposed for all and sundry to admire. 'No,' she said. 'Someone might come.'

'Yes, me.'

But he didn't persist, and settled for slipping his hand into her bra so that he could at least feel the smooth, silky skin and the full hardness of her nipples.

The sensation of his rough hand on her bare skin was so exciting that she barely noticed when he manoeuvred his leg between hers, but she did when he began to rhythmically push his hips against her, the hard length of his thigh pressing into the mound at the base of her belly. His hand went down and she felt the fabric of her skirt sliding up her legs until his fingers touched the bare skin of her inner thigh above her stocking. Then it was only a few incredibly erotic moments before his insistent fingers crept under the elastic of her knickers and pulled them aside.

Leila didn't think she was going to be able to stop either.

13

Jake and Leila spent every possible moment they could together, although frustratingly there weren't many. Leila was very busy at Whenuapai and Jake was training solidly with his regiment for the planned attack on Bougainville in the Solomon Islands. Their destination was now a badly kept secret. It was rumoured that the Third Marine Division would be leaving New Zealand shores some time towards the end of June, and they both dreaded it.

He bombarded her with deliveries of flowers and chocolates, nylons and cigarettes — and on one memorable occasion, a giant teddy bear he'd procured from God only knew where and sent out on the back of a motorbike with a fellow Marine making a courier delivery to the base — and she on occasion risked her job and her reputation by sneaking out of Whenuapai to meet him. They made love whenever and wherever they could, and although Leila had not been a virgin before she met Jake, she had never experienced anything like him in her life. She was enchanted by his charm and easy confidence, his heart-stopping looks, his American ways and talk of big cities and tall mountains and wide open plains. But most of all, she was besotted with his driving, insistent sexuality. He seemed to want to do it all the time and, when she was with him, so did she.

And then the inevitable had happened. Leila discovered she was pregnant halfway through May and had it confirmed by a doctor a week later — not the staff one on the base, of course, who would have been duty-bound to inform BJ immediately. Ten weeks on, the Mount Eden doctor said, give or take. She didn't tell anyone, not even Bonnie. On one hand she was secretly thrilled, but on the other there was a sense of shame at having been caught out in such a predictable way. They'd been careful to avoid such an eventuality, but obviously not careful enough.

She was nervous to her stomach when she told Jake, as she really had no idea of how he would react. He'd sworn repeatedly that he loved her, despite the fact that they'd only known each other a few short months, and she believed him, but there was no getting away from the certainty that this would change everything. There were plenty of stories of GIs who walked away from girls they'd made pregnant, avoiding them studiously until their units shipped out and leaving them alone and in desperate, shameful straits. Of course, there were other stories too, accompanied by girls proudly showing off engagement and even wedding rings. She'd gone over and over in her head how on earth to tell him, and had finally come to the conclusion that the best way was just to say it.

So she did.

Jake looked at her uncomprehendingly for a moment, then a slow smile spread across his

282

handsome face and he finally laughed out loud in delight.

'A daddy!' he exclaimed. 'I'm going to be a daddy!'

Then he scooped her up, whirled her around and then sat her down on his knee.

'What shall we call him?'

Leila giggled herself but more, she suspected guiltily, from relief than anything else. 'What if it's a girl?'

'What if it's a boy and a girl? You're a twin — isn't that sort of thing passed on?'

Oh God, I hope not, Leila thought, especially as he hadn't said anything yet about marrying her.

'What are we going to do?'

Jake kissed her nose. 'We're having a baby, aren't we?'

'Yes, but I mean, well . . . '

His eyes twinkled mischievously. 'Oh, I get it, you want to know if I'm going to make an honest woman of you, is that it?'

Leila felt a momentary stab of anger towards him, for making her have to say, yes, she did in fact want to know. So she held her tongue for as long as she could, but finally gave in.

'I do, Jake, if you don't mind,' she said slightly frostily.

'What do you want, honey? Whatever it is, you can have it.'

'No, Jake, what do you want?'

He cocked his head to one side and looked at her so fondly that Leila felt tears suddenly prick the back of her eyes. 'I want you to marry me,

Leila Morgan, that's what I want. I want you to marry me and come to America and be my wife and have dozens and dozens of children. So, will you?'

She felt as if a huge weight had been lifted off her — it was all going to turn out all right after all. She and Jake would be married, she would have their baby, and then she would go to America with him and they would be together, even if it did mean having to say goodbye to Bonnie and her parents and the rest of her family. Perhaps the war would be over even before the baby came, and then he could be here with her. That would be wonderful, she thought — perfect, in fact.

She hugged him. 'I will, Jake, of course I will.'

He heaved a sigh of relief of his own, and hugged her back.

'What was that for?'

'I thought, with you being the sort of girl you are, you might rather have the baby on your own,' he confessed. 'I thought you might not want to saddle yourself with an Oklahoma country boy like me and traipse all the way over to America. Some girls are like that, they'd rather be independent.'

None that I know of, Leila thought incredulously, especially not when there was an unplanned baby on the way.

'Would you have asked me to marry you anyway?' she asked.

Jake thought for a moment, and smiled again. 'I think so, honey, yes. I love you.'

He bought her a ring, a ruby flanked with

small diamonds, which she carried in her tunic pocket at work rather than invite attention by wearing it on her engagement finger, and they booked a date at the registry office.

She didn't tell Bonnie until the very last moment, for fear that her sister would give her advice she really didn't want to hear, advice that might concern the folly of marrying a Marine three weeks before he was due to ship out, even if a baby was involved. Bonnie had always been the more sensible twin, and although Leila was sure deep down that her sister would support her, sometimes you couldn't tell with Bonnie.

You certainly couldn't, she reflected later, after listening to Bonnie go on for a good ten minutes about what on earth Leila thought she was doing, and how could she have been so stupid as to let herself fall pregnant.

'I didn't *let* myself fall pregnant!' Leila protested when Bonnie had finally shut up. 'It just happened!'

'I'm not surprised, the way you two have been going at it like high country rabbits.'

'That's good coming from you!' Leila retorted. 'You and Danny have hardly been paragons of virtue!'

They glared at each angrily for a moment, then Bonnie asked, 'What *is* a paragon, anyway?'

'I don't know.'

Bonnie sighed. 'Are you sure you're doing the right thing? It's not too late to call it off, you know. You could go home and have the baby there. It wouldn't be the first time we've had a baby in the family conceived on the wrong side of the sheets. Look at us. And Liam,' she added. 'God, and Duncan, and Uncle Joseph. What's wrong with us all? What a dreadful family we are.'

'No more dreadful than anyone else, I'd say. But everyone got married in the end, remember. I'd be the only unwed mother.'

'Gran didn't, and neither did Liam's mother, whoever she was.'

'But that was only because Uncle Ian died in the war.'

'You don't know that for a fact.'

Leila ignored her, lit a cigarette and flicked the match out of her cubicle window. 'I'll probably have to go home anyway. I don't fancy having the baby up here in one of those homes for girls too silly to avoid getting themselves into trouble. Even though I am one. And Mum and Dad would be ropable if I did that, anyway.'

'I'd say they'll be ropable anyway,' Bonnie said gloomily. 'But really, it's an enormous step, marrying someone you've only known a few months and then trotting off to America after him, isn't it? And it might be ages before that happens, if it ever does.'

'What do you mean?'

'Well, we both know girls married to blokes in the RAF and they've been waiting two years to go to England.'

'But that's England, this is America.'

'I'll bet it's the same thing — no essential travel until after the war.'

'That's not really what you meant, though, is it?'

'Not really. What if you get there and it turns out that all the two of you really had was a wartime fling? What if he's already married?'

'He isn't already married.'

'Leila, what if he doesn't even make it back to America?'

Leila was losing her patience. 'Bonnie, he will make it back and I'm marrying him and that's all there is too it. I'd really like you to be there, and I know Jake's asking Danny to be his best man, but if you don't want to come, that's up to you.'

'Of course I'll come. I just want to make sure you've really thought about it, that's all.'

'I have. I've thought about nothing else. I'm pregnant, Bonnie, and I love Jake desperately. That's a good enough reason to marry someone, isn't it?'

'Maybe, but I think you should go and talk to Aunty Ri about it. She might be old but she certainly isn't stupid. She could give you some good advice.'

But Leila didn't want good advice, and she definitely didn't want it from Riria Adams *before* she married Jake. She was very fond of Riria, but knew in her heart that the old lady would say something extremely sensible and considered and wise, something that might start Leila really thinking about what she was about to do. No, she didn't want that at all.

Bonnie did attend the wedding, of course, and was as enthusiastic a bridesmaid as any bride could want. She helped Leila starch and iron her uniform to perfection the night before, and held Leila's posy of orchids while she and Jake signed their marriage documents. There were only the four of them at the short but rather sweet ceremony, plus the marriage celebrant, a benevolent old bloke in a dusty black suit with a perpetual smile on his face and an oddly high-pitched voice that made Bonnie and Leila avoid each other's eyes for fear of bursting into giggles.

And perhaps Bonnie too had been thinking about the boys' impending departure, because after they'd left the registry office and ventured into the lounge bar of a nearby hotel for a celebratory drink, she dragged Leila off to the ladies' and showed her the sparkling new ring on her left hand.

Leila threw her arms around her sister. 'Oh Bonnie, that's wonderful! We can be war brides together!'

'Except that I'm not a bride, am I? I'm only engaged. Which reminds me, how did Jake manage to get permission to get married?'

Leila gave Bonnie a funny look. 'What do you mean? He doesn't need to get permission. Does he?'

'Oh, *Leila*!' Bonnie shook her head and blew out her cheeks in frustration. 'He has to have permission from his CO, and a chaplain and God knows who else, and you're supposed to have been interviewed by all sorts of people and assessed for American citizenship and what have you. Haven't you done all that?'

'Well, no, and you know I haven't; you see me every day.'

'But weren't you . . . oh hell, ever since you've

been talking about getting married I've assumed all those times you sneaked off the base you were . . . oh, never mind. Leila, do you realise how serious this is?'

'No,' Leila said truthfully, and wasn't at all sure she did want to know.

They moved away from the handbasin as a woman came out of a toilet stall, and waited silently for her to wash her hands and leave, even though she must have heard every word they'd been saying.

'If Jake didn't get permission,' Bonnie went on, 'he'll be in an awful lot of trouble if you get found out. He could be shipped out tomorrow, or court-martialled, or, God, I don't know.' She grabbed Leila's hand. 'Come on, we're going to talk to him about this right now.'

She marched determinedly into the lounge bar with Leila trailing behind her, and sat down next to Jake, who was just starting on a large glass of beer.

'Hi, sis,' he said.

'Sis, my eye,' Bonnie shot back. 'Did you get official permission to marry Leila?'

Jake put his beer down. 'No, ma'am.'

'Don't you ma'am me. Why not?'

'Because she's pregnant and we're shipping out in a few weeks. I knew I wouldn't get it and I wanted to marry her. Simple. What the CO doesn't know won't hurt him.' He patted Leila's hand. 'I'm sorry, honey, but it was the only way I could think of to do it.'

Bonnie saw the logic in his argument, but she was still angry. 'What if it hurts Leila?'

'It won't. We're legally married. When the war's over I'll write and request that she join me.'

Bonnie's voice rose another octave. 'And how do you know you won't get found out?'

'Because the four of us here, and that old coot in the registry office, are the only ones who know Leila and I are married.'

Danny said uncomfortably, 'Bonnie, calm down honey, people are starting to look at us.'

'I don't care, Danny. And how long have you known about this?'

Danny went red. 'A week or so.'

'Why didn't you say something?' Bonnie demanded.

'I didn't think it was any of my business. And I still don't.'

That seemed to bring the conversation to a halt. Bonnie asked Danny to order two gin and tonics from the bar, and sat in silence until they arrived.

'I suppose,' she said eventually, 'it will be all right, providing it's kept a secret. Are we all agreed on that?'

Danny and Jake said yes immediately, and Leila nodded in agreement.

'It's still my wedding day, Bonnie,' she said after a moment. 'Couldn't we just enjoy it? The boys will be gone soon, and I'd like to make the most of it while they're still here.'

'Oh, love, of course we can,' Bonnie replied. She raised her glass. 'Here's to my sister Leila and my new brother-in-law Jake, and my fiancé Danny. Here's to all of us. May the road rise to meet us, and may the wind be always at our backs.'

★ ★ ★

Bonnie and Leila couldn't keep the secret, of course. For a start, they had to tell Riria when they went to visit her a fortnight later.

Riria's house in Parnell Rise was big, old and gracious. Her husband John Adams had operated his medical clinic from a downstairs room before he'd gone off and been killed in the Boer War, and Riria had lived in the house ever since.

She welcomed them with a kiss each, sat them down in the eclectically decorated front parlour, which smelled faintly of cinnamon and warm dust, and asked if they would like some afternoon tea.

'Yes please, but would you like a hand?' Leila asked. Riria waved her away.

'You should be resting in your condition, girl,' she said, and disappeared into the hall with a rustle of her long taffeta skirt.

Bonnie and Leila looked at each other. What?

Riria returned minutes later carrying a tray laden with a teapot, cups, a milk jug and a plate piled with three sorts of cake.

As usual she was dressed from head to toe in black. Her long silver hair hung down her back in stark contrast against the darkness of her clothes.

'Now, tamariki, what is it you need to see me about?'

'You said a minute ago, 'in my condition',' Leila began.

'You are pregnant, child.'

'Er, yes. How did you know?'

'Your smell. A woman's smell changes when she is hapu.'

'Oh. Well, that is sort of what we've come to talk to you about.'

Bonnie poured the tea and waited for her sister to explain further. And waited and waited.

Finally, she said herself, 'We have to be blunt about this, Aunty. Leila is, as you've already noticed, pregnant. She's about three and a half months on. The father is an American who is due to go overseas in three days.'

'Ah,' Riria said knowingly. 'The Third Marine Division, bound for the Solomons.'

'How do you know that?' Leila asked, surprised.

'Everyone does, dear.'

'Anyway,' Bonnie went on, 'Leila has married this Marine, without knowing that he hadn't received permission from his commanding officer. It's an offence according to the US Navy to marry without permission and there'll be hell to pay if anyone finds out. What do you think Leila should do about it?'

'No, Bonnie, that's *not* it,' Leila said tetchily. 'I'm very happy to be Mrs Jake Kelly, Aunty Ri. I need some advice on whether to stay here in Auckland to have the baby, or go home to Kenmore.'

'I would have thought that was not a difficult decision to make at all,' Riria replied. 'Who would not want to have their baby with their whanau?'

Leila sighed. 'All right, what I *really* want to know, Aunty, is how do you think Mum and Dad and Gran will take the news?'

'As well as you would if your daughter was pregnant to a man you have not met, who comes from a foreign country and who is about to go off to fight the Japanese.'

'I thought you might say that.'

Riria tut-tutted. 'But that does not mean they will not welcome you, e hine. Go home, that is the *only* thing you can do. You must think first of your child.'

Leila looked as if she were about to cry. 'I don't know how to tell them, Aunty.'

'Like this,' Riria replied. 'It is very simple.'

And she got up from her chair and went out.

'What's she doing?' said Bonnie after a moment.

Leila shrugged, and they sat there for several minutes until they heard Riria speaking to someone in the hall.

Then it suddenly dawned on Leila. 'Oh *Christ*! She's telephoning them!'

She rushed out of the room but it was too late; Riria had already been connected.

'Yes, we are all fine here, too . . . Really? Well, that is wonderful news. I am sure they will be very happy together . . . Yes, I expect they will. Tamar, I am ringing you about Leila . . . No, no, she is all right, but there is one small matter . . . No, she is fine, but it seems that she has married because she is three months

293

pregnant . . . ' There was a brief silence from Riria, then, 'Tamar, are you still on the line? . . . Yes, an American Marine . . . No, I have only just this minute found out . . . Yes, they are both here . . . I do not think that would be a good idea at the moment, e hine, do you? . . . No, it would be better I think if Keely comes up herself; it is a very long journey for someone of our age . . . Yes, I know, but these things can always be overcome, and sometimes they even work out for the best, as you know yourself . . . Wednesday? Yes, yes, I will. Goodbye, Tamar. Arohanui.'

She hung up and turned to Leila, who was waiting nervously for the verdict.

'That was your grandmother. Your mother will be arriving on Wednesday to collect you. Would you like to stay here, or go back to Whenuapai until she arrives?'

'I have to go back to the base — I haven't said anything to them yet. But I'll try to spend as much time with Jake before he goes as I can. I *love* him, Aunty. What if I never see him again?'

Riria watched as tears tricked down Leila's smooth, pale cheeks, and remembered the day that her darling John had left to join the New Zealand contingents in South Africa.

She held out her arms.

★ ★ ★

The girls went back to the base, and that night Bonnie helped Leila sneak out to meet Jake. They managed to spend one whole honeymoon night together at the luxurious Grand Hotel — after Leila had first produced their marriage certificate for the satisfaction of the concierge who would have nothing to do with unmarried couples using his lovely rooms as venues for their immoral trysts — and then two days later Jake, and Danny, were gone.

Leila and Bonnie were not able to see them off because they were on duty, but they appreciated the commiserations of their friends who knew they both had sweethearts shipping out. No one, however, knew yet that Leila had married hers, or that she was pregnant. Except perhaps for Peggy, whose knowing glance had lingered more than once on Leila's slightly swelling belly.

Keely arrived at the base the following day, and went straight to the administration block and asked to speak with her daughters. When Bonnie and Leila, working in the SWO's office, were advised that their mother was here, they glanced at each other apprehensively, took deep breaths and went to meet her in the visitors' room.

Keely sat gazing out of the window, watching a transport plane lumbering down the runway, her face pale and the bags under her eyes prominent after her long train journey. Her gloves were rolled up in her lap and she'd taken off her hat and set it on her small suitcase on the floor. She looked tired, and very sad, but she didn't seem angry. She stood and greeted them wearily.

'Hello, darlings,' she said as she kissed them. 'I'm sorry, I've come straight from the train station and I'm rather worn out.'

Bonnie and Leila were disconcerted — they had been expecting one of their mother's more spectacular tirades at the very least.

'Now,' she said resignedly once they were all seated, 'tell me everything, right from the beginning.'

So Leila did, hesitantly at first, but soon the whole story came out.

As she listened, Keely was flooded with memories of the day she'd become aware of her own unplanned pregnancy, and how hopeless and helpless she had felt. She had married Owen, of course, but had not loved him at first, although she'd certainly fancied him enough to sleep with him. Did these sorts of things perpetuate themselves in families? If certain events occurred often enough down through successive generations, did they became almost expected, and therefore acceptable? She had been very lucky with Owen — with his patience, his perseverance and his love — and she prayed that Leila would be just as lucky with this young American man she had chosen. She certainly hoped Leila would make a better mother than she'd ever been to her own daughters. And it would be even harder for Leila, because the father of her child would quite possibly be away for some time yet, and might not come back at all.

When Leila finished speaking, it was Keely's turn.

'Leila,' she began gently, 'your father and I were very disappointed when your gran told us what you'd done. But this pregnancy isn't the end of the world. We're very happy for you to come home to have the baby, and you know Gran would love to have a little one in the house again.'

Leila said in a voice that was beginning to wobble, 'I thought you would both be really angry with me.'

'Oh, we were, dear, very. Your father went off for most of the afternoon and wouldn't speak to anyone until the next day, and I threw one of Gran's best soup tureens against the kitchen wall. But we've had a day or two to think about it, and it isn't as if it hasn't happened in our family before, is it? We're still a little upset, though, about your decision to marry this boy, and rather hurt because you didn't tell us or ask for our advice. We didn't even know you had a young man. I would like to have met him before he left. Your father was all for rushing up and talking to the lad — at the very least — but after we'd talked about it we decided it wouldn't make much difference one way or the other, given that you'd already married him. We're hoping we'll meet him eventually.'

'Well, maybe not, Mum,' Leila said guiltily. 'He'll probably be sent back to America as soon as the war's over, and then he'll be discharged from the Marines.'

'So he isn't a career soldier?'

Leila shook her head. 'He was drafted for the duration.'

'And you want to go and live in America?'

'Yes, but there's no reason we can't come back for holidays.'

'It's a bit of a trek, dear.'

But Leila didn't want to talk about that. 'I won't be going for ages anyway, I'd say. Possibly not even until the war's over.'

'Mmm. Have you told this Mrs Buckley-Jones yet about your predicament?'

'Er, no, I was hoping you'd come with me when I tell her. I'll have to leave the air force straight away, I expect.'

'Well, there's no point in putting it off any longer. Where is she now?'

'In her office, probably. I'll go and ask if it's convenient for her to see us.'

'That's a good girl. Oh, and is there any chance of a cup of tea? I could really do with one.'

'I'll see, there's usually an urn on the boil in the mess.'

When she'd gone, Keely said to Bonnie, 'What's he really like, this Jake Kelly?'

Bonnie looked uncomfortable. 'Well, I don't really know, Mum. We all went out together but I never got to know him really well, but Leila thinks he's absolutely wonderful.'

'Clearly. And you don't?'

'Oh, no, he's nice enough. Very charming, very good-looking. I can see why she's fallen for him, I must admit. And he seems kind, and he's funny, and I do believe he genuinely loves her.'

'Where's he from? Do you know anything about his family?'

'He's from Oklahoma and his family are farmers. Cotton, I think he said.'

'Well, she's used to farm life, I suppose, but I

expect it's all very different over there.'

Bonnie shrugged. 'I don't know. He never really said much about his home.'

'I imagine that's the trouble with these American boys. You can never really tell what you're getting. What's yours like?'

'Sorry?'

Keely nodded towards the ring on her daughter's hand. 'I see you've formed some sort of an attachment too.'

Bonnie blushed. 'Yes, I'm engaged. I was waiting until after this to tell you. I thought Leila might be enough for you to go on with. His name is Danny Hartman, he's twenty-five and he comes from New Jersey. He was training to be a doctor when America came into the war, and he's a medic with the Marines. He's the youngest of five children, a surprise baby, he said, and his father's retired now, but he was a doctor too. An obstetrician. Danny's going back to medical school after the war.'

'At least he sounds like he has prospects.' Keely sighed. 'I suppose you'll be off as well, then.'

'I expect so, but I didn't think it would be a good idea to get married now. You know, with the way things are.'

'No, but then you don't have to.'

'No.'

Leila came back, and handed her mother a cup of tea. 'She can see us in ten minutes, she said, if we don't mind waiting.'

Mrs Buckley-Jones's office was small, and narrowly saved from military anonymity by

299

several pretty flower paintings on the walls and a vase of lavender hydrangeas on a bookcase behind her desk.

She ushered them in and introduced herself to Keely.

'You've a fine pair of girls, Mrs Murdoch, and it's a pleasure to work with them.' She sat down behind her desk. 'What can I do for you today?'

Keely looked at Leila expectantly.

In a way she was proud of her daughter. As Leila told Mrs Buckley-Jones what had happened she held her head up, her voice was steady and she didn't falter once.

Mrs Buckley-Jones made a steeple out of her hands, and rested the tips of her fingers against her lips.

'Well, Leila, I must say this is disappointing news; but these things happen, I understand that. You realise that you will have to leave the WAAF immediately? Your behaviour and your, ah, condition completely contravene the rules, and could be seen as a bad example to the other girls.'

Once again Keely was uncomfortably reminded of events from her own past.

Leila nodded. 'I'm going back home to Hawke's Bay. I'm sorry if I've disappointed you, Mrs Buckley-Jones. I enjoyed working here very much.'

'You made a notable contribution, Leila, and I liked having you. When you were actually on the base,' she added archly.

'Er, yes, thank you.'

'Right. Mrs Murdoch, will you be accompanying Leila home?'

'Yes, we'll be going back on the train tomorrow.'

'Then I'll see to the paperwork, and I suggest, Leila, that you go and pack your things and perhaps say goodbye to your friends. Unless, that is, you'd rather just leave?'

'I'd like to say goodbye, if that's all right.'

'Off you go then. Mrs Murdoch, you're more than welcome to give her a hand to pack.'

Bonnie was waiting in the reception area by the time Leila was ready to go. This was the first time in their lives they would really be apart, and she felt tears at the back of her eyes. She hugged her sister tightly.

'Take care. Look after that baby, and I'll be home as soon as I get a decent leave. Oh, sorry, I mean a *liberty*. And write me lots of letters. I want to know everything that's happening, all right?'

Leila nodded, and blew her nose.

Keely stood back and watched them, her own eyes filling up. She had something she needed to tell them, and now that Leila's affairs had been put in order she couldn't put it off any longer.

'Girls, I'm afraid I have some bad news. I didn't want to tell you before, but Drew has been taken prisoner by the Japanese. We think he might be in Burma now.'

14

Drew shook his head, but carefully, because he had another bad headache.

'No, I think the potatoes should be mashed, with grated cheese on top and then lightly grilled.'

'With roast beef?' Tim protested. 'No, you have to have roast potatoes with roast beef, lovely, crispy golden ones.'

'Well, all right then,' Drew said, 'I don't want roast beef, I want sausages. Pure pork ones.'

Don disagreed. 'Well, you're both wrong, as far as I'm concerned. The only way to eat potatoes, full *stop*, is to boil them, then add just a sprinkle of salt and serve them with lots of butter.'

Tim considered this. 'New potatoes?'

'Of course,' Don replied.

'Yes, but new potatoes are more of a summer thing really, aren't they, and we're having a roast.'

'You can have a roast in the summer,' Don insisted. 'We always had a roast every Sunday no matter what, summer or winter.'

Tim folded his arms. 'But Drew's having sausages now.'

But Drew had forgotten about his sausages and was wishing that Don and Tim would both shut up. His headache was getting worse by the

302

second, and he knew, with a sinking sense of dread, that it was going to turn into another migraine.

There would be no roast beef for dinner tonight, or sausages, or potatoes in any shape or form. What they might get was a small cup each of partially boiled rice and, if they were lucky, a shred of dried fish or perhaps a wedge of raw onion. Occasionally it was soya beans instead of rice, and from time to time there was a sort of pale watery soup with paper-thin slices of vegetable from the prison garden floating in it. Until recently this might have been supplemented with an egg or a tomato or a tiny piece of fresh fish bought or traded from the locals outside the prison gates, but this did not occur regularly enough to have any lasting nutritional benefit, and as the months had passed the Burmese people seemed to have had less and less to spare.

The food rations had been pretty diabolical ever since Drew had been captured nearly ten months ago when his ship, the Royal Navy cruiser *Exeter*, had gone down at the hands of the Japanese fleet in the Java Sea. At first they'd all thought they were going to be shot as they were pulled from the water by the Japanese sailors, but instead they'd been taken to the old Dutch barracks at Macassar, in Celebes. Well, some of them had. Where the other survivors from the *Exeter* were now, no one knew. The prison at Macassar had at least been clean and in fairly good repair, but even then the food was woefully inadequate. They were given the bare minimum of clothing — half of them were almost naked after their dunk in the sea — but no shoes. Drew, who'd arrived at the prison clad only in a pair trousers with one leg torn off at the crutch, was issued two pairs of shorts and a singlet, and, in retrospect, considered himself to have been lucky. They'd thought conditions at Macassar were appalling, but now he and the other chaps would give just about anything to be back there.

After a month at Macassar they were moved up to Burma and incarcerated in their current POW camp — Rangoon Jail, a huge, grim, imposing prison that had once, ironically, been operated by the British. The compound was configured like a wheel within a square: inside the high perimeter wall were half a dozen or so wedge-shaped sections divided off by barriers, and within each section were the 'spokes', long, double-storeyed blocks of prison cells surrounded by a large yard, along with various sheds and other smaller buildings, all in varying states of disrepair. At the centre of the wheel stood a tall, incongruously grand house where the Japanese commander lived. There were very few trees in the compound, but even they made a marked contrast to the miles and miles of grey concrete and tin. It was a thoroughly depressing and dismal place.

Drew went back to his rattan mat and lay down. Most of the time he counted himself very fortunate to be sharing a cell with three chaps from the *Exeter*, one of whom — Tim Scanlon — was also a New Zealander. Some of the other inmates, and there were hundreds and hundreds of them, lived in single cells, which he wouldn't have been able to tolerate — he liked company, and always had. But these days, when he was feeling so unwell much of the time, he could have done with a bit of peace and quiet. They played this game often, planning favourite menus, and Drew usually enjoyed it, especially when they got to the pudding bit, but today he just felt too sick.

Before banging his head leaping off the *Exeter* as she went down, and then hitting it again so hard when he was in the water that he'd been unconscious for nearly twelve hours, he'd never had a headache in his life. But now he seemed to be having them all the time. They'd started gradually, perhaps one a fortnight after he'd been taken prisoner, but now he was getting them every week, and sometimes they could drag on for three or four days. He could always tell when they were starting — first the extreme sensitivity to light, then sound and smell, and finally the excruciating pain — but the knowledge did him very little good because the medical care in the camp was dismal. The Japs issued about fifteen fresh bandages a month, to service the entire complement of prisoners, plus a small bottle of iodine and maybe a dozen assorted tablets, but there was certainly nothing suitable for severe headaches, or any other sort of pain, if it came to that. It was well known that the bastards had stockpiles of quinine for malaria and emetine to combat dysentery, but they kept those for themselves. There was no point to letting on you were sick anyway, as the Japs regarded illness as a sign of weakness and punished anyone forced to admit they were too weak to attend parade or work at prison chores.

Almost everyone had already contracted malaria or dysentery, or both — a month ago Drew had spent a whole week lying in a pool of his own reeking shit, despite the best efforts of his mates to keep him clean and comfortable — and squashy, swollen bellies and puffy ankles were clear signs that chaps were beginning to suffer from the malnutrition-related diseases, beri-beri and pellagra. The sanitary arrangements were extremely basic — a water tap per prison block, and the latrines were wooden seats mounted over basins on the ground which had to be emptied regularly into open drains at the back of the camp. It was probably only a matter of time before someone contracted cholera.

But there were doctors and medics among the prisoners, and they'd worked hard to set up a hospital in the camp for the sick and wounded, although they had almost no medical supplies, and only crude medical tools they'd fashioned themselves. The doctor in Drew's block, McCaffrey, was a major in the Royal Navy. When Drew had first gone to see him, he'd suggested that Drew was experiencing migraines, possibly brought on either by the stress of being a prisoner or the constant, debilitating heat, but more likely a result of whacking his head. He couldn't offer any treatment, except to mention that he was doing his best to get hold of some of the Thai opium he knew was available on the black market. It was a matter of coming up with something the guards were willing to accept as payment. He was talking to some of the RAF chaps at the moment: they were in a better position to offer some sort of currency simply because they'd been wearing more clothes — with more pockets containing items such as cigarette lighters — when they were captured. Along with watches and jewellery, those items had been very carefully hidden away for the day when they could be used for barter. And the chaps were also making decorative boxes, palm oil soap, wooden dolls, shaving brushes and other gadgets that appealed to the guards. If and when they were able to get their hands on some opium, McCaffrey had said, and if there was enough to go around, then there might be some for Drew. But he'd also told him, as kindly as possible, not to hold his breath; there were men in the camp, amputees and such, in severe need of pain relief, and any opium would have to go to them first.

McCaffrey was a decent bloke and obviously a competent doctor, but Drew had wondered afterwards if the man really knew what he was talking about when it came to migraines. He didn't have a clue himself — in his experience the only people prone to migraines were histrionic middle-aged matrons, or young women of nervous disposition who had to lie down in darkened rooms all day. But there was certainly something wrong. The headaches started innocently enough, a mere niggle at the base of his skull, and always in the same place, but then the pain worsened over a period of hours until it was immense and the nausea was chronic and he wasn't even able to move. Even the most shallow breathing caused sickening bolts of pain to blast and pound through his head, and it went on and on and on until he thought he might not be able to stand it any more. During several episodes lately, he'd been convinced that if he'd had a revolver he would have shot himself, just to stop the agony. As it was he could only lie there on his mat, with his mates tiptoeing around him, and pray that the pain would subside soon. The only good thing about the headaches was that he felt almost healthy in comparison when they'd gone, and there weren't many chaps in the camp who could say that.

But he too was beginning to suffer from malnutrition. The shorts he'd been given at Macassar now had to be held up with string as he'd lost a lot of weight. He was six foot one and had weighed over fourteen healthy, muscled stones at the beginning of the year; he estimated that he now weighed around ten, which was far too light for his big frame. His teeth were beginning to feel loose too, and he was covered in suppurating open sores, which were very difficult to heal in the heat and filth of the prison. There was talk that one poor chap in the block might even have to have his lower leg amputated shortly because of a huge ulcer on his shin.

He opened his eyes, closed them again quickly and rested his arm over his face — the light was just too bright to bear. At least it was marginally cooler inside the concrete cells than it was outside. The barred but open windows helped. And there was plenty of room in the cell, not that any of the chaps had much to put in it. Don and Keith, the fourth bloke in their cell who was currently on kitchen cleaning duty, had found themselves wooden boards and laid them across boxes to make beds, but Drew and Tim preferred to have their mats on the ground. The ceiling was criss-crossed with ropes on which their meagre clothes, threadbare blankets and cleaning rags hung to air, and two pails of water — boiled as per the doctor's instructions — sat against a wall, one for drinking and one for personal ablutions. They all shaved daily, and although it was pointless, really, it gave a man a sense of dignity to face the day with a cleanly shaved face.

Keith came in, dripping with sweat from the heat of the kitchen fires, slipped his home-made rubber sandals off and collapsed on his bed.

'What are we having?' Don asked immediately.

'Same old shite, rice an' a bit o' cabbage, one shred each,' Keith replied scathingly. Even though the dark lines of the tattoos adorning his forearms — a crown and anchor on the left and a very buxom mermaid on the right — were contracting as the flesh beneath them shrank, he, like the others, was not yet at the point where he felt grateful for anything at all to eat. 'Drew got one o' his heads again?'

'Started an hour ago.'

'Poor bastard,' Keith said.

309

Drew didn't even bother to uncover his eyes. He would not eat his food in case he threw it up and wasted it, but it would be kept for him — out of reach of the rats and cockroaches — for when he felt better, providing it was still edible by then. If it did look like going off before he could eat, then someone else would be allowed it. But he was grateful for Keith's commiseration. For months he'd been too scared to say anything about his headaches to the others for fear of ridicule, or of them thinking he was malingering to avoid having to do any work, but they'd all seen him vomiting until his nose bled, and then shitting uncontrollably when the migraine was beginning to subside, and they were quite sympathetic towards him, particularly Tim, who always brought him a rag soaked in cool water for his forehead. It would have been so much harder to bear if they weren't sympathetic, or even accepting. It was humiliating enough suffering bloody headaches when so many of the chaps were so much worse off.

His cell mates were good sorts. He'd been good mates with Tim — who had also made his own way to England at the start of the war to join the Royal Navy — for quite a while now, and he knew Keith and Don of course, because they'd been serving on the same ship. Tim was from a small settlement on the Taranaki coast, where his parents owned the local grocery shop, and had apparently spent much of his spare time sailing in the South Taranaki Bight in a small boat he'd built himself. He talked about the boat wistfully and often, and swore that the first thing he'd do when he got back home would be to take her out. Drew was older than Tim by two years, but they got on very well and had shared many drunken and raucous shore leaves together.

Don Kerr was an Englishman and Keith Wallace a Scotsman, originally from Glasgow. They were hard men, born sailors, handy with their fists and very capable. So was Tim, as he'd demonstrated many times in brawls, although he had a surprisingly compassionate side as well. Drew came from a different background, but any distinctions soon ceased to matter, especially as he refused to enter the navy as an ensign and chose to enlist as an able seaman.

None of them had yet lost their spirit, which was both a blessing and a bit of a wonder. They'd been in Rangoon for less than a year, but in that time had been starved, beaten, blatantly deprived of Red Cross packages, forced to work when they were unwell, and were completely at the whim of the temperamental Japanese guards and the camp commander, a man they rarely saw but hated with a vengeance. But they were managing all right, or at least that's what they told themselves. The doctors were doing what they could medically, and had set up rosters for regular inspection of the latrines, such as they were, and of the kitchens, in an effort to minimise the spread of disease. The doctors in fact copped a lot of flak from the Japs on behalf of the men too sick to work. They argued vehemently with the Japs at sick parade every morning to keep their patients out of the working parties, even the poor blokes too ill to stand, and were often severely punished for it.

Every man up to it had a job to do, not for the Japanese but for the benefit and morale of the prisoners. They kept their cells and environment as clean as they could, they made things to trade, and for themselves, and to keep themselves busy, they talked and congregated whenever they could, although the Japanese had forbidden meetings. This was a blow because it prevented any organised recreation, educational classes or even religious services — anything that would break the ghastly monotony of prison life. But it could have been worse; they could have been RAF, who were for some reason treated even more appallingly by the Japs. They were jammed together in the smallest cells, given filthy old sacks for bedding and only half the food apportioned to the other prisoners, and were beaten for merely talking to each other. Drew was extremely pleased he was a sailor, and hoped like hell that Liam was never shot down over Japanese-occupied territory.

He rolled over and bent his neck at a deliberate angle in an effort to relieve some of the agony in his skull. He closed his eyes and hoped for sleep. His headaches always followed him in his dreams, but the pain seemed further away then, muffled and just ever so slightly more manageable.

★　★　★

Mercifully, the migraine had gone yesterday afternoon, and he was back seeing McCaffrey

312

again. The hospital had been set up in a large wooden shed, and some of the chaps with carpentering skills had removed sections of the walls and replaced them with blinds made from bamboo held together with wool from unravelled socks. The blinds could be rolled up when it was really hot, or lowered to keep the patients dry when the rains came. There were about forty men in the hospital at the moment, so it was almost full.

McCaffrey had a screened-off cubby-hole at the end of the shed. He sat at his small table, looking gravely at Drew with his thin legs crossed and his hands in his lap.

'I'm sorry, old boy, but there really isn't much I can suggest. We do have a bit of opium now, and I hope there'll be enough left for the next headache, but I can't guarantee that. As you probably saw when you came in, we're pretty busy at the moment.'

Drew had tried once again to explain the extent of his misery when he had a headache — without actually mentioning that he had considered suicide, which would be seen as cowardly — but wasn't sure he'd succeeded. Oh, he knew the doctor was aware that the bloody things really hurt, but wasn't sure he'd grasped quite how hellishly awful Drew felt about it all, especially about not being able to do his chores. It made him feel inadequate and ashamed, as if he were letting the side down. And he was — every time he couldn't get off his mat, someone else, probably someone more ill than he was, had to do the work instead.

313

He opened his mouth to have another go at explaining himself, but McCaffrey held up his hand.

'Look, I do know how you must feel about all this. Well, I don't, because I've never had a migraine myself, thank Christ, but I know how damnably debilitating they can be so I've a fair idea of what it must be like at your end. But I'll say again that I think these headaches are a result of your head injuries, so there's no point going about thinking you've suddenly turned into some sort of sad sack with a 'delicate condition'. You haven't. Bad headaches aren't uncommon after a heavy blow to the head, and severe migraines aren't unknown either.' He twiddled his moustache for a moment. 'Does the heat seem to set them off?'

'Not so much the heat, but I think being in really bright sun might.'

'As in when you're working outside?'

Drew nodded.

'That's a bit of a bugger, given that we're in the tropics. Do you think you've the stomach to pick maggots out of a stinking great sore while the owner of said sore screams his head off?'

'Pardon?'

'Nursing duties, man, could you do it?'

'Er, I don't know.'

'Well, you're about to find out. You're now a medic attached to the hospital. It's never bright and sunny in here. Fortunate, really, because we're starting to get a lot of eye lesions from lack of vitamins, and bright light can be extremely painful.'

314

'But I'm not a medic. I'm only on the Japs' list as an able seaman.'

'Well, you're a medic now. I'll lie and say there's been a mistake.' McCaffrey uncrossed his legs and slapped his bony knees decisively. 'It's the best I can do, old boy. And if you do get a real stinker, you can just lie down yourself until it goes away. All right?'

Drew nodded, delighted. He could make a real contribution now, and if one of his sodding bloody migraines came on, well, where better to be than the hospital?

'But I have to warn you,' McCaffrey went on, 'it's hard work in here, a lot of it not very nice. It can be a bit stomach-turning.'

★　★　★

It was. His first job was to clean up a man brought in by his mates after twenty-four hours of constant vomiting and diarrhoea. The poor wretch was covered in shit and spew from head to foot, and was so weak he couldn't do anything to help himself. He was weeping as well from the pain of the severe griping in his bowels, and every time they moved he let out a moan he couldn't smother.

'I'm sorry, mate,' he said again and again, and Drew shook his head and waved his hand dismissively as he finally finished wiping him down.

'It's only shit, don't worry about it. I was up to my eyebrows in my own the other day. Stinks though, eh?'

And it did, too. It was absolutely eye-watering, and Drew wondered if he would stink of it constantly himself from now on.

The patient tried to laugh, but was suddenly gripped by another spasm. His bowels opened again and a great flood of watery green matter whooshed out from between his legs and soaked the mat beneath him, and the clean shorts Drew had rather short-sightedly given him.

'Perhaps if you just went naked, and put a bit of towel over yourself?' Drew suggested kindly as he got to his feet and picked up the bowl containing the dirty washing water. He'd have to get another lot now.

And it went on like that, day after day, although there was a fair bit of variety in what Drew was required to do. On his fourth day he was asked to assist when a doctor — not McCaffrey this time but an army doctor called Paterson — used a bamboo 'needle' and distilled rainwater with added rock salt, to rehydrate a man almost comatose from the effects of dysentery. A small cut was made in a vein in the man's arm — a vein which took four different attempts to locate because of his poor condition — the needle inserted and the water dripped in. It was crude, but the man recovered. Drew hadn't been involved in any of the tricky bits, and had only cleaned up the blood afterwards and kept an eye on the patient, but he'd been amazed at the ingenuity the doctors were using to help their patients. Crushed charcoal in water was also given to try and slow bowel activity, and the precious opium was administered when patients were unable to cope with the pain. Knives and forks were modified as surgical instruments, and sharpened spoons were sterilised in boiling water and used — without the benefit of anaesthetic — to scrape out the worst of the tropical ulcers that afflicted almost everyone.

Drew felt helpless, and sickened, a lot of the time, but he did everything he was asked. Sometimes the only panacea available was compassion, but he discovered he had a surprising reserve of that particular emotion and was more than willing to share it. But sometimes he suspected that his motives might be selfish, because the more he did for the patients, the better he felt himself. His headaches did not go away, far from it, but he found that being of some use to someone stopped him from thinking about himself too deeply.

He became very expert at detecting the early signs of emerging maladies in others, and was on at his cell mates constantly about washing their hands after using the latrines and before and after eating. Keith and Don tended to laugh at him, but Drew observed that they were actually very fastidious about their personal hygiene. Nobody actively courted dysentery, and even less the dreaded cholera that had now broken out in the camp.

The first victim had been brought into the hospital five days ago. The poor bloke, an RAF chap — so they had been bloody lucky to be allowed to bring him into the hospital at all — had been carried in by his mates at the instigation of his prison block's doctor, with intense muscle cramps, glassy eyes, a barely audible voice and a milky white fluid coming out of him at both ends. Over the next five hours his body dehydrated with incredible speed, in spite of the administering of the salt water. In fact, as the doctors had looked on in growing horror, he'd dried up and become unrecognisable — and then he'd died. So after that every cholera victim in the hospital — and there were a lot of them — had a small bamboo disc attached to his wrist so that he could be identified should his condition deteriorate. What had been particularly awful was that the RAF chap was fairly new in the camp, still quite a fit and healthy bloke, and he'd succumbed appallingly quickly. Drew had washed himself almost raw after that first one, but it seemed that the cholera struck randomly, and without any warning. The word went out again that absolutely all drinking and washing water must be boiled, and any food cleaned thoroughly in boiled water before consumption, an edict that was even endorsed by the camp commander, who had so far shown little interest in the welfare of his prisoners.

The only benefit from the death of a patient was that the doctor involved had the job of redistributing any personal effects. Drew received a pair of boots in this manner, although after a week he began to leave them off for two days at a time so that they, and his feet, had an opportunity to dry out. Tinea was a revolting affliction, and Drew had no intention of getting it if he could possibly avoid it. There was a man in the hospital whose tinea had started between his toes and had now spread all the way up to his groin so that his legs and genitals were a mass of weeping, burning sores.

At night, if he wasn't on night duty, Drew went back to his cell and collapsed with fatigue. Aside from the migraines, his own health was deteriorating at quite an alarming rate. He'd had two serious malaria attacks now, was still covered in sores, and his hip bones and ribs were protruding markedly. He usually ate at the hospital, so tonight he was very surprised to see a small mango sitting in the middle of his sleeping mat. A whole mango!

'Whose is this?' he asked in amazement.

Don and Keith watched on in amusement, and Tim sat up on his mat and beamed.

'It's yours. We got them from an old lady at the gate. It's a bit too ripe, but we didn't think you'd mind.'

Drew picked up the fruit. It was a little soft, but smooth and full and promised to be very juicy, and he could smell it quite clearly. He lifted the crimson and yellow globe to his nose and inhaled the heady scent, then bit straight into it. Juice squirted out and ran down his chin.

'My God, it's delicious!' he exclaimed, then he froze. 'Oh shit, you did wash it?'

'Christ, course we washed it!' Don countered, offended.

'Sorry,' Drew apologised, then took another bite. 'Mmm, it's indescribable.'

He ate the lot, any thoughts of saving some for later banished the second he tasted the rich sweetness of it, then put the stone in his mouth to suck the last tiny shreds of fruit off its rough surface. When he was sure he'd got it all he removed the stone and set it carefully on the box next to his mat; he'd plant it when it had dried, and then, if they *were* doomed to be in this God-forsaken bloody camp for much longer and it grew, they might at least be able to eat mangoes occasionally. He didn't know how long mangoes took to grow or fruit, but it would be something to watch and think about. He smiled as he thought of how his father, with his penchant for exotic fruits and vegetables, would approve.

He licked his lips one last time, slowly and carefully to make sure he didn't miss any remaining particles of juice, then looked up at the others to offer them a very heartfelt thank you for bringing him such a treat.

Don and Keith were still grinning, but Tim was staring at him intently, his face flushed, and when Drew met his eyes he looked quickly away.

Then he got off his mat and walked out.

Drew watched him go, then asked, 'What was that all about?'

Don shrugged, but Keith said, 'Them mangoes, we actually only got three. Tim said he didnae want his and that you should have it. Ah think he fancies ye.'

'What?'

'Tim. Ah think he might be one for the lads.'

'*Tim?*'

Keith shrugged this time, as if the idea didn't particularly bother him. 'It happens, ye ken, especially in the Andrew. Ye ken that.'

Drew did indeed. Homosexuality wasn't at all uncommon in the navy, especially on long voyages when the next port was weeks away and the memory of the women in the last was fading quickly. It was, he thought, more a matter of taking your pleasure where you could find it, and therefore usually it had a very masculine edge to it, but he supposed there probably were real nances among the men too.

But Tim? He'd never considered Tim in that light, not even fleetingly.

'I very much doubt it,' he said, convinced he was right. 'Have you seen him use his fists? He's as tough as they come when he needs to be.'

'Doesnae make a lot o' difference when it comes to where a man feels he really wants to put his prick.'

Drew sat down on Don's bed, stunned. 'Do you really think so?'

'Hard to really say,' Keith said. 'But he looks at ye a lot, just quietly mind, and he's always over to ye wi' wet cloths and drinks o' water when you're poorly.'

'That doesn't mean he's a nance, though.'

'No, but it might mean he's lonely, or looking for affection. Christ, we could all do wi' a bit o' company an' a cuddle.'

Drew couldn't believe it, and seriously doubted what Keith was suggesting. Tim couldn't be a nance — and Drew had encountered enough during his time in naval ports; they did tend to hang around the sailors' preferred haunts. He just didn't seem to be made that way, and he certainly didn't act like it. But what if Keith and Don were right?

'Well,' he said, 'if he is, does it really matter?'

Don said, 'Not here, it doesn't. Nothing matters here except staying alive.'

Drew thought about it some more, then finally shook his head adamantly.

'No, you're wrong, I'm sure of it.'

Keith crossed his arms. 'Then why could he no' keep his eyes off ye when ye were scoffing your mango, then go haring off like that when ye spotted him?'

'Look,' Drew said, irritated now. 'This is complete bullshit, and you know it. Tim is about as much of a molly as I am. I'm going to see what's up with him.'

As he walked out, and behind his back, Don and Keith raised their eyebrows knowingly at each other.

Drew found Tim sitting under the one tree in the yard. His knees were drawn up and he was systematically breaking a thin stem of bamboo, snapping it at regular intervals all the way down its length.

Drew sat down nearby and watched him. Like everyone else, Tim was wasting away. He'd been a big, strapping bloke before they'd arrived here, with long legs and arms and a well-muscled chest covered with curly gold hair. Now he was beginning to resemble some sort of stick puppet, all elbows, knees and shoulder blades. He was tanned, though, everywhere his tattered and baggy shorts did not cover, from working outside in the burning sun. He was due for a haircut

— for reasons of hygiene rather than vanity or fashion, as the lice and fleas in the camp were rife — and his fair hair flopped over his forehead. They were not dissimilar, the pair of them, and their likeness had been remarked upon more than once. They were — or had been — bigger than many of their English cohorts, and had rather proudly put it down to being New Zealanders and having had the benefit of plenty of milk and meat during their growing years.

There was no milk or meat now, though, and it showed.

'Had quite a good day in the hospital today,' Drew said casually.

Tim didn't look up from his stick.

Drew tried again. 'You know that chap I was telling you about, the one with the ulcer on his backside the size of a dinner plate? Well, Paterson has been packing it with a warm salt poultice three times a day, and we think it's starting to draw the infection out. The redness around the sore isn't as pronounced and there's a lot less pus. That's good news, isn't it? Mind you, the hole hasn't got any smaller.'

Tim nodded. 'It is good,' he said finally. 'You must be pleased.'

'Well, it was Paterson's idea, not mine. But, yes, it is good.'

Drew bent his head to the left as far as it would go, then to the right, stretching the muscles and tendons in his neck. There was an ominous crack, which he ignored.

'Look, thanks for the mango, it was delicious. But the chaps said it was actually yours.'

'Early Christmas present,' Tim replied.

'Well, I really appreciate it. I'm not quite sure why I deserve a Christmas present, though.'

Tim swept the bits of broken bamboo off his lap, and glanced up. 'I don't get . . . I mean, you're at the hospital most of the time now, I don't get to see you as often. I just wanted to make sure that, well, that we were still mates.'

'Why wouldn't we be?'

Tim shrugged. 'I don't know. I just thought . . . oh shit, I don't know what I thought. I was worried I was los . . . ' He faltered, and a pink flush crept up his neck and face. He was silent for a moment, then added angrily, 'It was only a fucking mango.'

But Drew, to his profound shock, was starting to suspect otherwise. 'It wasn't just a fucking mango, though, was it?'

Tim didn't reply, and reached for another stick.

Drew decided he had to have this out now, just in case, so that there couldn't possibly be any misunderstandings.

'Look, for God's sake don't be offended, but, well, we've been mates for a couple of years now, and we're both Kiwis and all that, but I'm not, well . . . ' Christ, this was difficult.

'Not what?' Tim asked, looking straight at Drew.

'I'm not . . . that way inclined.'

For a moment Tim looked as if he was going to deny any knowledge of what Drew was alluding to, but, to Drew's absolute horror, tears suddenly glistened in the other man's eyes.

324

'I thought I wasn't, either,' Tim croaked, his face a picture of dismay. 'At least, not until I met you.'

Tears trickling openly down his tanned cheeks now, he reached out and lightly ran the tip of his finger over the warm skin of Drew's shoulder. His touch was as deep and as powerful as an electric shock, and Drew leaped back instantly, appalled at the effect it had had on him.

Tim withdrew his hand and got to his feet. 'God, I'm so sorry,' he mumbled.

Drew watched him go in confusion, and unconsciously began to dig his fingers into the base of his skull. He was getting another headache.

15

As far as Jack Leonard was concerned, Ana
Deane had become indispensable to him, both as
a farm worker and as a friend.

She'd been with him for two and a half years
now, and he thanked God she had chosen to stay
rather than go home when the Women's Land
Service changed the rules about working for
relatives. He'd had Nola Butt and Betty Weaver
here for some time, too, but neither could really
compare with Ana, although Nola was pretty
good — a hard worker with an aptitude for
farming, even though she was a townie. But
Betty, buxom and cheerful, was hopeless on the
farm. She wasn't at all confident on horseback,
couldn't mend a fence to save herself and cried
every time a lamb died, but she gave everything
her best shot and laughed along with it, *and* she
was a truly excellent cook. It hadn't taken long
for them all to decide that her main duties would
be the cooking and the domestic work, looking
after the kitchen garden, feeding the animals and
mothering the orphaned lambs in springtime.
And all of that was essential, of course, because
it allowed the others to get on with the business
of sheep farming.

Ana, however, was a completely different
kettle of fish. The girl could do everything a
bloke could do, save all but the very heaviest of

lifting jobs, she had a stomach like cast iron when required, which was often, and she had the rare knack of being able to look at things from every angle at once. Jack had always planned at least a year ahead — you had to, on a farm — but Ana seemed to be able to see well beyond a mere twelve months, and he had already implemented some of the ideas she'd suggested. In a deliberately low key manner, of course, so that he wouldn't feel stupid for not having thought of them himself.

He was thinking exactly this as he trudged across the horse paddock and climbed wearily over the stile into the yard. It was almost dark, and his bones ached mightily after a full day in the saddle mustering. The sheep were all down now, and the first lot safely under the shearing shed for the night so they'd dry out in time for the start of shearing tomorrow.

The gang had arrived this afternoon — shearers, their wives, kids and all — but they would all have a role to play. They were Ngati Kahungunu, a family affair from Maungakakari, and Ana had organised them; this would be their second year on the Leonard farm. During Ana's first year with him he'd been able to get in only a very last minute, rag-tag gang, and the clip had suffered accordingly. Their general ineptitude had annoyed Ana quite spectacularly and the following year she prevailed on her family for assistance. As soon as the gang finished here they would be off to do the clip at Kenmore, and then on to somewhere else after that, so they only had a week at the most. Jack prayed that it wouldn't rain, as the wet always slowed things down.

The shearers' quarters had been tidied up and made habitable, thanks to Ana yet again. Her father and three men from Maungakakari had come over and set to fixing the roof and replacing the windows and the long drop that had been wrecked in a cyclone three years ago. He was a very decent fellow, Joseph Deane, Jack thought, and extremely able considering he had only the one leg. They'd discovered they'd both been at Gallipoli.

As he crossed the yard and dodged the sheets flapping on the line Jack noticed that the rickety old farm bicycle was propped against the wall of the house. That meant that Betty, who actually could ride a bike, had probably been into Kereru to collect the mail and perhaps some groceries. It was a twelve-mile pedal there and back, and the return journey always rather precarious if the purchases had included items such as a large bag of flour, but there just wasn't the petrol to go jaunting off to the tiny town in the truck for anything less than an emergency. Or the occasional beer.

He kicked his boots off at the back door and went into the kitchen. As usual there was the smell of something delicious simmering on the range, and on the table sat plates piled high with what he guessed — if his nose served him correctly — was baking, covered with damp tea towels. He lifted the edge of the closest and saw to his delight that it covered his favourite — cheese scones, nice big round ones with extra cheese on top. Betty's scones were a delight, always light and soft, never stodgy or prone to giving a man constipation. A good pat of butter would do these real justice, he thought, sneaking one out and raising it to his nose to savour the comforting, tangy aroma.

'Oi! Those are for the gang!'

Jack started guiltily and dropped the scone; it bounced off the table and landed on the floor, then rolled over to the sideboard. There was a furry streak of black and a cat pounced on it, batting it about merrily with one extended paw before crouching over it and proceeding to tear the cheese off the top.

'That was clever, wasn't it?'

Betty stood in the doorway, her arms filled with vegetables from the garden to make soup for tomorrow. A blue scarf covered her blonde hair, although it failed to prevent the curls from escaping in all directions, and the sleeves of her work shirt were rolled to her elbows. Her love of cooking was reflected in her figure, which strained the buttons at the front of her shirt and roundly filled out the seat of her trousers. Her pale blue eyes were bright and merry, and her cheeks their perpetual pink. Jack always thought she should be a poster girl for the WLS, she was that healthy and bonny.

'He'll be sick, he will, if he gutses all of that,' she admonished.

'Should I take it off him?' Jack asked, envisaging himself stepping into a puddle of cold cat sick on the back porch at five o'clock tomorrow morning.

Betty waved the suggestion away, a bundle of

radishes coming loose and rattling to the floor. 'Damn. No, leave him to it, he'll be all right. He hardly ever over-eats, that one.'

She crossed the floor, dribbling the radishes in front of her with her foot as she went, and deposited the vegetables on the table. There were silverbeet, potatoes, carrots, a cabbage and the last of the leeks.

'Did you go into town this afternoon?

Betty nodded. 'We were short of a few things. Oh, and there's a letter for you. It's on the mantle in the lounge.'

Jack snatched another scone and hurried out of the kitchen. Since the girls had come to the farm, the lounge, or 'front room' as he always referred to it, had lost its abandoned air. Betty had washed the curtains and the antimacassars over the back of the sofa and armchairs, cleaned the ancient ashes from the fireplace, dusted and polished, and regularly set out small vases of wildflowers. There was currently a pile of knitting at one end of the sofa — a tiny jacket in pale lemon Nola was making up for her sister's new baby — several copies of the *Woman's Weekly* strewn across an end table, and a bottle of Betty's pink nail varnish on the mantle.

Next to it sat an unopened letter.

Jack picked the envelope up, hesitated, then turned it over. It was, as he had hoped, from his son David, currently a patient in the New Zealand military hospital at Helwan in Egypt. David had been wounded three months ago, and there had been real concern that he not might survive. He hadn't actually said this in his letters,

330

but Jack knew his son well and had read between the lines. He'd been shot in the arm and the wound had become gangrenous; there had been 'a few dodgy weeks', according to David, but he was on the mend, although he didn't think he'd be going back to his old unit.

Jack tore the envelope open and unfolded the single page it contained, covered with his son's bold but messy writing.

Dear Dad,

Thanks for your last letter. It was great to hear about things on the farm. Good job you've got some decent land girls, otherwise you'd never get everything done on your own. It seems funny to think of girls doing a man's work, but if they're as able as you say they are, I don't suppose it matters, does it?

Well, I truly am on the road to recovery now. The bad news is I've been declared unfit for service because of this arm of mine, but the good news is I'm coming home very soon. The MO said with luck I'll be on the next hospital ship leaving Cairo, which apparently is next week. It hasn't been arranged yet, but hopefully I'll be on that one.

I'll miss my mates here, but I won't miss the flies and the heat and the bloody dust. It gets everywhere, you know, even in your tea.

You must be getting ready for shearing soon. Have you got the same gang you had last year? They sounded good. Good luck for it, anyway.

I'll write again when I can, and let you know exactly when I think I'll be home.

Your son, David

Jack read the letter twice, then checked the date at the top of the page: 29 August 1944. His heart lurched as he realised that David could be home any day now, if he wasn't already. But wouldn't someone have contacted him, if he was perhaps in a New Zealand hospital? Surely the bloody army would have? He'd get on to them as soon as he could, but the farm didn't have a telephone so he'd have to wait until the next time he went into Kereru. Which wouldn't be for a few days yet as they were just too busy.

He read the letter one more time, then took it to his bedroom and placed it carefully under the wooden jewellery box on the dressing table. The box had belonged to his wife, and he'd left everything in the room just as it had been when she was alive.

There was a discreet cough, and he glanced up to see Ana standing in the doorway. She was dusty and dishevelled after the day's mustering, the warm spring sun already encouraging freckles across her nose and cheeks.

'Everything all right?' she asked. 'Betty said you had a letter.'

He nodded; he didn't mind her asking at all.

'From David, he's coming home.'

'That's great news, Jack!' Ana exclaimed, and

then asked the question that everyone was compelled to ask when they learned that someone in the forces was coming home early. 'Is he . . . I mean, what . . . ?'

Jack sat down on the edge of the bed, the frame squeaking beneath his weight.

'He doesn't say, he just mentions his arm and that he's on the road to recovery. Doesn't sound too put out by it, though.' Jack pulled a face. 'But then David never was one for complaining. Broke his ankle once, when he was a boy, falling out of the big tree behind the lav, but didn't say anything to his mother because she was busy getting a roast into the oven. Just sat out on the steps waiting until she'd finished. It must be quite bad, though, for him to be sent home for good.'

Ana thought so, too, but kept her opinion to herself. Instead, she said, 'Nola's in too. We've done the horses and the dogs because Betty's too busy. Have you seen the baking she's done? It's enough to feed an army. She says it's a 'welcome' supper for the gang.'

But then, there was a small army on the farm now. There were at least fifteen people in the shearing gang, and she knew them well because almost all of them were her relatives.

She smiled. 'Actually, I think that's why they were so keen to come back this year — because of Betty's amazing scones.'

'Wouldn't surprise me,' Jack said as he got to his feet again and stretched until his spine cracked. 'I'm for a wash. What are we having for dinner, did she say?'

'Stewed neck chops with celery and dumplings, potatoes and vege bake, and rhubarb pie for afters. Yum.'

It was an excellent dinner, shared by the four of them sitting around the kitchen table. The animals had all been fed, the shearing gang had settled in, and everyone seemed to be happy. Especially Jack.

Dabbing at his lips with a napkin, which Betty made him use whenever he ate at the table, he said, 'When David comes home, two of you will have to double up, I'm afraid. Will that be all right?'

The girls looked at each other and shrugged.

Betty said, 'You can come in with me, Nola, if you like. I'm happy to share.'

Nola tucked a strand of dark hair behind her ear before she spooned up the last of her pie. Through a mouthful of rhubarb and cream, she replied, 'Fine with me, but I warn you, Betts, I'm not sharing anything else with you.'

'What do you mean?' demanded Betty, although they could all see the twinkle in her eye.

'You used my hair brush this morning, didn't you?'

'No,' Betty lied.

'You did. I left it on my dresser when we went out, and when I got in tonight it was on my bed, *and* it had blonde hairs in it!'

Betty inelegantly ran a finger around the rim of her pudding plate to collect the last of the cream. 'Well, actually, I might have used it. I've lost mine.'

'That wouldn't be the hair brush out in the yard on top of the dog kennels, would it?' Ana asked.

'Yes! Yes, that's where I had it last!'

Jack knew he shouldn't ask, but he did. 'Why did you need your hair brush out there?'

'Well, when you came in last night, the dogs were awfully mucky, so I thought I'd give them a bit of a tidy up.'

Ana rolled her eyes. 'Betts, working dogs get mucky, they're supposed to.'

'Mmm, I know, but they seemed to like it so I just kept going.'

Jack covered his smile with his napkin, and made a mental note to buy her a new brush next time he went into Kereru. If he could find one, of course.

★ ★ ★

They were out of bed the next morning at four-thirty, in time to have breakfast and get ready for the day's shearing. Betty had already been up for a while, and was away on the tractor up to the shearers' quarters with a couple of things they needed. They'd bought their own cook, who would prepare all of their meals and morning and afternoon smokos, but Leonard had offered them anything they wanted out of the garden, and given them a couple of hoggets.

They met her on the way back down and she waved cheerfully, nearly putting the tractor into a gorse bush.

Ana pulled Mako up. 'Are they ready to go?' she asked, anxious for the day's work to be under way.

'Yep, and they've got the most gorgeous little baby with them this time. You know Katarina? It's hers and he's so *sweet*! All cute and brown like a little button.'

'Actually, yes, I do know Katarina. She's my cousin, remember? Her father is my father's half-brother.'

Betty looked momentarily confused, then shrugged and put the tractor back in gear. 'Anyway,' she yelled over the racket, 'I'm off to start on lunch. I'll be back up at midday, all right?' And with an almighty jerk and a belch of petrol fumes she was off again.

When Jack, Ana and Nola arrived at the shearing shed the gang were sitting on the rails of the yards waiting. They were a fairly motley-looking bunch, but then shearing gangs always were when they were working. The men wore work trousers and open shirts over their black singlets, and boots that would be wrapped with sacking to stop them slipping once the shearing started, and the women were dressed variously in trousers or old frocks, depending on what their job was. The children looked as though they'd dressed in anything they could find.

Ana noted a new face, a tall, fit-looking girl with handsome features and sharp, dark eyes. Her wavy hair hung free halfway down her back, and she stood with hands on sturdy hips staring back at Ana.

'Who's that?' Ana asked her Uncle Haimona as she dismounted.

Haimona pushed his hat back off his brown face and scratched at the greying bristles on his head, his rolled shirt sleeves revealing fading vestiges of the tattoos from his days as a seaman in the merchant navy. 'Tangiwai Heke that was, Joshua's new missus. She didn't arrive until last night. Your father, when he was a boy, sailed with her koro. Cassius, his name was, a big bugger with a wooden leg.'

'Like my dad, eh?'

'Oh, no, bigger than your dad.'

Joshua was Ana's cousin, the eldest son of her Aunty Huriana.

'I didn't even know Joshua was married.'

'About three months ago now. She's a good worker, Tangiwai, but she's nearly as mean as her koro was.'

'Is that so?' Ana mused as she looked over at the girl, who was now removing her shirt to reveal a singlet, a spectacular bust and a pair of very well-muscled arms. 'Well, we'll see.'

'Just watch how you go, eh, girl. She's got a temper on her like a sow with ten new piglets.'

'Poor Joshua.'

Haimona snorted with amusement and walked off to round up his team, yelling at the top of his voice, 'All aboard!'

The day's shearing began as the first group of sheep were moved out from under the shed and into the yards, and Ngapere, Huriana's youngest daughter, climbed over the rails and positioned herself beside the race gate, signalling that she was ready to begin.

As sheep came belting down the race in single file she swung the gate to the left or to the right, separating the animals so they ended up in two different pens. It was a very skilled job, especially done at speed, and her brow furrowed in concentration under the shadow of her hat. The sheep in the near pen were for the clip, while the others, mainly lambs, would be docked, and castrated if they were males, then held until their mothers had been shorn. There was a hell of a noise as the lambs realised they'd been separated from their mothers, and the ewes answered by bleating pathetically for their babies.

The sheepos chased the ewes up a ramp and into the pens behind the shearing stands, and Ana nodded with satisfaction as the Anderson spluttered into life. There were five stands, but only four would be used this time around because there were only four shearers — her Uncle Haimona, his brother-in-law Piripi, Huriana's husband Anaru, and Joshua. Neither she nor Jack would be on the end of a set of clippers today; there was too much other work to be done with the lambs.

She watched as the pen doors opened and the first sheep, their hard little feet scrabbling for purchase, were pulled out onto the boards and wrestled onto their backs as the shearers bent over them, their wrists strapped firmly against the possibility of injury. They would work hard all day, competing for the coveted honour of gun shearer — the man with the biggest tally at the end of the clip, and the better rate of pay that went with it. Beyond the stands Katarina, the wool classer, stood at the sorting table with her baby in a sling on her back ready to check each fleece as it came past, alongside her sister Elizabeth who would be keeping note of the figures; the presser — Joshua's very well-built sister Rangimarie — waited in front of the one-man press into which the fleeces would go to be compacted before baling; and the five fleecos, women and the older children whose job it was to collect up the fleeces from the boards and pick off the worst of the dirt before they were classed, hovered in anticipation.

The remainder of the gang — several more children and the rest of the men — stayed outside to manage the smooth flow of animals up into the shed, and help out with the docking and castrating.

Satisfied that everything was progressing as it should be, Ana went outside and began to get her tools ready. But just as she was checking the sharpness of her docking knife, there was a loud and rather angry yell from Joshua. She glanced up at the shed and saw that he'd straightened up from his sheep and was gesticulating wildly at Tangiwai, who was in the empty stand next to him, attaching a set of clippers to the power cable.

'What are you doing, woman?' Joshua bellowed over the noise of the sheep. 'Get out of there!'

It appeared that Tangiwai could not hear him, as she carried on obliviously.

Joshua swore and began berating his wife

loudly. Ana, and no doubt everyone else, could hear what he was saying quite clearly. She glanced at Jack, who raised his eyebrows but shrugged, as if to say it would be more than his life was worth to get between the two. The other three shearers had stopped, and Ngapere had let the race gate close, backing up sheep behind it so that they were almost standing on top of one another.

'Get out in the yard!' Joshua demanded angrily. 'You're not shearing.'

'I bloody am!' Tangiwai shot back.

'You're bloody not!'

'I *am*!' she repeated, shoving her face forward until it was only inches away from that of her husband. 'I'm as good as these fellas, and twice as young! I can do it!'

Joshua stamped his foot so hard the boards shook. 'Maybe you *can*, but you're not *going* to!'

Tangiwai stamped her own foot. 'Why not?'

'Because shearing is not a woman's job, that's why not. Go and help Rangimarie with the press if you want to do something useful! You might actually learn something. Every cloud has a silver lining, you know!'

'*Make* me go and help Rangimarie!'

'I bloody well will in a minute!' he retorted, his face turning red.

Haimona stepped forward, although the shearers behind him looked on with interest, thoroughly enjoying the spectacle.

'Have some respect, boy!' he barked, irritated at his nephew for not being able to manage his wife. They would all be very busy over the next

340

few days, and there was not time for the tiffs of lovers settling into a new marriage.

Joshua spun on his heel. 'I would if *she* respected *me!*'

Haimona blew his cheeks out in frustration. 'You married her, boy.'

There were guffaws from rest of the gang at this, and Joshua blushed furiously. He turned back to his wife and held his hands out, palms up in supplication. 'Tangiwai, please, love, hop out of the stand, there's enough shearers for today.'

She considered him through narrowed eyes, her own cheeks flushed with indignation, then unhooked the shears from the cable. 'Only because you asked me nicely. Think of that next time!'

And she jumped down from the boards and strode out of the shed, her long hair bouncing behind her.

Ana rolled her eyes, and went back to her knife inspection. The shearers started up again and Joshua had his red face down over his sheep once more.

* * *

They had a very successful day. By nightfall the four shearers had clipped an average of three hundred sheep each, which kept them on their tight schedule. Betty had come out with extras to add to the food prepared by Arapeta, Haimona's wife, and with lemonade she'd made for the children.

341

By the time the sun was sinking behind the hills, even Ana had had enough. Her back was very sore, her arms stung from various nicks, scratches and mosquito bites, and she could do with a really good bath.

They packed up when the light grew poor, prepared the shears for tomorrow's work and packed their gear into the gang's two trucks. Everyone piled in — except for those who were on horseback — and headed slowly home.

Ana and Tangiwai trotted along in front of the truck, going carefully as the shadows of dusk turned rabbit holes and dips in the ground into hidden dangers. Ana admired Tangiwai's horse, on which she'd arrived at the Leonard farm late last night. The gang had also brought four other horses with them, all products of Kepa's breeding programme at Maungakakari, and they were fine animals, but none were quite as magnificent as Tangiwai's mount. He was a stallion, big and grey and gleaming in the dull light like polished pewter. Tangiwai sat him easily and confidently like the expert horsewoman she clearly was. Ana didn't think the horse was quite as lovely as Mako, but still, she wouldn't have minded a go on him.

She was about to ask Tangiwai how long she'd had him, when Mako suddenly shied violently to the left. Lulled by the gentle rhythm of his trot, Ana hadn't been paying much attention, and so had to clutch wildly at his mane to avoid being flung out of the saddle. Tangiwai's horse also shied, at exactly the same time, but in the opposite direction. Ana heard her swear as she gathered the reins and attempted to get him back in hand before he bolted. He bucked once, skittered sideways again, then settled, looking suspiciously back at the piece of ground they had just crossed.

'What was that?' Tangiwai asked. 'Did you see it?'

'No, was it a rabbit?' Ana replied, settling Mako by stroking his neck firmly.

Tangiwai shrugged, and they both turned back to the offending stretch of grass as if whatever had frightened the horses might still be there.

And then it happened. They watched in open-mouthed incredulity as Haimona's truck, with Anaru, Piripi, Joshua and four of the kids on the back, drove over the shadowed patch, then suddenly pitched nose first into the ground and partially disappeared. The children screamed and the men yelled out in surprise, and all but two of then were flung off the back.

There was a grinding creak as the vehicle settled further, and then quiet as the motor cut out.

Jack cantered up, dismounted and stepped cautiously over to the hole; it wouldn't do to have it cave in even further, taking him with it.

'Haimona!' he yelled. '*Haimona!* Are you all right?'

A muffled expletive came from the cab, together with a loud metallic screech as Haimona attempted to wind the window down. The cab was wedged two-thirds into the hole, and through the windscreen they could see the top of Haimona's jerking head, still in its hat, as he struggled with the winder.

He bent his head on an angle and yelled up at them through the glass, 'Come round here and put your foot on the window, it's bloody jammed!'

While Jack got down on his backside and eased his legs gingerly over the rim of the tomo, a subterranean cavity that had chosen that precise moment to collapse, Ana and Tangiwai checked to see that the dislodged passengers were unharmed.

Unfortunately, they were not. Piripi had jarred or perhaps even sprained his wrist as he'd hit the ground, and Joshua was grimacing and rubbing the small of his back. Anaru, however, was unhurt, and was checking the children for injury, who were starting to giggle now with the excitement of it all.

'They're fine,' he declared after a moment.

The two children who had not been thrown off the truck had jumped off under their own steam and were now standing watching Jack as he shoved his boot down onto the half-open window of the cab.

'Koro Haimona's saying really bad words!' trumpeted the smaller of the two gleefully.

So was Jack. 'Oh, for fuck's sake, the bloody thing's completely jammed now. Haimona, can you try the passenger window?'

Haimona hauled himself across the seat, causing the truck to lurch slightly and everyone else to jump back. He tried the window on the passenger side, and looked very relieved when it wound down quite easily.

344

It took some minutes but eventually they hauled him out of the cab, slightly bruised but other than that unhurt.

He stood looking ruefully down at his disabled truck, then said to Jack, 'Reckon your tractor can pull it out?'

'Probably. Backwards, though. Nose is in too deep.'

Haimona nodded. 'What's the damage?' he asked Ana, inclining his head towards Joshua and Piripi who were still sitting on the ground.

'A sprained wrist and a wrenched back, which leaves us with only two shearers. What the hell are we going to do, Uncle?'

Haimona said to Jack, 'You can shear, can't you?'

'Yeah, but there's still the docking and all.'

'Well, can't Tangiwai or someone help with that? We're on a bloody tight schedule, Jack.'

Jack rubbed his grubby hand thoughtfully across the bristles on his chin. Then he said something he suspected might make him the laughing stock of the district. Or perhaps not, depending on how it worked out. 'Why can't Ana and Tangiwai shear?'

Haimona's mouth fell open. He knew that both women could shear quite competently, because he'd watched them both at one time or another, but to let them loose on a clip as important as this? And in *his* gang? It was . . . it was . . . it was not a bad idea, actually, given their current predicament.

He raised his eyebrows, and Jack shrugged; they didn't have much choice at the moment.

345

And anyway, he could see the look of hope and expectation on Ana's face. He nodded, and grinned broadly as she whooped with elation.

Haimona said quietly, 'I hope you know what you're doing, Jack.'

'Oh, I think I do, but let's see, eh?'

On the other side of the truck, Tangiwai crouched on the ground watching Joshua, who was very cautiously twisting his back from side to side.

'Oh, Jesus,' he cursed. 'It keeps jamming up every time I move.'

'Can you shear, do you think?' Tangiwai asked solicitously.

Joshua nodded, but it was obvious to all that the constant bending would be beyond him in his current state.

Haimona approached, bent down and whispered something in Tangiwai's ear.

And a huge grin spread across her face. She reached out and patted her husband's hand. 'You know, love, you're right. Every cloud does have a silver lining.'

★ ★ ★

The clip count was only down by fifty at the end of the next day. The morning had not started well, with Joshua and Piripi hanging about the stands giving unsolicited advice about what the girls were doing wrong and how they could improve their techniques, until Haimona told them in no uncertain terms to go away and do something useful. So Piripi sloped off to help the sheepos, his wrist wrapped firmly in a bandage expertly applied by Betty, and Joshua went to assist Nola and Jack with the docking. The lambs were held up so that their back ends hung over a yard rail, to give easy access to their tails and, in the case of the males, testicles, so Joshua was able to stand quite comfortably and chop away nearly all day.

But by the time dusk had fallen, Ana and Tangiwai were in such pain they were barely able to straighten up, although both refused to admit it. The others saw, though, and even the men admired them for their fortitude and determination.

They were back the next day, of course, and the day after that until the clip had almost been completed. On the last day, they thought they might even finish by mid-afternoon, which was good news as Jack had promised a shout after the last sheep had skidded out of the shed, leaving its thick, pungent-smelling fleece on the sorting table to be classed then pressed. The wool would go off to the scourers after that, and the clip for this year would be over.

Jack, Haimona and Ana were sitting under the shade of a big kahikatea, sipping hot tea from tin mugs, when one of the kids, clutching the sticky remnants of a jam sandwich in his hand, ran up and announced breathlessly, 'There's a man!'

'There's lots of men, tama,' Haimona replied as he picked a small twig out of his tea.

'No! There's a man coming across the paddocks. On a horse!'

Jack squinted; there was indeed someone

347

approaching on horseback, although whoever it was was too far away yet to discern clearly. He got to his feet and made a shade of his hand over his eyes.

The rider appeared to be a bloke, wearing a town hat and a suit jacket slung casually over his shoulders, in spite of the early summer heat. And the cheeky bastard was riding David's horse! The horse ambled along easily, as if the animal knew its rider well.

Then Jack realised, with a surge of soaring joy, that the horse did indeed know its rider, because it *was* David.

'My boy!' he exclaimed delightedly to Haimona. 'It's my boy, back from the war!'

Everyone else was watching now too, waiting with interest for the rider to arrive. As he did, he reined in and looked down at Jack.

'Hello, Dad,' he said nonchalantly, as if it had only been four days since he had last seen his father, instead of closer to four years. 'You look well.'

Leaning on the pommel of his saddle with his left hand he swung his right leg over and dismounted, letting the horse drop its head and tear at the grass.

'My God, so do you, son, so do you!' Jack opened his arms to his son, but David stepped back.

'Hang on, Dad,' he said. He seemed to pause and take a deep breath, then in a single swift movement used his left hand to slip his jacket off his shoulders. Where his right arm should have been, there was an empty sleeve, folded and pinned just above the elbow.

The only sound for some moments was the insistent bleating of the sheep, and the look of agonised grief that flashed across Jack's face brought sudden and unexpected tears to Ana's eyes.

David shrugged awkwardly. 'Sorry, Dad, it was the only way to stop the infection. But I'm getting pretty good with my left hand.'

Jack made a noise that was half sob, half cry, and threw his arms around his son. 'You're home, boy, and that's all I care about!'

But Ana knew that there would inevitably be more to it than that. Farmers needed the use of both arms; what would happen now to Jack's dream of passing his farm on to his only surviving son? She felt desperately sad for the pair of them, the one who had stayed behind to keep the dream going and the other who had gone overseas to fight for it.

She blotted her eyes with the hem of her singlet and cleared her throat.

Jack stepped back, patted David on both shoulders and said in a voice that was just a little too cheerful, 'Well, boy, you're back just in time to help finish the shearing. This is Ana, one of my land girls. She's been shearing fit to burst for the last four days. Yes, that's right, *shearing*, and it's a rare sight to behold.'

Ana, her curls stuck to her head with drying sweat and her bare arms covered with wool grease and dirt, stepped forward and offered her left hand, even though she was normally right-handed. 'Nice to meet you, David. Your

349

dad's told me so much about you.'

David smiled, and his face lit up as if someone had turned a lamp on inside him. 'All good, I hope.'

'Oh, yes,' Ana replied, taking in his height and his strong, expressive face and his bright eyes. 'All good.'

16

Tamar thought the story about the truck going into the tomo was absolutely hilarious. And it was, the way Ana, home on Christmas leave for a week, told it.

'So you and Tangiwai actually did the shearing yourselves?' she asked after she'd dabbed tears of laughter from her eyes with her table napkin.

'Yes, but Uncle Haimona and Anaru did as well, of course.'

Tamar leaned forward and patted her granddaughter's hand. 'Well, I'm very proud of you, dear, and I'm sure your mother and father are too.'

'We are, very,' Joseph affirmed, stuffing one last spoonful of Christmas pudding into his mouth. 'I've no doubt Ana will make some lucky sheep farmer a wonderful wife one day.'

'But does Ana want to be a sheep farmer's wife?' Tamar asked archly.

Ana went pink and tried to hide it by leaning over her pudding plate, but was too late.

Erin pounced. 'Ana, you're not blushing, are you? Fancy that! Joseph, what do you think would make Ana blush like that?'

Kepa, sitting on Tamar's right, exchanged mystified looks with his son.

'Don't tease, dear,' Joseph replied, taking pity on his daughter.

Everyone at Kenmore knew that Jack Leonard had sent Joseph a puppy from his best working dog's latest litter as a Christmas-cum-thank you gift for his help over the past few years, and that David Leonard had delivered the squirming little bundle personally. They also knew that after the obligatory tea and cake, David and Ana had gone for a long walk up to the top of the daffodil paddock, and had held hands all the way. They knew this because Henry had followed them, believing himself to be cunningly hidden behind various tree stumps and bushes and thereby successfully avoiding detection. This had been rather spoiled when David had called out to him at the bottom of the paddock that he'd left his gumboots halfway up the hill, but Henry had been unable to refrain from telling everyone what he had seen.

Speculation had been rife at Kenmore since then, and Erin suspected that her daughter might soon have some news to announce. But she knew Ana, and knew also that she would not be hurried.

Tamar gazed contentedly around the long dining table, happy as always to have as many members of her large family about her as possible. Keely, Owen and Henry were here, Henry looking somewhat seedy after having consumed far more Christmas pudding than was good for an eight-year-old boy. Bonnie was at Rongotai Air Force Base near Wellington, where she'd been transferred at the end of last year, and had been unable to get away for Christmas, but Leila was of course at home.

Tamar watched fondly as Leila bounced her daughter on her knee. Daisy, two years old now, had a spoon in her fist and was whacking the table with it in time to the bounces. She was an absolutely delightful child, with shiny ebony curls and huge dark eyes. Her features were her mother's, but her colouring had obviously come from her father. The poor little thing hadn't even met her father yet, as he was still fighting in the Pacific. He did write often, though, if not very loquaciously, and had sent several photographs of himself, which Leila had framed and now had pride of place in her room. Tamar dreaded to think what might happen when they finally went off to America, and dreaded perhaps even more the spectre of her own disappointment when they did.

James and Lucy were here too. They had done very well during the war, as canned fruit and vegetables were in heavy demand. They had faltered somewhat after receiving the news of Duncan's injuries, but rallied as they began receiving letters from him insisting that he was doing well and that they shouldn't worry about him, even if he was going to look a bit odd for the rest of his life. And when he'd married Claire and written about what a wonderful girl she was and how utterly in love they were, James and Lucy had been thrilled and, Tamar thought, probably not a little relieved. She had always privately imagined that to go through life with terrible injuries would be bad enough, but to have to do it on your own would be unbearable. After all, look how wonderful Erin had been for Joseph.

And then had come the sketchy news of Drew's incarceration in a Burmese jail. This had frightened them all very badly, as everyone knew what sort of treatment Allied POWs were receiving in the Japanese camps. Lucy sent a letter off to him every week without fail, via the Red Cross, but had never received a single word back. There was the terrible possibility, which they all refused to say out loud, that he had died, but there were stories going around about the Japanese being too inhumane to allow their prisoners access to Red Cross parcels and mail from home, so perhaps that was it. But they were losing their grip on the war now, the Japanese, and the idea of Drew coming home no longer seemed quite so remote.

Kathleen was home at the moment, on leave from her job at a uniform factory in Wellington, and her presence at Kenmore over the holiday, Tamar knew, was at least some consolation to James and Lucy. Kathleen *had* left it too late to find herself a war job, and had been manpowered as a machinist because she'd put on her registration form that she could sew. Which she could, and very well, although she'd never imagined herself using her skills to make uniforms for soldiers. She had been offered the option of either going to Wellington to work at Cathie & Sons, or staying in Hawke's Bay and working in a factory that made canvas ground sheets, so the choice hadn't been that difficult in the end. And she'd since discovered that she really rather enjoyed it — not the endless sewing of nothing but khaki and two shades of blue, but the camaraderie that came with it, and life in the big city. Having been a country girl all her life, albeit an expensively educated one, she'd been initially rather startled at the pace of life in Wellington, but once she'd become accustomed to it and made some friends, had decided it was all really rather exciting. And Bonnie was in the capital too, which meant they could meet up quite often and go out together.

Kathleen had also run into someone else in Wellington. She had been with friends enjoying a night out at the Majestic Cabaret, when she'd gone into the toilet to powder her nose. While standing in the queue waiting for a cubicle she'd seen a familiar face — Liam's wife, Evie. Ignoring her burning need for a wee she'd rushed after her, but had received the shock of her life when she finally caught up; Evie was very obviously at least six months pregnant. Kathleen had been so flabbergasted she hadn't been able to speak. Evie had simply said 'Hello, Kathleen' as if they'd bumped into each other at the local grocery store, and walked coolly off.

That had been five months ago, and Tamar could only assume that Evie's baby had been born by now. She had not written to Liam — and she was damned sure Evie hadn't either — simply because she didn't know what on earth to say. She also didn't want to upset him while he was no doubt already under enormous strain. Bomber Command had been flying endless sorties over Germany of late, and bad news about his silly wife would be very unlikely to cheer him up. But still, she felt very uncomfortable with the knowledge that he would probably be the last one to find out what was going on. He hadn't mentioned Evie at all in recent letters, so Tamar had no idea of the state of their affairs. And 'affairs' was obviously the appropriate word. Perhaps she should have offered the girl money right at the outset and been done with it.

There had been good news during the week, though. Joseph and Erin had received a long letter from Robert, who was at the moment fighting in Italy. In August 1942 he'd returned from Fiji when the Americans took over the defence of the islands, then had been sent to New Caledonia and then the Green Islands north-west of the Solomons to mop up after the defeat of the Japanese forces there in February. The Third Division had disbanded after that, and its members, including Robert, sent to join the Second Division slogging their guts out in Italy. He'd missed the gruelling battle for Cassino and was now, according to his letter, enjoying a decent leave in the mountains.

He'd sounded reasonably content, Tamar believed — apart from the obligatory grumbles about terrible army food and not enough pay — and she hoped he would be fortunate enough to remain in one piece and in similar spirits until the war ended, which surely couldn't be far away now. Having Robert back safely would go some way towards helping Erin and Joseph adjust to a life without their eldest son. The papers were cautiously beginning to suggest that the light at the end of the tunnel was beginning to brighten, and Tamar fervently hoped that it was. She was feeling very tired and rather old now, and wanted nothing more than to have all her family around her again.

Thomas had telephoned recently with very good news, too. For some time he had been thinking about retiring, even though he was only fifty-four, and had finally made up his mind. He and Catherine, he had explained over the telephone, had a good mind to move up to Napier and spend their 'twilight years' enjoying the sunshine and fair weather of Hawke's Bay. Catherine had developed rheumatism over the past eighteen months, and her doctor had advised that a shift to a warmer climate would be very beneficial to her health. And besides, Thomas said, he had a hankering to come home; he'd lived in Dunedin for the last twenty-five-odd years, and although he and Catherine had enjoyed their life there and he'd done rather well from his law practice, he had no intention of dying in a city that was so cold in the winter that the water in the lavatory froze in the mornings, even indoors.

Tamar smiled as she remembered how sensitive and thoughtful Thomas had been as a child, always the one to think carefully about his actions and the effect they might have on the people around him. He hadn't changed, really. All her children had been delightful when they were little, and in spite of their markedly differing characters and the odd hiccup along the way, they'd all grown into wonderful adults. Except for poor Ian, of course, who had not been

357

allowed to grow into an adult at all.

She felt a pricking at the back of her eyes, and looked down at her hands, not wanting anyone else to see her tears on this special family day. She smiled again ruefully; her hands were certainly firmly ensconced in *their* twilight years. They were wrinkled and covered with liver spots and the skin no longer seemed to want to adhere to the bones of her wrists. Her hair was completely silver now, too, and her face quite heavily lined. Kepa, however, insisted that every time he looked at her he could still see the face of the young girl he had fallen in love with decades ago, and that always filled her heart with a warm glow and transported her back to their earliest times together. It was funny, really; she was eighty-two now, but in her mind she still felt young. She had somehow expected that when her body began to mature and then age, her thoughts and feelings would too. But although she was certainly much wiser now, she was still essentially the same person she had always been.

Kepa slid his hand over hers; he could always tell when she was feeling a little melancholic.

'Memories?' he asked quietly.

She nodded. 'Just of the children when they were young. And Andrew, even poor old Peter. Everyone who can't be here today. It's nothing, I'm just being silly.'

'I doubt it, my dear,' he murmured. 'You are not often silly.'

Henry suddenly let out an enormous, rumbling burp, interrupting their private tête-à-tête.

'Henry! You can sleep outside with the dogs tonight if you carry on like that!' Keely admonished.

'Beg your pardon,' Henry said, vaguely shamefaced, but trying not to smirk all the same.

'Yes, son, that was very rude,' Owen added, and belched even more vigorously himself.

'Oh, *Owen*!' Keely shook her head in dismay. 'See?' she complained to Leila. 'This is what happens when you have sons. You're lucky you only have Daisy.'

'She might have *hundreds* of sons, though!' Henry insisted. 'She might get to the United States of America and meet Mickey Mouse and Roy Rogers and eat loads of ice cream and hotdogs and have hundreds of sons with Jake! And then she can write to me and invite me over for the holidays and I'll show them all how to go eeling and play rugby.'

Keely pushed her chair back and got to her feet. 'That's enough, Henry. Go outside now, please, and run around for a bit after your dinner.'

'I don't want to, I want to stay here and listen!'

'Well, you can't. Unless of course you want to help with the dishes?'

Henry screwed his face up; his mother was always doing this to him — letting him do something he *really* wanted only if he did something else that was so awful or boring it wasn't worth it. He got off his own seat, left the dining room and marched down the hall, stomping his feet loudly enough to register his protest, but not loudly enough to get told off for it. But then he burped again, and it was such a good one he cheered up immediately.

'I wonder if he gets lonely out here with no other kids of his age living near?' Owen said pensively. 'Especially in the school holidays.'

'I wouldn't have thought so.' Keely started scraping chicken bones off plates and stacking them one on top of the other. 'He has plenty of little friends at school, and he's been to visit several since the holidays started, and they've been here.'

Owen was well aware of this. It had taken Joseph and him almost an entire day to dismantle the dam Henry and his friends had made in the stream last week — the stream that was the sole source of water for the big house.

He shrugged in acquiescence. 'Well, I suppose he's just bored. I'll take him with me the next time we go up to the top paddocks. In *fact*, why don't we get him a new horse? His feet nearly drag on the ground when he rides Amber now — he's far too big for her. Yes, what a good idea!' He turned enthusiastically to Kepa. 'What have you got at the moment that might be suitable? Nothing too fiery, just enough to keep Henry on his toes. Something about fourteen and a half hands, perhaps?'

Kepa thought for a moment. 'I have two ponies that might be appropriate. A bay and a grey, both broken in and ready to go. Would you like to come over and have a look at them?'

Owen nodded. 'I'll bring Henry with me. Give him something to look forward to.'

'Right,' Kepa said, setting his hands palms down on the table decisively, 'that is arranged then. Now, about these dishes?'

Tamar looked startled. 'Good God, you're not offering to roll your own sleeves up, are you?'

'No, but I am offering to take you for an after-dinner stroll around the garden.'

'Thank you, Kepa, that would be lovely,' Tamar said graciously.

Kepa got to his feet, slid Tamar's chair out with a very chivalrous flourish, then took her elbow.

Owen looked after them as they went outside, amused and rather touched by the way Kepa still treated Tamar — courted her, in fact — with the utmost respect, cherishing her as if she were still a beautiful young girl in the prime of her youth. It seemed the old man would never give up hope that Tamar might finally accept his proposals of marriage, even though he'd been making them for years and she, for just as long, had been turning him down. In a way Owen rather hoped that they would finally marry, because that would somehow make the circle complete, and he liked a happy ending.

Outside, the sun had not long gone down behind the Ruahine Ranges, leaving on the lawn spills of shadow that were blurring rapidly into a velvety dusk, and the air was still redolent with the warmth of the day. Tamar and Kepa strolled arm in arm around the paved borders of the formal flowerbeds, admiring the plants and enjoying the heady scents drifting up from the blooms. Tamar loved roses — but only the varieties with a strong perfume — and there was a mass planting of these in the garden's central plot, from ice white through to the deepest of burgundies.

'They have done well this year, have they not?' Kepa noted.

He too liked roses, but enjoyed even more Tamar's delight in them. He had a stunning new sunset-hued cultivar for her back at the village, but would not present it to her until New Year's Day. Perhaps they could plant it then together.

'Yes, they have, thanks to James's new underground watering system. It took him weeks to install the thing, the hoses and the sprinklers and what have you, but it's been worth it, I think.'

'He seems a changed man, James.'

'Very much so.'

'Do you think it was the move back out to Kenmore?'

Tamar sat down on a wooden garden seat, hooking the handle of her walking stick over the arm, and patted the space next to her.

'It certainly helped,' she replied when Kepa had seated himself, 'but I suspect the change occurred before he and Lucy actually moved back, which was part of the process of leaving his old life behind, if you like. I think it was partly to do with that business with the New Zealand Legion, and the appalling state of his finances because of the gambling, but I think the big thing was Duncan. His need to have his son back was greater than his desire to wallow in all that misery, so he finally decided to let the past go.'

Kepa grunted in acknowledgement.

'And,' Tamar went on, picking a rose thorn out of the fabric of her crêpe skirt, worn instead of her usual trousers in honour of Christmas dinner, 'I'm extremely pleased he was able to do that, not just for his sake, but for Duncan's too. When he comes home he's going to need support, and as a veteran himself James will understand. It would have been just too awful if they were still at odds and James missed the opportunity to help his own son, and of course if Duncan missed the opportunity to learn more about his father. God knows they never understood each other before.'

'Mmm,' Kepa said thoughtfully. 'And I gather he has now come to terms with you and I? We get on quite well these days, though he has never said a word to me about you. But then I do not suppose he would.'

'Oh, yes, he is much more understanding, although I must admit it did take a while, even after they moved back here. He came to me one evening, oh, about six months later I suppose, and actually apologised for his behaviour over it all and for what he termed his rudeness.'

'He was a little rude at times.'

'He was very rude, darling, most of the time, and you know it. And I admire you for never doing or saying anything about it. But he said he'd had a good think, and he understood it had nothing to do with his father, and I was entitled to some happiness even though Andrew had gone. I think he felt ashamed of himself, actually. And regretful, because underneath all that hostility he has always quite admired you.'

Kepa turned to look at her. In the growing darkness the planes of his face were even sharper than usual, and the silver in his hair glinted. 'Why have you never told me this?'

'I'm sorry, dear, but I promised him I wouldn't. But that was years ago now, and, well . . . it was years ago.'

'Did he ask you not to say anything?'

'Not at all, I just thought it wiser to keep it between the two of us. For his sake, really. I hope you're not offended.'

'Of course not.' Kepa took Tamar's hand. 'It was business between you and your son, not me. I admire you for respecting his feelings.'

They looked at each other and laughed until Tamar finally asked, 'So, do you think we've admired each other enough for one night?'

'I suspect so. One should not bask in the warmth of one's admirable qualities for too long or one might find that one's hat does not fit any more.'

Tamar chuckled again. 'Don't be pompous, dear. Although, is that why you're wearing a new one tonight?'

'A new what?'

'Hat.'

'Oh, no, this was a gift from my mokopuna, Ngapere, Makere and Rangimarie's little ones. They chose the style especially from a catalogue, saved up and sent away for it.'

'Yes, the emerald feather in the band really suits you. And it looks so striking against the blue felt.'

Slightly huffily, Kepa replied, 'I did not say they have good taste, my moko, but I will wear it because they gave it to me. It is precious.'

Tamar patted his arm. 'I know it is, I was only teasing. I received the latest copy of *Beano* from Henry for Christmas. Used, of course. But it was very important to him and he chose to give it to me, so I'll treasure that too.'

Kepa grunted again. 'It is funny, is it not, how we live through our children and grandchildren and great-grandchildren, and they in a way live through us? They need us to anchor them, to define who they are in the world, and we in turn need them because they are the part of us that will go on after we die.'

'That's rather morbid.'

'Perhaps, but it is true. And I think you are well aware of it these days, my love, as I am myself. We are old now and our time has almost come.'

'Or gone, if you want to look at it the other way around.'

Kepa looked at her quizzically. 'That depends on what you believe, does it not? If we are to go on to something else after this, then surely our time has come, not gone?'

'Well, it would be very nice to believe that there is something else, but I'm not entirely sure that I do,' Tamar replied.

'That is a shame, for surely that makes the contemplation of one's own passing even more frightening?'

'You're being pompous again. And I'm not frightened, not at all.'

'No?'

'No.' And she meant it. She shivered slightly. 'But I am getting cold. Shall we go in?'

'I'm afraid I must leave now. I promised to take Hemi and Rewi fishing in the morning.'

Tamar smiled and rose to her feet, Kepa's hand under her elbow to steady her, and they walked slowly around the house to his truck in the driveway.

They halted at the base of the steps leading up to the front door, Kepa turning her to face him.

'Merry Christmas, my love,' he said quietly, and softly kissed her cool lips, relishing the feel of her skin and the familiar scent of lavender she always wore. 'I love you, Tamar. No matter what, I love you.'

'Merry Christmas yourself,' Tamar whispered back. 'Drive carefully.'

'I will.'

She waited until he had climbed into the cab of his truck and started the motor, then raised her hand in farewell.

But suddenly, and inexplicably, she felt she needed to say something else to him. She hurried over to the driver's door and he wound the window down.

'Kepa? I love you too, very much. Remember that.'

He reached out and touched her hair. 'Always.'

★ ★ ★

He was up at six the next morning, and was rinsing his breakfast dishes under the kitchen tap

366

when he heard the sound of little voices arguing on his front verandah. He propped the rim of his plate against an upturned tea cup, and set the frying pan upside-down next to it to drain. Then, drying his hands on a tea towel, he walked down the hall to see what the fuss was about.

'Taihoa!' he exclaimed as he encountered two small boys, each hanging on to opposite ends of a wooden fishing tackle box, tugging it hard enough to spill the contents everywhere if they should drop it.

'I'm putting the hooks on!' one was complaining loudly.

'No, *I* am. You did it last time!' wailed the other.

'I . . . did . . . *not!*'

'You *did!*'

'I *didn't!*'

Kepa threw up his hands. 'Boys! *Boys!* Stop that, or no one will be going fishing!'

'But Koro, he started it!'

'That is enough, Hemi. There are plenty of lines and plenty of hooks. Enough for everyone.'

Hemi's bottom lip wobbled, but he hung onto his tears. It was always like this, his big brother pushing him around and telling him what to do. Rewi *had* put the hooks on last time, so it must be his turn today.

Kepa looked down at his great-grandchildren fondly, taking in their bushy dark hair and their bright brown eyes and chubby cheeks. Their feet were bare and they both wore baggy shorts and their special 'fishing' shirts, faded and full of holes, just like his own. They were constantly arguing, these two. Hemi was six and Rewi was seven, and competition between them was fierce. But they were good little boys, both of them, and he loved spending time with them.

'Do you have your canvas shoes, for the rocks?' he asked. The rocks where they intended to fish today were sharp and their feet would be cut to shreds.

'Yeees, Koro,' they answered in unison.

'Where?'

They both pointed at a rucksack lying on the steps.

'Mama made our lunch, too,' added Hemi.

Kepa nodded. 'Just let me get my hat and my fishing kit, all right? And then we will go.'

Ten minutes later they were in Kepa's truck, the boys bouncing all over the bench seat as they headed towards the sea and Kepa's favourite fishing spot.

It was a twenty-minute walk along the sand to the point and the rocks at the bottom of the steep cliff closing off one end of the bay. Kepa adjusted his blue 'mokopuna' hat to keep the sun out of his eyes, and enjoyed the warmth as he walked. The tide was half in, so they could not linger today — the swell around the point could come up very suddenly and cause the rock shelf from which they were to fish to become cut off, and it was a very challenging climb up the cliff.

Ahead of him, the boys were squatting curiously over something on the sand.

'What is it?' he asked as he caught up with them.

'Baby mako,' Rewi answered, poking the carcass of the small shark with a stick. Sea lice leaped in all directions and the boys jumped back. They itched like mad, sea lice, if they bit you.

'It *stinks*,' observed Hemi, holding his nose and screwing up his brown face.

'You would too if you had been lying out here all morning, and probably all of yesterday, as well,' Kepa said, amused.

'Then why hasn't something *eaten* it?' Rewi demanded.

'I do not know. Perhaps something will, today. Or perhaps it will be taken out to sea again with the tide, where it belongs.'

But the novelty of the dead shark had already worn off and the boys were away again, running ahead — leaving Kepa to carry their rucksack along with his own — and drawing long, sweeping lines in the smooth sand with their sticks.

Eventually they came to the rocks and Kepa called them back and made them stand still in front of him.

'Now, listen to me, carefully. These rocks can be very dangerous. The waves can sneak up on you. We are only going to fish off them if you do exactly as I say. Do you understand me?'

Two dark little heads nodded gravely.

'We are only staying for two hours. After that the tide will be too high and we will be cut off from the beach. If we have not caught any fish by then, too bad. All right?'

The boys glanced at each other and rolled

their eyes — silly old Koro and his rules. 'Yes, Koro.'

'Good.' Kepa hefted the rucksacks over his shoulder. 'Now, see that gap between the two biggest rocks? We will climb up there, and then walk over onto the flat shelf at the edge of the sea. When we get there we will bait the lines and I — I, you understand, not you — will cast them. Do you understand?'

'Yes, Koro,' Rewi said, 'but can we hold the lines?'

'You can hold them as long as you stay away from the edge. If a big wave comes you will be swept off.'

'Nah,' Rewi said, puffing out his skinny chest. 'We can swim! Eh, Hemi, we can swim, we'll be all right.'

'Boy!' Kepa snapped. 'Listen to me. You can swim, I know that, but are you strong enough to hold your head above the water while you are being bashed against the rocks? Can you keep afloat long enough for someone to pull you out? Can you pull *Hemi* out, if he is swept in too?'

Rewi looked crestfallen.

'No, I did not think so. But if you stay away from the edge, and do exactly as I say, you will not have to do any of those things. Tangaroa does not take kindly to smart-alec little boys who think they know everything about the sea when they do not know the first thing. Understood?'

The boys nodded, both rather soberly now.

'Good. Now, up you go. I will be right behind you.'

And up they did go, although they stopped at

least half a dozen times on the way to inspect crabs scuttling for their lives, and the occupants of various rock pools — the sea anemones that snapped into themselves at the blink of an eye, the starfish and miniature mussels and tiny darting shrimps and fish, and the opportunistic hermit crabs that made their way leisurely across the submerged rock as if they had all the time in the world.

There was less marine life at the top of the rocks, because the sea seldom came up this far, but there was still enough to entertain small boys grown bored with waiting for the fish to bite.

Kepa settled them at a safe distance from the edge, below which was a drop of eight or nine feet into the seething, grasping waters of the Pacific.

He left them to tie on their own hooks, which, he decided after twenty minutes, was an exercise in pure patience, for him anyway.

'Nooo,' Hemi wailed, holding his line in one hand and a fish hook in the other. 'You do the knot like this, and then you put the hook on and *then* the line goes through the loop.'

'No, you put the hook on first, and *then* you do the knot!' Rewi insisted.

'No, the knot comes first!'

'But if you do the knot first, how do you get the hook on?'

'You don't close it all the way up.' In his frustration, Hemi was close to tears. 'Koro, tell him he's doing it the wrong way!'

'But is he?' Kepa asked.

'Yes! His hook will come off, and the fish will get away!'

'Perhaps, but whose fish will it be?'

Hemi squinted up at his great-grandfather. 'Rewi's?'

'That is right. And do you care if *Rewi's* fish gets away?'

Hemi grinned suddenly. 'No.'

'Then do not worry about it.'

'They won't get away. I won't let them,' Rewi grumbled, although he was not entirely sure now about his hook-knotting technique.

They eventually got their hooks attached, then threaded on lumps of satisfyingly stinky dead octopus, guaranteed to attract fish from far and wide, according to their father. Kepa cast their lines for them, then set about hooking and baiting his own.

Within fifteen minutes they had their first catch — a nice fat snapper, its pink and silver scales gleaming in the sunlight, which Kepa tossed straight back into the sea.

'That one is for Tangaroa,' he said.

The boys nodded complacently. It was customary to throw back the first catch to appease the god of the sea, and therefore ensure the success of the fishing expedition.

And only a few minutes later Kepa had a second snapper, which he slipped into his sack then tightened the drawstring so the fish could not escape. The boys giggled as the sack thrashed about seemingly on its own on the rocks.

Then something tugged on Hemi's line, and he shrieked with excitement. He gave it several gentle but calculated jerks to secure whatever was nibbling the bait, then when the weight increased he began to pull the line in, his tongue poking out in concentration.

'Steady, boy,' Kepa urged. 'Do not yank it, the fish might get loose.'

Rewi, unable to control himself, reached out and grabbed the taut line.

'No!' Hemi squealed. 'It's *mine!*'

Kepa grasped Rewi's sleeve. 'Let go, boy, this one is Hemi's. Your turn will come.'

Rewi scowled, but his frustration soon turned to excitement as a silver shape began to ascend from the watery depths.

'It's a tarakihi. I can see it. A big one, too!'

Hemi's face was red from concentration and effort, but he managed to land the fish all by himself, and twist the hook from its mouth. Kepa held the sack open and Hemi flicked his fish into it with a shout of triumph.

In the next hour they caught three more fish, one each, and a very bad-tempered octopus. They broke for lunch, and while the boys were unpacking the food their mother had prepared for them, Kepa wandered over to the gnarled trunk of an ancient pohutukawa tree at the base of the cliff to relieve himself. But as he was doing up the buttons of his trousers, something in the air — a change, a slight shift in pressure, a sly rustling noise felt rather than heard — made him turn and look out to sea.

What he saw almost stopped his heart. Coming directly towards the rocks was a series of three huge, freak waves, not yet breaking, but getting bigger and bigger as they approached. He began to run at once towards the boys who, oblivious to what was coming, had their heads down over the fish sack.

'Run!' he bellowed. '*Run to the cliff!*'

The boys glanced up then, saw the expression on his face and turned to look behind them. They shrieked in unison and began to run.

The first wave broke against the rocks, its hissing fingers snatching up the fish sack and the boys' lunches. The second surged around their ankles as they raced towards Kepa and the cliff. The third hovered briefly then crashed down, sending spray and spume yards into the air. And when it receded, it had taken both boys with it.

Kepa groaned in dismay as he peered over the edge of the shelf and down into the churning sea, but then his heart thudded with hope as he spied Rewi clinging to the face of the rock below him. The boy looked up, and Kepa saw the look of pure terror on his face.

'Hold on,' he cried as he began to climb down, his hands and feet seeking small crevasses in the rock as he went. When he reached Rewi, he held out his hand for the boy to grasp. When their grip was firm, Kepa gave an almighty wrench — which surely must have pulled the boy's arm out of its socket — and hauled him up, then shoved him over the top.

'Go back to the cliff!' he yelled, even as he turned back to the water searching despairingly for any sign of Hemi. Another wave crashed against the rocks and he hung on desperately to stop himself from being sucked into the sea.

Could that be a little boy's head, that small black blob caught up in a knot of seaweed on the surface some yards out?

Kepa didn't think twice; he twisted his body around and launched himself off the side of the rock into the heaving sea. He went under but bobbed straight back up and made for the patch of seaweed, his arms moving freely but his feet dragging in their heavy boots.

In less than a minute he was there. He reached for the little ball and yanked, crying out in relief when Hemi's face appeared beneath it. The boy seemed stunned but his eyes were open, and at the sight of his koro his face lit up. Then he coughed up a great whoosh of seawater and started to cry.

Kepa rolled over onto his back and pulled the little boy into the crook of his armpit. 'Stay still, little one, and hold on around my neck,' he ordered, almost weak with gratitude from the feel of the child's body against him.

He set out, kicking with his feet and paddling with one arm, the other holding onto Hemi tightly. His choices were to paddle around the point and head for the beach, or return straight to the rocks; he chose the rocks, because he was not sure he would have the stamina to reach the beach.

He paddled a few feet then rested on the swell, paddled again, then rested again. He felt himself flagging and tried to conserve his energy. It was taking him much longer to return to the rocks than it had to swim out, and the sea seemed to be intent on dragging him, and his mokopuna, back out.

Finally he reached the rocks and turned over. Hefting Hemi in his arms, he held the boy until a wave rose beneath them and lifted them up. At the wave's peak, he placed one hand on the boy's narrow back and the other under his bottom, and gave an almighty, straining shove. Hemi flew out of the water and hit the rock face, where he clung momentarily like a small monkey.

'Climb!' Kepa urged. '*Climb!*'

Hemi did, and disappeared over the top.

Kepa let himself relax for a moment and hung on to the rock while he gathered his strength. They were both safe. Thank God. He could climb up himself now.

But he couldn't. The tiny pricking pain he had felt at the back of his head as he'd heaved Hemi up was growing into a massive burning sensation tearing through his brain, and a loud roaring filled his ears. He blinked, and suddenly all he could see was the crimson of the pohutukawa flowers. He was so very tired too, and cold, and his arms and legs felt like lead. When he asked them to move, they chose not to respond.

He clung to the rock for a moment longer, then felt his hands let go as he slipped back into the sea.

The pain in his head stopped just as suddenly as it had begun, and now he felt weightless, floating comfortably on his back, his limbs splayed like the starfish in the rock pools. It was warm again too, and he felt the sun caressing his blind eyes and the surface of the sea stroking his hands and his face lovingly. He smelled the scent of lavender, and smiled in his mind.

Then Tangaroa claimed him, and he slipped under.

On the rocks above, two terrified little faces peered over the edge. Below them, on the surface of the once-again placid sea, bobbed a blue hat with a green feather in its band.

The boys clutched each other then, and their spiralling wails of anguish silenced even the wheeling seagulls.

★ ★ ★

When the people from the village came that afternoon to tell Joseph that his father had gone, Tamar knew then that she had moved into the very last phase of her life.

17

Burma, April 1945

Drew dozed. He seldom slept properly these days. Or perhaps he did, but just didn't realise it. Not much at all seemed real any more, so it was quite likely he was asleep when he thought he was awake.

He shifted slightly on his sleeping mat, and felt Tim's forearm resting across his ribs. Tim's bones dug into his bones, and it hurt. Everything hurt now — his body, his soul and his mind.

The headaches had not stopped, although they had settled into a pattern he'd learnt to live with, like everything else in the camp. McCaffrey had died and Major Paterson continued to give him opium whenever it was available, and that helped, although he suspected he had become addicted to it. But what the hell did that matter now? He was already an outcast of sorts, a moving, breathing freak. He knew this because when he looked down at himself, he saw not the body of a man but only sharp, protruding bones and deep hollows where flesh should have been, and the sickly yellow of cracked, ulcerated and sagging skin. Under his loin cloth — which had replaced his rotted shorts long ago — his penis rested in its sparse nest like a small, shrivelled acorn above a pair of equally shrivelled balls.

The last time he had used it, for anything other than peeing through, had been at

378

Christmas time. The Japs — completely uncharacteristically — had given them all small amounts of surprisingly edible meat for several consecutive days, and it had provided just enough nourishment to get the juices flowing again. The experience had been both exhilarating and terrible, and had driven Tim and Drew to break the vow they had made to each other some months earlier.

Tim was his lover, and had been since Easter of 1943. Drew had not wanted things to turn out that way, but they had. It had taken him many weeks of agonised soul-searching, denial and argument with himself after the day in the prison yard when Tim had touched his shoulder and then walked away, but in the end he'd been unable to ignore the manner in which his own body had responded. He had not loved Tim then, although he'd finally had to admit he was physically attracted to him, but he needed him now. Tim, for his part, insisted he had loved Drew since the first day they'd met in England, and that he'd lived in hope that Drew would some day reciprocate.

The day of revelation might have taken place in the yard, but the night on which their relationship had been consummated had not occurred for another month. Tim and Drew found themselves the sole occupants of their cell, after Keith and Don had been relegated to a week of solitary confinement for some paltry misdemeanour. The separation left Drew and Tim feeling strangely bereft, as if their cell mates had died. Their spirits had been profoundly low and, when he looked back, Drew often wondered whether that had allowed the barrier between them to come down.

He'd been lying on his side on his mat, cocooned in that bright, still state between wakefulness and sleep when thoughts were not quite dreams. There had been a stealthy shuffling noise, no louder than the sound made by a rat scampering across the concrete floor of the cell, and he had sensed a presence behind him, the warmth of someone lying close but not touching. He held his breath, knowing that it was Tim, but not daring to acknowledge the other man out loud.

Finally, after what felt like an hour of long, individual seconds ticking slowly past, but was probably only five minutes, he did speak.

'Tim?'

'Mmm?'

Drew had no idea what to say next. He did not want Tim to move away, but neither did he want the seemingly inevitable to happen. If it did, everything could — no doubt surely *would* — change for ever.

In the end he'd not had to say anything, as Tim had moved his hand and set it gently on the sharp curve of Drew's hip. Drew placed his own hand over the long thin fingers and squeezed softly, feeling horribly nervous and excited and ashamed, but somehow relieved that whatever had flitted so feverishly back and forth between them for the past weeks would now be revealed and confronted.

Tim's fingers began to draw slow circles over

380

Drew's concave belly, and he wriggled closer so that his breath blew warm on Drew's neck. Drew, feeling disconcertingly as if he were standing at the top of a very high cliff and about to hurl himself off, relaxed back against Tim's chest and let it happen. The fingers crept lower, and Drew closed his eyes as what he belatedly realised he'd been longing for finally happened.

It was not particularly erotic, it was not very passionate, but it was a release. Most of all it was overwhelmingly comforting, this closeness to another human being and the sharing of something so absolutely intimate. It made Drew feel like a person again, a real, functioning entity, and not just a rotting body.

They fell asleep in each other's arms, and when Drew woke the next morning, he felt he might be able to last just a little longer in this fetid Burmese prison after all.

Their physical affair had continued for four months, at infrequent, snatched intervals because of the almost total lack of privacy in the camp, then Tim had become so ill with dry beri-beri he'd been admitted to the hospital for several weeks. Drew had had time to think then about what they'd been doing together, about what the others might say if they found out — if, of course, they weren't aware already. Some sailors might be a little more accepting of the idea of homosexual sex — although notably less of genuine homosexual love — but airmen and soldiers would almost certainly not be, and he didn't think he could stand the stress of being shunned by the men he had come to rely on for support, friendship and survival. He had no idea whether he was a true homosexual or not, but did know that he loved Tim as a friend, and as the person who gave him physical comfort when he so desperately needed it. But he still could not rid himself of his deep conviction that wanting comfort was not a good enough reason for having sexual relations with another man. The thought of it still disgusted him even as it settled and calmed him. It was wrong. He had joined up to defeat the wrongs occurring throughout the world, and now here he was adding to them. It had to stop.

So when Tim recovered enough to be discharged, Drew sat down one evening in the yard with him and talked for a long time. When he said he would prefer the physical side of their liaison to cease, Tim agreed almost immediately. Not because he also wanted it to stop, he said, but because he could see the effect it was having on Drew, and he didn't want to continue with anything that made him unhappy. They had made their vow then, and Drew had been relieved, but was left feeling hollow and somehow even more ashamed of himself.

Then conditions at the camp had deteriorated even further, as the Japanese directed their frustrations over their increasing losses and defeats at the prisoners. The food was reduced to such meagre, nutritionless portions that the men were lucky to find the energy to move, never mind anything else. There were deaths every day, and the hospital staff were no longer able to cope. It was as much as they could do to get the bodies decently buried.

Then Christmas had come, and the extra food, and Drew had found himself once again finding physical comfort with Tim. And once more he drew away as soon as his conscience became too much to bear. So now they were back to being just mates, although, as had happened last night, Drew occasionally woke in the morning to find Tim cuddled behind him. Keith had died three months ago, from a gangrenous ulcer on his thigh, and only Don shared their cell now, and if he had noticed that they sometimes shared the same sleeping mat — which he surely must have — he never commented.

Drew was tempted to think that perhaps nobody did care any more, and that what he and Tim did or didn't do wouldn't matter a damn. But he knew it would. It would matter to *him*, because he still believed it to be essentially wrong. And if the rumours that the British were getting closer by the day were true, then he might soon be faced with the task of turning back into the person he'd been before he was captured, and that person most certainly did not have relations with other men.

And the rumours must be true, because four days ago some of the Japanese had left the camp, taking with them about four hundred prisoners, about half of Rangoon's inmates — all those still fit enough to march.

A noise outside woke him fully, and he gently disentangled himself from Tim's arm, rolled over and very slowly got to his knees. He was so weak these days that any quick movement caused him to almost pass out, and he couldn't afford to bump into anything as his skin was so fragile it tore like tissue paper. Even a tiny contusion could grow into a festering great hole in the flesh, and he knew better than almost anyone that he could die from such an injury in less than a week.

He hauled himself upright, waited a few moments until his head stopped spinning, then slipped his feet into his boots. What the hell was going on outside? He glanced down at Tim, but he was still fast asleep. So was Don.

He was on duty at the hospital soon anyway, so he might as well get up now. As he trudged in semi-darkness across the central yard that connected all sections of the prison compound, he noticed it had suddenly become very quiet, but it was still several minutes before he spotted the small crowd of prisoners milling about the main gate. He stopped and blinked, then rubbed his eyes and blinked again.

The gate was wide open.

He approached cautiously, expecting at any moment to be shot or at least belted by one of the prison guards with a rifle butt. But then he noticed something else: there *were* no guards.

As he reached the nearest man he stopped; the bloke had his hands over his face and tears trickled between his fingers.

'What's going on? Why's the gate open?'

The man took his hands away and shook his head. He sobbed and a bubble of snot blew out of his nose, and he shook his head again. He seemed unable to speak.

Drew went on to the next man, an acquaintance from the compound next door to his.

'Bob, what's going on?'

Bob nodded at the gate. 'Watch.'

Wing Commander Bill Hudson, the most senior prisoner in the camp, stood in the open gateway with his hands on his hips, looking profoundly bemused. He glanced around then stepped through the gap, set one foot down on the ground outside the walls, then came back in and closed and locked the gates.

He turned to the small crowd. 'They've gone. The Japs have gone.' He held up a piece of paper. 'They've left a note saying we're free, and that they hope we might all meet again on the battlefield somewhere. Jesus Christ,' he added in disbelief, shaking his head.

Drew was stunned. They were free, they could go, they were free.

Soon the entire camp knew, although Hudson advised everyone to stay inside the walls in case they were shot by Allied forces, who were quite obviously very near.

They were; the RAF arrived not long afterwards and began bombing and shooting around the prison. Several men broke into the Japanese stores and took a bucket of whitewash up onto the roofs, and painted 'Japs Gone, British Here' to ward off the bombing. It didn't, and the RAF phrase 'Extract Digit' was also added, letting the circling pilots know that the occupants were indeed allies. The bombing finally ceased.

Four days later the British marched into Rangoon, and Hudson opened the prison gates. Drew and Tim were among the hundreds of men who spilled out onto the road outside, yelling and whooping and cheering madly.

But they stopped abruptly when they saw the expressions on the faces of their liberators — an appalled mixture of amazement, horror and profound pity. Drew looked down at his ruined old boots, emaciated yellow legs rising out of them like bleached sticks, at his grubby loin cloth and the skeletal form of his hip bones jutting out like a wire coathanger beneath ribs that could clearly be counted. The Rangoon internees didn't know it then, but they were the first Allied men to be released from a Japanese POW camp.

Drew raised his head and looked at Tim, and quietly began to weep. Tim reached for Drew's hand, then let his arm drop.

'It's over, Drew,' he said quietly. 'All of it.'

And then he started to cry too, and Drew nodded, because it was true.

They were given water and food, which made many of them vomit, then taken to the nearest air strip and loaded onto Allied aircraft as soon as they touched down. Before they could really grasp what was happening to them, they were on their way to a military hospital in Calcutta.

Kenmore, May 1945

By the time VE day was officially celebrated in New Zealand on 9 May, sixteen thousand men of the Second New Zealand Expeditionary Force had already returned home. These were the soldiers who had served overseas for three and a half years or more, and they were tired, worn down and bloody relieved it was finally over, for them anyway.

For some months now there had been clear signs that the German war effort was nearing collapse. The papers were full of stories of Allied victories in Europe, and most believed that it would only be a matter of time before the Germans surrendered, especially now that Germany itself had been overrun. Towards the end of April German units all over Europe began to lay down their arms, and then on the last day of April came the news that Hitler had killed both himself and his new wife Eva Braun. Berlin fell on 2 May, and five days later Admiral Karl Dönitz, Hitler's successor, met with Allied leaders outside Rheims in France and signed an agreement of surrender.

When the news that the war in Europe had ended came over the radio at Kenmore, Leila, finishing a bit of hand-sewing in the parlour, dropped it and clapped her hands with delight. Daisy, sitting on the floor with her own 'sewing' — a piece of hessian and an enormous wool-threaded darning needle with the point filed off — copied her gleefully until Leila snatched her up and tore around telling everyone that the war was finally over — upstairs to Tamar resting in her room, into the kitchen where Keely was baking, then outside to Owen, Joseph and Henry, tinkering with something in the implement shed. Then, breathlessly, she hopped onto the farm bicycle, tucked a thoroughly overexcited Daisy into the basket on the handlebars, and pedalled madly over to tell Erin, then back up the track to James and Lucy's house.

Lucy had already heard, as she kept the radio on all the time, and Leila found her and James waltzing up and down the rows of trees in the orchard. James lifted Daisy, shrieking with delight, out of the bicycle basket and popped her on his shoulders, then grabbed Leila and waltzed her around too.

Work stopped for the day and everyone gathered in the kitchen of the big house to celebrate. Everyone, that was, except Erin and Joseph who, understandably, wanted a little time by themselves to remember Billy before they joined in the festivities. They turned up an hour later, though, smiling widely if a little tearfully and bearing several bottles of beer and one of rather good champagne they'd been given by someone at Christmas and hadn't got around to opening. Whatever they'd needed to say to each other had obviously been said, and Tamar especially was delighted that they felt up to joining in.

Their impromptu party escalated as neighbours dropped by for celebratory drinks and the sharing of expert opinions on the final days of Berlin, Hitler's obvious lunacy, the certainty of Japan surrendering any day now and anything else relating to the 'sodding bloody war', as James kept referring to it within earshot of Henry.

Henry, thoroughly overexcited himself, amused himself by going around tapping people on the arm, waiting until they asked, 'Yes, Henry?' then saying 'Sodding *bloody* war' with such obvious relish that no one could keep a straight face. It wore off fairly quickly, however, and Keely was eventually compelled to tell him to stop it. But nothing could dampen his spirits today, not with all this excitement going on, so while no one was looking he pinched a bottle of beer and went outside with one of his school mates, whose parents lived nearby and had come over for a drink, to practise their burps.

Keely, Erin and Lucy ended up feeding about twenty extra people that night, and the evening was a great success, especially after the Murdochs, the Morgans and the Deanes had all had a turn talking on the telephone to Thomas and Lucy in Dunedin, Bonnie in Wellington — who kept saying she had to get off the barracks phone because other people were wanting to use it — and Kathleen, who said the same thing about the telephone in her lodging house. Neither of the girls knew when they would be coming home — technically the war hadn't really ended yet because of the bloody-minded Japanese — but they would keep their families posted.

Duncan, Liam, Robert and Drew couldn't be contacted, of course, because they were still overseas, but everyone vowed to write letters to each of them the following day, so that they wouldn't be left out of the celebrations at home. With the war in Europe now at an end, surely they must be back soon? And if the stories about the liberation of prisoners in the Japanese POW camps in Burma were correct, then Drew might even be home before the others.

At the end of the night they all raised a solemn toast to everyone who wasn't home yet, and to those who wouldn't be coming home, and it suddenly occurred to them all that it really was nearly all over — the endless working for the war effort, the making do and going without, and the ever-present worry about friends and family away overseas.

The party broke up at midnight because, German surrender or not, there would still be recalcitrant sheep, sagging fences and malfunctioning farm machinery to be tended to the following day. The visitors drifted off, and the Kenmore clan headed for their beds. There was a short panic when it was discovered that Henry seemed to have disappeared, but after he was discovered asleep in the garden next to an empty beer bottle and a small puddle of sick, all was well again, bar Keely and Owen's mystification over who on earth had given him alcohol to drink. But by the time he was tucked up in bed with his face and hands washed thoroughly with a warm, soapy flannel, they had forgotten about it.

They were thinking instead about what would happen when Bonnie came home from the air force, and how long they would have her and

Leila and Daisy to themselves before the three of them headed off for America. Keely hoped it would be ages before the red tape was sorted out and they were cleared to emigrate as war brides, although of course Bonnie was only a war fiancée. There was talk already of New Zealand women — many with small children in tow — bombarding the authorities to arrange passage overseas to meet up with their wartime husbands and lovers. She imagined it would be an absolute nightmare, sorting out who was legally married and who wasn't, who was entitled to go and who did not have the required credentials, and she could see that along with the excitement and anticipation there would be tears and heartbreak for those who discovered too late that the loves of their lives had disappeared without a trace, or already had a wife and five children at home. In bed, cuddled into Owen's comforting back, she crossed her fingers in the dark to ward off the possibility that Leila might turn out to be one of those poor wretches.

In their house half a mile away, James and Lucy were thinking about their own children. What would happen when Duncan came home? Would Claire come out to New Zealand with him straight away or would she have to wait in England for a while? What would he do for a job now that he was disabled, and was he in fact disabled? He couldn't be in that much of a state, James pointed out, if he'd been doing a perfectly good job in England for the RAF up until now, even if it wasn't flying. Lucy insisted that disfigured did not necessarily mean disabled, but

James was of the gloomy opinion that jobs might be thin on the ground when the men came home, and therefore it was likely that a fit, normal-looking man was more likely to be given a job over a man with a scarred face and hands. Lucy told James he was being a pessimist, and what about all those rehabilitation schemes everyone said were being putting into place for returned veterans? James said what about them, and that Lucy was being naïve — look what happened after the last war. But then he said that there was plenty of work for Duncan in the orchard if he wanted to do that, and perhaps they could even form a partnership if that suited everyone, and Lucy knew then that that was what he really wanted.

And there was Drew, too — he would have to find something to do as well. He'd mentioned in several of the letters he'd sent home before being captured that he very much enjoyed life at sea, and that he was considering — but *only* considering at that point, mind — joining the Royal New Zealand Navy as a regular after the war. Or the merchant navy, if the RNZN wouldn't have him, which would be very unlikely given his active service with the RN over the past eighteen months. But Lucy suspected that Drew might need some time at home to recuperate and build himself up again until he was fit to get on with his life. She knew James was thinking this too, but would not discuss it with her in case she became upset. Which was silly, because she'd handled everything else unpleasant that had happened in her life so far perfectly adequately.

In the Deane household, Joseph lay in bed talking about Robert rejoining him at Kenmore. The boy was a born sheep farmer, he said, and he'd like nothing better than to train him up to the point where he could hand him the reins when it came time to retire. And Ana, too, if that was what she wanted. But then Erin reminded him that Ana was likely to be flicking someone else's reins, if David Leonard got what he so obviously wanted. Joseph looked at his wife sharply, and Erin laughed at him and told him not to worry — she meant that David wanted to marry Ana, and if she wasn't mistaken, there would be a proposal in the not too distant future. Not too distant at all.

In the big house, Tamar sat in her bed alone, her back supported by a pile of pillows, the bedside lamp shedding a soft light on her unopened book. It was just over four months since Kepa had died, and she still had to squeeze her eyes shut against the tears whenever she thought about him. She had raged that she had not even had the opportunity to say goodbye to him, but after a couple of weeks it occurred to her that she had in fact done just that, the last time she had seen him. She was not a particularly demonstrative person by nature, and neither really was he, but she remembered he'd said quite emphatically that he loved her, and that she had made a point of saying it back to him. So perhaps they had known, somehow. They had of course been aware that their years together were limited, and that each one lived was a bonus and something to be savoured, but she'd always assumed she would precede him to the grave. She was the one with the damaged heart, after all, while he had always been as fit as a damned flea. In a way she was glad he'd had a stroke — she would have hated to watch him weaken and then fade away until he became someone who was not Kepa any more. And he'd died ensuring that his precious great-grandchildren would live, and she knew he would have considered the sacrifice worth it, even if it had robbed him of the last few years of his own life. She missed him so much it hurt her physically, in her heart.

She sighed. Kepa had gone, but Liam was still alive and would soon be coming home. He would have to be told about Evie, and she knew she would be the one to tell him. He could not be left to go charging over to Palmerston North to look for her when in all likelihood she wasn't there any more, or if she was, it might be with a toddler hanging onto her skirts, one that couldn't possibly be Liam's. She had toyed with the idea of sending him a letter before he arrived back in New Zealand, to prepare him, but decided against it. No, she would sit him down and tell him face to face, and then he would not have to absorb the news alone.

Japan, August 1945
On 26 July 1945, the United States, Britain and China issued Japan with the Potsdam Declaration, an ultimatum to surrender or face 'prompt

394

and utter destruction'. The Japanese chose to ignore it.

Consequently, at 2.45 a.m. on Monday 6 August, a B-29 Superfortress named *Enola Gay* took off from Tinian Island in the Marianas on a course for Japan. The aircraft was crewed by twelve members of the US Army Air Force. When the *Enola Gay* reached her target over the city of Hiroshima, the weather was fine and clear. At 8.16 a.m., the single, modified bomb bay opened in the aircraft's belly releasing the atomic bomb named 'Little Boy', killing two hundred thousand Japanese civilians.

Prime Minister Suzuki refused to accept a subsequent ultimatum from the Allied powers, and at 11.02 a.m. on 9 August, a second atomic bomb, this one named 'Fat Boy', was dropped on the city of Nagasaki, killing another one hundred and fifty thousand.

Five days later, Emperor Hirohito accepted the Allied terms of surrender. The following day, thousands of New Zealanders waiting by their radios heard the voice of British Prime Minister Clement Attlee declare that the war had finally ended.

★ ★ ★

In Wellington on VJ Day the weather was terrible, which is why Bonnie and Kathleen found themselves in the crowded, noisy lounge bar of a pub in Victoria Street. When the news had broken Kathleen and her workmates, still in their sewing overalls, had rushed out into the

395

street and had been flitting from pub to pub. By the time Kathleen spotted Bonnie in Willis Street, her apron had disappeared, her hair had fallen out of its victory roll and was whipping about in all directions in the steadily rising wind, her face was flushed from a tad too much Pimms, and her lipstick was smeared from the attentions of opportunistic kiss-grabbers in the revelling crowds.

'Bonnie!' she screeched over the noise of someone blowing a French horn less than two feet away from her ear. 'Bonnie Morgan! Over here!'

Bonnie, concentrating on avoiding the passionate embrace of an inebriated New Zealand soldier, didn't hear her, so Kathleen fought her way closer, almost breaking her ankle in the process when the heel of her shoe became stuck in a gutter grate.

'Damn!' she swore, and bent down to extricate herself. Her foot came out of the shoe easily enough but then the shoe wouldn't come out of the grate, which left her hopping in place on one leg wondering what to do next. She certainly wasn't about to spend the rest of the afternoon trotting about in only one shoe, and neither was she prepared to leave the stuck shoe behind — the pair had used up the last of her shoe coupons for this year and had cost an outrageous thirty-five shillings.

'*Bonnie!*' she bawled again. '*Over here!*'

This time Bonnie heard, her face lighting up as she fought her way towards her cousin. Then, as she noticed her cousin's predicament, she started laughing and found she couldn't stop. Kathleen began tittering herself and soon they were cackling their heads off, and had to sit down on a bench at an adjacent tram stop. Kathleen almost had herself under control until she caught sight of her stylish but lonely shoe again, caught in the grate all by itself, and off she went once more until her face was bright red and her eyes streaming.

It was then that a rather dashing moustached RAF airman appeared in front of them. Fair hair showed under his blue cap, and he had lovely brown eyes, currently screwed up against the wind, and the rain that was just starting to come down. He stood with his arms crossed — whether this was because he always stood like that or he wanted to show off his pilot's wings to their best advantage, Bonnie wasn't sure — and appeared to be struggling not to laugh himself.

Kathleen pointed at the grate and wailed, 'My shoe. Please, save it!'

She sounded so pathetic that the airman and Bonnie both burst out laughing, Bonnie with her hands pressed against her cheeks because they were already aching from the last bout of hysterics.

The airman whipped his cap off and bowed low. 'I see you're in a spot of bother, Miss. How can the RAF be of service?'

'My shoe, it's stuck in the grate. I have to have it back. It's . . . it's one of a pair, you see.'

'Really? Well, yes, I can see your predicament.'

He knelt down, getting the knees of his trousers wet in the process, and extracted a pocket knife from the top pocket of his tunic. Expertly flicking the knife open he wedged the blade between the grate and the concrete in which it was set. One or two forceful jiggles and he had the grate up and over, the heel of Kathleen's shoe still jammed between two of the bars. Then he did something that Kathleen seemed to think was awfully clever, judging by the daffy look of wonder on her face: he up-ended the grate, rested one side of it on the bench then pushed the heel rather vigorously back through with the heel of his palm.

'Voilá!' he said, and handed the rescued shoe to Kathleen with a flourish.

'Oh, thank you so much. I really don't know what I would have done if you hadn't come along.'

Bonnie rolled her eyes. She had never seen her cousin behaving in such a soppy manner; it must be the Pimms she could smell rather strongly on her breath. 'Hopped around for the rest of the day, I expect,' she said tartly. 'Thanks very much for your help, Flight Lieutenant. We'll be off now.'

The airman, who had been staring at Kathleen, looked a little disconcerted. 'Hang on a minute. I mean . . . well, is there anywhere I can escort you? Oh, I do beg your pardon, I'm Flight Lieutenant Jonathan Lawson, from Suffolk, England. I'm here on the Empire Air Training Scheme. But now I'm probably out of a job.'

'Never mind,' Kathleen replied gaily. 'Something's bound to come up.'

Jonathan Lawson looked as if he might want to say something rather risqué, but checked himself just in time. Bonnie suspected he was as tiddly as Kathleen, but somewhat more successful at hiding it.

The inebriated Kiwi soldier reappeared, and draped himself all over her.

'Found ya, darling! Thought you'd sneak away from me, didn't ya!' he slurred, puckering his lips in what he clearly believed was an irresistible fashion.

'Oh, get off!' Bonnie exclaimed, and gave him a good hard push that sent him staggering backwards.

'Playing hard to get, eh?' he said as he rebounded off someone in the crowd and lurched back again.

Jonathan jammed his cap back on his head and stepped gallantly forward. 'I say, excuse me, I don't think this young lady appreciates your attentions at all.'

The drunk looked him up and down and sneered, 'What would you know, ya big Pommy poof!'

'That's enough, pal. You're obviously not wanted so sling your hook.'

'Piss off yourself, ya whinging Limey flyboy!'

'Oh, fuck off!'

'Fuck off yourself, arsehole!'

Bonnie stood up. 'Hey! *Hey!* Stop it, the pair of you. This is supposed to be a celebration, not the start of a new war.' She hooked her arm through Jonathan's, and dragged him off, collecting Kathleen on the way.

They marched down the centre of the street, turned into Willeston then right again into Victoria Street and through the doors of the nearest pub. Fighting their way through to the lounge bar, Bonnie shoved a pound note in Jonathan's hand.

'A Pimms, a gin and tonic, and whatever you're having, thanks. We'll be sitting over there.' She pointed to a table that still had three empty seats, and Jonathan nodded and headed for the bar.

Bonnie steered Kathleen across the room and sat her down.

'How much have you had to drink?'

Kathleen shrugged. 'I dunno. Why?'

'You're acting rather strangely.'

'Am I? Oh. He's nice isn't he, that Jonathan?'

'If you like that sort of thing.'

'Don't you? Oooh, I do. It's that lovely English accent.'

'Yes, well, you be careful, all right?'

Jonathan came back, the tip of his tongue poking out as he carried the three drinks with exaggerated care.

'Nice daffodil,' he said, nodding at the yellow flower tucked into the lapel of Bonnie's WAAF tunic.

'Thank you. We pinched them from Bolton Street cemetery on the way in.'

'Jolly nice,' Jonathan said, then turned immediately to Kathleen. 'Look, I'm sorry, I don't even know your name.'

'Kathleen Murdoch. Very pleased to meet you.' She held out her hand.

Jonathan shook it with inordinate reverence, then asked Bonnie, 'And you are . . . ?'

'Bonnie Morgan. We're cousins.'

'You're a WAAF, I take it?'

'Mmm.' Bonnie took a sip of her gin and tonic and grimaced. It was rather strong — the barman must be feeling generous.

'Awful weather you have here in Wellington,' Jonathan noted cheerfully as he swept his wet hair back off his face.

'Can be a little windy,' Bonnie agreed.

'And what do you do, Kathleen?'

'Me? Oh, I make uniforms. I was manpowered into it.'

'Sorry? Oh, quite. We have that in England, too.'

There was a short lull in the conversation then, which they all tried to fill by speaking at once.

'Sorry,' Jonathan said again. 'I was just saying that my lot's having a bit of a do at the base tonight, in honour of the surrender and all that, and I was wondering if you girls would like to come along?' But he was looking at Kathleen when he said it.

Bonnie said, 'You're not at Rongotai, are you? I've not seen you there.'

'No, Anderson Park, and only for the last couple of months.'

'I'd love to come,' Kathleen said. 'Um, how old are you, Jonathan?'

'Don't be so rude,' Bonnie admonished.

'Twenty-three.'

'Oh dear,' Kathleen said, her pretty but pink

face crumpling. 'That makes me an older woman. I'm twenty-five.'

'You don't look it,' Jonathan replied chivalrously, 'and I don't care. Shall I pick you up?'

'Yes please,' Kathleen replied, and gave him the address of her lodging house.

'Kathleen, you don't even know him!'

'I do, we've both known him for at least half an hour.'

Bonnie leaned in to Jonathan and said quietly, 'I'll be around to see her first thing tomorrow morning, you know, and if you've treated her in anything less than a thoroughly gentlemanly manner, I'll have you. Is that clear?'

'Perfectly,' Jonathan replied, smiling sweetly. 'I take it that means you won't be joining us?'

'Unfortunately, no, thank you.' Bonnie held up her left hand. 'I'm engaged to someone who is, as we speak, probably still island hopping.'

'A Yank?'

'No, an American. Look after her, please. I mean it.'

Bonnie sighed. First Leila, and now Kathleen. She felt like somebody's mother.

Part Three

Aftermath
1946–1947

18

Kenmore

To Erin and Joseph's great disappointment, it seemed that Robert wasn't going to be coming home for some time. Because he'd joined the Second New Zealand Expeditionary Force quite late in the war, after a lengthy stand-down in Italy, he was sent to Japan as part of the British Commonwealth Occupation Force in February of 1946. The first letter Erin and Joseph received from him after he arrived in Japan was full of moans and groans about terrible billets, bad weather, bloody awful food and chronic boredom, but the second contained the news that he thought he'd be coming home in July, after replacements arrived from New Zealand. So he'd see them then, and would his mother rather have a silk kimono or a genuine Japanese tea set? Erin wrote back and said she didn't really mind, as long as he came home in one piece.

By September of 1945, almost all the New Zealanders serving in the RAF had been demobilised, including Duncan and Liam.

Liam arrived back in New Zealand two months later, in the company of two mates he'd flown with in England. They'd hitched a lift home in a series of noisy, uncomfortable RNZAF transports, and had landed at Rongotai early one November morning. He knew Bonnie had been demobbed by then so didn't bother looking for her. He said goodbye for now to his friends, telephoned Kenmore to say he was on his way home and went straight to the railway station. By lunchtime the next day, he found himself stepping onto the railway platform in Napier with his kit bag over his shoulder and not much else to his name. Tamar, Keely, James and Joseph were there to meet him, although everyone else had stayed at home because it would have meant bringing in two vehicles, and petrol rationing was still on.

Liam went straight up to Tamar and wrapped his arms around her. 'Oh, Gran, I was so sorry to hear about Kepa. I really was. And I'm sorry I wasn't here.'

Tamar hugged him tightly, blinking back hot tears. 'I know you would have come if you could, dear. It's all right, I'm all right now.'

He nodded and stepped back, and she gave him a watery smile and squeezed his hand.

There was plenty of backslapping from the men, and hugs from Keely, but no one said anything about Evie, including Liam himself.

By the time they arrived back at Kenmore, Tamar had worked herself into yet another state over how to tell him. Seeing him in the flesh made it even more difficult. Finally, after he'd had a cup of tea and something to eat and stowed his kit in his old bedroom, she asked him to come down to the study. He joined her a few minutes later, flopping into one of the armchairs beside the empty fireplace.

'It's great to be back,' he said cheerfully,

'although I have to admit I'm knackered. It was a long trip home with no end of stops and mucking about.'

Tamar seated herself opposite him, perched her spectacles on the end of her nose and sat back to allow herself a good, careful look at him. He was still the same Liam he'd always been, a little taller perhaps, but there was no denying he wasn't a boy any more. The golden curls were still there, and the merry blue eyes, but there was something wary in them now, something suggesting he'd seen things over the last few years he thought he'd never have to contemplate.

'You look well,' she said. 'Tired, but well.'

He nodded. 'You look well too, Gran. Your hair's gone completely grey. It suits you.'

'Yes, well, you can blame Henry for that.'

Liam lit a cigarette, inhaled deeply then let out a thin stream of blue smoke as he talked. 'My God, he's grown up, he was only a nipper when I left!'

'Yes, he has, hasn't he?' Tamar looked down at her hands for a moment. 'Liam, there really is no easy way for me to say this, and I'm so very sorry, but . . . '

Liam raised a hand. 'Gran, if it's about Evie, don't worry, I already know. I've known for ages.'

'About . . . ?'

'Yes, all of it. I know she had a baby. She gave it up for adoption, apparently. A mate from Ohakea, one of the ground crew, wrote and told me she was, well, she wasn't exactly pining for me.'

'Oh, Liam, I'm so sorry.'

'I was too, for a while. And angry. I really loved her, Gran. Or at least I thought I did. Anyway, I had a yarn to the CO about it, asked for leave to come home for a couple of weeks to sort it out. And do you know, he said something that really sort of put it all into perspective.'

Tamar raised her eyebrows. 'And what was that?'

'He said yes, I could have the leave, if I was one hundred per cent sure it was what I really wanted, but to think about it for a day or two first. So I went away and I did think about it. And I watched the chaps in my squadron busting a gut to get up there day after day — we were flying ourselves ragged at the time, bombing all over the place — and I watched the Luftwaffe coming over in formations so massive you couldn't see the sky through them, and one morning I decided I'd rather just stay with the squadron. Because if Evie was worth running home for, I shouldn't *have* to run home, should I? So I wrote her a letter instead, and said outright that I knew what was going on, and what was she going to do about it? And she wrote back and said she wasn't going to do anything about it, not while I was over there and she was stuck here bored and lonely in New Zealand, anyway.'

'At least she was honest,' Tamar said somewhat caustically.

'I suppose. So I thought about that for a while, too. She knew I was on the eve of going off when we married, she knew that perfectly well, so perhaps she never intended to be, well, faithful

408

to me. And now that I look back, she wasn't really that sort of girl at all, was she, the type to wait quietly at home?'

Tamar refrained from stating exactly what sort of girl she thought Evie was. 'What do you think you might do about it, now that you're back?'

'I've already done it, ages ago. I wrote and said I thought the best thing to do would be to divorce, then I filed for one on the grounds of adultery. And she was pregnant by then, so she couldn't really refute it. So I'm now single and fancy-free again.'

'Did she ask for money?'

Liam ground his cigarette out in an ashtray. 'She didn't actually. And I must admit that, by then, I had expected she might. But I don't think she was a bad girl, Gran, just an irresponsible one. I think she genuinely cared for me, but when I wasn't there any more, she needed to find someone else. Or a series of someone elses, which I gather was actually the case.'

Poor Liam, Tamar thought. But she didn't for one moment consider telling him she'd told him so. 'And have you, well, have you come to terms with it all now?'

'Oh, yes, although I still feel a bit . . . ' he trailed off, as if not sure whether to burden his grandmother with even more of his woes.

'A bit hurt?'

Liam nodded. 'It was my own fault, but it still wasn't very nice.'

Tamar imagined that it must have been devastating. 'Put it behind you, dear. Some lovely girl will come along soon, I'm sure of it.

Don't let your experience with Evie put you off.'

'I'll try not to, but I must say finding a new wife isn't exactly at the top of my list at the moment. I think I'd just like to concentrate on getting back to normal first. It's going to feel very strange for a while, I think, not flying every day, not trying to kill people.'

★ ★ ★

Drew had arrived home halfway through December, also via the RNZAF — preferential treatment because of his status as an ex-POW and because the journey by sea might have been detrimental to his health.

After four weeks in the military hospital in Calcutta, he and the other British survivors of Rangoon had been flown back to England for further rest and medical treatment. He'd put on weight and his malaria was more or less under control now — or at least treatable when he was suffering a bout — but the terrible headaches were still going on. He'd had five or six in the hospital in England, and after the first three the doctor in charge of his case had sent a shrink to see him. Drew had asked why the hell he needed to see a shrink when he was having physical pain, and the doctor, a major from the Royal Army Medical Corps, had muttered something about the headaches perhaps being psychological. They weren't, and Drew bloody well knew they weren't, but he'd agreed to see a shrink anyway.

The psychiatrist diagnosed severe stress from the prolonged incarceration in Rangoon Jail,

410

compounded by very poor physical health, and declared that Drew was in fact in a state of some mental disorder. But he also said he doubted that any of that was causing the headaches, although of course who could really know? In the psychiatrist's opinion it was more likely to have been the head injuries, which backed up what McCaffrey had said in the camp. Sometimes such injuries caused lasting damage to the brain; he was sorry but in his experience all that could be done was treatment of the symptoms, rather than the cause, and that would probably require very strong painkillers. He was no neuropathologist, of course, and could refer Drew if that was what he wanted, but it could be a very long and involved investigatory process in England. Drew said he would rather go into all that when he got back to New Zealand.

He had said nothing to the psychiatrist about the other matter that was causing him to lie awake at night, and making him want to burst into tears at the oddest and most inopportune moments during the day. He never did cry, of course, because it would have been terribly unmanly, especially given that he'd been out of the camps for some months and should be getting over it by now. But, oh God, he really did feel like crying, and he was terrified that if he started he might not be able to stop.

Tim had gone, two weeks before. He had simply risen very early one morning, made his bed neatly, then walked out of the hospital and disappeared. He'd left a note, though, in the top drawer of Drew's bedside locker. It had said:

Dear Drew,

I'm so sorry but I've thought about this very carefully, and I think the best thing for both of us is for me to just go. I love you, and I always will, but I know what this is doing to you. Deep down, I've always known what I am, but I don't believe that you have come to that point yet, if in fact you ever will.

We won't meet again, as I'm not going back home. People like me will always be more readily accepted in certain corners of England than I would ever be in New Zealand.

Being with you kept me alive in Rangoon, and I will never forget that, and I would rather do anything than continue to hurt you.

All my love, always,
Tim

Drew's first reaction had been to run down the driveway of the hospital and look for Tim, but Tim was a very resourceful and capable man, and Drew knew he would be long gone by now. He also knew that Tim always meant what he said.

In a way he was grateful, because now he would not have to make any sort of decision about their friendship, and everything that went with it, but in another way he was devastated. He had come to rely on Tim so much for companionship and comfort and support that he felt quite lost without him.

412

But none of this was the sort of thing he could discuss with anyone else — not the psychiatrist, even though he'd seemed like a sympathetic sort of bloke, and certainly not the major who was overseeing his medical treatment. He was a reasonable doctor, but Drew suspected that the second he mentioned anything even remotely concerning homosexuality — especially after the business with the headaches, which Drew knew the major already thought were effeminate — he would be shuffled off to a solitary room so he couldn't 'contaminate' any of the other patients, or even wired up to a machine designed to fry any such tendencies out of his head for ever. So he'd kept it to himself.

His homecoming had been everything he'd imagined it would be during his three long years in Rangoon. They'd all been there at the Napier railway station to meet him when he'd arrived on 19 December, just in time for his first Christmas in New Zealand since 1940. Even Tamar had made the trip in, which touched Drew deeply, as he knew from his parents' letters — although not her own, of course — that she was not keeping very good health these days.

He was quite shocked when he saw how old she was finally beginning to look, although not as shocked, he suspected, as she and the rest of his family were to see the state he was in. He knew he was still markedly underweight, that his skin was still yellow from the last malaria attack he'd had just before leaving England, and of course his hair had thinned noticeably from the malnutrition and he'd lost several of his back

413

teeth. He was grateful, as they stood silently, gazing at him with a horror they could not hide, that they couldn't see the deep, disfiguring scars on his legs and feet from the tropical ulcers which had now healed, but would leave their mark for ever.

But his family seemed at a loss only for moments; his mother was the first to rally, enveloping him in a huge, fragrant hug that almost knocked him off his feet. His father was next, and Drew was considerably disconcerted himself to see he was weeping openly.

After a bout of vigorous nose blowing into his handkerchief, James finally managed to say, 'Welcome home, son. It means the world to us to have you back.'

And it did. Having waited for months and then years for word of their son, James and Lucy had both been guilty of wondering from time to time whether or not he was still actually alive. James, as a veteran himself, was especially aware of the ease with which men on active service could and did vanish seemingly into thin air. In his time it had been into the greedy, grey mud of French fields, but now he supposed it could have been anywhere in the Indian Ocean, or in the hot, seething jungles of Indonesia. Neither the Royal Navy nor the Red Cross had been able to tell them how he was, only where they assumed he had been incarcerated. But they had been able to confirm that when POWs died, the Japanese did occasionally pass this information on, and as they had received no such notification regarding Able Seaman Andrew Murdoch, it

414

could only be assumed that he was still alive. Somewhere.

And so they had continued hoping, and praying, and Lucy had refused to let his bedroom be disturbed, not even for visitors. And it seemed to have paid off, because here he was, taller than he had been when he'd left home at the age of nineteen, certainly very much thinner and older-looking, but here all the same.

They would all be home soon, all of his and Lucy's children — the whole clan, in fact, when Duncan finally got back, except for poor Billy, and Robert who was still on active service — but he wondered how long it would be before they all started to go their separate ways again. He desperately hoped his sons would stay on at Kenmore and work with him, but knew he could only wait and wish.

Kathleen, he suspected, would be off soon enough, although where, he had no idea. Since she'd been released from her war job in Wellington she'd received an awful lot of mail from England from a certain Jonathan Lawson, a young RAF pilot she'd apparently met on VJ Day, and there had been talk about the chap coming back to New Zealand next year for a visit. Well, that would no doubt be very nice for Kathleen, who seemed rather smitten, but James wasn't sure if he fancied the idea of some bloke turning up out of the blue and wooing his only daughter away. And it would probably be back to England where they'd never get to see her again unless they made the effort of going there for a holiday and that could only ever be at the end of

415

the fruit-picking season each year. Lucy said he was being a worrywort and getting ahead of himself, but it didn't stop him fretting about it.

But at least Drew was back, and Duncan would be home soon, and for a while they would all be together again.

★ ★ ★

Drew thought it would be easy to settle in at home, but it was proving to be very difficult.

He had not been able to get used to sleeping in a comfortable bed again, for a start. In the hospitals, whenever he was feeling out of sorts, he'd simply spread a blanket on the ground next to his cot and slept there. Nobody had really seemed to mind, and plenty of the other POW patients had done it too, but here it didn't feel quite so right. It upset his parents, and the first time his mother had discovered him sleeping on the floor she'd burst into tears. He tried to explain to her that he just somehow felt safer closer to the ground, but she hadn't understood, although he knew she was trying hard. After breakfast that morning his father had come and had a chat with him and, surprisingly, he'd had some very helpful advice about what a bloke could do when that sort of thing was going on. He could go for a walk, even if it was two o'clock in the morning, or find someone to talk to who might understand how he was feeling, or go out and do some hard physical work, which James said he'd often found useful.

By the end of his first week home, Drew was

416

finally beginning to understand what had so plagued his father for so many years. And it shocked him, to think that James had carried all that fear and anxiety and confusion around with him for decades, and that no one had been there to help him. By the time he got around to asking his father why not, he was almost irrationally angry about it all.

'Oh, but I didn't have no one,' James replied. 'Not at all.'

'But . . . but if there was someone, well, I don't understand.'

James looked at his son thoughtfully and somewhat sadly. 'Don't you? I rather thought you might.'

Drew said nothing, but there was a horrible crawling feeling in his stomach at the sudden certainty that his father was seeing straight through him.

'You see, Drew, I did have someone to talk to, several people in fact. I had your Uncle Joseph, and Thomas and Owen — they all went through experiences during the war just as unpleasant as mine. Not exactly the same, perhaps, but certainly as upsetting. And they all offered me help, more times than I can count, actually. But I didn't want it. And I didn't want it because I was ashamed, not just traumatised, as the fashionable word for it seems to be these days. I don't know what's wrong with good old shell shock any more, I really don't. But I did something I was horribly ashamed of, and I just couldn't talk about it. No, it wasn't that I couldn't talk about it, I *wouldn't*. So it went on for years, I went on for years, making your life hell, making your mother's life hell, upsetting Gran constantly and everyone else I care about.'

'Why couldn't you talk about it?'

James shrugged. 'Pride, I suppose. Or ignorance. I was brought up to believe that there were certain things you just didn't do, and I did one of them. But instead of accepting that it happened, and coming to terms with *why* it happened, I spent years punishing myself for it, because I thought I should have been above it. But we're only human, you know, all of us, and all sorts of things happen in wartime.'

Drew looked at up his father for several long moments. 'What *did* you do, Dad? No one has ever said. Not to me, anyway.'

James stared back. 'I killed a man, a colleague, an officer in my company.'

'By accident?'

'No, on purpose.'

Drew continued to stare. 'But why?'

'At the time I believed he was seriously endangering the lives of my men.'

'And now?'

'I still believe that.'

Drew was stunned. 'But . . . weren't you court-martialled?'

'Yes. I was acquitted.'

'I don't understand.'

'No, I don't really, either. Evidently my men all lied for me.'

'Well, weren't you there? At the trial?'

'Not really,' James said, and tapped the side of his head.

Drew rubbed his hands wearily over his face. 'I had no idea. We just thought you were, you know, shell-shocked. When we were boys there were other kids at school whose dads were a bit barmy, too, from the war. Sorry, I didn't mean . . . well, yes, I suppose I do mean barmy. It was really hard living with you then, Dad. Apparently one poor boy's father woke up quite regularly in the night and ran about with a rifle in the paddock next to the house shooting at Germans. He was carted off to Napier Hospital, then ended up in Porirua. It drove his mother mad as well, they reckon. So we weren't the only ones. But no one really talked about it. It was just accepted, you know — some chaps had loony fathers because of the war and that was that.'

James didn't know what to say. But Drew was certainly concealing something, he was sure of it. And he was also sure it would come out when the time was right, and only then. Drew was exhibiting clear signs of shell shock himself — or whatever it was you developed after years of being starved and treated like an animal in a Japanese POW camp — but there was very little that James could do about it until Drew decided he was ready.

'Well,' he said, getting to his feet as it seemed the conversation had come to an end, 'if you do feel like a chat about anything I'm . . . well, you know where I am.'

Drew nodded, then listened to the sound of James's boots crunching on the gravel driveway as he headed out to the shed to start work.

He was grateful for the sentiment behind his

father's words, but appalled that he seemed to think his son had done something inglorious or ignoble while he'd been away. And he had, but not the sort of thing James could ever entertain, or perhaps possibly even imagine. It was inconceivable that he could ever talk to him about Tim — and that was what he wanted to do. Because amid the excitement of coming home and the love and support his family were giving him and the sheer relief of knowing he was finally safe and that it was all over, he'd realised, very belatedly, that he had loved — *did* love — Tim, and loved him in the way that Tim had always wanted to be loved. And it made him feel even more revolted with himself. Not only was his body tainted and ruined, but also his mind and his spirit. He could never go back to being the person he'd been before he went away, but who the bloody hell was he now?

★ ★ ★

He had his first 'New Zealand' migraine on New Year's Day. It was a bad one and went on for a week, during which he vomited all over himself, couldn't eat anything at all, wept with the pain and wished several times that he had the guts to kill himself. The headaches were getting worse again, and no matter what he told himself to the contrary, the fact was becoming impossible to ignore. Lucy insisted that Doctor Fleming was called in. He had been attending Drew regularly since his arrival back home, and was deeply concerned at his immediate and marked loss of physical condition as a result of the headache. Prescribing strong painkillers and a draught to settle Drew's stomach, he made a referral to the neurological specialist at Napier Hospital.

James went with him on the appointed day, and waited in the public waiting room for several hours while Drew was subjected to a battery of very thorough medical tests and an X-ray.

The afternoon was rather muggy, and Drew stood near an open window in Todd Bickham's large, airy office while the specialist went off to collect the pictures that had been taken of the inside of his head. Bickham seemed to be a bit of a virtuoso in his field, Drew noted, judging by the number of framed certificates adorning his office walls. He hoped so.

Bickham was back in ten minutes, holding a set of large, dark sheets of celluloid carefully by their edges.

'They're ready,' he said cheerfully, as if announcing the removal of a batch of particularly tasty scones from the oven. Clipping them onto a wire above a shallow glass case mounted on the wall, he flicked on a switch and stood back. 'Let's see what they can tell us, shall we? Please, do sit down, Drew, make yourself comfortable.'

Drew sat, and waited for some minutes while Bickham studied the X-rays, rocking backwards and forwards on his heels with his hands clasped behind his back.

'The head injury was severe, obviously. Were you knocked out?' He turned and looked at Drew over the top of his spectacles.

Drew nodded. 'For a few hours, apparently. I can't remember.'

'No, you wouldn't. Come and look at this.'

Drew moved closer to the screen. On it he could see a rather disturbing image of his own skull, complete with teeth — and gaps where some of them were missing — and the knobbly vertebrae at the top of his spine.

Bickham pointed with his pen. 'This crooked line across the back here, on the occipital bone, is where your skull was cracked when you sustained your injury. It seems to have healed well enough, but the ragged edges suggested it took some time. Did you receive medical treatment after the event?'

'No.'

'None at all?'

'The Japanese weren't too hot on it for POWs.'

'I suppose they weren't, no,' agreed Bickham as he went back to studying the X-rays. 'This dark patch here, do you know what it is?'

Drew shrugged. 'No idea, I'm afraid.' But suddenly he was very scared.

'Sit down again, will you, Drew.'

Bickham went to his desk and sat down himself, leaning forward with his elbows on his enormous blotter pad and his chin resting on his hands.

'It's not good news,' he said. When Drew didn't respond, he continued. 'You have a tumour in your brain. It appears that it may have started off as scar tissue — you can see where a small piece of bone has gone into the brain matter — but over the years, and without treatment, the scar has compounded and begun to generate cells of its own. Well, I can only guess at that without having a close look, but it's a very educated guess.'

'And it's the tumour that's been causing the headaches?'

'Without a doubt. That, and the original scar tissue.'

Drew contemplated his knees for a moment. 'Why do you think the headaches are getting worse?'

'I think, because the tumour is getting bigger.'

'Why now?'

'I'm not completely sure, and it would be terribly ironic if it is the case, but I suspect it's because you're getting decent food now. When you weren't, your body didn't have the nutrients to support the tumour's growth, but now it does.'

There was another short silence. 'Can you take it out?'

Bickham took his spectacles off and polished them absently with the end of his tie. It was clear to Drew that he was struggling to find the appropriate words.

'No,' Bickham said eventually, 'I'm very sorry, Drew, but I don't think we can. It's very advanced. In my opinion, surgery to remove it would almost certainly kill you.'

Calmly, Drew asked, 'Are there any other options?'

'I don't think so, no, not now.'

'Am I going to die?

Bickham put his spectacles back on. 'I'm so sorry.' He paused, then added, 'But we'll do our best for you while we can.'

Outside in the waiting room, James got to his feet and collected his hat as Drew appeared. 'All right?' he asked.

'Yes, fine. All sorted.'

'What's the problem, do they know?'

Drew shrugged. 'Mystery headaches, apparently. But the doc's given me a prescription for some pretty strong painkillers, so that should help.'

★ ★ ★

Duncan came home at the end of January, and brought Claire with him. In fact, technically, she brought him, because she was travelling with him as his nurse, as well as his wife. They would have left England earlier, but Claire wanted to work out a decent period of notice at Queen Victoria Hospital; she'd made a lot of very good friends there, and did not want to leave them in the lurch.

This time, Tamar was feeling unwell and did not go into Napier to meet the train. Instead, she waited nervously out at Kenmore, having counted down the days ever since James and Lucy had received the telegram saying that Duncan and Claire were finally on their way home.

She was resting in the parlour, reading, when she heard the sound of a car coming up the driveway. She marked her place, set her book down and composed herself.

She heard footsteps in the hall, but instead of Duncan in the doorway as she had expected, it was Henry.

'Are they here?' she asked.

Henry nodded, but he looked puzzled and rather disconcerted. 'It doesn't look like Uncle Duncs any more, Gran. It looks like someone else altogether!'

Tamar's heart suddenly began to pound as her mind conjured up all sorts of awful visions of what her darling Duncan might look like now, and her fear came out as anger.

'Not 'it', Henry, 'he'. Your uncle is not an 'it'. Don't be so rude!'

Henry hadn't intended to be rude at all, and was startled by his grandmother's tone. He looked down at his shoes and muttered, 'Sorry, Gran, but he does look, well, strange.'

'Well, so he might, but don't you dare ever say that to him, do you hear me, Henry?'

He nodded vigorously, and when he looked up he saw there were big, bright tears in his gran's eyes. And then he felt like crying himself, because he hated it when people got upset.

He glanced over his shoulder as the front door opened, and whispered loudly, 'Here they come.'

James and Lucy entered the parlour first. Lucy's eyes were red and a little puffy, but James looked happy enough.

'Well, the prodigal son's home!' he announced cheerfully, and moved aside to let Duncan in.

He was as big and as strapping as he'd always

been, and came forward, smiling broadly. She gazed directly into his eyes for a long moment then sat back, profoundly relieved to see that he hadn't really changed at all. His face was scarred and lumpy in places, and his features were blurred, but he was still Duncan. The tears came again, and she felt like getting up and giving Henry a good smack for upsetting her so much. But it wasn't his fault; he'd only been a small baby when Duncan left for England, and probably couldn't remember him anyway.

But her tears didn't want to stop, and when one trickled down her cheek, Duncan sat down next to her and gave her a hug.

'Gran, please don't be upset. It's all right. I'm fine now, don't worry.'

Tamar blew her nose. Why were her grandchildren so often saying that to her of late? It was her job to comfort them, not the other way around.

'I'm sorry, darling. I'm so pleased to have you home at last. We all are.' She gave one last honk into her handkerchief and brightened visibly. 'Now, where is this lovely wife of yours? We've all been dying to meet her.'

Duncan shot out into the hall, and came back leading a rather attractive girl, with a lovely figure, lots of dark hair and a smattering of freckles across her nose.

'Gran,' Duncan announced, 'I'd like you to meet Claire — Pearsall that was, Murdoch that is. Claire, this is my grandmother, Tamar Murdoch.'

Claire leaned down and kissed Tamar's cheek.

'Hello, Duncan's told me so much about you. It's lovely to meet you at last, Mrs Murdoch. I love your rose garden; you have some gorgeous varieties.'

Ana and Kathleen, who had been released from the WLS and the factory respectively almost as soon as the war had ended, clattered in then, and smothered Duncan with kisses. Kathleen started crying and Duncan said, 'You haven't changed much,' and Kathleen replied, 'Neither have you, you big bully,' and they hugged. Five minutes later the volume almost doubled when Bonnie and Leila, who had been up at the stream taking Daisy for a paddle, arrived, followed by everyone else, and the introductions had to be made all over again.

Tamar took an instant shine to Claire, and not just because she obviously knew a good rose when she saw it. It was the way she smiled at Duncan every time she looked at him, the way she stroked his face when she thought no one was watching and the way she disagreed with him when she felt so inclined. Tamar considered the last to be a particularly favourable portent of a well-matched couple and therefore a successful marriage. Claire was absorbed into the family with ease, because she was that kind of girl. And when it was revealed that she and Duncan were expecting a baby early in October, everyone was delighted. On top of that, Duncan had accepted his father's offer of work in the orchard for as long as he wanted it — for the long term, in fact, if he wanted to consider a partnership at some stage — and Tamar had been as pleased by that as she had been by the news about the forthcoming baby. It seemed that James and Duncan had finally, truly, put the past behind them.

19

Kenmore, 1946

David Leonard proposed to Ana in February, and although they were thrilled to bits for their cousin, Bonnie and Leila were miffed because it was likely that they would miss the wedding, which would not take place until the end of the year.

Jake and Danny had both written as soon as they had returned home, and requested formally that Bonnie and Leila join them in the US. The girls had had visions of just packing their bags and presenting themselves at the nearest port, but in reality it had all been a lot more complicated and frustrating.

First they'd had to apply in writing to the American authorities in New Zealand for permission to emigrate, which also involved presenting the letters from Danny and Jake, plus confirmation of the hefty bond required and their fares for the ship, and evidence that they had the personal means to purchase return fares to New Zealand if necessary. In response they were told they would have to present themselves for medical examinations at the nearest hospital, the results of which would be forwarded to the appropriate authorities, and agree to undertake a course of instruction in preparation for becoming American citizens. Unfortunately, no such course was available in Napier, which threw the girls into a temporary panic. Worst of all, they were told that, as war brides, their names would be put on a waiting list for berths, but that the list was very long owing to the numbers of New Zealand women seeking passage. The wait could be as short as two months or as long as twelve, but they would be notified as soon as berths became available.

This was extremely frustrating, especially for Leila who was terribly concerned that Jake would miss out completely on Daisy's early years. She was three years old already, and could well be four by the time her father finally met her.

But at the start of March, a letter came for each of them from the American Kiwi Club, an Auckland organisation sponsored by the YWCA and set up to offer advice, information, friendship and moral support to young women engaged or married to Americans and intending to emigrate to the US. The club, the letters said, was automatically informed when applications were made to the American authorities. Would Miss Bonnie Murdoch and Mrs Leila Kelly be interested in availing themselves of the club's services?

Folding her letter and stuffing it back in the envelope, Bonnie said, 'Well, that's all very nice, but we don't live in Auckland.'

Leila looked thoughtful. 'But we could, though, couldn't we?'

'What do you mean?'

'We could ask Aunty Ri if we could stay with her until we get berths!'

430

Bonnie pulled a doubtful face. 'God only knows when that might be. We could be sitting up there forever.'

'Oh, Bonnie, don't be such a pessimist.' Leila reached across the kitchen table and tapped the top off Daisy's soft-boiled egg for her. 'There, is that better? Now, remember not to put your spoon through the bottom of the shell, or the fairies won't be able to use it as a coracle to paddle across the river.'

Daisy's small pink tongue came out as she set about very carefully removing the contents of the shell without damaging it.

'We applied nearly six months ago,' Leila went on. 'They said the waiting list could be up to twelve months, so that means we've only another six left to wait, at the *most*. By the time we get everything organised here we'd probably only be in Auckland for a few months, so why not? And that's only if it takes that long. I'm sure Aunty Ri wouldn't mind.'

Bonnie thought about it. She had to admit she was desperate to see Danny again, and all this waiting around was nearly driving her round the bend. At least in Auckland they would have something to do, and she did think that learning as much about America as they could before they got there was an excellent idea. And it would be fun to meet some of the girls they would be travelling with. Perhaps one or two might even be bound for the same destinations as she and Leila were. It would be lovely if they could make friends before they even got there.

'We'd have to say goodbye to everyone early,'

431

she said, blinking back tears at the thought of it.

'I know, but I'm sure Mum and Dad would come up to Auckland to see us off. And Henry would do anything for a ride in a train, you know that.'

And so Bonnie and Leila left Kenmore several months before they actually departed from New Zealand. Tamar especially was upset to see them go, because she'd become convinced she'd never see them again. Everyone told her not to be so silly, but Tamar privately thought that they were rather naïve to expect anything else.

Bonnie and Leila said goodbye at the railway station on a warm March afternoon. The women all cried and cried, and the men stood about with long faces not knowing what to do with themselves. Claire was a great help, cheering Bonnie and Leila — who were having last-minute second thoughts in the face of the family's collective misery — and assuring them that moving to another country wasn't really such an enormous ordeal, especially when you had a lovely man and a new life waiting at the other end.

The girls cried on and off for several hours after the train left the station, and so did Daisy, who did not understand what was happening but certainly knew that her mother and her aunty were upset about something. In fact she cried herself to sleep, which was a relief because it gave Bonnie and Leila an opportunity to talk about what lay ahead without little, impressionable ears listening in.

But by the time night had fallen they both felt

better, having told themselves that they could, after all, come home if it all went wrong.

★ ★ ★

Riria was delighted to see them, as always, especially Daisy, whom she had not yet met. As soon as Leila set her down in the hall of Riria's house, she wandered off towards the kitchen, reappearing a minute later with a tiny fluffy grey kitten in a stranglehold under her arm.

'Kitty!' she said happily, 'Kitty-cat!'

'Careful, sweetheart,' Leila cautioned, 'the kitty has to breathe.'

'Yeees,' Daisy replied in a tone that implied that only a complete idiot wouldn't know that. 'It is breathing, see!' She held the kitten up to Leila, who could hear the little animal purring loudly.

'So it is!'

'I keep it? To take to 'Merica?'

Riria said, 'Of course you can,' at exactly the same time as Leila said 'No, dear.'

They looked at each other, and Riria put her fingers to her lips contritely.

Leila said, 'I'm sorry, sweetie, but I'm not sure if they let kittens on ships as big as the one we're going on.'

Whipping the kitten away from her mother so sharply that its little legs flew out and it squawked, Daisy said adamantly, 'They do!'

Leila sighed. 'We'll see, shall we?', hoping that Daisy would forget all about it by the time they received their departure date. It was unlikely, though — her small daughter could be extremely

433

stubborn about some things.

Riria showed them to their rooms and helped them settle in, then Bonnie telephoned the number they had for the American Kiwi Club: there was to be a coffee morning the next day at which she, Leila and Daisy would be more than welcome.

They caught the tram into the city, and arrived at the appointed time, smartly dressed and with Daisy in a new frock and a pink satin ribbon in her dark shining curls. They were welcomed by a tall, cheerful, slightly horsey-looking woman from the YWCA called Mrs Kendall, and introduced to a group of around forty other young women, just under half of them mothers. The children ranged in age from babies to little ones about the same age as Daisy.

First there was coffee and cake, then a short slide show depicting various American scenes — the New York skyline, Nebraskan wheat fields, the Nevada desert, the Mississippi River, San Francisco and the Colorado mountains. The girls in the club seemed to be bound for all points of the US, although Leila met only one headed for Oklahoma, a girl named Marjorie Callaghan. Her husband, also a Marine, lived in Stillwater, some distance from Harper County where Jake lived. Marjorie also had a child, a son, although he was only two years old.

Amazingly, Bonnie met a girl who was going to Philadelphia, where Danny lived. Her name was Sally D'Antoni and they hit it off straight away. Most of the girls at the club were nice, although Bonnie spotted a good handful whom she thought were rather fast and somewhat common. But everyone seemed to ignore this, particularly Mrs Kendall, and they all seemed to get on fairly well.

After the slide show there was a lecture on American customs such as Independence Day and the Fourth of July, and a promise that at the next coffee morning there would be an introduction to, and a discussion of, the Amendments to the American Constitution. Leila thought this sounded profoundly boring, but Bonnie was quite looking forward to it, having decided some time ago that the best way to get on when she did reach America would be to learn as much as she could about her new country. And Danny had occasionally mentioned American politics to her, and she wanted to be able to talk to him intelligently and knowledgably.

They all swapped addresses and telephone numbers and made promises to catch up with each other between coffee mornings. Bonnie suspected that some women wouldn't bother, but plenty of others seemed genuinely interested in forging real friendships before they left.

The next fortnight was spent attending lectures at the club three days a week, and shopping for the little bits and pieces they had been told they would need in the US, but might find it difficult to locate. Bonnie and Leila also shopped for New Zealand souvenirs for their American families. It was never said out loud in the lectures, but was certainly implied that if a girl hoped to get on in her new family, then it would certainly be prudent to start on the right foot with her husband's mother.

Bonnie purchased a pure New Zealand wool rug for her new mother-in-law, while Leila invested in a pair of luxurious sheepskin-lined house slippers for Jake's mother, and a bottle of whisky for his father, which, she joked, she could always drink herself if the going got rough. She also bought five new frocks, three jumpers, a dozen pairs of cotton knickers and half a dozen woollen singlets for Daisy, which prompted Bonnie to point out that there probably were shops in Oklahoma, and not to get too carried away. But Jake had told Leila that his family lived some way out of town, and she didn't want to run out of things, especially for Daisy.

Then, one morning at the club, the news came that berths were available on the *Robert E. Lee*, a former troopship departing Auckland for New York in seven days' time. There was a frenzy of excitement at the announcement, and Mrs Kendall had to clap her hands briskly and call, 'Girls! *Girls!*' to get their attention again.

The twins rang their parents that afternoon and it was agreed that Keely, Owen and Henry would come up on the train and spend a last night with Bonnie and Leila, before seeing then off at the wharf the following day. They also sent off telegrams to Danny and Jake, telling them when they expected to arrive in the US.

The week flashed past as they dashed about buying last-minute items. Leila finally decided that she was shopping as an antidote to her nervousness, and turned her attention to other things instead, such as attempting to force her and Daisy's things into their two large suitcases. It had become quite evident over the last few weeks that of all of the girls at the club, Bonnie and Leila were probably in the most comfortable circumstances. Some of the women seemed to have very little to take with them, although others appeared to have packed the most inappropriate items, such as nothing but dresses and hats and high heels. The twins themselves weren't exactly taking pots and pans and the kitchen sink, but they certainly had a few items that would contribute towards making a home.

By the time the day of departure arrived, everything was packed, their documentation was as it should be and they were ready. Owen ordered two taxis to take them all down to the wharf, and they were standing on the footpath outside Riria's house waiting for them to arrive when Daisy started crying. She'd refused to eat her breakfast that morning and had been irascible ever since, and Leila was worried that the little girl had suddenly realised she would probably not be seeing her grandparents or Henry for a long time.

She picked Daisy up and gave her a huge cuddle. 'I know it's hard, sweetie, but you'll have a new Gran and Gramps in America. And don't forget Daddy will be there too. He says there are lots of animals on the farm you can play with, and his sister has a little boy just your age.'

'Don't care!' Daisy wailed. 'Don't want to go!'

Leila felt absolutely awful. She wiped the tears off Daisy's cheeks with her thumb and said desperately, and with rather forced gaiety, 'All right then, what sorts of things could we do to make it better for you, do you think? What about an ice cream when we get down to the wharf? Or, I know, what about that big toy pussy cat we saw the other day!' To her father she whispered, 'Could we stop off and get it on the way? It was in Queen Street.'

But before he could answer, Daisy bellowed, 'No! Want a *real* cat!'

There was a short silence as Leila suddenly realised she was being shamelessly manipulated. Daisy risked a quick glance at her mother's face, and saw that the game was up. Her distress became urgent and real then, and she began to sob in earnest.

'Oh, God,' Leila sighed resignedly. 'Where is it?' she asked Riria, who was looking on with amusement.

'I will get her,' she said, and disappeared inside.

She returned a minute later carrying a square wicker box with a handle on the top. Daisy wriggled to be put down, and as soon as her feet touched the footpath she squatted down and opened the lid. Inside — of course — was the grey kitten, looking placidly up at everyone as if wondering what on earth all the fuss was about.

Bonnie couldn't help laughing. 'What are you going to call her?'

'Vagina,' Daisy replied without looking up.

Keely's hand shot up to cover her smile and Owen went bright red.

'Really?' Leila said a little too loudly. 'Don't you mean *Regina*?'

'No.'

Bonnie was laughing herself sick now, and Riria was trying unsuccessfully to smother her own titters behind a small lace handkerchief. Henry looked on in stony-faced bewilderment.

'What's so funny?' he asked.

'Nothing, son,' Owen said. 'Oh, look, here come the taxis.'

As two slightly elderly Morris Tens pulled into the kerb, Bonnie crouched down next to Daisy. 'I think the name Vagina is a bit, well, grand for such a little cat. What about Ginny instead?'

'Ginny, Ginny, Ginny.' Daisy tried the name out, and decided she liked it. 'All right, Ginny.' She reached into the box and the kitten obligingly raised her tiny head to have her throat tickled.

It was a bit of a squeeze, but everyone, plus the suitcases, carry-alls and the cat box, piled into the taxis and Bonnie and Leila waved madly to Riria as they drove off down the street.

It was only a short ride to the wharves at the bottom of Queen Street. The taxis deposited them at the gate to Princes Wharf, then puttered off in search of new fares.

Owen found a trolley and they heaped it with luggage and pushed it out along the wharf to the *Robert E. Lee*'s mooring.

Henry was most impressed. 'Can we come with you and have a look?'

'I don't see why not,' Bonnie said. 'We're not due to leave for another hour and a half.'

439

At the top of the gangway Bonnie and Leila's papers were inspected and approved, although their pile of bags received a doubtful look from a middle-aged ship's officer, with the title 'First Purser Woolley' on his name badge and a clipboard in his hand.

'That's rather a lot of luggage,' he said disapprovingly.

Leila gave him her brightest, most ravishing smile. 'Yes, it is, isn't it!'

Owen rolled his eyes and Keely had to look away.

The officer reached out with his highly polished shoe and nudged the cat box. 'What does this contain?'

'My hats,' Leila said, fluttering her eyelashes furiously. 'I don't own a hat box,' she added, hoping like hell that the kitten wouldn't make a noise.

Faced with two very attractive young women, not to mention the rather delightful little girl with them, the man didn't really stand a chance.

He frowned slightly. 'All right, then, ladies, on you go. You're on B deck, cabin 46. We hope you enjoy your voyage.'

They wound their way through the narrow corridors on B deck, which was above the waterline but only just, until they found their room. It was a big cabin, with a window, a handbasin and eight bunks, so obviously they would be sharing. There were suitcases on two of the bunks already, but the remaining six seemed still to be unclaimed. Bonnie and Leila piled their things onto two of them, and slid the cat

440

box under a third, which Daisy declared she had to have because it was a bottom one and she couldn't be too far from Ginny.

'What are we going to do about, you know, when the kitten has to . . . ?' Leila asked.

'Hang her botty out the window,' declared Daisy.

'No, darling, I don't think that's a very good idea, do you?'

'A nappy?' Daisy tried again. It was clear she had been thinking about this for some time.

'Kitten's don't wear nappies,' Henry said in disgust as he bounced on one of the bunks. 'God, this is a bit hard!'

'Don't swear, Henry,' Keely admonished absently.

'I wasn't. I could run round all the lavs and pinch loads and loads of toilet paper and she could go on that!' he suggested enthusiastically.

'Let's not worry about it now, shall we?' Bonnie said. 'I'd like to have a look around.'

So they all went exploring. The ship was quite large, with four passenger decks. As well as the other girls from the American Kiwi Club in Auckland there were another seventy war brides who had already boarded in Wellington, plus roughly a hundred young English evacuees on their way home, and a few dozen US military personnel — mostly men but a few navy and army nurses who'd stayed on at the American hospitals in the Auckland area until their patients were fit enough to be shipped home.

They'd been right round the entire ship and arrived back at the girls' cabin when the announcement came over the Tannoy that all visitors must leave the ship, as she would be sailing in thirty minutes.

Keely, who had been putting on a very brave face, burst into tears, followed closely by Bonnie and Leila, and then Daisy. Henry hung on for as long as he could, but finally succumbed as well. They all lingered on deck near the gangway, then it was time for Keely, Owen and Henry to go.

They hugged each other ferociously amid promises to keep in touch regularly by letter and telegram, and pleas from Keely and Owen to for God's sake come home if it didn't all work out.

When all non-passengers had left the ship and the gangway was raised, Bonnie, Leila and Daisy hung over the bulwark waving furiously as the *Robert E. Lee* began to shudder away from the dock. As the people left behind on the wharf grew too small to see clearly, they held hands and cried and cried.

England

At exactly the same time as Bonnie and Leila were saying goodbye in New Zealand, a girl was leaning over the rail of an English ship docked at Southampton, waving goodbye to her own mother and father.

Beside her was a little boy almost five years old, with dark hair and skin, and brown eyes as big and as lively as his father's had been. But at the moment they were filled with tears, because he didn't know if he would ever see Granny and Pop again. His name was Sam, and although he had never known his father, his mum told him all the time that he looked exactly like him. They were on their way to visit his dad's family in New Zealand, and it was supposed to be a secret. From whom, Sam couldn't quite work out, because he knew, and his mum knew, and so did his grandparents, so the only ones left who didn't know must be the people in New Zealand. He'd asked Mum lots of times why it had to be a secret, but all she would say was that it was meant to be a surprise. He knew about surprises, but he wasn't at all sure now about secrets.

Violet had been thinking for a very long time about going to New Zealand to seek out Billy's parents. She wanted nothing at all from them, because she had everything she needed in Dogmersfield, but she did want them to meet Sam. He was their grandson after all, and if they were half as decent as Billy had said they were, then she certainly wanted Sam to meet them.

When Harry Tomoana had written after the Battle of Crete and told her that Billy had been killed, she'd known for three months that she was expecting his baby. The shock of learning about his death — especially after she'd worked so hard to convince herself that he would come back for her just as he'd promised — was awful, and she had ended up in such a state she'd almost miscarried. But Sam had arrived later that year in August — big, healthy and unmistakably brown-skinned. At first she'd been shunned by some of the villagers, then their censure had turned to curiosity as she'd begun to take Sam out in his pram, and finally he'd been accepted into the small community as just one of those things that happened in wartime. He was a lovely, contented baby and, as he grew, a bright, inquisitive and perpetually happy toddler, and in a way he'd come to embody the sense of fun and exuberance that the Maori lads from New Zealand had brought to the village during their time there in 1940.

As a single woman Violet had been manpowered into war work, despite having a child to look after, so she had left Sam in the loving and very capable care of her parents and gone to work in a munitions factory in Guildford, coming home whenever she could to be with her son. But that was all over and done with now and she'd had plenty of time to consider what would be best for Sam. He was an English child, there was no doubt about that, but he also had another heritage, and Billy had spoken so passionately, if briefly, about that side of his own life that Violet believed Sam had a right to at least know about it first hand, if not to live it. So she'd talked it over for months with her parents, and finally decided that she would take Sam to New Zealand, just for a visit.

Her mother and father had been very understanding about it all, as they had been about her pregnancy, to her surprise and relief. They had provided the money for her and Sam's return fare, which she would never have been able to cobble together herself. She'd promised to repay them as soon as she could, as she knew the money had come from their retirement fund, and she meant it, even if she had to work six

444

days a week in the bakery for the rest of her life.

And now the day had come for them to leave. Poor little Sam couldn't understand that they would be coming back, and she felt for him as tears trickled down his cheeks, even though he was trying hard to be really brave. She picked him up and held him high so he had a better view of his grandparents, waving energetically back at him from the dock and putting on brave faces themselves. She had taken photos of them so Sam could look at them whenever he was feeling homesick, and kept them in her purse next to the only picture she had of Billy — the one they'd had taken together by Dogmersfield's one and only photographer, which was now creased and dog-eared because she'd looked at it so often.

He'd been a lovely man, Billy Deane, and the only one she'd ever loved, and she still mourned him deeply. It seemed so unfair that they'd only had a few months together, but at least she'd been left with something of him, a child who was so precious to her that she sometimes wondered how she would have survived without him. Other women regretted the moments of passion that had transformed them from carefree young girls to mothers in the wink of an eye, but she never had. Because as long as she had Sam, she would also have Billy, and some days she even managed to tell herself it was almost enough.

* * *

Two hours after the *Robert E. Lee* had steamed out through Waitemata Harbour and into the Hauraki Gulf, and the girls had gone below because the wind on deck was giving Daisy an earache, a knock came at the door of cabin 46. On opening it, Bonnie was confronted with First Purser Woolley, standing next to a trolley on which were stacked an assortment of sand-filled boxes.

'Will you be requiring a sand-box in this cabin?' he asked impassively.

'I'm sorry?' Bonnie knew her face had flushed scarlet.

'A sand-box, for the disposal of cigarettes. It is a safety measure.'

'*Oh!* Yes, of course! Four of us do smoke. How thoughtful!'

'Indeed,' the first purser said, his eyes straying over to Daisy's bunk where she sat blinking her huge eyes ingenuously and holding the cover down over a wriggling Ginny. 'And perhaps you might require a second box for, oh, I don't know, whatever hitherto unplanned-for contingencies may arise during the voyage?'

'Er, yes, thanks, that would be very helpful.'

First Purser Woolley gravely handed Bonnie two sand-boxes. As he turned to go, Daisy bellowed, 'Ta, Woolley!' making everyone in the cabin laugh.

As the door closed Bonnie crossed to her bunk. 'That was close,' she said, sinking onto it. 'Thanks, girls, for not letting on.'

The twins were sharing with Sally and Marjorie, and another girl named Gail Spano, whom they had also met at the American Kiwi Club, and had not liked very much. Gail's husband, like Sally's, was Italian, and she was headed for New York and then, according to her, Hollywood. She was certainly an attractive woman, and her baby was gorgeous too, a dear wee eighteen-month-old with black hair and cornflower-blue eyes that matched her mother's, and the most adorable little nose and rosebud lips in a pink-cheeked face.

But Gail was what the twins — and Marjorie and Sally — considered to be rather fast. Bonnie and Leila were worldly enough themselves, and were happy enough to admit it, but they liked to think they were worldly in a sophisticated and (usually) tasteful sort of way. They drank, they smoked — but then who didn't these days? — they wore make-up and fashionable clothes and were usually first onto the dance floor and last off. And God knew they weren't innocent, but they didn't believe they advertised the fact as Gail Spano did.

Bonnie had announced ages ago that they shouldn't judge how other people chose to behave, especially given that Daisy's date of birth was always going to be six months after the date on her parents' marriage certificate, but Gail had a way about her that did invite, if not comment, then at least speculation. Her clothes were flashy and she wore so much jewellery that she clattered whenever she moved. She certainly turned heads — especially men's — with her bright outfits and her undeniably spectacular figure, but did not seem to have very many female friends. She had a good sense of humour and was obviously intelligent but, in Leila's opinion, her bad language and predatory attitude towards men alienated other women.

Unfortunately, because they were all sharing a cabin, they would be seeing a lot of Gail, but it couldn't be helped, and anyway she wasn't that bad, just abrasive. And her little girl Jennifer (named after the film star Jennifer Jones) was absolutely lovely. There were five women and three children in the cabin, and Bonnie hoped that the weather would be fine most of the way, as she didn't fancy being cooped up with them all for weeks. The ship would be stopping off at Pago Pago in American Samoa, but no one knew yet whether they could go ashore. They would sail on from there through the Panama Canal and the Caribbean, then up to New York along the US eastern seaboard, where the American-bound passengers would disembark and the English evacuees would continue on across the North Atlantic to Britain.

If any of the war brides travelling on the *Robert E. Lee* had harboured hopes of having a high old time on the voyage to their new homes, most of them soon discovered they'd been sadly mistaken. The rules were very strict, with clear and frequently repeated instructions regarding where on the ship the women were and were not allowed to go. According to the general consensus, this discipline was for their own protection because the ship was crewed by sex-starved men. Members of the American Red Cross were on board too, with daily programmes for the women including lessons on how to knit and sew and cook — as if most New Zealand women did not have these skills already — and yet more lectures about life in America. But they also ran a nursery for the children, which gave mothers a very welcome break. Leila was particularly grateful. Daisy was one of the oldest children on the ship, inquisitive, energetic and easily bored, and by the time she had been around the deck with her a dozen times over the first two days, she was more than ready to hand her over to the kind and enthusiastic care of the Red Cross women for an hour or so.

Many of the children were only babies, however, or toddlers. Disposable nappies were preferred, since washing and drying cloth nappies on board was impractical, and by the end of the third day the captain had had to issue an edict stating that disposable nappies were not to be tossed overboard as they were forming a trail all the way back to New Zealand.

Seasickness struck, but most passengers had found their sea legs by the fourth day, and that was when boredom began to set in. One evening, after dinner, it was discovered that Gail had left Jennifer in the cabin by herself and gone off. When the others had returned from the dining room, they found the toddler tied by one chubby wrist to her bunk, screaming herself blue in the face and wearing a reeking nappy and the grubby clothes she'd been in all day.

Marjorie rushed over immediately, untied the little girl and picked her up, crooning and rocking quietly until her shrieks had subsided to irregular, hiccupping sobs.

'God, she pongs,' Marjorie said, pulling a face. 'Pass me a nappy, will you, Leila?'

By the time she had been cleaned up, changed and dressed in fresh clothes, Jennifer had recovered somewhat. She could only speak a few words, and one of these was 'Mummy'. She kept intoning this over and over until the other women thought their hearts might break.

'Where the hell is she?' Sally asked angrily. 'Was she at dinner, did anyone see?'

Nobody had, and the hunt began.

While Leila stayed in the cabin to look after the children, Sally and Marjorie began a thorough search of every part of the ship in which they thought Gail might be holed up — except for the prohibited crew's quarters, although they both agreed that flat on her back on some sailor's bunk was the most likely place for her to be.

Bonnie went up on deck and prowled around in all the dark corners, peering behind the huge funnels and beneath badly lit stairwells. It really wasn't on, she thought angrily, leaving your baby to scream her head off alone while you were out gallivanting about, not on at all. Of course, they might all be seriously mistaken and find that Gail had been unavoidably detained in the toilet for the last three hours because of a dodgy stomach, or something similarly unfortunate, but she doubted it.

She especially doubted it as she spied one of Gail's high-heeled shoes dangling over the side of a lifeboat. The shoe had a foot in it, attached

450

to a slim leg which disappeared under a tarpaulin loosely covering the boat. The boat itself was swinging slightly on its thick chains, as whoever was in it moved rhythmically up and down. Or perhaps it was from side to side; Bonnie couldn't tell from where she was standing. She felt like giving the heaving hump under the tarpaulin a good kick, but instead she turned on her heel and went straight back to the cabin.

When Gail finally put in an appearance several hours later, everyone else was in bed, although the lights in the cabin were still on. Jennifer was tucked up in her own bunk, fast asleep and surrounded by the other children's toys to keep her company.

Sally snapped, 'Enjoy your night out, did you?'

Gail sat down and lit a cigarette. 'I did, actually.'

'Seaman or an officer?'

'Oh, an officer. I always aim high.'

Bonnie snorted in disgust. 'We don't care what you get up to, but how could you leave Jennifer on her own like that?'

Gail shrugged. 'Easily. I don't really give a bugger.'

The others looked on, stunned and speechless.

'Well, it's true! She was an accident, a mistake, but her father was stupid enough to marry me so I'm entitled to American citizenship now, and *that* means I can work in Hollywood.'

'What as?' Bonnie retorted, but Gail ignored her.

Leila finally found her tongue. 'But what

about Jennifer? What will happen to her, the poor little thing?'

'Poor little Jennifer will be going to her father. He dotes on her. Sends her a letter every week without fail, toys, clothes, you name it. So don't worry, she'll be okay. And let's face it, girls, she'll be far better off with him than she ever would be with me,' Gail added with unexpected frankness. 'I just wasn't cut out for motherhood.'

This was so patently obvious that no one bothered to refute her.

'Has anyone ever told you you're a cold, calculating bitch?' Marjorie asked.

'Several times, but at least I'm an honest one.'

Leila asked indignantly, 'And what's that supposed to mean?'

'Well, look at you lot, for a start. You've all married your American Prince Charmings after five-minute whirlwind romances, and in exchange for sex and a marriage certificate you're now off to the promised land for a life of mod cons and big cars and lovely palatial homes. What's that if not dishonest? At least I'm straight up about what I do.'

There was a collective gasp of outrage.

'You nasty, mean-spirited cow!' Leila spat. She climbed out of her bunk and sat down beside Daisy, who was awake now and beginning to whimper at the mounting tension. 'I married Jake because I love him. His family owning land has nothing to do with it at all.'

'Are you sure about that, sweetheart? Where did you say he comes from? Oklahoma? There aren't too many nice big prosperous farms out that way, I can assure you, so I sincerely hope in your case that love can conquer all.'

'How the hell would you know what's in Oklahoma?'

'Because I talk to people, a lot, and I listen, and if there's one time a man's going to tell you the truth, girl, it's right after you've just given him a great time. The streets of America aren't paved with gold, unless you make it yourself. And just about none of those boys who came over to New Zealand had any of that gold, because if they did, they would have used it to buy themselves out of the military.'

'Look, Gail,' Sally said, getting angrily out of bed herself, 'what exactly are you trying to say?'

'I'm *saying* that you're having yourselves on if you think everything's going to be rosy when you get to wherever it is you're all going. How long did you know these husbands of yours before you married them? How much of what they told you do you *really* think was the truth, eh? You know, when they were swanning about all over Auckland in their smart uniforms with bags of money and hero written across their foreheads in capital letters, but deep down terrified about where they were heading next and wanting nothing more than a good time with a pretty girl? You don't think they might just have said things to you that weren't quite true?'

'So what?' Marjorie shot back. 'I'm not interested in money. Or property.'

'You will be when you find out he expects you to live in a disgusting little basement room in some slum somewhere.'

'Are you trying to tell us we've all been had on?' Bonnie demanded. 'I can't believe you can be so cynical. What about *your* husband?'

'Believe me, sweetheart, he's the one who got the rough end of the stick, and we both know that already. But he'll get Jennifer, and I'll get my ticket to fame and fortune, so who's really lost out? No one, right? It was a deal. Admittedly, he didn't quite know all the details when he said he'd marry me, but it was still a deal. What are you girls getting if it turns out you *have* been led up the garden path? Bugger all, I'd say, except your ticket home, which you have to pay for yourself anyway.'

Leila glanced at Bonnie and they shook their heads. What a strange and bitter girl Gail was, and what a lot of rubbish she was spouting.

Sally said, 'Yes, well, you're entitled to your own opinion, although I for one don't care about your view of the world. What I do care about is Jennifer. If you leave her on her own again I'm reporting you to the Red Cross people *and* the captain.'

'Mmm,' Gail said, frowning. 'That's a pity, because I'm probably going to be quite busy for the rest of the trip.' She looked at Sally contemplatively. 'Look, if you care so much about Jennifer, why don't you look after her?'

Sally opened her mouth to protest at the absolute cheek of the idea, then shut it again. She exchanged glances with Marjorie, Bonnie and Leila, then said, 'All right, I will. We all will, if it means that Jennifer gets the care she deserves. On one condition.'

'What's that?' Gail replied as she retrieved a file from her handbag and began to shape her long painted nails.

'That one of us is there when you hand her over to your husband. I for one won't be able to live with myself if I'm not satisfied she's going to be well looked after. It isn't fair; she's only eighteen months old, for God's sake. Is that all right, girls?'

Everyone else nodded. Daisy pulled Ginny out from under the blankets and made her nod her little furry head, even though she had no idea what the grown-ups were talking about.

'Oh, well, that should be a piece of cake — he's meeting me as soon as the ship docks. Okay, ladies, it's a deal.' Gail smiled. 'I like a good deal.'

20

Naturally, Ginny escaped from cabin 46, and ran amok throughout the ship. She wandered out after Marjorie left the cabin door open on her way to the toilet, and as soon as Daisy noticed that the kitten had disappeared she became inconsolable.

A search party was assembled and sent out in all directions, but to no avail — Ginny was nowhere to be found. Then the reports of sightings began to come in: children in the nursery that morning had been transported with glee as a small fluffy creature had been spotted playing among the soft toys before tearing off again; something unmentionable had been discovered on the carpeted floor of the A deck corridor; and the head chef had very nearly gone berserk when he'd glimpsed what he insisted was a very cheeky-looking small grey rat loitering about in the ship's galley.

Daisy was informed of these sightings — to help her to feel better, as she had convinced herself that Ginny had fallen overboard — and it was then that she came up with the most sensible idea anybody had had so far.

'Woolley can find her.'

Leila looked doubtful. 'Sweetie, how would he know where Ginny is?'

''Cause he owns the ship.'

Leila suspected, as Daisy had assumed, that

First Purser Woolley probably did know just about everything that went on above and below decks.

'Well, I suppose we can ask. Come on then, let's go for a walk.'

So off they went, hand in hand, along the corridor and down onto the deck where the staff had their offices.

Leila knocked on the door marked 'First, Second, Third and Assistant Pursers', and pushed it open as a voice from within invited entry.

First Purser Woolley was seated at his desk, in front of a large stack of papers.

'Ah, Mrs and Miss Kelly, what can I do for you?' he asked, carefully replacing the cap on his fountain pen.

'Ginny's run away!' Daisy blurted.

'Ginny? One of the children, perhaps?'

'Er, no, actually,' Leila replied sheepishly. 'The kitten.'

'Oh, yes, the kitten. The one that wasn't in the wicker box.'

Leila blushed, but only slightly this time. 'It's Daisy's kitten, and she's very upset about her going missing. We were wondering if you could help us find her?'

'This wouldn't be the kitten that has recently been sighted in, let me see . . . ' He consulted a sheet of paper on his desk. 'Yes, the nursery, the galley, twenty minutes ago in the dining room, in the corridor outside the engine room, and, well, there's no need to mention that particular little matter.'

'That's her!' Daisy exclaimed. 'She's very naughty!'

First Purser Woolley looked at Daisy over his spectacles, and smiled kindly. 'Unfortunately, I don't know where she is at this instant, but I expect I can find out. Why don't you take your mother back to your cabin and wait there? I'm sure we'll have good news for you soon. A kitten shouldn't be too hard to find.'

Under her breath Leila mumbled, 'I wouldn't bet on that,' but she smiled brightly. 'What a good idea, that's exactly what we'll do, and thank you so much for your help. It's most appreciated.'

'Yeah, ta, Woolley!' Daisy added.

First Purser Woolley lowered his head to hide his smile, then rummaged in his drawer and withdrew a handful of wrapped toffees. 'I keep these especially for young ladies who have temporarily misplaced their kittens. I'm told they help.'

As they rose to leave, he said quietly to Leila, 'You do understand that animals are not permitted to wander about the ship? They should be caged in the hold at the very least. Running about, they are a danger to themselves and to others.'

'Er, yes, I do understand that. Sorry.'

'On the other hand, I gather this kitten of Miss Daisy's is very small. When it's returned to her, please make sure the creature remains within sight of someone, ah, *responsible*, let us say.'

'Oh, of course. Yes, I'll certainly see to that. Thank you.'

Daisy was still chewing enthusiastically as they arrived back at their cabin.

'No news?' Leila asked as she flopped onto her bunk.

Bonnie shook her head. 'Sorry, not yet.'

'We spoke to Woolley, and he said he'll keep an eye out.' Leila lowered her voice. 'God, I hope she turns up soon, those toffees he gave Daisy are only going to last so long.'

As it happened, Ginny was delivered back to cabin 46 by the first purser himself, standing to attention and holding a silver serving platter with a domed lid.

'Miss Daisy Kelly, I believe that this is your order?' he announced rather grandly.

'No. Mum, what's a order?'

'I think it *is* your order, Miss Daisy,' he repeated and handed her the tray.

She removed the lid and shrieked with joy. '*Ginny!* Mummy, it's Ginny in a dish!'

Ginny stretched, stepped off the tray, climbed up Daisy's chest and settled in the crook of her neck. Daisy gave Woolley's smartly trousered leg a big, heartfelt hug. In response he reached down and patted her head, and allowed himself to smile openly this time.

'All part of the service, Miss Daisy, all part of the service.'

★ ★ ★

The *Robert E. Lee* docked at Manhattan on the Hudson River on an afternoon in the third week of April.

459

The Statue of Liberty, on an island all by itself in the bay, had been a bit of a disappointment because it turned out to be green, and not the defiant burnished bronze the war brides had been expecting, but the imposing and truly spectacular skyline of New York city made up for it. The weather was pleasant and springlike, and the girls from cabin 46 carried their coats over their arms as they stood on the dock, wondering where to go next.

Sally, whose husband could not meet her, had sent her the money for the rail fare to Philadelphia, but Bonnie had suggested during the voyage that she hitch a ride with herself and Danny, who would be waiting when the ship docked. Leila and Daisy were to stop off in Philadelphia too, before they boarded the train that would take them to Harper County, Oklahoma.

But Danny was nowhere to be seen, and there was also the matter of the rendezvous involving Jennifer and her father to be sorted out. Gail had dressed the toddler in a very charming little outfit of pink and white lace, and she looked irresistible, but they were all worried — Gail perhaps more than anyone — that he would not appear to collect her.

'Where *is* Danny?' Leila asked, giving voice to the question that had been on Bonnie's mind for the past half-hour as they milled about the crowded immigration hall.

'I don't know,' Bonnie said, the slightest hint of panic in her voice. 'He said he would definitely be here.'

Gail looked at her, but wisely kept her mouth shut. She couldn't have cared less whether Bonnie's fiancé turned up or not, as long as her husband did, and took Jennifer off her hands.

There was a minute's uncomfortable silence as the others contemplated the awful possibility that Danny might not appear at all, leaving Bonnie high, dry and jilted thousands of miles from home, when suddenly there was a commotion near the wide glass entrance doors.

Hurrying towards them across the marbled floor came what appeared to be a huge bunch of red roses on legs. The roses were lowered and suddenly there was Danny, looking completely different without his Marine's uniform, but with the same wide, happy smile.

He thrust the roses at Bonnie and almost put her eye out, then picked her up and swung her around so that her handbag flew out and her hat nearly came off.

'Bonnie, Bonnie, *Bonnie*!' he crowed. 'I was so worried you might have changed your mind!'

Bonnie laughed in delight, and rescued her hat as he set her back on her feet. 'How very odd,' she said, 'I was thinking just the same thing myself.'

'I'm so sorry, I couldn't find anywhere close to park the car. Did you think I wasn't coming? Oh, my poor, poor darling, I'm so sorry,' and he gathered her in another huge hug.

'Hello, Danny,' Leila said when he finally let Bonnie go.

'Hello, Leila, you're looking great. And, oh my

gosh, this isn't Daisy, is it? What a gorgeous little lady!'

'Yes, this is Daisy. Ah, Jake isn't here, is he?'

'Jake? No, why, did he say he would be?'

'Oh, no, I just thought he might have, well, that you might perhaps have heard from him lately.'

Danny looked a little uncomfortable. 'I'm sorry, Leila, but I haven't seen Jake since we were demobbed last year.'

Leila was a little taken aback; for some reason she'd thought that Jake and Danny would have maintained their firm friendship after the war ended.

'But don't worry,' Danny insisted. 'He'll be waiting for you in Harper County, if that's what he said he'd do. He's a good man, Jake.'

Leila nodded, and turned her attention to Gail, who was eyeing up Danny in his smart and obviously expensive suit, hat and stylish city shoes. She curled her lip ever so slightly, and Gail scowled back.

Holding her huge bunch of roses awkwardly, Bonnie introduced Sally and Marjorie, and explained that Sally needed a ride to Philadelphia. Then she added, 'And this is Gail Spano and her daughter Jennifer. Jennifer's father is collecting her while Gail, well, Gail's not stopping.'

Danny raised his eyebrows, but said nothing.

'So, now that we've found you, all we have to do is find Jennifer's father. Isn't that right, Gail?' Bonnie added somewhat aggressively.

It was clear to Danny that something was

going on here, but he wisely decided it would be best to remain ignorant.

'I don't know exactly what time he'll be here,' Gail said calmly. 'Only that he said he'd meet me in the immigration hall on the afternoon the ship arrived.'

'What does he look like?' Marjorie asked.

'Tall, dark and handsome.'

Leila looked at Gail for indications of sarcasm, but she seemed genuine.

Eventually, after they'd all had their first cups of American coffee and a doughnut each, and Daisy had had a hotdog and slopped ketchup down the front of her frock, Gail announced, 'Here he is.'

Anthony Spano *was* tall, dark and, if not devastatingly handsome, then at least really rather pleasant-looking, and clearly of Italian heritage. The girls noted that he too was smartly dressed, in a dark three-piece suit and a charcoal trilby. He approached the table with his hat in his hands, and stood staring at Jennifer. His face was pinched, and there was tension in the way he held himself.

He nodded at the others politely and said curtly to Gail, 'Have you sorted her things out?'

'Yes, don't worry, you won't have to wait around.'

She selected the smaller of her two cases and pushed it across the floor towards him. He ignored it and moved around to where Jennifer was sitting on Gail's knee.

He bent down. 'Hello, honey,' he said in a gentle voice that held a hint of tears. 'I'm your daddy, and we're going home.'

Jennifer reached out and bopped him on the nose with a small fist, smiling happily. He picked her up, sat her on his hip and kissed the top of her dark head.

'Shall we go?' he asked her. 'Your grandparents have been waiting to meet you for a very long time. And so have I.' Then he reached into his jacket pocket, extracted an envelope and handed it to Gail. 'Here's your money. The divorce papers are in there too. Please sign them and return them to my lawyer as per the instructions.'

Gail nodded and stood up. 'Good, I will. Well, ta ta girls, nice to have met you.'

She picked up her case and walked off, her heels clacking on the polished floor and her hips swaying pertly from side to side.

Jennifer watched her go for a moment, then suddenly burst into tears, shrieking hysterically, 'Mummy, *Mummy!*' and reaching out with chubby arms.

Gail didn't look back.

Anthony pulled his daughter's little body against him and rocked and soothed and patted. 'Ssshh, ssshh, don't cry, baby, it's all right, it's all right.'

He looked at the women helplessly. 'I'm so sorry about all this,' he said. 'I really am.'

'God, so are we, believe me,' Bonnie replied. 'If there's anything we can do . . . '

'Thanks, but my mother knows all about kids — she's had seven of her own. We'll be fine.'

He turned to leave but Leila, her eyes bright

with tears, put a hand on his arm to stop him. 'May I have your phone number? We'd like to know how she's getting on. We've all become very fond of her during the trip over.'

'Of course,' Anthony replied, and handed Leila a card. 'This is my work number. Call whenever you like. Perhaps you could come by and visit some time? Bring your little girl, too.'

'Oh, no, thank you, but we're heading for Oklahoma in a few days, so we won't have the chance.'

'Could I possibly get in touch with you, then? Just to let you know.'

'Er, I'm sorry, but my husband doesn't have the telephone on.'

Anthony Spano looked disappointed, but not, Bonnie suspected, because of the lack of telecommunications at Leila's future address. It was the mention of her husband that had caused his face to fall.

Leila blushed slightly. 'But thank you anyway.'

★ ★ ★

She waved through the window as the train pulled away from the platform. Daisy was crying again, but quietly this time, huddled into the corner of the seat holding Ginny in her box on her knee. It was so hard on the children, Leila thought, all this travelling about, but they would be there soon, and Daisy would at last meet her father.

They had thoroughly enjoyed their four days in Philadelphia. She and Bonnie had both

465

gasped as Danny had driven up a circular, shrub-lined driveway and parked his car — a big Lincoln Continental coupe that looked as if it had come straight out of the movies — in front of a very grand, two-storeyed house in one of the city's obviously more affluent suburbs. It was his family's home, he'd explained, and he and Bonnie would be staying there until they were married, if that was all right with her. In separate rooms, of course. His parents were quite modern, but not that modern.

His mother had been busy making wedding plans since before Christmas, so he sincerely hoped that Bonnie had not changed her mind. No, she hadn't, she assured him, but she'd rather thought she might have quite enjoyed planning her wedding herself.

'Oh, but you still can,' Danny insisted after Daisy had been put to bed, having fallen asleep in her dinner. 'All she's done — well, this is according to *her* — is investigate venues and caterers and what have you. Oh, and she's notified the designer who made my sister's wedding dresses when they were married, but you don't have to go there if you don't want to.'

Bonnie was feeling rather bowled over. She had known, of course, that Danny came from an old and reasonably well-off Philadelphia family, but she hadn't been at all prepared for this. The Hartmans were clearly rolling in it, and enjoyed a level of comfort and privilege that surpassed even that of her own family.

Cordelia Hartman, Danny's mother, was a patrician-looking woman with a well-defined

466

nose, lovely skin and dark hair that had a striking sweep of silver at one temple. She dressed impeccably, spoke with a cultured accent, and had very definite opinions about everything. Bonnie and Leila felt compelled to be on their best behaviour in front of her, but they managed quite admirably, and considered that their mother and Tamar would have been very proud of them. Their father, on the other hand, would have laughed at their exaggerated manners and efforts to not put a foot wrong. Daisy, unfortunately, did not have the skills to maintain her own personal social decorum for long, and during breakfast the following morning yelled at Cordelia's miniature dachshund to 'Get in behind!' when it wandered into the dining room looking for tidbits, while at the same time stuffing a piece of bacon into her pocket for Ginny. Barnard Hartman, a jovial, friendly man considerably older than his wife, roared with laughter — he'd fallen in love with Daisy the moment he'd met her, and Bonnie suspected he rather wished she was his grandchild. She could see that there would be pressure before long for she and Danny to start a family.

Danny had tentatively selected a wedding date at the end of July — mainly, Bonnie guessed, to shut his mother up — and Bonnie had agreed. In fact, she would have married Danny tomorrow, but it was clear that nothing less than a big, swish society wedding would satisfy Cordelia, and that sort of event took time to arrange. And then there was the matter of their own home. Danny had purchased (with the help of his parents) a very nice house in the same neighbourhood — but thankfully, Bonnie thought, not too close. It was sitting empty at the moment, except for great heaps of wallpaper, paint and fabric samples, which he hoped Bonnie would have a look at as soon as she felt rested and settled. He would leave it all up to her. While he was poring over books about rare and revolting diseases, and techniques for setting recalcitrant bones, he could rest happy in the knowledge that their new house would be a lovely, welcoming home.

Bonnie was delighted, as she'd always wanted to have a go at interior decorating, but she felt a little guilty at having landed so squarely on her feet when poor Leila hadn't even seen Jake yet, and was so clearly dying to. So she'd brushed everything else aside, even Cordelia's offer to go shopping for fabric for her wedding gown, and made a point of spending as much time with her sister and niece as she could. They went sightseeing, had a good look at downtown Philadelphia and sent postcards to everyone in New Zealand they could think of. Leila bought Daisy two pairs of the cutest little denim dungarees to wear on Jake's farm, and herself a cowboy hat to keep the sun off her face in case she went riding. She also sent a telegram to Jake to let him know when the train would be arriving.

There had been more tears and hugs as she and Daisy boarded the train, and promises that they would most definitely be back for Bonnie and Danny's wedding in three months' time. But now, as she sat back and watched the city streets turn into suburban roads and then fields, she thought about what Danny had said when he'd taken her aside last night after dinner.

They'd sat down on a bench on the wide stone balcony overlooking the garden, and he'd given her a glass of cognac and lit a cigarette for her.

'What I said on the day you and Bonnie arrived about Jake being a good man, well, I meant that.'

'Yes?' Leila wasn't quite sure what Danny was getting at.

'I really did, but, well . . . ' He ran his fingers through his hair hesitantly, as if he didn't know how to phrase his next words.

'What? What are you trying to say?' Leila demanded, feeling a stab of panic.

'Don't worry, it isn't anything really. It's just that, well, it was rough on Okinawa, and it sort of affected Jake.'

'What do you mean? He hasn't got shell shock, has he?'

'No, nothing like that, but he was very quiet afterwards though. And he hit the bottle for a while. Mind you, we all did that.'

'He didn't go with . . . well, you know what I mean.' Leila wasn't sure if she wanted to hear the answer to this.

'Other women? Hell, no. He talked about you and Daisy all the time. No, it's more like he lost a bit of his spirit, but I'm sure he'll be back to normal by now because it's been almost a year. I just wanted to say that if he seems a little subdued and not like he was when we were in New Zealand, well, that's probably why. That's

469

all, nothing serious.'

Leila exhaled in relief. Without being conscious of it she'd been steeling herself against hearing news a lot worse than that. Almost cheerfully, she said, 'Well, thanks for telling me, Danny. I'm sure he'll have come right by now, and if not, well, Daisy and I will just have to see what we can do about it, won't we?'

'That's what I thought.' Danny raised his glass. 'So here's to you and Jake, best of luck and may you prosper. And tell him I fully expect him to see him with you and Daisy at the wedding, okay?'

So it hadn't been bad news, not really. Just something she might have to watch out for.

Daisy fell asleep almost as soon as the train left Philadelphia, and Leila drifted off half an hour later. When she woke it was almost lunchtime and they were both hungry, so they made their way to the dining car. If they had boarded the train from Manhattan they would have had the company of the girls from the *Robert E. Lee*, including Marjorie, who were travelling across country, but now it was just the two of them. The train stopped at regular intervals to let people on and off, and the other passengers in their compartment were friendly, and interested in where the young woman and her pretty daughter were from and where they were heading. Leila thought that was a good sign. And the scenery changed often, so there was always something to look at.

They spent the first night on the train stretched out on the seats, which wasn't very comfortable, but it was better than having to sit up. When they woke early the next morning they were in Arkansas, according to the signs on the railway stations they went through. They would be getting off at a city called Alva in Harper County, the nearest railhead to the settlement of Wyman, beyond which Jake lived.

She surreptitiously sniffed her armpit. A bath would be very nice, but all they'd managed was a quick wash in a tiny handbasin in the train's toilet. At the next stop, she and Daisy dashed off and bought several newspapers and a comic to occupy them as the hours and the miles rattled past. It had been exciting at first, heading off across America by train, but now it was merely boring, and all the sitting was very hard on a person's bottom. Daisy was extremely fidgety, and had been up and down the length of the train many times already.

On the tenth excursion, she came back leading an elderly black man by the hand. Leila could see from his uniform that he worked on the train.

'Mum, here's Mr Brakeman,' Daisy announced.

The man laughed, showing dazzling white teeth in what was probably the blackest face Leila had ever seen.

'No, Missy, I *am* the brakeman, my name is Jackson T. Phelps.'

'Oh. Anyway,' Daisy added, 'he's never met a lady from New Zealand before.'

Jackson Phelps offered his hand. 'Pleased to meet you, Missus Daisy's Mother.'

'It's Mrs Kelly, Leila Kelly. Hello, Mr Phelps,

I'm very pleased to meet you.'

'We've never met a black man either, have we, Mum?' Daisy said.

'Daisy, manners!'

'But we haven't!'

'It's all right, Missus Kelly, she's just a child. And ain't it probably true, with y'all coming from New Zealand?'

'Well, plenty of people from New Zealand are dark-skinned, but I have to be honest, Mr Phelps, hardly any are as dark as you are, if you don't mind me saying so. I think it's a bit of a novelty for Daisy, so please don't be offended.'

'It definitely ain't no novelty for me, Missus, but no, I ain't offended, not in the least. In fact I was just sitting on my little stool wondering what to do next when your Daisy appeared in the engine. As we don't allow no children up in the engine, we thought we'd walk back together. Ain't that right, Miss Daisy?'

'Yep, it sure is,' Daisy replied, having picked up some of the American vernacular already. 'We're going to live with my dad in a big house on a big farm, aren't we, Mum?'

'War bride?' Jackson Phelps asked interestedly. 'Seen a few of those over the last twelve months or so. Quite a few from New Zealand, too. So, where you heading?'

'Someplace near Wyman. My husband has some land there. He's meeting us at the railway station tonight.'

'Is that right? Well, there's plenty of land out that way, sure enough.' He took his cap off and scratched the grey stubble on the back of his head. 'But what I come to ask you was, your Daisy seems mighty bored and my old momma always said idle hands do the Devil's work, so would you have any objection to me teaching her a few card games? Nothing like poker, just some simple tricks I teach my grandchildren when I'm at home, to give her something to do. I got nothing to do myself 'til we hit the next station.'

'Whereabouts?' Leila asked cautiously.

'Right here, if that's all right with you, Missus. I ain't supposed to fraternise with the passengers, but who the hell's going to see?'

Daisy giggled. 'Jackson swore, Mum.'

Jackson made exaggerated spitting noises. 'So I did. Wash ma mouth out with soap!'

Leila giggled herself this time. 'Well, I suppose so. Just say when you've had enough, though. Daisy's been known to wear down the most patient of people.'

'Not me, Missus,' Jackson chuckled. 'You ain't met my grandchildren.'

They played cards for two hours without a break, giving Leila the opportunity to doze, then go for a walk up and down the train herself. Outside the scenery was changing yet again. It was starting to look very dry and dusty, and flat for almost as far as the eye could see.

Then it was lunchtime, and Jackson had to go back to work. The afternoon passed just as slowly, although Jackson came back for an hour. Leila asked him about the history of the area, and he told her a rather depressing story about the dust storms that had come during the 1930s and destroyed almost all the crops and forced the landowners and workers to pack up everything they owned and drive away for ever. But there were still people working the land, he said, and the federal government was starting to set up programmes to get the fields and the soil back to a state where crops could be grown again, although it was a slow and very expensive business. It was a fascinating and heartbreaking story, and Leila never once connected any of it to where she and Daisy were going to live.

At 10.30 that night, Jackson came through the car to let them know that they were about ten miles outside of Alva. Daisy bounced up and down on her seat excitedly, and Leila got to her feet and set about gathering their things.

Soon, the rhythm of the train changed and began to slow, and the occasional house flashed past in the semi-darkness of the night. It seemed that Alva wasn't really a city at all, perhaps not even as big as Napier, but by then nothing could dampen their excitement. As the train came to a slow and noisy stop, Leila and Daisy waited at the end of the car to step down onto the station platform.

From the engine, Jackson watched as the woman and the little girl got off, and smiled to himself as a tall man appeared out of the shadows and stood with his arms spread wide in greeting.

There were no passengers or freight to pick up, so the train pulled out almost immediately.

The engine driver followed his brakeman's gaze. 'Where they headed?'

Jackson's smile disappeared. 'Wyman.'
'Oh my Lord.'

★　★　★

Jake helped Leila and Daisy up into the cab of his rickety old truck. He couldn't stop smiling, and Leila was far more relieved than she wanted to admit to see that he looked exactly as he had in New Zealand, except of course that now he was wearing overalls and an old work shirt, instead of his smart Marine uniform. He'd clearly been in the middle of working when he'd set off to collect them.

Daisy, who had suddenly become uncharacteristically shy the minute her father said hello and picked her up for a big hug, had fallen asleep.

Unexpectedly, Leila felt shy and tongue-tied herself, and almost as if she were sitting in the truck with a stranger. And she was, really; it had been almost four years since she had last seen Jake. She'd looked forward so much to this meeting, and now that it had arrived she didn't know what to say.

They drove in silence for a while, then he asked her how she was and how things had been since he'd last seen her. So she told him, and then he talked about what he'd done since leaving Auckland, but not about the bit on Okinawa, and how it had been for him coming back home and being demobbed. And she talked about her family, and how most of her cousins were home from the war now, and what they all planned to do now that it was over. And all the

475

while she watched miles and miles of identical, flat fields sweep past in the dark, while snatching glances at Jake when she thought he wasn't looking. But he always was, and now and then she thought she caught a hint of sadness in his eyes, as if he were seeing something she couldn't even begin to imagine.

They talked about Daisy, who was slumped against Leila and snoring her head off, Ginny at her feet. Leila spoke of what she wanted for their daughter, and Jake said nothing, just nodding as she talked.

His hair was longer now, curling where it touched his collar. He was as handsome as he'd ever been, and his body was still strong and hard. But the more Leila looked at him, the more her heart sank. There was absolutely nothing about him to justify what she was trying so hard to deny, but she knew that Jake had somehow changed. The flame that had once burned in him — the one that had made him swing her around to 'Boogie Woogie Bugle Boy', the one that had made her knees weak and set her on fire, the one that had so much made her want to say 'I do' when they were married — had gone out. He wasn't cold, he was just . . . somewhere else.

But, she told herself, this was to be expected. She was probably the same; it had been such a long time and they would have to get to know each other all over again. It might take time but they would get back to the way they'd been before. They would.

The truck was a particularly elderly one, with

476

a hole in the floor through which Leila was convinced she could see the gravel road, and it was rattly and draughty and the window at the back of the cab was missing. The headlights worked, though, and in them she caught brief glimpses of small animals — looking suspiciously liked stripey possums — as they dashed from the fields on one side of the road to the fields on the other.

'What are they?' she asked Jake.

'What are what?'

'Those little animals running across the road.'

'I didn't see. Gophers, maybe? Raccoons?'

'What does a raccoon look like?'

'Well, it looks like a . . . raccoon.'

'Do they have stripes on their tails and sort of goggles on?'

Jake laughed. 'Yep, sounds like a raccoon all right.'

Leila contemplated waking Daisy so she could see them too, but decided against it — there would be plenty of opportunities for her to see the local wildlife.

They were silent again, until Leila eventually asked, 'How far now?'

'About another thirty miles or so. The road gets quite rough just a bit further on.'

And so it did, but Leila didn't feel the bumps and swerves as the truck went over and around various potholes, because she too had fallen asleep.

She woke with a jolt almost an hour later, wondering where she was.

Jake had pulled up in front of a small,

L-shaped house in the middle of what appeared to be an endless field of stunted little bushes. By the moonlight she could see that the house had never been painted, and that the yard surrounding it was of bare earth. In front of the house stood a single tree with a tyre swing hanging from it, swaying gently in the breeze. A decrepit shed stood to one side, empty. Somewhere, not too far away, a dog was barking; otherwise the silence was total, except for the ticking of the truck's motor as it cooled down.

She sat up. 'Why have we stopped here? Are we lost?'

Jake looked at her, and in the moonlight his eyes were unreadable. He reached for her hand. 'No, Leila, we're home.'

21

Violet and Sam had been on a train too, the one
that travelled from Wellington up to Napier.

Violet had been fine all the way across the
Atlantic and Indian Oceans until they'd reached
Australia, but then she had woken one morning
in the cabin she and Sam shared, wondering if
she was doing the right thing.

What if Billy's parents rejected them? What if
they denied that Sam was Billy's son and wanted
to have nothing at all to do with him? He was
only a little boy, but he was very perceptive and
Violet feared that such a rejection would harm
him badly. He knew all about his father being a
soldier from New Zealand, and that he and his
mum had fallen in love but that his father had
died in the war before they could be married.
There had been no secrets between mother and
son, and no silly stories to explain away the fact
that Sam had no father. But the possibility that
his grandparents might not want to know him
might prove too much for him. She hadn't even
written to them in advance, for that very reason.
If she had, and they'd declined, she would
eventually have had to tell Sam that they weren't
interested. But perhaps she should have done it
that way after all. Billy had said his parents were
wonderful people, but Billy was dead, and he
would not be there when they finally did meet.

But it had been too late by then. So here she and Sam were, having trudged to the outskirts of Napier because she didn't have the money for a taxi, standing on what she had been assured by a passing cyclist was the road out to where Billy's parents lived, with their thumbs out hoping that some kind motorist would give them a lift. It was cool and they both had their winter coats on, but it was nowhere near as cold as early spring in England. They had one suitcase between them, and Sam was sitting on it with his head down, almost asleep he was so tired from all the travelling. He was wearing his little cap as well, and Violet bent down and pushed his dark hair back under the brim.

'Won't be long now, love,' she promised. 'Someone will come by soon and give us a ride.'

Sam said nothing, and continued to stare unseeingly at the stones on the road. He was exhausted and hungry, and his feet hurt in his new boots.

Violet gave him a kiss, and dug an apple out of her bag for him to eat while they waited. New Zealand was a very pretty place, she thought, almost like England in some ways, and there were all sorts of things in the shops that you couldn't get at home, although the shopkeeper she'd spoken to earlier today had said that some items were still being rationed. But he'd given Sam a biscuit out of a huge jar on his counter for nothing.

They waited for another half-hour and still no one stopped. In fact, hardly any motorists went past at all. Finally, though, a man in a big black car did stop for them. His name was Doctor Fleming, he said, and he'd been into town to pick up medical supplies but was heading home. He lived on the road beyond Kenmore Station so he would be happy to give them a lift.

Violet climbed into the passenger seat and Sam hopped into the back, lay down and went to sleep immediately.

'Come a long way, have you?' Doctor Fleming asked. 'I note you have an English accent.'

Violet nodded. 'We arrived in Wellington yesterday morning, and caught the train straight to Napier.'

'Oh, I see. I didn't realise you'd come that far! You *are* a long way from home, aren't you?'

He was curious as to the nature of the pretty young woman's business at Kenmore, but refrained from asking out of propriety. On the other hand, there had been serious upheavals out there lately, and he didn't want her to arrive without being forewarned. She had come a long way and it would probably be the decent thing to at least give her the essential details.

'Visiting, are you?' he asked casually.

'Yes, we are,' she replied, and left it at that.

He tried again. 'Anyone in particular?'

The woman turned and looked at him directly in the eye. Her own remarkably blue eyes were full of weariness and something he suspected might be close to anxiety. Her lovely English face was drawn, and there was dust and grime on her smart but clearly inexpensive coat and hat.

'Does it really matter?' she asked.

'I'm afraid it does, actually. The family have

481

suffered a bereavement recently and, well, forgive my directness, but I'm not entirely sure who will be welcome at the moment and who will not.'

Violet closed her eyes. This was the last thing she had expected to hear. She fixed the doctor with her gaze again, and he saw that his news had upset her.

'Did you know Billy Deane?' she asked cautiously.

'Billy? Of course, a fine young man. Killed on Crete, a hero apparently. Tragic.' He glanced quickly into the back seat, then back at Violet again, and his bushy eyebrows shot up as he suddenly put two and two together. 'I say, the boy, he isn't . . . ?'

'He is, actually.'

'Hell's bells,' Fleming exclaimed, 'I didn't even realise Billy was married.'

'He wasn't, we weren't.'

'Oh, I see.' He shrugged, a man who had seen the ways of the world change markedly in the last six years. 'And you're bringing him home to meet his grandparents?'

'Something like that.'

'Do they know?'

Violet grabbed at the door handle as the doctor swerved to avoid a rabbit on the road. 'No, not yet.'

Fleming straightened the wheel, then thought for a moment. 'Well, I should tell you then that it was Drew Murdoch who died, James and Lucy's son, and Billy's cousin. He'd been in a Japanese prisoner of war camp in Burma for several years and had developed a brain tumour, although he'd apparently taken it upon himself not to tell anyone else, not even me and I'm the family doctor. The tumour was progressive, and inoperable, and when it became unbearable he took all of his medication at once and wandered off up into the hills to die.' The doctor was silent for a moment. 'But he was a troubled lad, Drew, apart from the tumour.' Then he reddened, as if realising he might have gone a little too far with the Murdoch family's confidences. 'But I suppose we'll never know about any of that, and perhaps it's not our place to know. Who's to say?'

★ ★ ★

Violet declined his offer to drive them up to Kenmore's front door, and he let the pair of them off at the gate.

They stood at the end of the long, tree-lined driveway for several minutes, staring in awe at the elegant, two-storeyed colonial house set in beautiful, manicured gardens.

'Come on, love,' Violet said as she hefted their suitcase. 'Let's go and meet your grandparents, shall we?'

Sam was feeling better after his nap, and he smiled, transforming himself into a miniature version of Billy. He held his hand out to Violet and she took it, and together they walked towards the house.

But before they reached the front entrance, Violet stopped. There was no sign of anyone about.

'Let's not knock on the front door, shall we? Let's go around the side. I'd rather do that.'

Sam shrugged — he couldn't care less, as long as there was a lav when they got there. He was dying for a wee.

So they went around the side of the house and into the garden that lay beyond the french doors of the parlour. And then they stopped.

A tall young man was working in the rose garden, wearing scruffy trousers and an old shirt, the sleeves rolled up to above his elbows. His head was bare and his curly blond hair flopped over his forehead as he bent over, hoeing the soil around the roses, stopping now and then to pick up a weed and toss it onto the lawn, and humming to himself as he went.

Violet knew the tune. It was 'Blue Smoke'.

Oblivious to the woman and child standing quietly next to the big, fragrant daphne, he started singing. He managed, 'Blue smoke goes drifting by into the deep blue sky', and then, to Violet's shock, he burst into tears.

Dropping his hoe, he wandered over to a bench under a tree, sat down and put his head in his hands. After a minute he looked up through bleary eyes, and it was at that moment that he saw them.

If Violet was shocked a moment ago, she was mortified now.

What he saw was a young woman with the bluest eyes he'd ever seen, and long, fine hair the colour of eggshell that lifted in the breeze and settled again on her shoulders. She was holding Billy's hand, except it was Billy when he'd been

484

a little boy, not Billy as he had been when he'd gone away.

'Which one are you?' Violet asked gently.

'I'm Liam.'

Violet nodded, because she'd already known that — he was exactly as Billy had described him, although perhaps a little older-looking than she'd expected.

'Who are you?'

'I'm Violet Metcalfe. This is Sam, Billy's son.'

Liam nodded, for some reason not at all surprised at the appearance of the woman and her child. He opened his arms, and when Billy's son shyly approached, he hugged him close and felt his tears starting again. If there was nothing left of Drew, then at least it seemed they would now still have a part of Billy.

He held out his hand to Violet, and she came forward, took it and hung on tight.

Philadelphia, July 1946
In all likelihood, it had never been going to work, and she could see that now, quite clearly.

Leila moved her breakfast tray off her knee, set it on the floor and walked over to the window, where she sat in an upholstered chair and gazed out at the gracious trees and gardens surrounding the Hartmans' house. She and Daisy were going home to New Zealand in three days' time, and she was grateful to the Hartmans for allowing her to spend her last week in America in peace and comfort.

It had not been Jake's lies that had destroyed

it, because they hadn't really been lies. His family did have land, and he was a farmer. What he had not said was that the Kellys were sharecroppers who merely rented their small patch of dirt on which to grow cotton. He also hadn't mentioned that they hadn't had a successful harvest in almost a decade, and that his family were dirt poor, although his father, Roscoe Kelly, refused to load everything into the truck and leave, as many other sharecroppers in the north-western reaches of Oklahoma had done. He was a stubborn man, and a patriarch, and apparently would rather see his family starve than admit defeat.

It had not even been his mother, Wynne Kelly, who after years of trying unsuccessfully to scratch out a living and feed her family from the mean and sterile soil, was an embittered and angry woman. She had resented Leila even before they met, and made no pretence about the fact that she had not wanted Jake to marry a foreign woman — especially one with such 'airs and graces', as she put it. As she had bluntly said on the morning following Leila's arrival, there were enough single young girls — all of whom would have given their right arms to marry a handsome, virile buck like Jake — for him to have had the luxury of being able to pick and choose. But no, he had to go and get himself a fancy girl from New Zealand, who didn't know the first thing about cotton farming, had a funny accent no one could understand and who didn't look capable of having produced the child she already had, never mind five or six more, which was the number of grandchildren Wynne had set her heart on. And although Leila could understand her disappointment, she could not condone Wynne's offhand treatment of Daisy. It was almost as if Wynne did not believe that Jake was the little girl's father, even though her parentage was patently obvious when you looked at them together.

Leila was expected to pull her weight in the house and around the farm. She stood for hours in the kitchen baking and cooking in the near-primitive conditions, and in almost continual silence, as Wynne and her daughter Faith would not talk to her unless they had to. There was no electricity or running water — the stove was powered by wood, and water had to be collected in buckets from a pump in the yard and then heated on the stove. Laundry day was a nightmare, because although Wynne Kelly was a fairly basic sort of a woman she was a very clean one, and insisted that every piece of household linen, threadbare as it was, be laundered once a week without fail. It was a job that took all day, and almost broke the back of the woman allotted the job of scrubbing and rinsing, which usually turned out to be Leila.

Jake had done his best to act as a buffer between Leila and his mother, but it was very difficult when they all lived in a house that was only the size of Kenmore's kitchen and parlour put together. Faith and her two children lived there too, Faith's husband having disappeared some time ago, as well as Wynne's mother, an ancient woman who, in Leila's opinion, was even

487

nastier than her daughter. It was extremely crowded, and although Jake and Leila initially had the luxury of a bedroom to themselves, they were soon sharing it with Daisy, who refused to sleep in the front room with the other children because they were mean to her and teased Ginny.

Poor Daisy had perhaps been affected most of all. She had spent all her short life waiting to meet her father, whom Leila had built up to be such a hero, such a wonderful, capable, larger than life person, that the reality had fallen well short of any expectations. Jake liked Daisy, and was very kind to her and took her out into the fields each day, teaching her about cotton farming and all the little field animals and the ways in which the weather changed and what it meant, but the bond that should have developed between them simply had not. He was aloof at times; Daisy could not understand why and naturally thought she was the cause of it, and became upset herself, and grizzly and difficult. Leila assured her day after day that things would get better, that Daddy had to get used to having a wife and a daughter after such a long time by himself, but as the weeks then months passed, even she stopped believing that.

Jake knew it was not going well, and would become upset himself and drink at night to cover his disappointment. He was not a violent drunk, and never once shouted or raised his hand to them, but he often came to bed reeking of the dreadful moonshine he consumed by the pint, and would subside into what seemed closer to a coma than natural sleep. It gave them little opportunity to talk, and even less to make love, which Leila found extremely frustrating and disappointing. The lover who had once transported her physically and emotionally to unimaginable heights of pleasure and passion had gone, and in his place was a tired, sad man barely able to sustain an erection even if he managed to produce one. At first Leila had thought it was her fault, that she had lost her appeal, and went to great lengths to tempt him sexually, but nothing had worked, and then Daisy had moved into their room, and the opportunity had been lost. But finally, and in spite of that fact that her ego was taking an immense battering, she had decided that the problem lay not with her but with Jake, and she stopped telling herself that she was responsible for the failure of her marriage.

There was no chance of her, Jake and Daisy packing up and going to live somewhere else: there was simply not the money. Leila could have asked her parents for help, but she wouldn't, and Jake never asked her to. And he made it quite clear that he couldn't, or wouldn't, leave his father to run the farm on his own. Leila had accepted this, and even reluctantly admired him for it.

She opened the window and lit a cigarette. A scent wafted in — she thought it might have been magnolia. In spite of everything, it might have worked if Jake had not changed so much. Physically he had been the same, except for his problems in the bedroom, but mentally, or spiritually, he was a different man. The essential, vibrant, New Zealand Jake had gone, leaving behind only a person who looked like him. Because of her Uncle James, she knew that the root of the problem lay in what had happened on Okinawa, but he flatly refused to talk about it. Every time she cautiously raised the subject, he either changed it, or simply walked away. His face would close over, and his eyes would take on a distant, disconnected look, and that would be that. It had been hurtful, and terribly frustrating.

So after three months, she'd come to a decision. When she told Jake, he had not argued and had not defended himself. He had cried, but he hadn't tried to stop her. The next day, he'd driven her and Daisy into Alva, where she purchased tickets for the train back to Philadelphia. They said goodbye and he'd driven off. Leila stood on the platform and waited and waited, but the plume of dust rising up behind the truck had not faltered, and finally it had disappeared altogether.

She had sat down and put her arm around her daughter.

'I'm sorry, darling, I'm so sorry it hasn't worked out the way we wanted it to.'

Daisy had Ginny on her knee. 'It's all right, Mummy,' she said as she stroked and stroked the soft, sleek fur. She looked up. 'But we tried, though, didn't we?'

Leila blinked back tears. 'Oh, yes, sweetie, we tried.'

'That's all right, then.'

The train had pulled in an hour later, and Leila and Daisy had been very pleased to see a familiar face waving at them from the engine.

They boarded and found themselves an empty compartment, and Leila had to physically restrain Daisy from tearing through the cars to find Jackson, whom she was sure would be busy at the moment. But he appeared five minutes later, knocking on the compartment door and waving through the glass.

'Jackson!' Daisy cried, and bounced out of her seat.

Leila's heart hurt a little as it occurred to her that Daisy had never greeted her father with such enthusiasm.

Jackson came in and took off his brakeman's cap. 'Mind if I sit, Missus?'

'Not at all, Mr Phelps, please,' Leila replied, indicating the seat opposite.

He sat down, elbows on his knees and hands dangling, and watched Leila thoughtfully. Daisy was busy extracting Ginny from her box to show her friend how much the cat had grown.

After a moment Jackson asked, 'Heading back to Philly for a vacation?'

Leila knew full well that he knew, but was grateful he was too polite to let on.

'No, we're going home. My sister in Philadelphia is getting married in a week's time, then we're going back to New Zealand.'

Jackson nodded wisely. 'Best time for a wedding, summertime.'

'Yes, my sister's future mother-in-law thinks so.'

'Hope it works out for her. Your sister, I mean.'

'I'm sure it will. Her fiancé is a very nice man. Very decent.'

Jackson sat back and stretched his old legs out in front of him. He was wearing one black sock and one grey one, which Daisy thought was hilarious.

'Sometimes, though,' he said eventually as he patted Ginny's grey head, 'it don't make much difference. Even if the man and the woman is both decent, it still ain't going to work. Sometimes, it just ain't meant to be, no matter what.'

Leila stared at him.

He went on, softly but surely telling her what she so much needed to hear. 'And when that happens, according to my old momma anyway, and she did know about these things, there can't be no blame. The things that was there to start with just ain't there after a while. No one's fault, it just is. So you just got to pick yourself up and keep on going, 'cause there's always something better around the corner. For them that wants to believe that, anyway.'

'Thank you, Mr Phelps,' Leila said in a wobbly voice, then burst into tears.

Jackson extracted a large, meticulously folded mauve handkerchief from his uniform pocket and handed it across to her.

He sat with her for an hour, occasionally saying something quietly to Daisy who was amusing herself by trying to put a nappy on Ginny made from her own handkerchief, and simply waited.

Then he asked Daisy to go along to the dining car and order a cup of coffee for her mother and a soda for herself, and to say it was to go on Jackson T. Phelps's tab, and it had all come out.

Leila felt immensely better afterwards, mainly because it had been the first opportunity she'd had to talk to anyone who hadn't actually been involved. Hearing the story out loud in her own words, it all sounded quite hopeless and naïve, and in retrospect doomed to failure, but she understood that what she knew now she hadn't known then, and that made it a little easier to accept.

Jackson went away after a while, but he made sure that no other passengers encroached on Leila's compartment, and over the next seventy-two hours she had plenty of time to think. By the time the train reached Philadelphia, she was feeling somewhat better. Still desperately sad and bereft, but a little less raw.

Bonnie and Danny were at the station to meet them, although they'd had to wait for some minutes while Daisy went to look for Jackson to get his address so she could send him a postcard from New Zealand.

Mr and Mrs Hartman had been very understanding, and offered to put Leila and Daisy up until after the wedding. Nothing was said about what had happened, although everyone knew, but Leila took care to limit her discussion of recent events to her sister and occasionally Danny, because she just didn't think it was anyone else's business.

Bonnie and Danny's wedding had been truly

spectacular, with Bonnie in a gorgeous white satin dress and long lace veil looking exactly like the sort of bride the twins had marvelled at in magazines, and Danny in a smart grey morning suit and top hat. It had been decided at the last minute that Daisy would be a flower-girl and she too looked delightful in a pale apricot lace dress that would have done justice to a Christmas-tree fairy.

But Bonnie and Danny had gone now, off on their honeymoon, and there was not much left for Leila to do except pack for the voyage back to New Zealand. She had written to her parents and told them briefly about what had happened, with a promise of more detail when they got home, and that she and Daisy were well and very much looking forward to being back at Kenmore again.

So when the Hartmans' maid knocked on the bedroom door with the message that a Mr Spano was on the telephone for her, and did she want to take the call, she was surprised to say the least.

He was telephoning, he told Leila, because he thought she might like to know how Jennifer was settling in.

'When we met you said you weren't on the telephone, but I thought I'd call your sister for your address so I could drop you a line. I had no idea you were back in Philadelphia yourself.'

'Yes, we are,' Leila replied, 'but only for a few more days. We're going back to New Zealand very soon.'

There was a short silence at the other end,

then Anthony Spano said, 'Would you and your little girl like to come and see Jennifer? She's doing very well, as it happens, and she's very happy, but I know she'd like to see you.'

Leila paused. She would love to see Jennifer again, but didn't know if a visit to Anthony Spano would be appropriate, or if indeed it was what she felt like doing.

'Look,' he said as she dithered, 'why don't I bring Jennifer to see you? What about tomorrow? It's only a short drive from where I live.'

In the end Leila said yes, knowing that Daisy would probably be cheered up by seeing Jennifer too. But before she hung up, she asked, 'How did you know the telephone number here?'

'Oh, that was easy. I rang the shipping company you came over with and asked for the forwarding address given by Miss Bonnie Morgan. Then I checked in the phone book.'

'Why didn't you just ask for my forwarding address?'

Another short silence. 'I thought it best to check with your sister first. I thought your husband might not appreciate you receiving letters from strange men. I'll see you tomorrow then. Goodbye.'

Leila replaced the telephone, sensing that Anthony Spano had just changed his story somewhere along the line, though she wasn't at all sure where.

★ ★ ★

He had been right about Jennifer; she was thriving, and dashing about madly in the most adorable little pale yellow dress with matching Mary Janes and white socks with lace around the tops. The colour suited her perfectly, a lovely foil for her shining black hair and blue eyes. She was talking well now, too, and chattered on to Daisy as they both played with Ginny on the lawn.

Leila and Anthony sat on the patio and drank coffee. She complimented him on how well Jennifer looked, and he explained that he couldn't take all the credit as he'd recently hired a nanny, with whom Jennifer seemed to get on very well.

A nanny, Leila thought, raising her eyebrows. But Anthony Spano did seem to be quite well off, judging by his clothes and the car he'd arrived in. He hadn't said what he did, but she'd gathered it was something rather profitable. He hadn't mentioned Gail either, so she thought it best that she didn't herself; she had the distinct feeling that he was more than happy to put the whole episode behind him. Except for Jennifer, of course, whom he clearly adored.

He did ask her about Jake. Leila said as little as possible, other than to state that her marriage had ended owing to irreconcilable differences, and that she had decided to take Daisy back to New Zealand. He hadn't said anything else on the matter, but when it was time for him to take Jennifer home, he had asked if he could write to her at her parents' address. She saw no harm in it, so they parted on friendly terms after a very pleasant afternoon. During the voyage back to New Zealand, however, Leila found herself thinking about Anthony Spano more and more as the days went by.

22

Kenmore, March 1947

Thomas and Catherine had moved back to Napier at Christmas time, and had bought a rather nice house in town, one of the stylish, modern ones built after the earthquake. Thomas was still practising law, but only two days a week, and Catherine was resting, enjoying the summer warmth that gave such relief to her arthritis.

Robert had also come home, and was working with Joseph and Owen on the station again, and thoroughly enjoying himself after his long sojourn overseas.

Ana married David Leonard, and was now living at the Leonard farm. They were expecting a baby in September, but Ana, characteristically, was refusing to let her 'condition' hamper her activities and was belting about on Mako and helping David and Jack get the farm back into some sort of order.

As he'd promised in his letters, Jonathan Lawson had come back to New Zealand, and he and Kathleen had set their wedding date for October. Jonathan was occupying himself helping out on the station, and was staying in one of the little shearers' cottages, James having decided that it wasn't quite the thing to have your future son-in-law sleeping under the same roof as your daughter before they were married. After they were, though, Jonathan was taking

Kathleen to England on an extended honeymoon so she could meet his family. They would decide after that where they wanted to make their home. Jonathan was seriously considering joining the regular air force, given that he'd been trained as a pilot during the war and couldn't really do much else, but whether it would be the RAF or the RNZAF, he hadn't decided. He adored Kathleen, and would do anything to make her happy, so it was highly likely that he would make his decision around her.

Duncan had settled into life as an orchardist remarkably easily. James and Lucy had at first thought he might not take to the slow pace of the work but he was adapting very well. He had to wear a hat all the time to keep the sun off his damaged face, and gloves to prevent the thin skin on his hands from being scratched by branches, but his enthusiasm for the propagation, cultivation and harvesting of the various fruits James grew was increasing by the day. Rather than becoming bored, he seemed to enjoy the gentle, reliable rhythms of horticulture and watching day by day as leaves went from bright green to the darker hues of maturity, and blossoms became fruit. The war had changed him, as it had changed everyone else, and he seemed to revel in Claire and their new baby.

Now and then he would tell hair-raising tales of his flying exploits during the war, stories that made his mother go pale at the very thought, and very occasionally would mention the names of men who had died — Terry Finch who had gone down in flames, his plane a fiery coffin, and

Jacko Ebbett, who had been caught on the runway when the Luftwaffe bombers had flown early one misty morning over Biggin Hill — but, like Liam and Robert, he kept most of his war experiences to himself. Every few weeks they would pile into the farm truck and go into the RSA in town, and join the new, younger generation of veterans who had started congregating there to talk about things that no one else would have a hope of understanding, but generally the war had been relegated to a private and increasingly sacred place.

Duncan's contentment was a great comfort to James and Lucy, who had been deeply and profoundly bereft when Drew had taken his own life. It had helped just a little to learn that he had been suffering from a terminal illness, but the knowledge that he had not been able to share that with them had been another heavy blow. He had not wanted to worry them, and there was nothing they could have done, but they grieved intensely for him nevertheless. Their greatest regret was that he might have died thinking he was alone, and the thought ate away at them for months until they were finally able to accept that they had done what they could for him — and that had to be enough.

Liam, who had rather naïvely thought that once the war ended all the dying and the grief would stop too, had been shattered by Drew's death. He had been sliding inexorably into depression when Violet and Sam had arrived on that September afternoon. Since then, he had perked up markedly, and had taken Sam under his wing as if the boy were his own. Despite Violet's fears, Erin and Joseph had been delighted to discover that Billy had a child, particularly one who looked so like him, and that their son had had the comfort and pleasure of a genuine love affair before he'd died. They had asked Violet to consider staying on in New Zealand. At first she had very politely said no, explaining that her life, and Sam's, was in England, and that they had only come out so that her son could meet the other half of his family. She was very grateful for the offer, but her parents were expecting them back, and she was needed to help with the family business.

But as the weeks passed, she found she was beginning to change her mind, for two reasons. The first was Sam; since their arrival, and after he had overcome his initial shyness, he had flourished. He had suffered from asthma all of his life, but there had been no sign of the ailment here in the hills of Hawke's Bay, not even when it was cold and damp. He was spending much of his time with his grandfather now, and had learned to ride a horse (after a fashion), could tell the difference between various types of sheep and had decided he knew all about dagging and shearing and docking. He could also make an eel trap, one that actually caught real eels, which was his proudest achievement to date. He'd met some of his cousins and aunties and uncles from the settlement at Maungakakari, the village that Billy had spoken of with such fondness, and had been awed to discover that his grandfather was a real, live Maori chief, even though he wasn't covered in tattoos and went around in ordinary work pants and a tatty old hat. He had been a happy child in England, but here he seemed really at home, and a whole new side of him was beginning to emerge. Violet didn't know whether she could deprive him of all that now, by taking him back to England.

The second thing was Liam. Violet had assumed, vowed even, that after Billy had died, she would never be interested in another man for as long as she lived. Billy had been the one for her, and if she could not have him then she did not want anyone else. But, to her surprise, she was changing her mind about that too. Liam was almost the complete opposite of Billy, in looks as well as character. Billy had been assertive and quite loud and very sure about everything he did, and the power of his personality had swept her off her feet, literally. But Liam, who was as fair as Billy had been dark, was a much gentler soul, though equally kind and generous. He was attractive, though, because of it, and becoming more so as the weeks passed. She knew without even having to ask that he had been through some very unpleasant times during the war, and Kathleen had told her that he had once been married to a woman who had taken him for a complete patsy and treated him very badly. She sensed, too, that he was a sensual man, or at least that's how she felt when she caught him looking at her. Her own body's responses told her that beneath his calm and thoughtful exterior, he was a man who could be very passionate, and she also knew that if she went back to England, she would never discover exactly how passionate.

Leila, too, had settled in well again at Kenmore, and was slowly recovering from her disastrous marriage. Daisy seemed to have put the whole experience behind her and was back to her happy, cheeky and inquisitive self, but she talked often of Jackson T. Phelps, and had recently sent him a photograph of Ginny now that she had grown into a proper, and rather fat, cat. Leila realised that the old man's kindness, patience and words of wisdom had been exactly what the child had needed at the time. They certainly had been for her, and she would be for ever grateful for what he had said to her on that train returning to Philadelphia.

She had her family and was in regular contact with Bonnie, who was thoroughly enjoying being Danny's wife, and there was never any shortage of beaus wanting to take her out. She said yes now and then, and enjoyed the odd night out in Napier, but she suspected that the old days of carousing and dancing until dawn might be behind her now. She had not grown up during the war, she had to admit, but she had come back from America with a new maturity and the knowledge that, whatever happened to her in future, she had the strength to survive.

This was something she had written to Anthony Spano not long ago when she'd replied to one of his many letters — always accompanied by photos of Jennifer and amusing stories, told with pride and affection, of what she had been up to lately — and his response had given her a lot to think about. She believed she knew

Anthony better now than she had ever known poor Jake, and she very much liked the person he was turning out to be. She was not yet ready to make a commitment, but she knew that Anthony Spano would be waiting when she was.

So life at Kenmore was as good as it could be, given the enormous upheavals and awful losses of the past six years, and the Murdochs, the Deanes and the Morgans were beginning to adapt again to a life without war, one that promised long stretches of calm, stability and prosperity, and opportunities for their children and their children's children to grow up in a happier, more settled world.

It was a terrible blow, therefore, when Tamar, at the age of eighty-seven, had another major heart attack, and Doctor Fleming pronounced that she only had a matter of weeks to live.

★　★　★

Leila telephoned Bonnie in Philadelphia straight away, pacing backwards and forwards next to the phone in the hall waiting for her call to be connected to the international operator in New Zealand, then to America, then to the operator on the exchange at Bonnie's end.

Bonnie, distraught, had agreed to come home as soon as she could. She arrived from Sydney five days later on TEAL Airlines, after having flown there from San Francisco in a DC-6, part of British Commonwealth Pacific Airlines' new air fleet. Danny was with her, and as soon as they landed in Auckland they flew on in a rather

504

noisy twelve-seater passenger plane to Napier's Beacons aerodrome.

It was almost dark when they pulled up in a rented car in Kenmore's driveway, and Bonnie barely stopped to greet anyone before rushing upstairs to her grandmother.

Tamar was lying in her bed, her head propped against pillows that were the same shade of white as her face, and Bonnie gasped in shock at her appearance — she had deteriorated so much over last twelve months. Her skin seemed as fragile as tissue paper and she had lost a significant amount of weight, so she now looked more ethereal than human. She wasn't moving at all, and Bonnie wondered, but was too scared to ask, whether she was in fact too late.

Keely read her daughter's mind. 'No, darling, she's still with us, but barely. Doctor Fleming came this morning, and told us we must prepare ourselves.' She retrieved a crumpled and sodden handkerchief from her sleeve and dabbed her puffy red eyes. 'He thinks it won't be long now.'

Bonnie moved across to the bed and looked down. Tamar stirred then, and opened her faded eyes.

'Bonnie, dear,' she said in a voice that was barely audible. 'You came. I'm so pleased.'

Bonnie took her hand, which felt smooth and cold against her own. 'Did you think I wouldn't, Gran?'

'I knew you would, if you could. You're a good girl, Bonnie, you always were.'

Bonnie lifted her free hand to her mouth to stifle a sob. 'I want you to get better, Gran,' she blurted, as Keely lay a comforting hand on her shoulder.

'No, dear, it's time.' Tamar closed her eyes again wearily, or perhaps they closed by themselves. 'I'm tired, darling, it's time.'

Bonnie burst into tears then, and Keely led her out of the room and downstairs to sit with the others.

They waited another four hours, fortifying themselves with cups of tea, and brandy when necessary, each suspended in their own grief and the memories that grief always summons. Everyone was there, filling the kitchen and the parlour, and they all — Tamar's children, her grandchildren and her two great-grandchildren — said their goodbyes to her over the course of the afternoon. Doctor Fleming would not be coming back, he had advised them earlier, because there would be no point unless it was to sign the death certificate. He was not being cruel, merely pragmatic. It was a wonder she had hung on for as long as she had, he said, and it would be unkind to interfere medically any further. Better to let her slip away when she was ready. She was not in any real pain, but her heart was gradually slowing down as the hours ticked past, and when it finally stopped, she would go.

The atmosphere was sombre but from time to time there was a ripple of laughter as someone told a funny story involving Tamar, or an anecdote she was particularly fond of herself. She had not quite gone yet, but they were girding themselves with all the good things she meant to them before she did, so that it might be a little easier to bear.

At a few minutes before seven o'clock that evening, Keely came down and asked James, Thomas and Joseph to accompany her to their mother's bedroom. They filed upstairs in silence and arranged themselves around her bed, trying very hard not to cry in front of her as, even at this late stage, they did not want to do anything that might cause her anguish.

After several minutes Tamar took a deep hitching breath, opened her eyes and said quite clearly, 'I love you all, very much. You have been my life and I want you to remember that.'

They waited and watched, and when a bright, dancing light came into their mother's eyes they hoped against hope that the inevitable was not, after all, going to happen.

And then she smiled, a small, private smile, and raised her hand as if to place it into the hand of another.

We do hope that you have enjoyed reading this large print book.

Did you know that all of our titles are available for purchase?

We publish a wide range of high quality large print books including:
**Romances, Mysteries, Classics
General Fiction
Non Fiction and Westerns**

Special interest titles available in large print are:
**The Little Oxford Dictionary
Music Book
Song Book
Hymn Book
Service Book**

Also available from us courtesy of Oxford University Press:
**Young Readers' Dictionary
(large print edition)
Young Readers' Thesaurus
(large print edition)**

For further information or a free brochure, please contact us at:
**Ulverscroft Large Print Books Ltd.,
The Green, Bradgate Road, Anstey,
Leicester, LE7 7FU, England.
Tel:** (00 44) 0116 236 4325
Fax: (00 44) 0116 234 0205

TAMAR

Deborah Challinor

The first volume in a three-volume family saga. When Tamar Deane is orphaned at seventeen in a small Cornish village, she seizes the chance for a new life and emigrates to New Zealand. In March 1879, alone and frightened on the Plymouth quay, she is befriended by an extraordinary woman. Myrna McTaggert is travelling to Auckland with plans to establish the finest brothel in the southern hemisphere and her unconventional friendship proves invaluable when Tamar makes disastrous choices in the new colony. Tragedy and scandal befall her, but unexpected good fortune brings vast changes to Tamar's life. As the century draws to a close, uncertainty looms when a distant war lures her loved ones to South Africa.

WHITE FEATHERS

Deborah Challinor

The second volume in a three-volume family saga. In 1914, Tamar Murdoch's life is one of ease and contentment at Kenmore, a prosperous estate in Hawkes Bay, as storm clouds over Europe begin casting long shadows. Tamar's love for her children is sorely tested as one by one they are called, or driven, into the living hell of World War One. During the Boer War, Joseph, her illegitimate eldest son, fought as a European, but this time he is determined to enlist in the Maori Battalion. As loyalties within the Murdoch clan are divided, and the war takes Tamar and Andrew's only daughter far from her sheltered upbringing, the people and experiences their children encounter will shape the destiny of the Murdoch clan for generations to come.